Simon Blake is an investigative journalist who has reported on some of the most controversial stories of the last two decades. He lives in London and France.

The Butcher Bird

Simon Blake

First published in Great Britain in 1998 by
HEADLINE BOOK PUBLISHING

Fisrt published in paperback in 1998
by HEADLINE BOOK PUBLISHING.

A HEADLINE FEATURE paperback

10 9 8 7 6 5 4 3 2 1

ISBN 0 7472 5312 9

Typeset by Palimpsest Book Production Limited,
Polmont, Stirlingshire
Printed and bound in Great Britain by
Mackays of Chatham PLC, Chatham, Kent

HEADLINE BOOK PUBLISHING
A division of Hodder Headline PLC
338 Euston Road
London NW1 3BH

The Butcher Bird

Prologue

He stood on the jetty as the sun flared and died. From the jagged skyline on the far side of the Chao Phraya river, velvety shadows spread across the water, transforming it from chocolate brown to inky black. The current gulped and sighed as it coursed past the jetty's rusting stanchions, each surge bringing more of the city's detritus drifting past: a cluster of vegetable leaves, a bobbing beer bottle, a posy of red and yellow paper flowers, the odour of decay made more sickly by the pall of humidity that had thickened with the dusk. Antoine Cabrini dabbed at his forehead with a pale blue handkerchief. He was a weighty man, barrel-chested, with dark receding hair, carrying a grey attaché case in his right hand. His cream linen jacket had long been saturated and, although he had folded it over his arm, sweat still trickled from his armpits, the stains spreading inexorably towards the middle of his matching cream shirt. Cabrini was accustomed to the knife-like heat of the Mediterranean. Sure, it could burn. But it didn't leave you drenched like this.

Out in the main stream, lights danced like fireflies. Bangkok's ferries and water-taxis were plying their trade, ceaselessly transporting their human cargo the length and breadth of the river. Cabrini was all too aware that soon he would have to venture on to the river himself. He had done his best to persuade Kain to meet him in Bangkok – even now, the lights of the air-conditioned bar of the Oriental Hotel were beckoning from above the jetty – but Kain had refused. This was Kain's territory, and if Kain insisted, then too bad: there was nothing more to be done.

A solitary light had detached itself from the fleet and was heading towards the jetty. It took shape as it neared, a narrow wooden craft, painted blue, throwing out a rooster-tail of spray like the water taxis Cabrini had seen before night fell, dodging and weaving among the larger boats. It was powered by a clattering diesel engine that reached a crescendo as it turned into the current to approach the jetty, then subsided as it eased alongside. A man wearing a red bandanna was working the tiller and a girl was crouching in the prow. The girl, wearing jeans and a faded red T-shirt, clambered on to the jetty clutching the painter. She walked towards him, her bare feet padding on the boardwalk, and fixed him with her ebony eyes.

'You come,' she said. Her voice was as high as a flute.

'Come where?'

'You waiting for Mr Kain?'

'That's right.'

'Red say you come.'

Cabrini felt irritated. Kain was playing his games again, and he had no choice but to comply. The girl beckoned and he followed her to the edge of the jetty. The boat was heaving on the swell below, no more than five metres long, its grimy wooden deck containing only an upturned beer crate which served, Cabrini guessed, as its passenger seating. The man with the bandanna, his face lined like a sailor's and timelessly old, was still gripping the giant tiller while nursing the diesel engine with his bare foot. Cabrini climbed down into the boat and sat on the crate, his arms and sturdy legs splayed across the deck, his jacket on his lap, his attaché case by his feet.

The man kicked at the gear lever beside the engine, then opened the throttle with his foot. The engine roared as the boat lurched away from the jetty, heeling over so far that Cabrini feared it would capsize. He grabbed at the side of the boat and braced his feet against the deck until it righted itself and sped towards the opposite shore. He was sure they would run aground but at the last moment the man heaved on the tiller, the boat bucking and bouncing as it headed into the current.

The girl had perched beside the engine, watching Cabrini with the unembarrassed stare of a child. Her boyish body made it hard to tell how old she was: anywhere from 15 to 20, he supposed.

'What's your name?' he shouted.

She smiled but did not answer. Cabrini tried again.

'Tell me your name.'

'My name is Kop.'

'Is that your real name? Or is it what Kain calls you?'

She looked puzzled. 'I am Kop,' she said.

'Do we have far to go?'

She smiled again and looked away. The river was curving now, making a broad sweep to the right, and there was a yellow glow on the water. A temple came into sight, its layered roofs curled like petals, glinting in the rising moon. As it passed by, Cabrini saw a brighter orange light ahead. At its heart was an ornate palace, tiered with minarets and flanked by two slender towers, illuminated by floodlights so dazzling that Cabrini had to look away. Even after the palace disappeared, the orange aura lingered before it too was consumed by the dark.

Without warning, they veered to the left. At first Cabrini supposed that they were searching for somewhere to land but as they approached the shore the boat slid into a narrow waterway that he took to be a canal. The man eased back the throttle and the boat shrugged and settled as it glided across the canal's viscous surface. They were passing between high banks, with shadowy houses set back on both sides, hurricane lamps in their porches reflecting weakly on the water. There was a sudden splashing, followed by shouts and a burst of shrill laughter from children swimming somewhere out of sight. The shouts faded, to be replaced by the sucking of the prow.

Kop stood up and edged past Cabrini to kneel in the bow, shining a torch ahead. Cabrini wondered if they had arrived but all he could see in the thin yellow beam were long sinewy tendrils trailing in the water, then a momentary flurry as some unknown creature – a rat? an otter? – dived for cover among a cluster of tree-roots. He looked at his watch: more than an hour had passed since they had left the jetty. The canal was narrowing and Cabrini supposed they were nearing its navigable limits, yet still they pushed on. The night was pressing in and he heard himself drawing deep, rasping breaths as if oxygen was in short supply. A pair of mosquitoes whined around him and he put on his jacket, pulling up the collar to his ears. Damn you, Kain, he thought.

Kop was leaning out over the water as she prospected with the torch.

'How much further?' he asked.

She called back but Cabrini could not tell whether she was

addressing him or the man. Then, at the extent of her beam, he glimpsed a crude landing stage, nothing more than a plank supported by two poles, projecting into the river. She called again, and the man slowed the engine to little more than idling speed. It coughed and stuttered as the boat slid towards the bank, jolting to a halt beside the plank. Kop turned round.

'We here,' she said.

She stepped on to the plank and gestured to Cabrini to follow. He was halfway along when there was a growl from behind. He turned to see the boat slipping away. When he looked ahead, Kop had vanished. There was no sign of Kain.

'Hey Kain,' Cabrini called. 'It's me, Antoine.'

The engine noise faded and died. For a moment it seemed that everything was still. Then the air was filled by the sawing ululations of crickets, breaking the silence as if cued by a mischievous conductor.

'Kain,' Cabrini called again. 'Are you there?'

There was a chuckle from above, cutting through the incantations of the crickets.

'Antoine, old buddy. Glad you could make it.'

'*Merde!* Hey Kain, stop screwing around.'

'Why don't you come up and have a drink?'

There was a short line of steps above the landing stage. As Cabrini reached the top, he saw a low bungalow, set back a dozen paces from the canal. Kain was standing in the doorway, silhouetted by the light, his face indistinct. He raised a bottle of beer to his mouth, turning his head so that a ponytail was visible behind. As Cabrini approached, Kain reached out his hand to greet him, drawing him inside.

The house Kain occupied was built of teak, a relic of the colonial days in Bangkok when the merchants and administrators constructed their homes as far as possible from the sounds and smells of the city, its poverty and its despair. Kain had acquired the house, he liked to boast, from a former business contact: 'a guy,' he would elaborate, 'who couldn't complete his side of the deal.'

Did this former contact object?

'He didn't get the chance,' Kain would say, a grin displaying his perfect teeth, reflecting in his china-blue eyes.

The house had a verandah, raised from the ground as a precaution against Bangkok's propensity for sudden torrential rain. Kop lay on the verandah, barely cushioned with a mat, her face turned towards the river. The *farangs* were talking about her, the floorboards creaking as they moved around the room by the doorway, its window casting its light on the verandah just beyond her head.

'You like my little brown bunny?' said Kain.

'She doesn't have much to say,' his visitor replied.

'She came with the house.'

The visitor laughed. Kop didn't know if he would be staying until the morning. She thought of her father, who would be cooking noodles and drinking gin in their shack, perched on stilts beside the canal a short way from the landing stage. If Kain ordered him to take the visitor back to Bangkok that evening, no matter what time it was, he would have to go. Whatever Kain wanted, her father had to obey, as he too had come with the house. The *farangs* were speaking again. She closed her eyes in concentration, trying to register the words.

'I brought her details. Take a look.'

That was the visitor. There was silence, then Kain asked:

'Where is she now?'

'In Spain. Palma de Mallorca.'

'Spain, for fuck's sake. What's the use of that?'

'It's okay.'

'I told you, day one. No screw ups.'

'Listen, my friend. It's risky if she stays in France all the time. The authorities will get to know too much about her.'

'So what's your plan?'

'It's very simple. Your people fetch her from Palma. It's thirty hours to France, no more. There are quiet places where they can wait until you tell them to bring her to you, two hours away, three at the most. When you've finished then puff, she's gone. Provided everyone is careful, no-one will notice her. Why don't you take another look?'

Another silence. Finally Kain said: 'Okay, she's fine.'

'That's settled then?' said the visitor.

'Settled,' said Kain. 'You want another beer?'

'Sure.'

'Kop,' Kain called.

She waited, stirring as though she were emerging from sleep. He called again and this time she answered. 'I'm coming.'

'Get in here and get us two beers.'

She walked through the doorway, passing the room where they were talking and going to a refrigerator at the back of the house. She removed two bottles and took them into the front room, unscrewing the caps and averting her eyes as she passed them to Kain. She glimpsed the visitor with his attaché case open on a table, papers scattered. She stood still as if expecting further instructions but Kain waved her away. She returned to the verandah and lay down, waiting for the talk to resume. It was quieter now; the crickets' chorus was muted and the humidity was weighing on her like a blanket, the signs of an approaching storm.

'Pictures?'

'It's done,' the visitor said. 'They'll be waiting when I get back.'

'Done where? How?' Kain was spitting out the words. 'Any chance your people were spotted?'

'*Calmes-toi*, my friend. They were very careful.'

'Where?' Kain asked again.

'In England, of course. Outside the school. Nobody saw them.'

'How will I get them?'

'The same way as you pick up messages.'

'On the computer?'

'That's right. No meetings. No phone calls. Nothing in writing. That's the rule. You're okay with the laptop?'

'Sure,' said Kain. 'I've used these things before. So long as it works.'

'It will, don't worry. What else?'

'This cousin of yours.'

'Sanpiero.'

'You're sure his place is safe?'

'Of course I'm sure.'

'Entrances?'

'Two. But most people only know one.'

'What about the police?'

'No problem. We own them. How long do you need it for?'

'Two weeks, three weeks max. It depends on how much he wants the kid back.'

'Sanpiero is a patient man. What about you?'

Kop was still. Even though she was used to the humidity, she could feel her skin grow clammy as the storm clouds poised to break.

'It depends,' said Kain.

'On what?'

'Whether I get what I want.'

'And if not?'

The rain exploded on the roof of the bungalow, hammering on its wooden tiles, sheeting off the verandah barely a foot from where Kop lay, swamping all other sounds. She could no longer hear the words from inside, only murmurs of the *farangs*' talk. Then Kain's voice briefly rose and she realised he had come to the window, his shadow breaking the pool of light beside her head. He stood there silently and she remained motionless until she sensed he had gone back inside. The rain was easing already, then stopped as abruptly as it had begun. There was the patter of dripping water, and the sawing of the crickets began again. Inside the house, the conversation seemed to be coming to an end.

'I'd better be getting back,' the visitor was saying. 'Before it rains some more.'

'Suit yourself,' said Kain.

He called out to Kop. She knew what he wanted and she cupped her hands to her mouth, giving three hoots, like one of the marsh owls that live along the canal. She imagined her father taking a last gulp of gin before hurrying down the steps to bring up the boat. She heard it come clattering through the darkness, saw its shape easing alongside the landing stage. Kain and his visitor were waiting on the verandah, then shaking hands.

'Kop,' said Kain.

She went ahead of the visitor, guiding him to the river bank, holding his case as he stepped on to the boat, following him aboard. There was a roar as her father opened up the engine and moved it into gear. Behind them Kain was framed once more in the doorway, staring at the point where the boat had disappeared, his eyes fixed on the night and the dark.

Part One

1

On the balcony of his room overlooking the swimming pool at the Hôtel Le Bosquet, Mark Carlson watched his prey. It was not as easy as he had hoped. The hotel, with its curving driveway, its pillared entrance, its gleaming white cupola topped by a navy blue flag that hung listlessly in the afternoon heat, had been constructed on a wooded promontory extending into the Mediterranean from Saint Jean-Cap-Ferrat. The myriad trees which surrounded the hotel, from orange and palm to blue cedar and cypress, provided welcome relief against the Provençal sun. The problem for Carlson was that a luxuriant eucalyptus was obstructing his view of the pool. He had already rearranged the furniture on his balcony, pushing the white wrought iron table with its two matching chairs into the corner, to give himself the best vantage point. By inclining his head against the balcony wall so that it lowered his line of vision by six inches, he found that he could obtain a clear sight-line to the pool and the four people beside it. He extracted another Marlboro from the packet that lay on the table. Cigarettes were a useful prop: who would look twice at someone indolently smoking on his balcony while taking in the view of the trees, and the azure sea beyond? Then he concentrated on each of the four figures in turn.

There was the laughing girl called Fiona, just emerging after completing a dozen lengths in a strong, athletic crawl. As she climbed the steps on to the pool-side, revealing a vivid yellow bikini, the water glistened on her long auburn hair. Then there was the boy, Josh, with his long, clean limbs, flashing his smile that showed off his well-kept teeth, winning a laugh from her with his banter.

Sitting beneath an ample parasol at a table at the far end of the pool, with a fresh *citron pressé* in her hand, was the woman, Mrs Beaumont – Ms Suzanne Beaumont, of Austin, Texas, as she had signed herself in the hotel register. She too was wearing a bikini, if rather less revealing than the girl's. With her fine, creamy skin – Carlson thought of a white peach – she was taking more care to shield herself from the sun than the kids. Her honey-coloured hair was fastened behind her head with a tortoise-shell barrette. He guessed she was around forty, but could pass for a lot less.

Finally there was the boy the others called Olivier, who so far had not ventured into the pool. He was a less perfect specimen: his shoulders were bony, his ribs pronounced. Carlson had found it hard to learn anything about him. He was not staying at the hotel, and the receptionist had been no help. But that was an hour ago. Now Carlson knew all that he needed to know.

Twice he had seen Olivier grow restless, fidgeting with his fingers, paying little attention to what the others were saying. Twice Olivier had excused himself and withdrawn to the whitewashed *cabanon* set back from the pool that served as the changing room for Le Bosquet's guests. Twice he had come back sniffing and rubbing his nose.

Olivier wasn't on amphetamines or anything else that comes in a pill – of that, Carlson was sure. If he'd been taking pills, he would have been able to palm them into his mouth without the others noticing. Whatever Olivier's drug of choice, consuming it required privacy of the kind he could find in the *cabanon*. He was in and out so quickly he had to be snorting; almost certainly, that meant cocaine.

Carlson stubbed out his cigarette and stood up. It was going to be easier than he'd thought. Without a further glance at either the trees or the sea, he withdrew inside, into the shadows of his room.

'Oh hi, dad.'

Tom Stewart could see his daughter's hair trailing down the back of her chair and one slender leg sprawled over its side. On the television screen beside her dressing table, Jack Nicholson was flashing one of his manic grins.

'Guess the movie,' she said, without turning round.

'*The Last Detail*?'

Her face appeared above the chair, her hazel eyes teasingly bright.

'Come on dad, you must know this one. It's about a journalist.'

He racked his mind. 'Give me a clue.'

'Directed by Antonioni?'

'*The Passenger*?'

'About time too. Haven't you seen it?'

'I kept missing it.'

'You can't have done. It's about this reporter who goes to Africa. A gun-runner dies and it's just got to the bit where Jack Nicholson takes on his identity.'

'So you've seen it before?'

'I got it out on video a couple of months ago.'

'Do you know where Antonioni lives?'

'Rome?'

'Not any more. He's got a villa at Lake Como. There was a piece about him in the *Herald Tribune* I read on the plane. He holds court in a local café every morning. He can't speak since he had a stroke, but he loves to listen to his fans talking about his films.'

Fiona stood up. She was wearing a mauve T-shirt inscribed with the words 'Natural Born Lovers'.

'I came to tell you about dinner,' he said. 'I've booked a table for eight.'

'Who are the other six?' she asked, in a deadpan voice.

It took Stewart a moment to get the joke, even though he was used to his daughter's sudden shafts of wit. 'I walked into that, didn't I?' he laughed. Then he added: 'You've got less than an hour to get ready.'

'Oh shit,' she said. 'I'd better unpack.'

Her suitcase lay across the bed, clothes spilling out from beneath the half-open lid. She removed a pile of shirts and placed them in the top drawer of the dressing-table. Stewart opened the French windows and walked on to the balcony. The blue-green leaves of a eucalyptus tree shimmered in the breeze. A salmon pink bird with black and white wings was showering spray on the top step of the swimming pool.

'There's a hoopoe having a bath out here,' Stewart called.

Fiona joined him at the rail of the balcony just in time to see a blur of plumage disappearing through the trees. Stewart put his arm across her shoulder. 'I'm so glad we're here,' he said.

'So am I. I've really been looking forward to this.'

'Did you enjoy the pool this afternoon?'

'It was all right.'

Stewart assumed that meant she had enjoyed herself. She returned to the room and continued unpacking.

'What did you do?' he said from the balcony.

'Sitting around and swimming. Sitting around, mostly.'

'What do you think of the Beaumonts?'

'She's cool. She runs her own company in the States. It does medical research, biotechnology, that kind of stuff. They find treatments for illnesses no one else has been able to cure.'

'What sort of illnesses?'

'Viruses, blood diseases, especially in children. She's done really well.'

'That's very impressive. What about Josh?'

'What about him?

'Do you like him?'

'He's all right.'

'That's what you said about the pool. Only all right?'

'Well – he's all right.'

'So you do like him?'

'Yeah – sort of.'

He had played these verbal duels with her before, trying to penetrate the air of indifference with which she liked to cloak her feelings. It sounded as if she fancied Josh.

'I didn't think much of his friend,' she said.

'Who's that?'

'He's called Olivier. He's French but they go to the same boarding school in England. His father lives somewhere near here.'

'What's wrong with him?'

'Nothing really.'

'I thought you said you didn't like him.'

'He just seems a bit weird, that's all.'

'What does that mean?'

'If you'd turned up at the pool, you might have found out.'

Stewart looked abruptly at his daughter. The barb had

struck home. They had given the Beaumonts a lift in the car he had rented at Nice Airport. As they arrived at the hotel, he had suggested that Fee join them at the pool while he finished the work he had brought with him from London. 'I didn't promise I'd come,' he protested. 'I said I'd try.'

'That's what you always used to say,' she replied. 'I think that's one reason mum got so pissed off with you.'

'Fee, that's history. Don't let's get into it now.' He went inside, to find her in the bathroom arranging a small collection of moisturisers and creams. 'Anyway, I've just spoken to her.'

'Is she all right?'

'More or less. There was a delay at Heathrow and she was three hours late getting into Baltimore. She sends you her love and says not to worry about her – just make sure you have a great time.'

A frown crossed Fee's face. 'How's gran?'

'She's okay for the moment. She's having more tests in a day or so. We should know the results by the end of the week.'

Fee had finished unpacking. She picked up a silky white shift that seemed impossibly short.

'I think I'll wear this tonight.'

'It looks terrific,' Stewart said. She appeared to take no notice, but Stewart was relieved. The last time he had taken her to dinner, in a modish brasserie in Soho, she had worn torn jeans and what looked like a pair of army boots. He so wanted the evening to be a success. He had already asked the *maître d'hôtel* to give them a table on the terrace, overlooking the Mediterranean. He glanced at his watch. 'I'd better go and sort myself out. I'll call for you on my way down.'

Fee lay the dress carefully on the bed. Then she reached up and kissed him lightly on the lips.

'I'm really happy, dad,' she said.

'That's cool,' he said with a grin.

Olivier Lavar, nearly nineteen, currently residing in the toytown principality of Monte Carlo where his father maintained an apartment mainly for tax purposes, ordered bourbon on the rocks. It was his second drink of the evening and it was not yet seven thirty. In the cocktail bar of Le Bosquet, a measure of bourbon cost the equivalent of ten dollars. Not having ten dollars to spare, Olivier signed for his drinks with Josh Beaumont's name and room number. That's what buddies were for.

It shouldn't have been necessary. Olivier Lavar should have been able to afford his own bourbon but the allowance his father gave him, generous though it was, stretched only so far. Cocaine is expensive when it gets to be a habit.

'Can I buy you a drink?'

The man who said this was tall, blond, his accent American. He stood beside Olivier's chair, smiling down at him in a disarmingly familiar manner.

'Do I know you?' Olivier asked.

'Not yet, but I'm pretty certain you know your way around this town. I figured I'd buy you a drink and maybe you'd show me.'

Olivier's internal alarm system was ringing.

'What do you want?'

The American pulled out a chair and sat down at the table.

'The bartender thinks your name is Josh Beaumont, but it's not. You're Olivier, right? I think you may have a little liquidity problem.'

A waiter arrived bearing two glasses of bourbon on a tray.

'Your drinks, Monsieur Carlson. Shall I charge them to your room?'

'That's fine,' he said.

'I have to go,' said Olivier.

'That's a shame.' Suddenly earnest, the American leaned across the table. 'What's the problem? You think I'm a cop?'

That was precisely what Olivier thought: a cop, or some other kind of trouble. He wanted to stand up, but the American's fingers were pinning his wrist to the arm of his chair.

'Look, Olivier, if I was a cop out to bust you, I'd try to sell you something or buy it. I wouldn't give.'

The American withdrew his hand, dropping into Olivier's lap a small square of folded paper.

'You're looking a little ragged. I know the feeling. The men's room is over there.' He grinned.

Olivier looked down at the folded paper, then back at Kain, wondering if this was a trap. Kain smiled, providing the assurance Olivier needed. He picked up the paper and headed across the floor of the bar.

The stuff was superb, the best he'd ever had. When he returned from the men's room his gums were tingling. He took a shot of the bourbon and swilled it around his mouth. It tasted like nectar. He looked at Carlson inquiringly.

'I have the same needs as you, Olivier,' Carlson said 'I'm stuck here for three weeks and you've just had the last of my stash.'

From his pocket the American produced a plump roll of five hundred franc notes. 'I don't have a liquidity problem. Help me, and I'll help you.'

Olivier looked at the roll of notes for a moment.

'So what is it you want me to do?'

Stewart read the passage again:

Among the hundreds of visitors to the Vietnam war memorial in Washington that crisp, late-summer's day, one figure stood out. While others surged past he remained in one spot, as if examining his reflection in the ebony marble of the memorial wall. Maybe he was; for sons are given to contemplating their father's image, and wondering how much of themselves they can see. He was called Luke Meriwether Lewis, after the renowned explorer who, with his partner William Clark, opened up Luke's native Kansas almost two hundred years ago. And the father who had christened him was Captain Barney Lewis, of the US Marine Corps, whose name had been etched into the marble at the very place where his son now stood. But Captain Lewis was not among the fifty-six thousand American dead of the Vietnam war, not officially. Instead, like more than two thousand others, he had been consigned to a nether land, occupied by those classified as Missing In Action. And so Luke was fated to wonder what had happened to his father, and even to dream that he might not be dead at all, and in that dream to reflect who he was himself; and how much of his father might have been preserved in him.

It's getting better, Stewart thought. Before going to see his daughter, he had spent several hours reworking the opening pages of his manuscript: chiselling at his words, sharpening their focus. But he knew that it was not his opening chapter, or the subsequent four hundred pages, that were the problem. It was the last chapter, which he knew he still could not write.

He stood up from the desk, clasping the towel he had secured at his waist after his shower. From the floor of his wardrobe he retrieved the bottle of Glenmorangie malt whisky he had bought at Heathrow airport. He poured some into the tumbler he had found in his bathroom, watching as the silky liquid settled in the glass. He sat on his bed and dialled his home number. When he heard his own voice answer, he keyed in a code to listen to his messages. As the unctuous tones of the British Telecom recording told him, there were four in all.

Stewart was ready for the first. It was his editor, calling from New York. 'I'm surprised not to have heard from you, Tom,' he said in the gravelly voice he used to chide his authors. 'I'm longing to hear how you got on in Bangkok. Call me.'

'Do you want to repeat that message?' asked the recording.

'No,' said Stewart, and erased it.

The second message did not surprise him either.

'Tom, this is Luke Lewis in Washington. I'm keen to hear what happened on your trip. Get back to me, will you?'

Stewart kept the message, then listened to the third.

'It's Luke again, Tom. Please call me, any time.'

The fourth was even more pressing.

'Hey, Tom, what's going on? What did you find out? Call me. Please.'

Stewart let a measure of Glenmorangie swill around his mouth, savouring its tang before swallowing it down. He picked up the receiver and dialled a second number in London. It was engaged.

He took the tumbler into the bathroom and peered at the mirror. He ran his fingers through his long, tousled hair and smoothed his face with his hand to check there were no stray bristles, particularly in the dimple cleaving down his chin. There seemed to be a new depth to the semi-circles beneath his pale blue eyes. Was it the fallout of his ceaseless travelling over the past weeks, doing his best to grab some sleep in departure lounges and economy class airline seats? Or was it the more permanent talisman of a man in his early forties? The short, elliptical scar on his right cheek, which at first he had assumed would fade with time, seemed more vivid too. Six years after acquiring it in Beirut – nothing heroic, merely the legacy of a shard of glass tumbling out of the air following an explosion a half-dozen blocks away – he realised that it would be his for life.

He returned to the bedroom. It was time to dress, but he could summon no enthusiasm for his suit, which hung from the wardrobe door. Some people, he had come to realise, managed to look well turned-out no matter what they wore. He wasn't one of them. Even though he had bought the suit in a rash moment at a hideously expensive tailor's in Jermyn Street, he knew that it would persist in drooping from his angular shoulders. He returned the suit to the wardrobe and selected the loose pale blue shirt and chinos he always seemed to fall back on.

He re-dialled the London number. This time an answering machine replied.

'Hi. This is Jonathan Baxter. Leave a message after the tone, and I'll get back to you.'

Stewart replaced the receiver and looked at his watch. He had bought it in Bangkok, from a street vendor who told him that his life would be incomplete without a watch that contained an altimeter. Since he was a sucker for gadgets, he had easily succumbed. But he had still not mastered the sequence of controls which took it through the functions, from timepiece to altimeter via stopwatch, alarm, countdown and barometer. Although it had displayed the time in Fee's bedroom, it now insisted on informing him that he was ten metres above sea level. Stewart tried in vain to switch modes before admitting defeat by dialling the hotel reception. 'It's ten to eight,' the cheerful receptionist told him.

Stewart took a final swallow of malt. He contemplated the empty glass before concluding that it was probably too late for a refill. He picked up his manuscript and placed it inside a grey box folder which he slid into the bottom of the chest of drawers beside the wardrobe. For the evening at least, he was determined to put it, and thoughts of Luke Lewis, to one side.

* * *

'Everything's perfect,' Stewart said.

The head waiter smiled and placed two menus on the table. Beyond the terrace, the Mediterranean merged seamlessly with the sky and the evening air was laden with a heady aroma of eucalyptus and pine. Fee's white dress hung in filmy folds and she was wearing the strand of pearls he had given her for her sixteenth birthday almost exactly a year before. Stewart thought she looked stunning: a mix of innocence and knowingness that would surely break some man's heart one day, if not his own.

'You look terrific,' he said.

'Cheers, dad,' Fee said with an air of nonchalance, though he thought he detected a blush before she turned to look at the view. A blue-hulled catamaran glided past the tip of the promontory on its way into port, its crew lowering the sails with military efficiency.

'Have you ever been sailing?' he asked.

'No. Have you?'

'I did a bit before I met your mother. I used to go off at weekends with a friend around the Solent and across the Channel. The boats are rather cramped and it can be dangerous if you're hit by a storm, but that's all part of the fun.'

'So why did you give it up?'

'It was partly meeting your mother. She wasn't keen at all. Plus I started getting a lot of assignments abroad which meant I wasn't around so much at weekends. Why, do you fancy having a go?'

She looked back at the yacht as it made a lazy turn around the buoy marking the entrance to the harbour. 'Why not? We can do it while we're here.' She added, with sudden enthusiasm: 'You can teach me if you want.'

Stewart had not expected her to take up his offer with such alacrity. 'I'll see if we can hire a boat somewhere,' he said vaguely. He saw a waiter hovering and asked Fee if she had looked at the menu. The day's catch, an extraordinary array of local seafood, was hand-written alongside the carte.

'What about the sole?' Stewart suggested. 'That's what I'm going to have.'

'They've got bouillabaisse,' she said.

'It's the classic Mediterranean dish,' Stewart told her. 'Why don't you try it?'

Fee agreed. For the first course, she asked for melon while her father chose a salad with goat's cheese. When the sommelier arrived, Stewart ordered a bottle of Puligny Montrachet – a little smugly, Fee thought.

'What's so special about that?'

'It's one of the great white burgundies,' Stewart said. 'I thought we should celebrate.'

'Celebrate what?'

He took in the restaurant, the sea, the immaculate sky, with a sweep of his hand. 'All this,' he said. 'And being here with you.'

A waiter came and unfolded their napkins. 'So we get to do this every night?' Fee asked.

'We'll see,' Stewart replied teasingly. 'What have you been up to at home?'

'I've got a job,' she announced brightly.

Stewart was startled. 'What about school?'

'No, dad. It's a summer job, for when I get back. I'm going to work for a television company called First Rate Films. Mum sorted it out for me. She's worked with them at Channel 4.'

Stewart harboured dark suspicions of the television world inhabited by his former wife, where independent production companies seemed to have the life-span of a mayfly on a good day. 'Are they well known?' he asked.

'Sort of,' said Fee. 'They made a drama-doc last year about a British army patrol that deserted during the Gulf War. The one I'm working on is about what happens in a village in Wales when the last pit closes. I'm going on the shoot, then I'll be working in the edit suite during post-production. Everything's cut on computer now, so I'll learn how it all works.'

Stewart felt the same irritation as when Rachel used to slip into film production jargon. 'It all sounds very worthy,' he said guardedly. 'How much are they paying you?'

'Not a lot,' Fee admitted. 'About ten pounds a day.'

'*How much?*'

'Honestly, dad, it's not for the money. It's the chance it gives me.'

'The chance to do what?'

'To learn about making movies. Mum's been bringing home loads of videos, which is cool. We've watched nearly all of Antonioni's movies. We saw *L'Avventura* last week.'

It was twenty years since Stewart had seen Antonioni's saga about a coterie of bored Italian aristocrats moving listlessly between relationships, with Monica Vitti the most inscrutable of all.

'What did you make of it?' he asked.

'It was all right.'

'All right as in okay? Or all right as in, I really enjoyed it?'

'No, I enjoyed it,' Fee assured him. 'But I didn't understand it all.'

'It's about a woman who disappears, isn't it?'

'Thanks, dad,' said Fee, a touch sarcastically. 'I did manage to figure that much out.' Then she said: 'I liked *Blowup* best. David Hemmings and the Sixties and all that. And that really tall supermodel.'

'Verushka.'

'That's her. I thought it was clever the way Hemmings enlarged the photos and saw the guy with the gun and he went to the park and found that body.'

'And when he went back the next day it wasn't there.'

'So you've seen it?'

'I saw it with your mother a long time ago.'

'But you never saw *The Passenger*?'

'No.'

'Jack Nicholson was brilliant, especially when he was pretending to be the gun-runner. An actor acting someone acting someone else.'

Stewart remembered Fee's part as Viola in her school's production of *Twelfth Night* at Christmas, when she portrayed the character pretending to be a boy with particular aplomb. 'I can see why that would appeal to you,' he said.

The Puligny Montrachet arrived. After the ritual uncorking and tasting, Fee took her first taste.

'What you do think?' her father asked.

'It's lovely,' she announced, to Stewart's relief.

Two waiters brought the first courses. Fee spooned into her melon and let the chunk dissolve in her mouth.

'How's school?' he asked.
'All right,' she replied, cautiously.
'How did you get on in your exams?'
'Fine.'
'What does that mean?'
'To be honest, I couldn't be bothered with them.'
'Don't the exams matter?'
'Only if you want to go to university.'
Stewart was about to take a sip of wine but he put the glass back on the table. 'I thought that's what you wanted to do?'
'No, dad, that's what *you* wanted me to do. I think it's a waste of time.'
Ever since the divorce, Stewart had assumed that Fee would go to university, and had agreed with Rachel that he would meet the cost. 'Who on earth gave you that idea?' he said suspiciously. 'Was it your mother?'
'Don't be stupid, dad. It wasn't mum's idea, it was mine. Having a degree doesn't mean you're going to get a job any more. Plus you end up with a massive debt. If I'm going to work in movies, I'd be better off starting at the bottom and working my way up. Like you.'
'But I didn't know you wanted to work in movies,' Stewart protested.
'That's what I keep trying to tell you.'
'Fee, how much have you thought about this?'
'I've thought about it a lot. And mum says she doesn't mind, as long as I'm sure it's what I want to do.'
Stewart was beginning to feel conspired against. 'But are you sure you know what you're doing?' he asked, trying to keep his voice even. 'The film industry is about as insecure as it gets.'
'I don't need you to tell me that,' she snapped. 'Someone's got to succeed. Why shouldn't it be me?'
'Why not go to university first?'
'I've *told* you, dad.' She was sounding pained. 'Because I don't want to waste three years listening to lectures when I could be learning how to make films. Do you know where Quentin Tarantino studied?'
'No, I don't,' Stewart admitted. He suddenly felt his age.
'The Manhattan Beach Video Store. He learned how to be

a director by watching great movies. Including Antonioni's, as it happens.'

'Come on, Fee. Tarantino's a one-off. Wouldn't it be sensible to get a degree first, so that you've got something to fall back on?'

'Why?'

'In case things don't work out,' he said as gently as he could.

'You mean in case I fail. Thanks a lot, dad. Don't worry, I'm not going to fail.'

'And I'm sure you won't,' Stewart replied, with as much reassurance as he could muster, just as the waiters arrived with the main course. Fee looked on quizzically as a steaming tureen was placed on the table beside her.

'Do I help myself?' she asked, peering into its depths.

'That's the general idea,' Stewart said.

She ladled some chunks of fish on to her plate. 'What's classic about this?'

'Try it and see, he said.

His sole was deliciously fresh. 'What's it like?' he asked, as she completed her first mouthful.

'Not bad,' she said.

They ate in silence for a while, and then Stewart asked: 'Would you like to go to Monaco tomorrow?'

She frowned. 'What for?'

'It's a bit touristy but we can take a look at the royal palace, and the casino's fun – very kitsch. And I know a terrific restaurant on the quay where we can watch the boats.'

Fee wrinkled her nose. 'You remember what you said about Antonioni going to a café at Lake Como every morning?'

Stewart knew what was coming next.

'Why don't we drive to Italy? I'd love to see him, even if he can't speak.'

'It's a hell of a long way.'

'No it isn't,' Fee persisted. 'I've looked it up on the map. It's about two hundred miles but most of that's on motorways.'

'We'd have to get up terribly early. It said in the *Trib* that he leaves the café around midday to go home for lunch and a siesta.'

Fee was clearly not to be diverted. 'I don't mind. We can make it if we leave by seven. Come on, dad.'

'I'm sorry, I can't. Not tomorrow, anyway.'

'Why not?'

'I've got to go into Nice first thing to get a copy of the *Trib.*'

'What for?

'The same reason I was reading it on the plane. There's something I'm looking out for.'

'Well, what?'

'It's very complicated. I don't really want to go into it now.'

'Don't they have it here at the hotel?'

'I've already asked the receptionist and they don't.'

'Can't it wait until we get back from Lake Como?'

'I'm afraid not. Because if what I'm looking for is in tomorrow's *Trib*, then there's something else I'll have to do in the morning.'

'Is this work?' She made it sound like an accusation.

Stewart hesitated. 'In a way.'

Fee looked pained. 'But dad, you *promised.* You said when we came on holiday you wouldn't bring any work. But you have. You worked this afternoon and now you're doing it again tomorrow. That's what you've always done.' She put down her spoon and fork. 'Anyway, why can't you tell me what it's all about?'

'Honestly, Fee, it's not that important.' Even as Stewart spoke, he knew he had set himself another trap. She saw it at once.

'Just now you said it's too complicated. Now it's not important. But it's important enough to stop us going to see Antonioni.'

'Look, I'm sorry about tomorrow. We can go and see him one day next week.'

'He might not be there next week.'

'There's no guarantee he'll be there tomorrow either. We'll have to take the chance whenever we go. Now, about tomorrow. If we go to Monaco, we can see about hiring a boat after lunch. Would you like that?'

Fee seemed placated. 'All right,' she said. 'But next week's a promise.' It was more a statement than a question.

'Promise,' Stewart replied.

Fee was making progress with her bouillabaisse. She took another sip of wine.

'What was Bangkok like?'

'I don't like it much,' Stewart said. 'It's incredibly crowded, the pollution's dreadful, and it's full of disgusting middle-aged men on sex tours.'

'But what about the palaces and the temples with all the carvings?'

'I never got to see them. I spent most of my time in girlie bars.'

'Doing what?'

'Research for my book.'

'What kind of research do you do in girlie bars?'

'You don't want to know. They're really sordid places. A lot of the girls have been sold to the bars by their parents, and some of them are even younger than you.'

'But what's that got to do with your book? I thought it was about Vietnam and the war.'

Stewart felt trapped again. 'Look, Fee, I'm sorry, but I just can't tell you. At least, not yet.'

'Why the hell not?'

Until now, he had absorbed Fee's more barbed remarks. For the first time he feared that the conversation was moving beyond his control.

'I can't even tell you that, because then I'd have to tell you what it is I can't tell you. Please trust me. I promise I'll tell you as soon as I can.'

He met her eyes to see if his appeal had succeeded. It had not.

'Why *can't* you tell me what you're doing?' Her voice was suddenly hard beyond her years. 'Why should I trust you when you won't trust me?'

He reached across the table and let his hand rest on her arm. 'Fee, please.'

'Work's always come first for you, hasn't it? Holidays, birthdays, things at school – if anything came up on the far side of the world, you went off and didn't care what happened to us. Now, on our so-called perfect holiday, you're doing it again – and you won't even tell me why.'

Her voice was rising and she pulled her arm away. 'If you want to keep me out of your life, fine. But don't get angry when I tell you what I want to do with mine. Because it's *my* life and I'll live it how I want.'

Heads were turning across the restaurant and the bouillabaisse was congealing on Fee's plate. He had an irretrievable sense of loss, as if his daughter had just slipped from his grasp.

'Please, sweetheart,' he said softly. 'Don't spoil the holiday. I've been looking forward to it so much.'

Fee gripped her napkin but she could not stop her hand from trembling. 'And you can spare me the emotional blackmail,' she said. 'You know you're spending all this money just so you don't feel so bad about leaving mum and me. Well, it doesn't work any more. You can't buy me off.'

Stewart lost his patience. 'That's enough,' he said harshly. 'Don't you dare talk to me like that. I'm your father.'

'And?' The single syllable was laden with contempt.

'I know sometimes my work still gets in the way. And sometimes I don't get things right. But I do my best to be there for you when you want me.'

She stood up, knocking over her glass of Puligny Montrachet. The wine flooded across the table. Tears were coursing down her cheeks.

'Dad, you just don't have a fucking clue.'

She fled from the restaurant without looking back.

Ten years before, Tom Stewart had given up smoking. It had been a quick, decisive break of which he was proud. Sometimes the urge returned, particularly when the adrenalin was racing, as it had done most recently in Bangkok. Always he had fought off the temptation. But this time, standing on the hotel terrace, he would have given anything for just one cigarette.

He replayed the conversation with Fee in his head, trying to work out where it had all gone so horribly awry. He recognised that, on the eve of her seventeenth birthday, his daughter had become sharper and more aware, less tolerant of his old evasions. She was right, of course: in the past he had fought a losing battle to balance his family and work responsibilities, with work usually winning out. But this time . . .

'How nice to see you again.'

The woman who had interrupted his thoughts was holding out her hand. She was wearing a stole across her shoulders, and her honey-coloured hair framed her face.

'Mrs Beaumont,' said Stewart, shaking her hand.

'Please, it's Suzanne. I wanted to thank you again, for giving us a ride from the airport.'

'A pleasure. And thank you for letting Fiona spend the afternoon with you.'

'Now that really was a pleasure.' She smiled. 'Josh and I liked her a lot. She's so bright. You have a very special daughter, Tom.'

Don't I just, he thought.

'And she's very proud of you. So how was dinner? It's a beautiful restaurant, isn't it?'

'The food was just fine,' said Stewart.

'It's none of my business,' she said, 'but we couldn't help noticing that Fiona seemed upset in there. Is there anything I can do to help?'

'That's kind of you,' responded Stewart stiffly, 'but I don't think there's anything you can do. Her grandmother has had a stroke. Fee is very fond of her and naturally she's worried. She lives in Maryland and Fee's mother's over there now. We can only hope she's going to be all right.'

'Do you think she'd like to spend some time with Josh tomorrow? If you're going to be busy?'

'I appreciate the offer, but we're going to Monaco. She's quite keen to go, and I'm hoping it'll take her mind off her grandmother.'

'Well, have a good time,' she said. 'You will take care of her, won't you?'

* * *

What is life to me without thee?
What is left if thou art dead?

In the softly-lit study of a substantial house in London south of the River Thames, Victor Canning lay motionless on a large off-white sofa, listening to the true contralto of Kathleen Ferrier coming to him through the speakers of his stereo system. There were occasions when her voice was the only thing that could soothe him.

His eyes stared, unseeing, at the ceiling. The irises were deep blue but in the shadows of the room their colour seemed to come from further down the spectrum. They were violet, and when his pupils contracted they resembled points of molten gold, as if the retinas were on fire. His body was sturdy, of not much more than medium height. Even inert on the sofa, he gave the impression of a raw power at odds with the fragile beauty of the music that absorbed him.

Though he was at home, and it was late in the evening, he was formally dressed. He wore a cream shirt with French cuffs and a lightly-starched collar, together with a sober tie patterned in grey and maroon. The trousers of his suit were charcoal-grey and well-pressed, and the jacket, single-breasted, cut with one vent in the back, was carefully draped over the back of a chair. Alongside sat his black shoes, highly polished, with the laces undone. It was as if he was awaiting the late arrival of visitors – guests rather than friends – who would expect a degree of decorum. This was not the case. He rarely allowed anyone to enter his home, apart from his housekeeper. He had no friends.

As Kathleen Ferrier brought *What is Life* to its poignant end, he got up from the sofa, crossed the room to his stereo system and considered his next choice. When detectives from the Criminal Intelligence Section of the London Metropolitan Police found a way to place a listening device in Canning's lair, they became familiar with Ferrier's exquisite interpretations of Gluck and Handel and Bach. Those who drew the listening duty learned nothing to their advantage, but some of them became quite taken with Handel's 'Art Thou Troubled?' It was also one of Canning's favourites and he chose it now.

Art thou troubled?
Music will calm thee.
Art though weary?
Rest shall be thine.

2

NL, no response received before deadline. It's now or never. St Germain, Thursday, usual time. ALEX.

AUNT MUSI. Ratman ate Preacher Paul. Need replacement. Call me.

REWARD. Anyone knowing whereabouts of Gayle Susan ARCHER, last heard of in Geneva, please call +33 90 72 48 11.

SACRED HEART OF JESUS and Saint Jude, thank you for answering my prayer. DC.

Nothing there.

Tom Stewart thought of the note he had pushed under Fee's door on his way out of the hotel.

'Fee, I've gone into Nice to get the *Trib*. Sorry, but I have to do it. We can still make lunch in Monaco. I'll call you later. Love, Dad. PS: I've left something for you at reception.'

The 'something' was a package he had bought at the Dubai Duty Free on his way home from Bangkok. He had intended it as Fee's birthday present but, on impulse, had decided to give it to her now – a kind of peace-offering, he hoped. That left the problem of what to give her on her birthday, but there were still two days to sort that out.

He returned to the *International Herald Tribune* he had bought at a kiosk on the Promenade des Anglais, spreading it out on the table of a beach café in the shade of the promenade's celebrated rows of palms. Beneath the ads for 'Escorts and Guides' – 'NICKY: Charismatic, beautiful – you will NOT be disappointed' – were rows of so-called business opportunities: save money importing from China; set up a company in the Channel Islands; buy a Belize passport for $50,000 and gain entry to eighty countries, from Bolivia to Venezuela.

Still nothing.

He drained his coffee cup and beckoned to the waiter who had served it fifteen minutes before.

'Do you have a payphone?'

The waiter pointed to a *cabine* fifty metres along the promenade.

'I'll be back in a moment,' Stewart told him. 'Would you bring me another coffee?'

The *cabine* took phonecards. Stewart still had one from a previous visit to France, and the display beside the receiver told him he had three units left.

'Jonathan,' he said, when his call went through. 'It's Tom. Did anything arrive for me?'

Jonathan Baxter was his neighbour, an acquaintance more than a friend, but somebody he could call on for a favour.

'Well, I picked up your post like you asked. There's nothing from Bangkok, or anywhere else exotic, I'm afraid. All you had was three bills and what looks like a bank statement. Do you want me to open it?'

'No, spare me the bad news.'

'You want me to keep checking?'

'Yes, please.'

'How's the weather?'

Stewart heard a succession of staccato beeps. The screen told him his phonecard had run out.

'Jonathan, I'll call you . . .'

He was about to say 'tomorrow' when the line went dead.

The café was beginning to fill. Next to his table a German couple, who had just staked out their place on the beach with straw mats, were drinking Orangina. His coffee, still steaming, was waiting for him. He turned the pages of the *Tribune* but could find no more small-ads. The news from Britain was predictably dreary: the so-called beef war in Brussels, the quest for peace in Northern Ireland, each of them mired in rhetoric and impasse. Then his eye was caught by another headline:

Vietnam – the search for MIAs goes on

In rugged terrain, investigators still cherish hopes

In rugged terrain . . .

Stewart was back in Vietnam, at the heart of a stark landscape, a jumble of mountain peaks, with twisting ridges on their flanks, intersected by ravines where turbulent rivers flowed. Everywhere was green: the green of bamboo and elephant grass, the green of the forest canopy, made luxuriant by the rain of the monsoon. There was a clammy heat that seemed intensified by the hoots and cries echoing from the forest around. He remembered the US general in his battle fatigues who had beckoned to him across a clearing, and shown him the searchers' booty, carefully stored under a tarpaulin canopy. And he thought again of his last chapter, and what he would have to tell Luke . . .

An ashtray clattered on to the table.

'Is there anything more, monsieur?'

Stewart saw a line of people waiting to be seated. He looked at his watch. It was coming up to noon – and he hadn't called Fee. He paid the waiter and started walking briskly to the *cabine*. Then he remembered he needed another phonecard.

He returned to the café, where the waiter was showing a couple to his table. 'Where can I buy a phonecard?'

'The *tabac*, monsieur. Along there.' He pointed back down the promenade.

Stewart reassured himself that if he got back to Le Bosquet by twelve thirty, they could easily get to Monaco for lunch. The drive back to the hotel – given luck – was twenty minutes, plus five minutes for the phone call: there was still time.

The *tabac* was five hundred metres along the promenade. It was closed. There were three *cabines* outside: they all took cards, not coins. He saw another cluster of *cabines* in the distance. Should he head back to his car, parked in the warren of side streets behind the promenade? Or take the chance of finding a *cabine* that took coins?

He took the chance.

The package her father had left at reception contained a camera: the latest, most hi-tech model available, of course.

When Fee touched the shutter button there was an intriguing *beep* and the image in the viewfinder swam into focus.

There was Josh, lying on one of Le Bosquet's towels at the edge of the swimming pool. Beside him, watching him from a table, was Olivier, his fingers strumming at a bottle of beer; behind them was the pool. She pressed the zoom button and the water seemed to dance before her eyes, points of light sparkling like crystals across its surface. She moved the camera to the left and there was Josh again, a book in front of him on the towel, open at the first page.

'Hey, Josh – this way.'

Josh looked up, grinned when he saw the camera, and flexed his biceps. There was another *beep* when Fee pushed down the button and the shutter clicked.

'What else can you do?' she laughed.

He gave her a boy-model pose, sullen, lips pouting, eyes lowered.

'You're so up yourself, Josh,' she said.

'My turn,' he said, reaching out for the camera.

'Don't get it wet.'

'Yeah, yeah.'

In the viewfinder, Josh saw a young woman in dark glasses looking at him disdainfully from beneath her parasol.

'You're full of it yourself,' he said, pressing the shutter. 'What zoom has it got?'

'Power driven. Three hundred mil.'

'Excellent,' he said, adjusting the zoom until Fee's face, her glasses now pushed forward on her nose, filled the frame.

'One more,' he said, pressing the shutter again.

'Jo-osh.'

'Okay, okay,' said Josh. He handed back the camera, then asked: 'What was happening with your father last night?'

'What are you on about?'

'Over dinner, I mean.'

'Oh, that. It was nothing, really. You know what parents are like.'

Fee wandered away from Josh and sat on a bench, scanning the surroundings through the viewfinder. She panned into the trees near the hotel entrance, so that they appeared as a barrier of greens and browns, then followed the ribbon of the driveway winding its way back to the hotel. A line of balconies appeared, overlooking the pool. She zoomed in and found that she could see into the darkened room behind. A man was sitting on his bed watching television. She pressed the shutter, which suddenly seemed terribly loud. She half-expected him to come running on to the balcony but he stayed where he was, scratching his stomach. She photographed him again: *click*.

She focused on the next balcony: empty. At the entrance to the next a woman was drying her hair: *click*. The next was half-obscured but in the corner sat a man drinking coffee: zoom, *click*. In the next, two children were running in and out; she heard a muffled shout, presumably from their mother. *Click*.

'Naughty,' said Josh, who had walked over to where she was sitting. 'Did you get anything good?'

'Like what?'

'People at it?'

'Don't be sad, Josh.'

Josh had the grace to laugh. 'The camera must have cost a fortune,' he said.

'Probably,' she said.

Not probably, she told herself. Certainly. Her father had done it once again: lavishing presents on her, this time to compensate for their row. She knew him well enough to guess that it had been intended as her birthday present. She had tried to push the row from her mind but it came surging back. She didn't want to tell Josh what had happened: he was too new a friend for that. She felt angry and confused: angry with her father for provoking her and with herself for upsetting him; confused over what she wanted him to do now. But where was he? She stole a look at Josh's watch: already past twelve. Perhaps he was trying to buy her another birthday present. So much for his idea of going to Monaco for lunch. She suddenly didn't want to see him, not yet anyway, even if he did come back in time to go to Monaco. She hadn't really wanted to go there in the first place.

She put the camera on the table. 'Shall we go and explore?'

'Explore where?' replied Josh.

'Anywhere. Anywhere not here.'

'I've got this book to read,' Josh said.

Olivier was just swallowing some beer. 'We could go to Villefranche,' he said as he put the bottle on the table.

'What's at Villefranche?' Fee asked.

'Lots,' Olivier said. 'It's got bars and clubs. Or we could go out in a boat.'

'Sounds cool,' said Fee. 'What about it, Josh?'

'God, my mother would go ballistic. I'm grounded. I can't go anywhere until I've finished this book.'

Fee picked up the book, which was open at the first page. '*Les Enfants Terribles*,' she read out. 'You don't seem to have got very far.'

'That's why I'm grounded,' Josh said. 'Anyway, I thought you were having lunch with your dad.'

'So did I,' she said. 'At least, I was supposed to be.'

'I've got my car here,' said Olivier. 'We can get there in no time.'

'What about this book?' asked Josh.

'There's masses of time to finish it before you go back to school,' said Olivier.

'Besides, if you read it now, you'll forget it all anyway,' added Fee.

'What shall I do about my mother?'

'Leave her a note,' said Fee. 'I'll write one for my dad too.'

'I'm still not sure about this.'

'Come on, Josh,' said Fee. 'Get a life.'

The woman in the *tabac* peeled a phonecard from the pack she kept in the top drawer of the counter. 'It's a pretty one, isn't it?' she said. In other circumstances, Stewart might have agreed. The card – one of a series illustrated with stills from classic French films – depicted Simone Signoret with one hand on hip, the other holding a telephone to her ear. She looked impatient, as though she was waiting for the operator to answer.

None of the *cabines* further along the promenade had taken coins. Ruing his gamble, Stewart had decided to search for a *tabac* that was open. He had taken another twenty minutes to find one. Stewart, who would not have noticed if the card had depicted a troupe of naked dancing girls, seized it from the shopkeeper and thrust a fifty franc note into her hand.

The *cabine* outside the *tabac* was occupied, of course. A youth in motorcycle leathers lounged against the glass. As Stewart met his eyes, he responded with an insolent fuck-you stare. There was no other *cabine* in sight. The youth kept talking until beeps from the phone indicated that his card was about to run out. Stewart prayed that he did not have another one. It was now ten to one, and lunch anywhere, let alone Monaco, was a rapidly evaporating prospect. To his relief, the youth quit the *cabine*. Stewart dialled the hotel and asked to speak to his daughter.

There was a pause, then the operator came back on the line.

'I'm sorry, Monsieur. There is no answer from your daughter's room.'

He asked to talk to the receptionist. Outside, the youth was revving his scooter's engine as if it were a Harley-Davidson. Above the noise, Stewart thought he heard the receptionist say his daughter had gone.

'Gone where, Maria?'

He pressed the receiver hard against his ear to block out the crescendo of the scooter's departure.

'She said she was going out for the afternoon, Mr Stewart. She's left you a note.'

'Did she seem upset?'

'Not at all.'

'Could you read me the note, please?'

'*Dad,*' Fee had written, '*We've gone to Villefranche for the afternoon. Hope you're okay. See you later. Love, Fee. PS: Thanks for the brilliant camera.*'

'She's underlined brilliant,' Maria added. 'And there are two crosses at the end.'

Stewart thanked her and hung up. So, the camera was brilliant. His tinge of irritation that Fee had not waited for him was far outweighed by his relief that she appeared to have consigned last night's debacle to history. Although he had long overstayed his time, there was no parking ticket taped to the windscreen when he returned to the Renault. Things were definitely looking up.

He drove out of Nice and retraced his journey towards Cap Ferrat. His first thought was to return to the hotel but he could see the seductive rise of the Alpes Maritimes beyond, their white caps etched against a cloudless sky. He had always liked the mountains. They stood for family holidays with his parents, who had led him on walks along desolate glens to the remote lochs and corries of the Scottish Highlands. When Fee was growing up, Rachel preferred beach holidays, and he'd been in no position to argue, particularly as he never knew until the last minute whether he would be able to join them.

On an impulse, he ignored the Cap Ferrat turning and continued on the coast road towards Menton. After Beaulieu, he took a minor road that climbed, in a long series of zigzags, to the village of Eze and beyond it, still higher, to the *Grande Corniche*, the dizzying cliffside road built for Napoleon's armies. He followed the *corniche* until it dropped towards Menton and then struck off again, winding steadily upwards as the road followed the line of a river dropping steeply through a wooded gorge. Then the road emerged above the treeline and cut across a bare mountainside, with streaks of bleached scree fanning out from jagged limestone crags. Stewart stopped the car. He remembered his watch: this was the moment he had bought it for. He pressed the display button repeatedly. No matter what he did, it persisted in telling him that the altitude was twenty minutes to four.

He took it off and stuffed it into the glove compartment. As he pushed the lid shut, an unwelcome image returned to him: of the grey cardboard box file, containing his manuscript, stowed in the bottom of the chest of drawers back at the hotel. He dispelled it from his mind and got out of the car. Above, the road worked its way towards a gap between the crags on the skyline. Below, stretching along the horizon like some timeless artifact, lay the Mediterranean. The air was perfectly still, the silence broken only by the rustle of cicadas. He walked a few yards off the road and sat down on a block of white quartzite rock, its smooth surface radiating the heat of the day.

In the distance he could see the smudged shape of ships and their wakes – on their way, he fancied, to distant lands. For a moment he felt the traveller's urge to be on the move, savouring the expectation of arriving at an unfamiliar destination, imagining the cacophony of new sights and sounds coming at him from all sides. He quelled it, and looked again at the vessels poised in mid-journey, wondering where they were bound, and what tales they enshrined.

Victor Canning's live-in housekeeper had taken the afternoon off to visit her sister in Dorking. She would not return until 10 p.m. or even later – far too late to prepare his evening meal. His instructions to her were, as always, that he would fend for himself. Nevertheless, as was her routine, she had left a supper for him wrapped in cling-film on the top shelf of the refrigerator, and a tray set for one. Canning, who invariably dined at eight, picked at the plate of cold meats as he waited for the kettle to boil. He made tea in a bone china pot and then carried the tray up two flights of stairs and along a broad corridor to his study.

Beside the door was a keypad, recessed into the wall. Canning entered the code that deactivated the alarm and waited five seconds until the signal light turned from red to green, telling him it was safe to enter. A motion sensor turned on a table lamp, for although it was still light outside, the thick curtains at the study's windows were, as always, tightly closed. There was a soft click as the sensor activated his hi-fi equipment. Placing the tray on a large walnut writing desk, he removed his jacket and hung it carefully on the back of his chair while he waited to learn how this evening's Kathleen Ferrier concert would begin. Ten compact discs containing her life's recorded work were always kept loaded in the CD player, with the programme selection menu set to 'random' so that he never knew what treat lay in store. This evening, plaintive strings announced the beginning of Pergolesi's *Stabat Mater*, in Canning's view the greatest work of an unrecognised genius who completed it only weeks before he died at twenty-six, to be buried in a pauper's grave.

As the chorus made its entrance, Canning unlocked a drawer of the desk and removed a notebook computer equipped with a modem which he connected to the telephone line. His fingers moved swiftly over the keyboard as he entered a set of instructions that were transported to an electronic mailbox in Zurich. Last month the mailbox was in Vienna. Next week it could be in Hamburg, or Caracas, or Los Angeles, or any one of a score of cities at his disposal. Changing some of the patterns of his life was only one of Victor Canning's precautions.

Ferrier began the second verse:

Through her heart, His sorrow sharing,
All his bitter anguish bearing . . .

As her voice subsided, the computer made the connection with Zurich and logged on to the remote system. Line after line of hieroglyphics raced across a screen that glowed a ghostly white, casting Canning's broad face in the same unearthly light. The messages were in code and to read them he typed in a password that also changed from month to month. It was formed from six digits which he had derived from significant dates in Kathleen Ferrier's short life. The current password came from the date of her unsuccessful marriage.

There were eleven messages in all for him to read. He scrolled through them rapidly until one seized his attention. The message had been sent by RED BIRD and was addressed to RAVEN. It read: THE BIRD IS IN THE NEST.

3

'Is my daughter back yet, Maria?'

The receptionist smiled and inspected the rows of pigeon-holes behind her. 'No, Monsieur Stewart, her key is still here.'

It was five o'clock. Whatever she was doing in Villefranche, it could be another couple of hours before she was back. He wondered where they should go for dinner. Better not the hotel, after the previous night's disaster; perhaps to one of the quayside restaurants in Villefranche. He thought briefly of trying to find her there, but dismissed it as hopeless. He had no idea where she was.

Stewart went to his room, passing Fee's locked door on his way, and stepped out on to the balcony. There was nobody to be seen in the grounds; the swimming pool was deserted, and seemed suddenly enticing.

It was twenty-five metres long, generous for a hotel, and Stewart resolved to swim forty lengths. Normally he reckoned he could cover one thousand metres in twenty minutes. After so long spent travelling, twenty-two minutes sounded a more realistic goal. As he pushed away from the edge and moved into an easy crawl, he felt his shoulders loosen and some of the day's tension drain away. He reached the far end and made a somersault turn, kicking firmly off the wall, getting into his rhythm.

Four lengths passed, then eight, twelve. You're doing fine, he told himself. Sixteen. Twenty. Halfway there.

It was on the twenty-first length that Stewart became aware of someone beside him, matching him so precisely stroke for stroke that he thought at first he was seeing his own reflection in the water. After they kicked simultaneously at the next turn, he realised that his second self was edging ahead. He notched up his own pace a fraction and drew level. This was no mirage but another swimmer, laying down a challenge.

Twenty-six lengths. Thirty. His rival was still there, bubbles streaming from his body as he hit each turn. Stewart's shoulders were aching. He told himself to stay relaxed, swim through the pain, come through the other side. Thirty-two lengths, thirty-four. His lungs gulped for air each time he turned his head out of the water.

Four lengths to go. He nurtured his strength for a final surge.

Two more left. *Kick away. Go for it.*

As Stewart channelled all his remaining energy into the final length, his rival eased away. He performed a perfect turn and was already heading back down the pool when Stewart's last despairing stroke took him to the wall. He grasped the edge and threw back his head, gasping for air. His heart was still pounding when he heard an American voice say: 'Hey, good swim. I didn't have much left, I'll tell you. I'm glad you quit when you did.'

The American climbed out of the pool, showing his powerful haunches and calves. His chest was tanned and muscular and he certainly wasn't breathing like a man who had just exerted himself unduly.

'Carlson,' he said, stretching out his hand. 'Mark Carlson.'

'I'm Tom. Tom Stewart.'

'Good to know you. How about a beer?'

They sat down at one of the pool-side tables and Carlson beckoned to the waiter.

'On vacation?' he asked.

'Sort of,' said Stewart. 'Half holiday, half work.'

'Two beers,' Carlson said as the waiter appeared beside them. 'The kind that comes out of a tap. That okay with you, Tom?'

Stewart said it was fine. The waiter returned bearing two glasses of foaming *pression*. Carlson signed the bill and Stewart savoured the first bitter taste of the beer as it hit the back of his mouth.

'So which half are you on now?'

'Sorry?'

'Is this the vacation part?'

'Sort of. I'm a writer and the trouble is, you never really stop writing.'

'What do you write?'

Not very much at the moment, Stewart thought. He dodged the question. 'Books, articles, as it comes. What about you? What do you do?'

Carlson drained half his beer in one swallow and said he was in computers: software development for the Internet. He told Stewart about the licensing deals that had brought him to Europe and looked like keeping him there for the duration.

'You people can't get enough of our stuff, I'm glad to say.'

'So where are you headed next?'

There was a sudden commotion at the far end of the pool. An Italian family of at least three generations had arrived, and were colonising the tables and loungers with their beach-bags and towels. Closer by, Stewart saw an elderly woman sitting on the edge of the pool, stretching a green bathing cap over her snow-white hair. She lowered herself stiffly into the water but was then transformed, swimming with a graceful breast stroke that seemed to take her through the water with the ease of a swan. Carlson said it was a good thing she hadn't been around earlier, as she'd have made fools of the pair of them. They both laughed.

'Where's home?' Stewart asked.

Carlson said he came from Baltimore, Maryland, and perhaps Stewart had been there. Stewart said he had indeed, as his wife's parents also lived in Maryland. Carlson said it was a small world.

'Is she here – your wife?'

'No. I should have said ex-wife. I'm here with my daughter. That's the holiday part.'

'Oh, right. I guess I saw you both in the restaurant last night. What's her name?'

'Fiona.'

'Pretty name. Is she having a good time?'

Not last night, she wasn't, Stewart thought, but he wasn't going to admit that to Carlson. 'Seems to be. She loves the pool and she's already made a couple of friends.'

Carlson must have signalled to the waiter for he materialised at their table with two more glasses of beer. Stewart said it was his turn to pay, but Carlson insisted. He begged a booklet of matches from the waiter and lit a Marlboro. My only vice, he said, exhaling a trace of smoke. Stewart turned to look at the elderly woman in the green cap and reckoned she was already into her fifth length.

'Do you live in London?'

'Some of the time,' Stewart replied.

'What about Fiona's friends? Are they from England too?'

'Not exactly.' Stewart explained that although they both went to school in England, one was American, the other French.

'That's nice,' Carlson said. 'A sort of family of nations. Now, the American boy, would he be the one who's staying here with his mother? Tall, good-looking woman, from Texas. Suzanne something. What's her second name?'

Stewart felt a flicker of unease, but could find no reason not to tell him: 'Beaumont – Suzanne Beaumont.'

'That's it. Got her own business, I understand. Do you know what she does?'

This time Stewart hesitated. 'Hey, don't mind me, I'm as curious as a cat,' Carlson said. 'You see, I was chatting to her boy this morning – Josh?'

'That's right.'

'And he told me his mother was here for a conference, something to do with biotechnology. If she's got her own hi-tech company, she could be in the market for some software.' He grinned. 'I never turn down the chance to do a little business.'

Stewart said he didn't know much about her, and even less about her business. Carlson waved his hand, as if to say it was of no account.

The noise from the Italian encampment was growing. A fat man, whose body appeared to be completely hairless, performed a belly-flop that cleaved the water into two matching tidal waves. The elderly woman in the green cap swam serenely on.

'So, is Fiona at college?' Carlson asked.

'Not yet. She's barely seventeen. In fact, she's not seventeen for another two days.'

'Hey, so you get to spend her birthday here together. That's great! I suppose she lives with her mother most of the time?'

Stewart said that she did, and then stood up. 'Look, talking of Fiona, I'd better be going. I've got to find out what's happened to her.'

'Is there a problem?'

'No, I don't think so. She went off to Villefranche for the afternoon and she hasn't come back yet.'

'Well, it's not that late, is it? I'm sure she's fine.'

'I hope you're right.'

Carlson stubbed out his cigarette and offered his hand. 'Good talking to you, Tom. You be sure you enjoy the rest of your vacation.'

Stewart woke with a start and looked at his watch. To his surprise, it had remained in time mode, and showed that it was almost 7.30 p.m. He had only meant to close his eyes for a few minutes, but he had slept for more than an hour. He picked up the telephone and dialled room 212. There was no reply. He called reception and asked if there were any messages for him. None. Was his daughter's room key still in its pigeonhole? Yes, it was.

Where was she?

He went to the bathroom and splashed cold water on his face. A sudden thought came to him, and he hurried back to the phone and called reception again. What about Josh Beaumont's room key, he asked? Was that still in its pigeonhole?

'Yes, Mr Stewart.'

'What about his mother?' Stewart asked.

'Her key is also here,' said the receptionist. 'I haven't seen any of them this afternoon. Perhaps they are together?'

Perhaps they were. Perhaps that explained it. Perhaps there was nothing to worry about, after all. He found himself standing by the desk in his room. He picked up his manuscript and read his opening words again. He noticed the repetition of the word 'one' in the second sentence and wondered whether to change it. Then he realised that this was a diversion from his greater preoccupation. He dialled his own number in London and heard the prim voice report: 'You have no messages.'

He looked at his watch again. It said 7.57 p.m. In three

minutes, he would check at the reception desk once again, this time in person.

At 7.59, Stewart left his room. As he neared the bottom of the stairs, he saw Suzanne Beaumont talking to Maria, who, for once, was not smiling. Suzanne was wearing a lemon yellow linen business suit with a straight skirt and matching yellow strap sandals. There was a black leather attaché case at her feet, and she looked tired. As Stewart approached, she turned towards him, holding a sheet of the hotel's blue notepaper in her hand.

He was about to speak when she said, 'Do you know where your daughter is?'

'I was hoping she was with you.'

'With me?' she looked puzzled. 'I've been working all day, setting up an exhibition stand.'

'Is that a note from Josh?'

'Yes. Did you get one from Fiona? What did it say?'

'That she'd gone into Villefranche for the afternoon. Actually, she said "we've" gone into Villefranche. I presumed she meant her and Josh. What about yours?'

She let him read it.

Mother dear,
With the best will in the world, there is only so much of Monsieur Cocteau's prose a boy can take at one sitting. There's a chapel in Villefranche where he painted the walls, or so I'm told. So we've gone to see it. Is a Cocteau painting worth a thousand Cocteau words? I certainly hope so.
Josh.

It was Stewart who now look puzzled.

'He's supposed to be studying while he's here,' explained Suzanne. 'At least part of the time. French literature in general, Cocteau in particular. He didn't do too well at French Lit last semester.'

'I see.'

'The thing is,' Suzanne added, 'it's getting pretty late.'

He could measure the anxiety behind the tiredness in her eyes. Although he knew the time perfectly well, he looked at his watch. 'It's only just gone eight o'clock.'

She didn't look reassured. 'It's a pathetic excuse,' she said.

'What is?'

'Going to look at a chapel.'

Stewart laughed. 'I don't know. It sounded like a pretty ingenious alibi to me.'

'I'm glad you think it's funny,' she said. She picked up her attaché case. 'If you hear from your daughter, you might let me know. Good night, Mr Stewart.' He watched her stride away.

Twenty minutes later, the telephone rang in Stewart's room. He was sitting by it and picked up the receiver instantly.

'Fee?'

It was Suzanne who replied. 'I'm afraid it's me. And I'm sorry for the way I over-reacted just now.'

'Don't worry. I could have been more sympathetic. No news, I suppose?'

'No, nothing at all.'

'Listen, were you thinking of having dinner?' he asked.

'I don't think I can face food.'

'No, you're right. How about a drink?'

There was a pause and then she said she would settle for a walk in the grounds.

'Larry's dead,' her father-in-law had said. There was no warning, no softening of the blow. He reported it as if it were a matter of fact, another bit of business data to be factored into his calculations, even though he was talking about the death of his only child.

At first Suzanne responded in kind. She assimilated Jesse's information about the crash, and how there must have been some kind of engine failure to make Larry's Cessna fall out of a clear blue sky. 'I carried on tidying the kitchen, I made the beds. Then it hit me like a kick in the stomach.' Her arms and legs were trembling and she had to sit down. She called a neighbour, who hurried round, bringing others with her. One of them went to fetch Josh from school. They were left alone while Suzanne tried to tell him what had happened.

'Josh, you know what it is when someone dies?'

He stared at her with uncomprehending eyes. Then, when she spoke the fateful words – 'Your father's dead' – he hurled himself at her, head buried in her lap, his body heaving as he sobbed. She took his head and cradled it in her arms, looking at him through her own tears. His face turned to hers and she could see him imploring, without words: 'Mom, tell me it isn't true.' But it was true, and there was no comfort she could offer him. His tears chilled her again now, even in the soft warmth of a summer's night in the south of France.

'You're getting cold,' said Stewart gently. 'Let's go back.'

She said she was all right. At his suggestion, they had walked the length of Le Bosquet's driveway and now stood at its entrance, watching the swallows swoop and dive in the dusk. Stewart was surprised that this comparative stranger had opened up to him about one of the most painful moments of her life. Then he presumed that talking about it still had a cathartic effect for her, and he was grateful for the diversion it provided from his own growing anxiety.

'When did it happen?' he asked.

Almost five years ago, she said; five years next month, in fact. To be even more precise, on the twenty-third of next month, at eight minutes past ten in the morning, Texas time. The plane had exploded on impact. Later Jesse had told her that investigators found dirt in the Cessna's carburettor, and the engine had cut out as Larry was climbing away from Austin's municipal airport on his way to his father's ranch. It was Jesse who had asked him to make the flight.

'How did Jesse take it?'

'At first it was as though he didn't care,' said Suzanne. 'But when I saw him that night, he broke down and cried. He's never done that before or since. It has to be the worst loss of all, when your own children die before you.'

'What about Josh? He was, what, eleven?'

'Twelve.'

Older than Luke, Stewart thought. What was worse? To know for certain your father was dead, and try to come to terms with that? Or nurture hopes that slowly died?

'How did Josh cope?'

'From that moment, he had two huge burdens. He'd lost his father, and he had to carry all his grandfather's hopes.'

'You make it sound as if it was too much for him.'

'It was. You see, nobody could love Larry as much as Jesse did,' she said. 'At least, not in Jesse's eyes.' It wasn't bitterness Stewart thought he could hear in her voice so much as resignation. 'He'd invested so much in him.'

Suzanne fell silent, and Stewart decided to go back to the beginning. He asked: 'What was Larry's business?'

Suzanne composed herself. 'He and Jesse started a biotechnology company together. About twelve years ago. The company was Larry's idea – at least, the science was. When Larry came back from college he had a science degree, *summa cum laude*, and a yearning to get into genetic engineering. He was passionate about it. There were all kinds of diseases he thought it could cure one day – from cystic fibrosis to some kinds of cancer. Of course, it was futuristic stuff. Replacing defective human cells with functioning ones seemed a pretty long way off. But a lot of the early research was very promising, especially in developing pharmaceutical compounds and vaccines. And the potential rewards were sensational. That was what appealed to Jesse, of course.'

So, she explained, Jesse had raised the start-up capital, while Larry recruited the scientists and directed their research. Larry also looked after most of the day-to-day running of the business. 'It worked,' she said, 'because each of them knew what they did best. Boy, did it work.'

With a certain bravura which typified Jesse's approach, they called their company BioGenius Incorporated. On Larry's advice, its research was first directed at finding a cure for an immune deficiency disease known as CHID syndrome, whose victims were first and foremost young people. Much like AIDS, CHIDS was caused by a virus that attacked the T-cells, a key defensive element in the human immune system. Larry and his colleagues had focused on finding a way of enabling the T-cells to resist the virus's attack. In a key moment of inspiration, they concluded that the best way of doing that was to genetically re-engineer the T-cells so that they were no longer recognised by the CHIDS virus – in effect, to camouflage them.

They manufactured a protein in their laboratories which did precisely that. It also brought a bonus they had not expected. It was not just that the CHIDS virus ignored the T-cells; the T-cells retained their own aggressive properties and destroyed the virus. The early testing on MycoGene, as

Larry had dubbed the new protein, produced phenomenal results. Barely three years after the first clinical trials had been completed, MycoGene was on the point of receiving 'fast-track' approval from the Food and Drug Administration in Washington. 'You can imagine what that did for the stock price,' she said.

Then Larry was killed.

'Jesse's hopes were in ruins – above all, his dreams of a family dynasty.'

'So he transferred all that to Josh?' asked Stewart.

'Right. Everything he'd wanted Larry to be – everything Larry was – Josh had to fulfil. He simply wasn't ready.'

The family had used the Cessna all the time, and as soon as Josh was old enough to reach the controls, Larry had let him fly the plane for part of the flight. On his twelfth birthday, they all flew up to Jesse's ranch together. This time Larry had let Josh take over as soon as they got clear of Austin. Josh flew all the way and even made the landing. Larry liked to say that Josh was a natural – born to fly, just like his dad. Josh was so proud. That was one week before his father died.

Josh never wanted to fly a plane again. But two years after the crash, Jesse was flying him and Suzanne to San Antonio. He'd taken his hands off the controls and said: 'You have command, son.' Josh sat there as though turned to stone, and no amount of cajoling on Jesse's part had helped. That was when it all started.

'Of course he didn't want to fly the plane, not after what had happened to his father. But Jesse thought he should snap out of it. He wanted someone as driven as Larry, and as ruthless as himself, and this was some kind of test. As Jesse saw it, if Josh could get over his fear and take control of the plane, then one day he would take over BioGenius. But he was only fourteen. I told Jesse he had to give him time.'

'Did Jesse understand?'

'I don't know,' said Suzanne. 'But I made the working assumption that he did.'

'What do you want for Josh?'

'I want him to be happy. Doesn't any mother? But I know he's got his father's best qualities, and if he does eventually get involved with the company he could achieve some wonderful

I made a deal with Jesse. He paid for the schooling – it doesn't come cheap – and he got me.'

Stewart stopped and looked at her. 'I'm sorry?'

The deal was, she said, she went to work for him. Jesse was the entrepreneur, the deal-maker, not the nuts and bolts man. 'He always needed someone he trusted to run the show while he concentrated on what he calls the bigger picture. Originally, of course, that someone was Larry.

'After he died Jesse did his best to manage everything himself. But when things began to go wrong with Josh, he saw I had qualities he could use.' Larry had built up a strong team of scientific researchers who could more or less run themselves, but what was needed was somebody to take charge of the business. She had a Masters in Business Administration and, no less important, she was 'family', and Jesse felt he could trust her. For Suzanne's part, 'I thought it was important to carry Larry's banner and hope that one day Josh would want to pick it up himself.' She joined the company a month before Josh went to England, Jesse rewarding her with the title 'Vice President of Marketing and Corporate Affairs'.

'It suited me,' she said. 'Of course, it's hard work. Jesse thinks everyone should work seven days a week, like him. But I've learned how to cope with his demands and make them fit my life.'

'So how did you escape?

'You mean here?' To Stewart's relief, Suzanne laughed. 'Oh, I'm only out on parole. There's a big biotech conference going on in Nice. Usual kind of thing: academics arguing about their results, and a trade show going on at the same time. It's the sort of occasion BioGenius can't miss. But it suited me perfectly. Josh's school has just started the summer break, so I could bring him down here to be with me. Afterwards we'll go back to Austin together for the rest of his vacation. Of course, Jesse thinks he's studying, and he's partly right. It should help improve his French. That's the theory, anyway.'

They had reached the hotel and were standing near the entrance when a taxi entered the driveway. As it approached, Stewart could see two people in the back – a young man and woman. His stomach gave a start.

'Is that them?' he said.

The taxi drew up. A young couple got out and went into the hotel without looking round. The insignia on the taxi's sign said 'Voyages Orange – Villefranche.' Stewart bent down to question the driver. Was it difficult getting a taxi in Villefranche? Not tonight, said the driver. Business wasn't exactly booming.

'You know,' said Suzanne, 'I'm just wondering if they took a taxi at all. Maybe they're with Olivier. He's got a car.'

'Wouldn't Josh have mentioned it in his note?'

'Maybe not. He knows I don't entirely approve of Olivier. There was some trouble at school last month. They both got caught going into an exam with crib sheets in their pockets, in Josh's handwriting. Josh took the blame, and said it was his idea, but I'm not so sure. There's something about Olivier that I don't quite trust. And if they went off with Olivier, Josh wouldn't necessarily tell me.'

'Maybe that's it,' said Stewart. 'Perhaps Olivier did pick them up here, or perhaps he met them in Villefranche? And if he did, maybe he's taken them somewhere? A party, or something? Do you know where he's staying?'

'I'm not sure. I know his father owns an apartment in Monaco. I think Olivier uses it when he's in France, but I don't know the address.'

'Do you know his father's first name?'

'Yves. Yves Lavar.'

'Well, it can't be too hard to find.'

They went into the hotel and approached the reception desk where Maria looked as cheerful as she had that morning, when Stewart had entrusted her with Fee's camera. When he told her they needed to find a phone number, she showed them the Minitel computer, which, she assured them, listed every telephone number in France. She typed in 'Lavar, Yves', followed by 'Monaco'.

The screen flickered briefly and she gave an apologetic smile.

'I'm sorry,' she said. 'He's on the *Liste Rouge*.'

'Meaning?' Stewart asked.

'The number is not available. At Monsieur Lavar's request.'

It was Suzanne who spoke first. 'So what the hell do we do now?'

'Let's go into Villefranche.'

'I don't know where that will get us.'

Neither did he, but it was better than doing nothing.

They said little as they drove across Cap Ferrat towards Villefranche. The car's headlights picked out the trunks of roadside trees and beyond them the night. As the lights of an oncoming car flared in Suzanne's face, he wondered why she had confided so much to him.

'Any theories?' he asked.

'What about?'

'The children.'

'I have some instincts. What worries me most is that I thought I knew Josh well. But I have no idea what he could be doing.'

'What's the worst thing that can have happened?' Stewart asked.

'They've gone off in Olivier's car and there's been an accident, I suppose. But I keep telling myself we would have heard by now. Isn't that what they say? No news is good news?'

'What sort of things is he into?'

'What do you mean?'

'Does he like to go to parties? Have a good time?'

'Sure. What teenager doesn't?'

'Does he use drugs?'

Suzanne fell silent and Stewart wondered if he had gone too far. Finally she said: 'It's a fair question, but I'm pretty sure he doesn't. I didn't tell you this before, but that's another reason I thought that sending him to school in England would be a good idea.'

'What makes you think it's any different in England?'

'Are you saying that Fee's using drugs?'

The question struck home, but not in the way she had intended.

'I honestly don't know. Sometimes I wonder if I know her at all.'

He thought of the night before, and Fee's icy voice and blazing eyes.

'Are you talking about what happened over dinner?'

'Yes. You said you'd seen that?'

'It was pretty hard to miss. I should think everyone in the restaurant saw it. Why was she so upset? Was it really about her grandmother?'

'I know that's what I told you, but I was pretty embarrassed at the time. One moment she was my beautiful and charming daughter. The next it looked as though she was behaving like a sulky brat. That's what she's like. She can be rather unpredictable, wonderfully sweet or terribly angry. Sometimes I simply don't know what to expect.'

'What were you talking about?'

'About her mostly. How she's been getting on at school, her summer job, was she enjoying the meal. Then we got on to my book and suddenly she went spare. I tried to calm her down but nothing I said made any difference. It was like talking to a stranger.'

They passed a sign that said: 'Welcome To Villefranche'. It seemed as if the good people of the town were all safely tucked up in bed. But after they turned off the main road and headed down the steep hill that led to the old cobbled harbour, another world opened up. The waterfront was lined with cafés and bistros whose tables spilled out on to the quayside. It was bathed in a pool of light, as if it were a film-set, with a line of elegant Italianate houses rising like a backdrop behind. The scene was alive with diners and drinkers and strollers, and there was a hum of talk and laughter. Normally Stewart's gregarious nature would have drawn him into its midst but now it left him disconcerted. Suzanne said: 'How on earth are we going to find them in this?'

They drove slowly along the waterfront, both of them searching for a familiar face among the throng. As they looked into the depths of one particularly crowded restaurant, he took his eyes off the road and a man crossing in front shouted at him and banged on the bonnet of his car. He braked hard and lifted his hand in contrition but they shouted at him again. Heads in the restaurant turned their way.

'This is hopeless,' he said. 'We've got to find somewhere to park.'

Ahead the street squeezed between a hotel and an angular chapel perched on the edge of the quayside. Stewart spotted a space at the end of a line of cars. When they got out they discovered that they were on the edge of a square which was markedly narrower at one end than the other. It was almost deserted, save for a young couple walking across it. Stewart turned to Suzanne, who was a pace or two behind. When he looked back, the couple had gone.

'What on earth?' he said.

'What did you say?'

'Where did they go?'

'What are you talking about?'

'Look. Over there.'

He pointed to the far side of the square, where a narrow arched entrance led underneath the ramparts of houses. A second couple emerged from the shadows beside the hotel and disappeared through the arch.

'Why don't we split up?' he said. 'You take the waterfront. I'll see what's up there.'

Suzanne agreed. 'Let's meet back here in an hour.'

It was the echoes which Stewart noticed first, as he walked through the archway and found himself in a low vaulted passageway. From somewhere ahead came the sound of footsteps, followed by a girl's shout, reverberating off the grey stone walls. A young man, standing in a doorway, followed Stewart with his eyes. Then the passage divided: one branch ran parallel with the waterfront, while the other seemed to lead further into the bowels of this subterranean world. High on its wall was a sign. Through the gloom he could just make out the words: 'Rue Obscure'.

A group of young people the same age as Fee and Josh brushed past him and disappeared around a corner. He decided to follow them. The passage became narrower, with smaller alleys leading off into the shadows on either side. Then came a throbbing that seemed to make the walls and ground shiver. He followed the group to the source where, beside a stout wooden door, a sign on the wall said in sloping scarlet letters: 'The Red Parrot'. When the door opened, he followed them inside.

He felt as if he had been the victim of a violent attack. The noise seemed to come from above and below, even from inside himself. A young woman seated at a table shouted 'one hundred francs', and he pushed a note into her hand. Ahead was an amphitheatre, where pulsating red and blue lights rebounded from the walls and young men and women were gyrating to to a hammering beat. The pulsating lights gave way to a series of brilliant white flashes that had the effect of freeze-framing the dancers. They seemed oblivious to their surroundings or even to each other, locked in their own worlds, gleaming with sweat.

He scanned the dance floor, moving from face to face, but he could not see Fee or Josh. He needed a better vantage point. On the far side of the room, near a raised platform where two disc jockeys were hunched over their console, he spotted a flight of stairs winding up from the dance floor.

The stairs took him up through a series of mezzanines. He kept climbing until he reached the highest one, set above the lighting gantries, so there was some relief from the effect of the strobes. When he peered over the balcony, the mezzanines made it seem as if he was looking down into a doll's house with cut-away floors – and if Fee and Josh were anywhere down there it was even harder to tell.

At the back of the mezzanine were several doors marked 'Private'. He knocked on one but there was no answer and when he tried the handle he found it was locked. He was about to try the next one when a hand gripped his wrist. It belonged to a man with greying hair and a stubbled chin.

'Who are you?' the man asked.

With his matching black linen suit and turtle neck sweater, Stewart thought he looked and sounded like something out of Central Casting.

He pulled his wrist free. 'What's it to you?'

'Because you're in my club.'

'You're the *patron*?'

The man nodded.

'I need your help. I'm looking for my daughter.'

Stewart took a photograph of Fee from his jacket pocket.

'As you can see, she's very young. She left our hotel this afternoon and never came back. I'm very worried. Have you seen her, please?'

The *patron* took the photograph and studied it for a few seconds before handing it back.

'She's not here,' he declared flatly.

'How can you be so sure?'

'It's my business to be sure who comes into my place. Is that a recent photograph?'

It was.

'Then she's never been here.'

He was so adamant that Stewart knew it was useless to persist. He put away the photograph, nodded a brisk thank-you, and began to turn away.

'Are you staying in Villefranche?' the *patron* asked.

'No,' said Stewart, turning back. 'Cap Ferrat.'

'Did she come to Villefranche alone?'

Stewart explained that she had been with a young American, and possibly a second man, who was French. But he had photographs of neither. The *patron* shrugged: without photographs what could he do? Stewart gave up and headed for the stairs. Above the blare he heard the *patron* shout: 'Try Le Mustang. Four doors along.'

He tried Le Mustang, and two other clubs much like it, but there was still no trace of them.

Suzanne was waiting for him, sitting on a low wall beside the chapel, when he retraced his steps to the square.

'Any luck?' he asked.

'Nothing. And you?'

'The same.'

'What do we do now?'

'Try the police, I suppose.'

The Villefranche bureau of the *Police Nationale* was set above the harbour, a newish barrack-like building with small square windows that sat incongruously among the more venerable architecture of the old town. The entrance lay beyond a pair of plate-glass doors that gave on to a broad corridor, with an enquiry desk at the far end. The glass doors were locked. A sign read 'Open: 8 a.m. to 10 p.m.' It was almost midnight.

'Let's call it a day,' he said, taking Suzanne's arm. 'There's nothing more we can do now. We'll start again in the morning.'

4

'*Votre nom, monsieur?*'

'Thomas Stewart.'

The desk sergeant at the Nice headquarters of the *Police Nationale* typed the foreigner's name with two fingers. He inspected his handiwork, selected a bottle of white-out fluid from the cluster of office equipment on his desk, made a correction, and waited for it to dry. Then he looked up to the wooden counter.

'Your birthday?'

'December 18, 1952.'

Tap, tap, tappa-tap, tap. Stewart could feel his anger rising as the sergeant embarked on this second test of his typing skills. Mercifully, he passed.

'Your father's name?'

'Richard Stewart.'

Tappa tap tap.

'Your mother's name?'

'Angela Stewart.'

Tap tappa tap.

'The name of your mother's mother.'

'Jesus Christ!' exploded Stewart. 'What is this?'

The sergeant watched him implacably, his fingers posed over the keys.

Stewart said: 'It's Henderson. H-E-N-D-E-R-S-O-N. Now can we get on? Don't you understand? *Our children are missing.*'

It took a further ten minutes to record all the details the sergeant required before Stewart and Suzanne were given the chance to explain what had happened.

'So where do you think they may have gone?' the sergeant asked.

'We don't know – that's the whole point,' said Stewart testily. 'That's why we're here.'

'Sergeant,' said Suzanne, 'our children wouldn't just go off without telling us. Something must be wrong. We're worried they might have been in an accident. But surely we'd have heard something by now?'

'Not necessarily. Were they carrying identification? The name of your hotel?'

'I really don't know.'

'In that case, the first thing we will do is check the hospitals.'

'What's the second thing?' asked Stewart.

'First, we'll check the hospitals.' He beckoned to his assistant and handed him the forms that now described Josh and Fee in clinical detail: height, weight, colour of hair, colour of eyes, complexion, shape of face, distinguishing marks. Stewart watched as the young officer sat down at the sergeant's desk and picked up the telephone.

'Tell me more about them,' the sergeant asked as he came to the counter. 'How do they know each other?'

'They met here on vacation,' Suzanne replied.

'Did they get on well?'

'Sure.'

'Very well?'

'They seemed to.'

'Well enough to want to go off with each other, perhaps?'

'That's preposterous,' Stewart protested. 'They've only known each other for a couple of days.'

'We have to consider all possibilities,' the sergeant replied. 'Has there been trouble at school?'

'No,' said Stewart.

'Do they use drugs?

'Not as far as we know.'

'Were they happy?'

'They were very happy.'

'Quite sure?'

'Of course I'm sure.'

'There were no arguments? No rows?'

Stewart did not hesitate. 'Certainly not.'

'Do you have pictures of them?'

They had come prepared for that. From his wallet Stewart

produced his favourite photograph of his daughter: an informal portrait he had taken himself the last time Fee had come to see him at his converted loft in Wapping overlooking the Thames. It had been a cold Sunday and they had just got back from a walk along the river. She was wearing one of his old sweaters, several sizes too large, and her hair was pulled back behind her head so that she looked like a waif. She was sitting by the picture window with an artist's pad on her knee, making a pencil sketch of the skyline, and he'd managed to catch her unawares. She'd just had time to look up from her pad when he'd taken the shot, capturing her expression at the instant it changed from surprise to amusement.

The sergeant accepted the photograph without comment and wrote her name on the back in neat capital letters. At the desk the assistant put down the telephone for the fifth time. 'Nothing, chief,' he called. The sergeant turned around and spoke quickly; too quickly for Stewart to catch.

'What did he say?'

Suzanne said: 'He said to check the morgue.'

'And your son's picture, Madame?'

She'd been holding back, as if she was reluctant to part with it. Now she placed on the counter a small presentation folder made of ivory-coloured card. The photograph inside had obviously been taken in a professional portrait studio. Against a blue backdrop, their heads close together, Josh and his mother smiled radiantly. Underneath, in grey italic script, were the words '*The Beaumont Family – Christmas 1995*'.

The sergeant removed the photograph from the folder and held it up to the light. He carefully drew a circle on the back so that it framed Josh's head and wrote the boy's name inside. Then he removed a bulging black ledger from beneath the counter and flicked through it in search of the current page. He had just found it when his assistant called out: 'Nothing. Nothing at all.'

The sergeant ran his thumb across the page and found the reference number for the most recent entry: 3791. He took his pen and inscribed the figures 3792 on the back of each photograph. Then he looked up at Stewart and Suzanne.

'So, that is good news. We know there hasn't been an accident.'

'How can you say that?' Suzanne demanded. There was a sudden sharpness in her voice. 'Supposing they've gone off the road? They could be lying at the bottom of a cliff somewhere and no one would know.'

'They have a car?' He seemed surprised at the possibility.

'No,' said Suzanne, 'but we think they might have gone to Villefranche with a friend of my son. Or they might have met him there. He has a car.'

'His name?'

'Olivier Lavar. L-A-V-A-R.'

He printed the name on his pad. 'His address?'

'In France, I don't know. He goes to the same school in England as my son. When he's here I think he uses his father's apartment somewhere in Monaco. Surely it's easy for you to trace him?'

The sergeant nodded. 'The number of the car?' he asked.

'I don't know.'

'The make of the car?'

'I don't know. I've never seen it. But you must be able to find out?'

He pushed his pad to one side. 'Our patrols will keep a look out, of course,' he said. 'But there would be skid-marks, a gap in the crash barrier. It is most unlikely.'

'Well, *something* has happened.' Suzanne was still more insistent.

The sergeant leaned across the counter and spoke quietly, as though he was imparting some great confidence. 'There is something I have to tell you both. Parents like you come in here all the time because their children have not come home. In most cases the children turn up – one day, two days later. Sometimes it's a week, maybe a month, but they usually come back. Most of them. The parents are furious at first, then they are just happy to have them home. It will be the same for you, I am sure.'

He stood up and gathered the forms into a neat pile. He secured it with a paper clip and placed it in a manilla file.

'If you hear anything, please let us know. We will do the same, of course.'

'You mean that's it?' asked Stewart.

'In one week, if nothing has been heard, you may file a

deposition with a magistrate. If he thinks a crime has been committed, he may order an investigation.'

'*May* order an investigation? *In a week*?'

'It is the law, Monsieur. There must be evidence of a crime. It is not a crime if a young woman does not wish to return to her father.'

'She's a child,' protested Stewart.

'She is seventeen.'

'Not yet she isn't,' said Stewart. 'Not until tomorrow.'

The sergeant closed the file. 'She's old enough,' he said with finality. 'There is nothing more we can do.'

They were leaving through the stone-flagged vestibule of police headquarters, Stewart feeling in his pocket for the car key, when she said: 'What in hell's name did you think you were doing?' He looked up in surprise and saw Suzanne standing directly in front of him, her jaw set.

'I'm sorry?'

'Why did you lie to them?'

'What are you talking about?'

'Come on. They asked if you'd had a row with Fee. You said no. Why?'

'It's got nothing to do with it, that's why.'

'Oh really? How do you know?'

'That's ridiculous. It was just a silly argument. In any case, if I'd told them about it, they would have decided that was the explanation and done nothing.'

'They're not exactly busting a gut as it is. And it's not ridiculous at all. Anyone can see your relationship with your daughter is in deep trouble.'

'How can you possibly say that? Just because we had a row?'

'*Just because we had a row.* You think that's all there is to it? Have you any idea what's going on inside her head? Or are you totally lacking in imagination?'

'This is outrageous. You've known me for two days and you start hurling accusations around! What happened over dinner was between me and Fee. It's got nothing to do with it – or you.'

'Oh, yes it has. It's not just Fee we're talking about. You appear to be forgetting that my son's gone too.'

'So how do you know this wasn't Josh's idea?'

'I don't. But I do know we didn't have a row just before he disappeared. You and Fiona did.'

Stewart pulled the car key from his pocket. His voice was cold as he said: 'I think we should get back to the hotel. In case there's any news.'

He left her no choice, setting off towards the street where he had parked the Renault an hour before. The pavement was narrow, and they had to thread their way through shop display signs, parking meters and bicycles tethered to the railings of windows. Stewart reached the car first but Suzanne was quick to climb into the passenger seat beside him. He was trying to find the ignition when she spoke again. Her tone was more even now.

'You know she thinks the world of you, don't you?'

'After the other night, I'm not so sure.' He was still fumbling with the key.

'Grow up, Tom. She thinks you're wonderful. When we were at the pool together she told me how you used to travel the world, glamorous places one day, war zones the next, sending back your reports, getting your name in print. You know she's kept a lot of your articles, don't you?'

'She never told me that.'

'She told me about the book you're writing. How you met this boy in Washington, and how you're trying to find out what happened to his father in Vietnam. She said you'd nearly finished it. She's really proud of you.'

'Shame she doesn't always show it.'

'Oh, stop feeling sorry for yourself. It's quite plain how she feels. I certainly saw it in the restaurant before you started fighting. Listen, you told me last night that Fee was all mixed up. But I'm not sure she's the one with the problems.'

He had found the ignition at last. He started the engine and edged out of the parking space. 'We go left at the lights, don't we?'

Suzanne was still looking at him.

'Face it, Tom. You're avoiding your emotions. It's about time you dealt with them – and hers.'

He kept his eyes on the street ahead. 'Let's drop the

psychobabble, shall we? I know perfectly well what I feel about my daughter. I love her, and she knows it.'

'Do you know what she feels about you?'

'Of course I do. You just said it. She thinks I'm wonderful – some of the time, at least. I imagine she loves me too.'

'You still don't get it, do you? Of course she loves you. She adores you. She's had to accept that you can't always be there when she wants you. But even when you are there, you're still not giving her what she wants.'

The traffic lights were red.

'You're talking in riddles.'

'Then I'll spell it out for you. You bring her to the south of France, shower her with presents, eat at expensive restaurants. I suspect it's the same old routine, but I'm sure she loves it. What you don't give her is yourself. That's what she wants more than anything. This isn't just about your book, and whether you should have brought it on holiday. It's about her and what you mean to her. You breeze in and out of her life whenever you feel like it. Then you try to buy her affections, and it doesn't work. That's not what being a father means.'

The driver behind hooted. The lights were green. Stewart turned into the Promenade des Anglais, accelerating past the line of palm trees on the central reservation.

'So what makes you such an expert?'

'I have to be.' Her tone was icy now. 'My son doesn't have a father, as you know. Fiona does, but you're throwing it all away. What do you talk to her about? How much do you really know about her? Do you know how she really feels? Do you care?'

The palm trees were receding in the mirror. A car was close behind, jostling to overtake.

'Of course I care,' said Stewart forcefully. It was the easiest of her questions to answer.

At 11.01 that morning – Maria Scarletti was later able to time it precisely, by the clock of the nearby Eglise de Sainte Martine striking the hour – Mark Carlson checked out of Le Bosquet. He explained that he was leaving several days early because urgent business had called him to Paris. When Maria sympathised – such a pity that he should have to leave

Provence for the metropolis, and with the weekend coming up – Carlson thanked her for her concern, adding that when you were in business for yourself, there was no such thing as a weekend off. He handed Maria his ticket and asked her to call Air Inter to check the time of the first available flight.

Maria, confirmed that there was a flight at 12.45 p.m. and that there were plenty of seats: would monsieur like one reserved on his behalf? Monsieur certainly would: aisle, smoking, please. Alas, said Maria, it was no longer possible to smoke on an internal flight, thanks to those European bureaucrats in Brussels. How would Monsieur Carlson be getting to the airport? A taxi? Right away, monsieur.

When the car from Voyages Orange arrived fifteen minutes later, Carlson handed Maria a one hundred franc note in appreciation of all her help. He asked her to be especially sure that the driver took him to the correct terminal, since he understood that there were two, and that they were some distance apart. 'It's the terminal for Paris,' he told Maria again. 'Of course, monsieur,' Maria murmured, and told the driver loudly that his passenger was taking the twelve forty-five Air Inter flight to Paris and wanted to be at the domestic terminal in plenty of time. The driver promised there was no problem. He asked monsieur if he would like his case – a soft Gucci carry-on bag – to be placed in the boot, but Carlson said he would prefer to keep it with him.

The taxi arrived at Terminal Two at Nice Airport at 12.10, comfortably in time. Mark Carlson paid the driver the fare, plus tip, amounting to a round 150 francs. The departure board indicated that the Paris flight was still being checked in. Carlson walked across the entrance hall, pushed open the door of the men's lavatories, and went inside.

Ten minutes later, a new Mark Carlson emerged. In place of his blue shirt and trousers he was wearing a white cotton shirt, jeans and a pair of tan cowboy boots, which although well-worn displayed an impressive sheen. His hair was still blond and comparatively short but was no longer combed to one side, instead appearing tousled, even unkempt. His eyes had been transformed from blue to brown, thanks to contact lenses. A pair of granny glasses, fitted with plain glass, perched on the end of his nose. There was a leather thong on his right wrist. A silver medallion depicting two pioneering settlers standing by a rock, together with the inscription *Montani Semper Liberi* – the slogan, in Latin, of the state of West Virginia – hung from his neck.

He now looked passably like the photograph of Edgar Bartlett, a sound recordist from Trenton, New Jersey, who had come to Europe at the end of May as part of a documentary crew making a film about the music of the Gypsies, and who had stayed on for a few days in Amsterdam. Back in Trenton, it should be said, Edgar Bartlett's live-in partner was beginning to worry that she had not heard from him for almost two weeks.

The former Mark Carlson – or the new Edgar Bartlett – deposited his carry-on bag in a luggage locker and walked out of the terminal with a neat blue rucksack on his back and a canvas satchel on his shoulder. Outside, its engine running, he found a bus bound for the railway station in the centre of Nice.

Little more than an hour after Mark Carlson had left Le Bosquet, Edgar Bartlett walked into the lobby of the Aston Concorde, and approached the Avis car rental desk. Using a Master Card issued to Edgar Bartlett, and confirming his identity with his passport, he rented a modest Renault Clio, asking the desk clerk if the insurance was valid for Spain. The clerk assured him that it was valid throughout Europe. Bartlett said that France and Spain were all he needed, since he was going to Cadaqués, the fishing village midway between the Pyrenees and Barcelona that had been much loved by Salvador Dali. He expected to return the car in two weeks' time.

Stewart was dreading the call. He thought of his former wife in the large open space that served as the kitchen and dining room of her parents' home in Bethesda, Maryland. It was a comforting house that managed to be tidy and homely at the same time. His dominant memory was of a warm, open family who had quickly made this tall, gangling man from across the Atlantic feel welcome. He pictured Rachel again, this time sitting on her parents' bed, her mother's hand in hers, her father keeping silent watch from the stiff-backed chair alongside. As he sat down at the desk in his room at Le

Bosquet he felt a pang of anxiety and took several deep breaths to compose himself. He picked up the phone and dialled.

Her voice was surprisingly faint.

'Rachel?'

'Tom?'

'How are things? Can you talk?'

'I'll just shut the door.'

He heard her heels clicking on the wooden floor, and knew she was in the kitchen.

'Mom's not too good, I'm afraid,' she said when she came back on the line. 'The stroke was worse than I thought. It could go either way.'

'Oh God, I'm so sorry. Let's hope there's some improvement soon.' He knew this sounded inadequate, but he pressed on. 'Listen, there's something I have to tell you.'

'I'm listening.'

'It's about Fee. I'm afraid she's missing.'

'Missing? What do you mean, she's missing?'

'She's been gone since yesterday lunchtime. She went into a small town near here with a couple of new friends she'd made and they haven't come back. The police seem to think they'll turn up eventually, but it's very worrying.'

'Oh, Tom. I don't believe it. Tell me it isn't true.'

It came not only as a cry of fear, but also as an echo across the years. As Stewart tried to recount what had happened, he felt that he was reliving their past. He could hear himself trying to justify the unjustifiable, as when he had struggled to explain why he had to miss another of their daughter's rites of passage. He prepared for the reproaches from Rachel, knowing how precise and devastating her accusations could be

There was no escape, as he related the bare details he knew, and had to answer her implacable questions about just where he had been when Fee had disappeared. What were you doing in Nice? Why did you want the *Herald Tribune* so badly? How long did that take, in any case? You were thinking about your book? So you were working? What do you mean, not really? You weren't there when she needed you, were you? *For God's sake, you bastard, you've lost our daughter.*

'Rachel, I know, I know. I feel terrible about this. I know it's my fault. I'm doing everything I can to find her.'

He recounted the fruitless search of Villefranche the night before, and the visit to the police station that morning, which – while frustrating – had at least established there hadn't been an accident. He told her that the key to the mystery might lie with Olivier Lavar, and of his attempts to track him down.

'I'm trying to get his father's address in Monaco,' he said, 'because that's where we think he's staying. He goes to the same school in Kent as the Beaumont boy, and I've been calling them on the phone most of the afternoon. The problem is, of course, they've broken up for the summer. But I managed to get hold of the village bobby, and he's given me the number for the caretaker's lodge. There's no reply so far, but I'll keep trying. If that doesn't work, I'm going to ask Jonathan Baxter to go down there tomorrow.'

'Tomorrow?' said Rachel. She made it sound an age away.

'We have to be a little patient,' Stewart said, uncomfortably.

'I'm coming over,' she said. 'I'll get a plane tonight.'

'Rachel, what's the point? I'm doing everything that can be done. The minute I hear anything, I'll let you know. Besides, what about your mother?'

There was a pause.

'You're needed there,' he said.

He heard her blow her nose. 'You're right. I can't just leave. Even if I could get her into hospital today, there's still Pop to think of. He's only just holding on.'

Stewart promised again that he would call the instant there was any news. He wished her mother well and sent his love.

'You're being very brave,' he told her.

'Goodbye, Tom.'

He sat at the desk, replaying the conversation in his mind, until he heard a knock on his door.

'It's open,' he called out.

Suzanne Beaumont walked into the room.

'Are you okay?' he asked.

'No,' she said. 'No, I'm not. I've just called the police again. That's the fourth time today. All I get is this crap about having to wait seven days before they'll even classify them as missing. Well, I'm not going to sit around here for a week while they do nothing.'

'So what do think we should do?'

'I've already done it. I called Jesse.'

'What can he do? This isn't Texas, Suzanne.'

'We'll see,' she said. 'Knowing Jesse, my guess is he'll achieve a darn sight more than we have.'

From her glare, Stewart was left in no doubt who she meant by 'we'.

It felt like an abandoned stage. The last time Stewart had stood in the doorway of his daughter's room, she was watching Jack Nicholson. Now the furniture, and Fee's belongings, resembled the props left in place after the actors had finished their performance, and the theatre was closed.

He picked up the notepad beside the telephone, hoping to find a message or some other clue as to where she had gone. It looked as if the top sheet had been torn off, but the waste-bin was empty: the maid had done her work several hours before. He opened the drawer beneath the telephone but it contained only a brochure advertising the attractions of the hotel.

He turned to the chest of drawers beside the bed. He was startled to discover how meticulously she had allocated her clothes: one drawer for T-shirts, one for shorts, one for her underwear, all of them neatly folded. Must be her mother's influence, he thought, remembering the disorder of his own room: she certainly didn't get that from me. Nestling among the pullovers was the soft felt pouch containing the pearl necklace, her first piece of adult jewellery, that he had given her when she was sixteen. Gingerly, trying to dispel the feeling of being an intruder, he lifted out the pouch. The necklace was inside, together with several other items – a pair of inlaid earrings, a butterfly-shaped brooch, a second necklace made of silver – he did not recognise.

He opened the wardrobe. The first thing he saw took his breath away, just as it had when he had taken her for dinner. The shimmering white dress that had clung to her body was at the front of the line of hangers. Whatever her mood when she came back to her room after the restaurant debacle, she had put away the dress with impressive care. On the floor of the wardrobe were her shoes, four or five pairs in an orderly line. He looked into the bathroom: nothing but half a dozen jars and tubes of moisturisers and creams, set out on the glass shelf above the basin.

He was no longer sure what he had come to Fee's room to find; he also sensed that he was learning things about her he had not suspected. He pushed open the French windows and stepped on to the balcony. On the table in the corner was a small sketch pad. He recognised the scene on the first page at once.

Fee had been looking down on a line of jagged roofs; beyond was a bridge carrying a railway line; beyond that, a cluster of high-rise towers. It was the view he had confronted so often from his flat in Wapping when he broke off from his writing, paced across the room and stared at this segment of the London skyline. He realised that she was trying to put herself in his place, see the world as he saw it; and yet she had not shown him what she had done. He had not even realised how far her skill at drawing had progressed.

He turned to the next sheet of the pad and saw himself staring full-face from the page. He saw his worry lines and the scar from Beirut; but he also saw a gentler person than he imagined. He guessed she had adapted it from the dust-jacket photograph on one of his books, but could not tell when she had drawn it. And was this, he wondered, how he really was? Or how she wanted him to be?

The phone rang. Stewart gave a start. For a brief moment his anxiety fell away. He imagined Fee saying: 'Dad, it's me – I'm sorry to have worried you.' When he picked up the receiver he heard the hotel operator, telling him he had an urgent call. She had tracked him to Fee's room after the receptionist told her he had borrowed the key. 'Tom, this is Luke Lewis. I'm glad I've caught up with you. I've been expecting you to call.'

Not this, Stewart thought. Not this, not now.

'I'm sorry Luke. I've been very busy . . .'

Lewis interrupted. 'Don't bullshit me, Tom. We've gone too far for that. I left three messages on your answering machine. Didn't you pick them up?'

'Yes, I did. I'm sorry, I was going to get back to you. How did you find me?'

'The fourth time I called, your neighbour Jonathan was there, picking up your mail. He told me where you were.

things. MycoGene was just the start. We've got a new therapy coming along for another immune disease that looks as though it's going to be just as successful. When something like that happens, you feel you can really do some good.'

'Is that what Josh wants?'

'I don't know yet. I don't suppose he does either. But he was proud of his father, and he knows how much Larry contributed to the company's success. If we can get it right, then I'm sure – or I think I'm sure – that Josh would love to carry on his father's work. Provided Jesse agrees, of course.'

She fell silent, and Stewart wondered if she thought she had said too much. The swallows had retired, their feasting on insects ended. Headlights from approaching cars occasionally lit the entrance to the drive. None slowed. 'I think we should be getting back,' Stewart said. 'In case they've tried to call, or something. Maybe they can't find a taxi.'

As they retraced their steps along the driveway, Stewart asked why Josh went to school in England.

'I thought it was sensible to get him away from Jesse for a while. He wasn't doing well at school in Austin, which was only to be expected. But Jesse took a strict view – felt Josh should pull himself together, that sort of thing. I thought of sending him to school in Connecticut, but Jesse doesn't hold with the East Coast. Then I heard about this school in England that specialises in "intensive learning" for "problem children". It has a lot of American kids.'

'You saw Josh as a problem?'

'No. But Jesse did.'

Suzanne explained that the school was in Tonbridge, not far from the airforce base in Kent where Jesse had been stationed during World War II. Jesse had returned an anglophile, full of admiration for Winston Churchill and always saying how the British had guts. She had sold it to him, on the basis that a year in England, at a school that boasted of teaching on traditional lines, might be just what Josh needed. Suzanne thought it was a good idea for other reasons: it would broaden his horizons, show him a country with a long history and traditions, give him a chance to visit Europe and imbibe its culture.

'Of course I had mixed feelings,' she said. 'I didn't want to lose Josh. But I thought that all round it was for the best. And

What the hell is going on? What happened on your trip? Why haven't you let me know?'

Because he couldn't face telling Luke the truth, that was why.

'A lot happened on the trip, Luke, and it wasn't what I expected. But this isn't the time. I was going to call you, but my daughter's gone missing and that's the only thing on my mind right now.'

Luke's voice softened as he asked Stewart to explain. Stewart heard himself recite the details, acutely aware that he was using his own misfortune to excuse himself from fulfilling his obligation to Luke. He listened to Luke saying how sorry he was and that he quite understood. He mouthed his promise to call and explain everything as soon as he had found Fee. He heard the receiver click as Luke rang off.

'You shit,' Stewart said. He was talking to himself.

5

Early that morning, a mile after Ben White Boulevard becomes Route 71, just beyond the city limits of Austin, a white Lincoln Continental took the exit for Cedar Creek Park. It glided down the ramp, made a sharp turn under the arches of the highway, and headed into the fold between two low hills. Seated in the back, Saul Bates, the Senior Senator from Texas and one of the most influential power-brokers in Washington, waited impatiently to reach his destination.

Anyone arriving at Cedar Creek Park for the first time and expecting to see trees or a lake would be disappointed. The 'park' consists of a dozen sprawling buildings, constructed with copious use of steel and reflective glass in a palette of shades of brown, blue and green. Together with their immaculate lawns and ordered parking spaces, they have the look and feel of a university campus, fulfilling the architect's aim of creating an ambiance imbued with the twin spirits of academia and commerce. The Lincoln pulled up outside the largest building of all, marked by a grey marble plaque inscribed 'BioGenius Incorporated'. At this hour there was only one other car in the parking lot. The senator eased his ample frame out of the car and told his driver he would be back in fifteen minutes.

He knew little more than that Jesse Beaumont needed help. From the brief conversation setting up their meeting, it sounded like familiar territory: BioGenius's latest product, HaemoGene, was bogged down in Washington as it waited for approval from the Food and Drug Administration. As he walked up the pathway to the entrance to BioGenius, Senator Bates was in little doubt that the problem could be resolved.

The electronic lock guarding the double glass entrance doors clicked open and he passed into the atrium that was the most striking architectural feature in Cedar Creek Park. At its centre was a granite statue entitled 'Woman and Child'. The mother sat relaxed, her back comfortably supported, her head angled forward in a position of tenderness and solicitude. In her arms she cradled a baby wrapped in a swaddling cloth; mother and child gazing into each other's eyes.

Bates did not give the statue a second look. He climbed the open circular staircase to the first floor. A second set of doors opened in front of him and he followed a corridor to Beaumont's office. He entered without knocking, to find Jesse walking towards him, smiling broadly, ready to shake his hand.

'Senator,' said Beaumont. 'Good of you to stop by.'

The office reflected the man: sparsely furnished, economical in its assertion of power. Instead of a desk, there was a circular table, a sofa and a pair of elegant easy chairs. There were two bookcases lined with technical manuals and business directories, with a cluster of photographs on the wall nearby. They showed Jesse with his bomber crew in England; Jesse with Larry on his graduation day; Jesse with Larry, Josh and Suzanne. To one side was a photograph of a smiling President Reagan, standing between Jesse and Senator Bates, his arms around their shoulders. The senator had the same photograph in his Austin office, enlarged almost to life-size.

The senator thought that Beaumont looked tired. Normally his flowing white hair, swept back to cover his ears, gave him a distinguished look but today his broad forehead and moon-shaped face seemed to lack their customary lustre, and his voice sounded drained. Beaumont gestured to one of the easy chairs while he took the sofa.

'You're looking good, Jesse,' said Bates. 'What's on your mind?'

'You know what, I just can't figure it out,' Beaumont replied. 'These folks up in Washington, do they want to see our children dying?'

'I wouldn't have thought so,' said the senator non-committally.

'You know how many kids are dying?'

'Tell me.'

'Thousands in the States. Maybe a million worldwide.'

'That many?'

'That's minimum,' said Beaumont. 'And all of them die. It's a terrible disease, Saul. They get trouble with their blood – not enough red blood cells to get oxygen round their bodies. If they're diagnosed early enough, some of them make it to puberty, provided they get regular blood transfusions. But then the iron overload from all those transfusions kicks in. They get heart problems, liver, glands too. Aren't many that make it beyond thirty.'

'Is that right?'

'That's not the worst of it. The ones that don't get transfusions, most of them are dead within a year. Even if they last a while longer, they get severe anaemia, enlarged spleens, deformed skulls. They're like haemophiliacs – cut them and they bleed like stuck pigs.'

'Sweet Jesus,' said Bates. 'What did you say this is called?'

'Cooley's Anaemia.'

'Who's Cooley?'

'He's the guy who figured it out. It's a form of thalassaemia.'

'Thala what?'

'Thalassaemia. Comes from the Greek word for sea, because it's most common around the Mediterranean. Leastwise, that's where it was first identified. Now we know it's everywhere. Everyone who gets it suffers from some kind of blood problem. Cooley's Anaemia is the worst kind.'

'So where does HaemoGene come in?'

'Well, you see, Saul, Cooley worked out that it's not a virus. It's inherited. If both your folks have got defective genes for haemoglobin, you've got Cooley's. If you can't get oxygen from your lungs to your blood cells, you're going to die.'

'And you've found a way of fixing those genes?'

Beaumont got up and walked stiffly to his bookcase. 'Can't fix the genes, senator. But we sure can fool them. That's what HaemoGene's all about, if we can ever get those damn fools at the FDA to move. The guys out back came up with a way of persuading the body to make more blood cells. It's the same kind of trick we pulled with MycoGene – messing around with the genetic signals so the body does what you want it to do. In this case, synthesise more globin chains so that it makes more red blood cells.'

'You've lost me there, Jesse.'

Beaumont pulled a manual from the bookshelf. 'It's all in here. Background on the research, trials, results. Anything else you need, I'll get one of the science guys to talk you through it. Point is, with HaemoGene we can give these kids a fighting chance.'

He handed the manual to Bates, who put it on the table beside him. 'It's as effective as MycoGene?' Bates asked.

'More effective. At least in the trials. Within a month, close to ninety per cent of the kids were making more red blood cells, and those counts are still going up. Shit, Saul, in the first MycoGene trials we were getting a sixty per cent success rate, tops. Even so the FDA gave us fast-track approval. MycoGene was with the doctors inside five years from start to finish, and there are a million kids out there alive today who would otherwise have died of CHIDS. If we could get approval for HaemoGene, there's thousands of kids in the US alone we could get off death row. But those sons-of-bitches at the FDA won't get off their fannies to help. You figure it out. I can't.'

Bates picked up the manual and flicked through the pages, pausing once or twice. 'You sure they've got the plot?'

'Good question. I used to be able to talk to Frost whenever I wanted. Now he won't even return my calls.'

Beaumont leaned over the senator's shoulder and found a tab marked 'Exchange of Correspondence with the Food and Drug Administration'. The most recent letter, announcing yet another delay in the FDA's approval of HaemoGene, was signed by Forster Frost, deputy administrator of the Regulatory Control Division.

'Look at this bureaucratic garbage,' said Beaumont. 'It's bullshit.'

'I tell you frankly, Jesse, I find this alarming,' said Bates.

'There is another point. We need HaemoGene. You seen the stock price lately?'

Bates smiled. 'Doing well, I hear.'

'Sure is. It's gone through the roof in the past few weeks. That's because folks think HaemoGene is about to be approved. Any more delays and they're going to start wondering if something's wrong. There's a lot riding on this. Jobs. Contractors. Research. You know how these things work, senator. Word gets out that HaemoGene's in trouble, and the stock's likely to go back down through the floor. The investors won't be too comfortable with that.'

'I hear you, Jesse,' said Senator Bates. 'I'm going back to Washington this afternoon. I'll call you. End of next week at the latest.'

'Sounds good, Saul.'

'You bet.' Bates put the manual in his briefcase. 'We through?'

'There is one other thing.'

'Shoot.'

Beaumont rubbed his leg again. 'There's a problem with Josh.'

'Your grandson?'

'That's right.'

'Something serious?'

'Hard to tell. His mother called this morning. They're over in France, and he's gone and got himself lost. Went off yesterday afternoon with some English girl and hasn't come back.'

Bates smiled. 'You think it's in the genes?'

'Hell, I hope so. Thing is, Suzanne's got herself all upset. She says the French police don't seem to be taking it seriously. Told her she has to wait a week before it even becomes official.'

Bates took a slim leather-skin notepad from his jacket pocket.

'Sounds like somebody needs a kick up the ass. Where exactly in France?'

He noted the details Beaumont gave him.

'You got someone you can call?' Beaumont asked. 'Someone who can get those Frenchies moving?'

Bates put away his notepad. 'Count on it,' he said.

'Appreciate it, senator.'

'You bet.'

Beaumont escorted Bates down to the main entrance where the two men shook hands. As the doors closed behind him, the senator heard the electronic locks close. The driver was waiting, the rear door of the Lincoln open. Bates glanced at his watch. He'd been right: exactly fifteen minutes had passed.

* * *

Victor Canning was seven years old when Kathleen Ferrier died of cancer. Her death, at the age of forty-one, made little impact on Victor at the time. Kathleen Ferrier was no more to him then than a disembodied voice which came from the loudspeaker of his mother's gramophone whenever his father was away. Since the voice continued to reach him after Ferrier's death, continued to fill the house during his father's daily absences, Canning saw no reason to grieve. Nothing had changed.

It was only later that he realised how much his mother had been affected by the singer's death. Like Ferrier, she was a naturally gifted pianist and, like Ferrier, her talents had been recognised. Both women were told at the age of seventeen that they had the ability to become concert pianists. Both chose marriage instead. Both worked as telephone operators, Ferrier in Blackburn, Victor's mother in Croydon.

There the similarities ended. In 1937 – as Victor's mother never tired of relating – Ferrier entered a singing competition at the Carlisle Festival. She did so in order to win a one shilling bet from her husband, whom – 'incidentally', Victor's mother would say – she soon divorced. She sang Roger Quilter's 'To Daisies' and the *Carlisle Journal* recorded that she had 'one of the finest voices ever heard'. A star was born.

Victor's mother, meanwhile, whose husband did not encourage her talents, remained a telephone operator, in her case in Croydon. But through Ferrier she found a vicarious meaning to her life, until it was cruelly taken away by Kathleen's death in October 1953. When Victor's mother died, also from cancer, four years later, Victor registered a connection, for he, unlike his father, had recognised his mother's decline.

But in one important sense, Kathleen Ferrier did not die, and nor did Canning's mother. Forty years on, they continued to live on, through the speakers of his superbly modulated Quad sound system.

This afternoon Victor Canning sat motionless at the walnut desk in his darkened study, retrieving his latest encoded messages from Zurich.

The first was a long one, a report from Antony Palmer, who was formally Canning's lawyer. Palmer filed his report once a week; a detailed summary of what had moved, what had sold, who had paid, who had not. It was Canning's habit to study Palmer's reports with great care because, based on what they contained, he would make decisions involving millions of pounds and affecting countless lives. He often worked late into the night, preparing his comments and instructions so that he could reply to Palmer the next morning. But on this occasion he seemed distracted.

He scrolled rapidly through Palmer's report and then opened the file containing his second message. It was addressed to RAVEN and it said: RED BIRD HAS FLOWN. In the light of the computer screen his violet eyes glowed.

He got up from his desk and went to the bank of hi-fi equipment that occupied most of one wall. He pressed a button and the room was filled once again with Ferrier's anguish as she embarked on the opening lines of Gluck's 'What is Life'. He found it especially affecting, as Ferrier had made the recording just two months before she died.

There are nights when it is only dark, and there are nights when it is utterly black. The first kind is when the moon lights the trees and the lake at Indian Point, casting shadows across the path that runs from the house to the edge of the Potomac River. Special Agent Phil Brady of the Federal Bureau of Investigation preferred the second kind, when you have to use instinct and fieldcraft to find your way to the shoreline, and only the flickering lights on the far side of the river suggest that there is anyone else alive in the universe.

It was one of those nights. Brady placed the book he was reading on the floor of the porch and sat motionless in his cherry-wood rocker, listening to the timbers of the house as they shifted and creaked – the echoes of previous generations, he sometimes fancied, calling to him across the years. Then he softly called 'Zola' to the labrador lying at the far end of the porch and the two of them set off, the dog running ahead, Brady feeling the stones of the path beneath his feet as he anticipated its meanders among the trunks of unseen pines. The stones turned to sand when he reached the shore but the water was perceptible only as a brooding mass. He stood at its edge, absorbing the night, and the silence and the solitude.

Through the trees came the sound of a telephone.

'Damn,' muttered Brady. 'Who on earth?'

He already knew who it was likely to be. Much as he wanted to ignore it, that was out of the question. He started back up the path. When he reached the house he entered a four-figure code which automatically redialled the number of the caller.

'Miller.'

'Jim, it's Phil Brady here.'

'Phil, I'm sorry to call you so late. I don't have to tell you it's important.'

'I guess you know I started my vacation' – Brady looked at his watch – 'less than twenty-four hours ago.'

'I know, Phil, I know. The problem is, we've got a case with a French connection, and I need your expertise. Saul Bates has got himself involved, and he's taken it all the way to the Oval Office. Believe me, if there was any other way . . .'

Brady believed him. It was one of the saving graces of working for the FBI that Assistant Director James Miller was as straight as top brass came. If it was serious enough for Miller to call him when he was not even on the Bureau's emergency roster, it had to be very serious indeed. Brady listened mutely, jotting notes on a pad, as Miller laid out the problems. An American boy had disappeared while on vacation near Nice, together with an English girl. It was French jurisdiction, of course, but that hadn't stopped the senator using his inside track to call the White House. No one yet knew how serious it was – the best bet was that the kids had just gone on a jaunt together. Nor was it exactly clear why Bates had used his influence so dramatically. But since Bates was who he was . . .

'Well, I don't need to spell it out for you,' said Miller.

Brady remembered Bates. He had once been called to testify before the Senate Judiciary Committee, and recalled his leathery face, his tongue flickering like a lizard's, as he'd harried Brady over some detail of a case involving a supposed bomb threat in Chicago. Brady had considered the point ridiculously arcane, but he knew that Bates was pursuing his own political agenda – see how tough we are when American lives are at risk – and answered with all the concern he knew the senator expected. He also knew that Bates was as well-briefed as any veteran of the Hill's infighting. He was not surprised when Miller told him that Bates knew Brady had served a stint as the Bureau's attaché in Paris.

'He put your name up to the President,' Miller said. 'If he had his way, you'd be on a plane to France by now. We told him it's not quite that easy. But you'd better reckon on being back there within the week.'

Brady thought of the small suitcase he had brought with him from Washington. There was hardly any point unpacking it now. And he knew there was no point protesting. He had been around headquarters long enough to understand how the political commerce of Washington worked.

'I'll be in the office first thing. My biggest problem is Zola.'

'He's going to be upset?'

'You bet he's going to be upset. I told him he had me for two weeks.'

'Tell him I owe him one, if that will help.'

'I doubt it.'

'Phil, is there anything you can do tonight to help us persuade Bates we're on top of the case? Is there someone in France you can call? Cut through the bullshit and find out what's going on over there?'

'I'll give it some thought,' said Brady.

He knew precisely who to try. After Miller had rung off, he dialled a number in Paris that he had no need to look up. It answered on the second ring.

6

'Daddy.'

She called again, elongating the words, so that they whispered through the trees.

'Da-dee. Da-dee.'

'Fee,' he called back. 'Where are you?'

'I'm over here. Over here. Here, here, here.'

The words echoed softly around him. He could not see her, only the trees disappearing into the gloom of their own shadows. A path cut through them, dappled by the fractured sunlight, but he could not see the end since it rounded a bend a hundred yards away. Her voice was becoming fainter and he set off down the path to look for her. No matter how far he walked, the bend was always another hundred yards further on.

'Fee,' he called, in increasing desperation. 'Fee. Fe-eeee.'

He heard a twig crack underfoot. There was a sudden hammering which sounded like a woodpecker. A crow croaked. He pressed on until the trees parted and he found himself clambering up the flank of a ridge. There was scree underfoot, loose stones which subsided as he took each step, so that he had to redouble his efforts to gain height. Above him grey crags rose like ramparts. At first they seemed to bar his path but mercifully he found a narrow gully that twisted its way through.

When he reached the crest of the ridge the view opened up like a map spread out in front of him. The forest was far below, a patch of dark green that swathed the valley floor. From within the trees he could hear the roar of rushing water that must have been a waterfall. He'd thought he was in England but now he seemed to have arrived in Vietnam. Ahead the ridge snaked upwards. Wraiths of mist were drifting over it but they parted just long enough for him to glimpse a lone figure climbing carefully along the ridge. Just as his eyes focused, mist swelled over the ridge again and the figure disappeared.

He thought it was Fee. But she seemed older than when she had disappeared in the forest. Was it her? And had he brought her here to Vietnam? He racked his mind but could not remember if she had been with him on the plane. He looked at his watch. It was getting late. Time to get off the ridge before the clouds thickened and before it was dark. With an overwhelming sense of sorrow he plunged down the scree until the found the path through the trees.

'Rachel,' he said when he arrived home. 'I've lost Fee. I'm very sorry.'

'What on earth are you talking about?' Rachel asked.

'Don't you understand? I've lost her. We were in the forest, and she was a little girl. Then I think we were in Vietnam. But she's gone.'

'Don't be silly. She's here with me. It's her birthday. Don't you remember?'

He turned round. Fee was sitting in an easy chair, reading.

'Hi, dad.' She seemed surprised to see him. 'Where have you been?'

'I've been looking for you, Fee. I thought you were lost.'

Fee's wide eyes fixed his. 'I wasn't lost, dad. You must have been dreaming. We've been waiting for you to come home.'

In the moment Stewart awoke, he was flooded with a sense of joy and relief. *She isn't lost. My daughter isn't lost after all.* He groped for his watch. It was ten minutes to six. A shaft of sunlight lay across the dishevelled sheets of his bed, testimony to a wretched night of intermittent sleep. Now he remembered. He was in the south of France, where he and Fee were supposed to be on holiday. It was supposed to be her birthday, too.

Room service had not started yet, the night porter at Le Bosquet regretted, when Stewart telephoned reception; he could get coffee at half past six. By then Stewart was already on his way to Villefranche. Once there, it was the waiter at the Café du Progrès who brought him an espresso as he sat in the market square watching the town come to life. Farmers and growers were erecting their stalls and unloading their produce from their battered vans.

The waiter glanced at the photograph of Fee lying on the table.

'Do you work here every day?' Stewart asked.

'What's it to you?'

'The girl in the photograph is my daughter. She was here two days ago. I'm trying to find her.'

'I didn't see her. Do you know how many people we get here every day?'

'It's important.'

The waiter shrugged. 'I'm busy,' he said, although only a handful of customers had chosen to take refreshment at the Café du Progrès. Most of the farmers in need of their morning *petit rouge* had congregated at other cafés around the square: in view of the waiter's surliness, Stewart now understood why. On the far side a cluster of people had gathered outside the *boulangerie*, and Stewart went to join them. The door opened with the tinkle of a bell just as he arrived, and he followed the others inside. He waited while they selected their bread and exchanged greetings and gossip with Madame behind the counter. When his turn came he chose a croissant and a *pain aux raisins* and debated with Madame the prospects for the weather.

'That's sixteen francs, monsieur.'

Stewart took out his wallet and paid her. Then, speaking loudly to make sure everyone could hear, he said: 'Madame, I need a favour. I'm looking for my daughter. She's been missing for two days and I'm extremely worried. Can I show you her photograph?'

He took Fee's photograph from his wallet and laid it on the counter. As Madame picked it up and stared at it, the customers crowded round, awaiting her verdict. She replaced it on the counter and said: 'I'm sorry, monsieur. I haven't seen her.'

Soon the photograph was being passed from hand to hand.

'A pretty child. How old is she?'

'Have you told the police?'

'What about the Missing Persons Bureau?'

'They're useless, they just keep lists. When my neighbour's boy disappeared . . .'

Stewart let the chattering take its course. Then a woman

asked: 'Did you say two days ago? I might have seen her. Was she by herself?'

He showed her a picture of Josh. 'She was with this young man. An American.'

'No, the girl I saw was with a woman. Your wife, perhaps?'

'I'm afraid not.'

'Come to think of it, the girl I saw was younger.'

The babble resumed.

'What a worry for you.'

'Have you tried the cafés?'

'What about Madame Dufour at the *épicerie*? She doesn't miss much.'

'She's in hospital.'

'Is it bad?'

'Nothing serious. She fell and broke her hip.'

'You should try the butcher's.'

'And the flower shop.'

'What about the harbour? There are plenty of cafés down there.'

It was another five minutes before Stewart left the *boulangerie*. Over the next half-hour he repeated the performance in the grocer's, the butcher's and the flower shop, hoping that Villefranche would soon be buzzing with talk of the pretty English girl who had gone missing.

There was a *bar-tabac* in the corner of the square, with rust red shutters half-closed against the heat of the sun. Stewart went inside.

'Any luck?'

The man who spoke was one of the customers from the *boulangerie*. Stewart shook his head.

'Too bad,' the man said. 'Try Madame Robert.' He nodded towards the counter. 'If she's seen your daughter, she'll remember.'

Madame Robert, a sturdy woman in a denim smock, sat beside an antiquated cash register. Stewart handed her the photograph and steeled himself for the apologetic shaking of her head.

'*Bien sûr*,' she said brightly. Stewart felt a surge of adrenalin. 'She came in to buy some film. Such a nice young woman. Most polite.'

He handed her the photograph of Josh. 'Was she with this boy? He's American.'

She nodded. 'Yes, he was with her.'

'Did they seem all right?'

'What do you mean?'

'Did they seem worried? Or frightened?'

'No, not at all. They were laughing together, all three of them.'

Stewart almost missed it.

'*Three* of them?'

'That's right.'

From Madame Robert's description, Stewart was in no doubt the third one was Olivier. French, she said, the same age as Josh, thin and pale. She had good reason to remember him, for she had spoken to him a week earlier, when he had blocked the delivery bay with his car.

'The beer lorry arrived but when I asked him to move it he was very rude. I had to call my son.'

'What kind of car was it?'

'I don't know anything about cars,' she said, raising her shoulders in resignation. 'You'd better ask Philippe.'

Philippe Robert was polishing glasses at the far end of the bar.

'The monsieur wants to know . . .'

'I heard,' he said.

Philippe was a car buff. Olivier's car, he told Stewart, was a black Peugeot 205 1.9 litre GTI with racing tyres and a blue-print engine.

'What's that?' Stewart asked.

He leaned across the bar. 'Hand-built, hand-tuned. Twin carburettors, twin exhausts. Black metallic paint with a thin red stripe down each side. Tinted windows. Monaco registration plates. A year old, maybe a little more. Not much wear on the tyres. There was a small dent on the front bumper, driver's side.'

Stewart was writing the details in a spiral-bound notebook. 'And how many kilometres had it done?'

Philippe laughed. 'I like cars,' he said. 'I notice details.'

'You think he would notice if his mother fell over in front of him?' Madame Robert asked.

Stewart smiled. 'So what happened when your mother asked for your help?'

'He moved the car. No problem.'

'Have you seen him since?

'Him, no. But I've seen the car several times. Most nights last week.'

When the bar closed at night, Philippe said, he liked to walk down to the harbour to clear his head and stretch his legs. He had noticed the Peugeot, usually in the same place near the chapel, and supposed that its owner had gone to one of the clubs in the old town.

'How late are they open?' Stewart asked.

'Some don't close until three or four. I never saw him, but my guess is he was in one of those.'

'Can you give me some names?'

'The Black Cat. Zara's. There's another one in the Rue Obscure that's very popular with the kids. It's called the Red Parrot.'

Stewart stiffened.

'You know the Red Parrot?'

'I've met the owner,' Stewart said.

'Jean-Luc Fratoni,' said Madame Robert. She curled her lips in distaste.

The alleyways of the old town, with their vaulted walls, felt almost as claustrophobic as they had at night. The Rue Obscure was deserted, the door of the Red Parrot firmly closed. Stewart pressed the bell-push but there was no answer. He backed towards the far side of the alley and craned his neck to look up at the windows. There was not even the twitch of a curtain or a glimmer of light.

'Fratoni!' he called. 'Hey, Monsieur Fratoni!'

His shouts ricocheted from the walls. He shouted again, turning to scan the windows on each side.

'Fratoni! Are you there?'

High above a window was thrown open and a woman's head appeared.

'Are you mad?' she called. 'Stop making that racket.'

He took a couple of steps back.

'I'm looking for Fratoni.'

'The club's closed. Come back later. Tonight.'

'I know it's closed. I have to talk to him now. Where does he live?'

The woman withdrew and he heard the window being closed.

He was about to shout again when he saw a man hurrying down the Rue Obscure, a pair of baguettes under his arm.

'Good morning,' said Stewart. 'I'm looking for Fratoni. Do you know where I can find him?'

'Why?'

He was a small, wiry man with thin lips and a sharp nose.

'I need to speak to him.'

'Fratoni won't give you the time of day.'

'Well, that's up to him. Tell me where to find him, and I'll see what he has to say.'

He looked Stewart up and down.

'You're the Englishman who's trying to find his daughter?'

'That's right.'

'What do you want with Fratoni?'

'My daughter was here in his club.'

'Is that right?' Stewart recognised the glint that had entered his eyes. 'So you'll want to see him urgently?'

'Very urgently,' he said.

'Trouble is, Fratoni doesn't like people meddling in his business. Doesn't like people talking about him.'

He inserted a key in the lock of the door next to the Red Parrot.

'He values his privacy,' he said.

Stewart waited. He knew what was coming next.

'It's not worth a man's while to upset Fratoni,' the man said as he pushed open the door. 'No profit in that.'

Stewart took a two hundred franc note from his wallet, folded it in half and held it in the fork of two fingers.

The man looked both ways along Rue Obscure. It was still deserted.

'Try Mario's. It's on the waterfront. Last one at the end.'

He reached out to take the note and disappeared inside.

Mario's Restaurant stood alone at the end of the quayside, as far along the crescent-shaped bay as it was possible to go.

Stewart pushed through the door. As his eyes adjusted to the shadows, he saw Fratoni at a table nearest the bar, still dressed all in black, still looking in need of a shave. There was a ledger open in front of him and he was working through a pile of bills.

'You're a man of many parts, Mr Fratoni,' said Stewart.

Fratoni did not look up. 'Still trying to find your daughter?'

Stewart sat down opposite him and placed Josh's photograph beside the ledger. 'When I came into your club the other night, I said I thought my daughter was with two young men. This is one of them.'

Fratoni's eyes flicked across from his ledger. 'I haven't seen him.'

'The other man is French,' Stewart said. 'I don't have a photograph, but I can describe him to you.'

A waiter placed a jug and a tall, thin glass containing two inches of *pastis* on the table. Fratoni poured an equal measure of water from the jug, and the mixture turned milky white. Stewart sat forward in his chair.

'He's eighteen but may seem older. He's a bit shorter than me. He's skinny and pale and has short dark hair and brown eyes. He drives a black Peugeot GTI with Monaco plates. He's a regular at one of the Villefranche clubs. I suspect it's yours.'

Fratoni sipped his drink. 'You're wrong.'

Stewart slumped back in exasperation. 'Come on, Fratoni! His car was parked near your club nearly every night last week. All I'm asking you to do is check your records, just in case he's a member. All I want is his address. His name is . . .'

'I know his name,' Fratoni said.

Stewart stared at him. 'You do?'

'Lavar. Olivier Lavar.'

'But you said he doesn't come to your club'

'That's what I said.'

'So how do you know him?'

Fratoni took another sip of *pastis*. Something in Stewart cracked. He slammed the table with his fist, making Fratoni's glass jump. 'Why are you making this so fucking hard?'

Some of the *pastis* had spilled on to the table. Fratoni beckoned to the waiter who began mopping up the puddle.

'You don't listen, do you?' he said when the waiter had

finished. 'I've told you, I've never seen your daughter, or the boy. And I haven't seen Lavar since Easter. I don't know where he lives – I don't care where he lives. I can't help you. Stop wasting my time.'

'I will,' said Stewart, 'if you'll just tell me one thing. How do you know Lavar?'

'I told you before, it's my business to know who comes into my place. It's also my business to know what they get up to while they're there. You sell drugs in the Red Parrot, you don't come back.'

'You're saying that Olivier is a drug dealer?'

'I'd say he's mainly a user, but, yes, he deals on the side. Like most addicts.'

The previous Easter, Fratoni told him, Lavar had been caught by one of the club's security guards selling drugs in the men's lavatory.

'Selling what?' Stewart asked.

'Junk.'

Stewart felt a surge of panic. 'Heroin? Oh, Christ!' he said.

'Doesn't mean he uses it. I made him show me his arms and there weren't any needle tracks. Maybe he was selling junk so he could buy whatever poison he prefers. It happens.'

'What did you do?'

'I made him show me his identity card, then I threw him out. I told him never to come into my club again. That's it. That's all I know.'

Fratoni picked up the pile of bills and began working through them, writing numbers in the ledger. Stewart watched him, saying nothing, until Fratoni put down the bills and glared at him.

'What are you, my accountant? You're beginning to annoy me.'

Stewart had already decided he had nothing to lose. 'My daughter is seventeen years old, Fratoni. Today. It's her birthday. She's vanished off the face of the earth with a man you tell me deals in heroin. I don't care who I annoy, I have to find Lavar. Help me, and I'll get out of your hair.'

It was Fratoni's turn to raise his voice. 'What do you want me to do?' he said angrily.

'Get Lavar's address for me. He's got to be a member of one

of the clubs round here, or at least a regular. Call the other owners. One of them might know, and they'll talk to you a lot sooner than they will to me. Just call them, please. Then I'll go.'

Fratoni stood up and looked at Stewart as if he was sizing him up for a fight. Then he said: 'Wait here.' He stepped across to the bar and picked up the phone. He dialled a number, then a second and a third, and each time there were terse, muttered conversations Stewart could not hear. The third time Fratoni replaced the receiver he scribbled a note on a pad. He returned to the table and handed it to Stewart. It read: Apartment 14B, 119 Avenue Princesse Grace, Monaco.

'Which club . . . ?'

'Don't ask,' said Fratoni. 'Now, get out.'

When Stewart reached the door he looked back intending to wave his thanks. But Fratoni had his head down over his ledger, engrossed once more in his pile of bills.

Wolfgang Kaufman winced in anticipation. He gripped a pair of tweezers, embraced the surplus nostril hair that was so aggravating him, and tugged. As the offending hair came away, his eyes brimmed with tears. He dabbed them with his silk handkerchief then inspected himself again in the mirror of his office at Le Bosquet. He was satisfied with what he saw. Chin smooth and perfumed with cologne from the morning shave. Grey silk tie perfectly knotted. Black dress jacket spotless. Not a hair out of place.

He inspected his office. His oak desk, with its sturdy wooden legs, was immaculate, with the spaces between its blotter, writing pad, and pen precisely judged. A computer sat on a side-table awaiting his instructions. A cabinet stood in a corner, the in-tray on top stacked neatly with letters ready to be filed. His wife, Elspeth, looked on approvingly from her photograph. He peered through the narrow inspection window, with its one-way glass, towards reception. Two newly-arrived guests were being attended to by Maria, her smile as ingratiating as ever. The currency exchange rate chart was up to date. The clock above the reception desk showed just after noon. The first customers would soon be arriving at the restaurant, overlooking the terrace beside the pool. Everything was as it should be. He rubbed his chubby palms in a gesture of satisfaction.

There was a sudden commotion from outside. Cars raced to a halt on the driveway, gravel flew, doors slammed. Through the inspection window, Kaufman could see a dozen men flooding into the reception area. He hurried into the lobby where bewildered guests were being shepherded against the wall. Maria turned to him helplessly.

'It's the police,' she said. 'They want to talk to you.'

A hand at his elbow steered him back into his office. A woman wearing a loose-cut navy cotton suit with an open-necked white shirt followed him in. She showed him a blue card, embossed with a seal, the *tricolore* running diagonally across one corner.

'Commissaire Halard of the *Police Nationale*,' she said. 'I am attached to the Ministry of the Interior and I'm here on the authority of the Minister himself. I have come to investigate the disappearance of Joshua Beaumont and Fiona Stewart.'

Halard. Kaufman knew the name. She was one of France's most renowned police officers, with a string of dramatic cases and headlines to her credit. He remembered her face from the cover of *Madame Figaro*, with her short curly hair, cropped tight around her face, and her intense brown eyes. If Halard was here, it had to be serious. He had already called head office in Berne about the missing teenagers, to be reminded of standing orders in such circumstances. First: cooperate fully with the police. Second: avoid upsetting the guests. Third: do everything possible to keep the matter out of the press.

'Wolfgang Kaufman,' he said. 'General manager. At your service.'

She gave a perfunctory nod. 'I require access to your records and I intend to interview your staff and guests. Nobody is to leave the hotel until I say so.'

The second rule was crumbling already.

'The guests?' Kaufman said. 'Is that really necessary?'

'Absolutely,' she said. 'This is a matter of great urgency.' She nodded over Kaufman's shoulder. 'Detective Inspector Desiry will organise the interviews.' Kaufman glanced behind to see a man in a blue suit, a little overweight, with a balding head and a bushy moustache, who stared back impassively.

'First, I need to know of any guests who have left the hotel since the children went missing.'

Kaufman's palms went damp. Pray God, he thought, the files are in order. He moved to his computer and pressed a key. The screen flickered alive and presented him with the staff roster for the coming week. He tried again. Success.

'Five people have checked out since yesterday,' he said. 'Four were couples who departed this morning. One British, one French. The fifth was an American. He left yesterday. He was by himself.'

'Did any of them leave earlier than you had expected?'

He consulted the screen again. 'Yes, the American. He was originally booked in until Thursday. A Mr Carlson.'

Inspector Desiry hovered into Kaufman's view.

'Tell us about him,' Halard said.

Kaufman slid open the top drawer of the filing cabinet and searched through the folder marked C. Carlson's bill was missing. What had gone wrong this time? He looked again and found it under K.

'He stayed five nights,' Kaufman read out. 'His room bill was 3,750 francs. He spent 380 francs in the restaurant, 476 francs at the bar, 395 francs on room service, 230 francs on extras.'

'Extras?'

'Laundry. The total was 6,282 francs – including tax.'

'How did he pay?'

Kaufman saw Desiry riffling through the papers in his in-tray.

'How did he pay?' Halard asked again, more insistently.

'By cash.'

'Isn't that rather unusual?'

'Not really,' Kaufman said. 'We require our guests to provide a credit card on arrival. But when they pay their bills, there are always some who prefer to use cash.'

'But you've got his credit card slip, anyway?'

'I'm afraid not. We always destroy them if they're not used.'

Kaufman saw that Desiry was scrutinising the photograph of his wife. 'Presumably you kept a note of the number,' Desiry said.

'We don't do that either,' Kaufman said. 'If the guest pays cash, there is no need.'

'This isn't very helpful, Mr Kaufman,' Desiry said, with heavy sarcasm.

Kaufman felt the knot of his tie. 'I'm trying to be as helpful as I can.' Halard took Carlson's bill from his hand. 'We'll need this,' she said.

Stapled to the bill was the registration card Carlson had filled out when he arrived at the hotel. He'd written his full name – 'Mark Andrew Carlson' – and nationality – 'American' – in a confident script, but nothing else.

'Why isn't his passport number here?' demanded Desiry.

'French law no longer requires that, inspector,' Kaufman said.

'That doesn't stop you asking for it, does it?'

'It wasn't necessary because . . .'

Desiry cut across him. 'What happened when Carlson left? Did he go by car? By taxi? Did he say where he was going?'

Kaufman fingered his tie again. 'I don't have those details,' he replied. 'But I'll see if our receptionist can help.'

Kaufman dialled the reception desk and asked Maria to come in. There was only a vestige of her customary smile. 'Some of the guests are very upset,' she said.

Halard took no notice. 'We want to know what happened when Mr Carlson checked out.'

'The American gentleman? Who checked out early?'

'That's right.'

Maria recalled how Carlson had asked her to book him on to the next plane to Paris, saying he had been called there on urgent business. She confirmed that he had paid his bill in cash. 'When I tore up his credit card slip, he asked me for the pieces.' He had given her a hundred-franc tip and left for the airport in a taxi from Voyages Orange.

Halard told Desiry: 'Get on to them right away.'

When Desiry had gone out of the room Halard turned to Kaufman again. 'What about the children's parents? Do you know where they are?'

'There's something I'm trying to tell you.'

'Please be quick, Mr Kaufman.'

'I have a photocopy of Carlson's passport.'

Halard's look was like stone. 'Why didn't you tell us this before?'

'I tried to, but your inspector wouldn't let me. I'll get it for you now.'

To his relief, Kaufman found the folder in its place in the filing cabinet. He placed the copy of the last two pages of Carlson's passport on the desk. There was the number, alongside a photograph of a man with a broad forehead and penetrating eyes.

'Do you always make copies of your guests' passports?' Halard asked Kaufman, in a tone which left him uncertain whether or not she approved.

'Usually,' he said. 'It's a precaution against credit card fraud.'

'Is that what he looked like?' Halard asked Maria.

'More or less,' she said. 'Except that his hair was lighter than in the photograph. I think he tints it.'

Halard picked up the photocopy. 'I'll take this as well. Now, what about the parents?'

'Mrs Beaumont is attending a biotechnology conference at the convention centre in Nice,' Kaufman said. 'She left us a phone number, in case there was any news of her son.'

'And the girl's father? Stewart?'

Desiry came back into the office. 'The driver who took Carlson to the airport will be here in twenty minutes,' he said.

'And Stewart?' Halard repeated.

It was Maria who replied. 'He left the hotel in his car early this morning. The night porter told me when I came on duty.'

'Do you know what time he left?'

'I came on duty at eight. I think he went out around six.'

'Did he say where he was going?'

'I don't think so.'

'Do you know what car he was driving?'

Kaufman flourished Stewart's registration card, which he had just retrieved from the filing cabinet. 'He has a Renault Laguna hired from Hertz – licence number 3628 VC 06.'

'What's he up to, Commissaire?' Desiry asked.

'Let's ask him,' Halard replied. 'I'll deal with Mrs Beaumont.

You put out a full alert for Stewart's car. When you find it, bring him in.'

Stewart followed Avenue Princesse Grace as it passed under Monte Carlo's casino and parked the Renault opposite number 119, one of the towering apartment blocks which crowd the tiny principality. Apartment 14B was clearly marked among the columns of bellpushes beside the entrance, but there was nothing to show who lived there. He pressed the bell and listened at the grille of the entryphone. No reply.

Stewart's intention, when he'd set out for Monaco, was to find Olivier, or some way of tracing him. As he jostled through the speeding traffic from Villefranche, a new hope had crystallised in his mind: that Fee and Josh had come here for the weekend. Perhaps Olivier had thrown a party, lubricated with alcohol and drugs, and they had crashed out and even now were still asleep – or just waking, bleary-eyed and in search of coffee, or the telephone, to let their parents know they were safe. It seemed an entirely reasonable scenario. They had to be *somewhere*. Why not here?

Through the windscreen of his car, he studied the passage of Monaco's well-heeled residents along the avenue. In fifteen minutes he had found the pattern he was looking for. As they approached the entrance, the residents of number 119 usually slowed while they searched for the key cards required to open the heavy glass front door. Several more people strode by without pausing. Then came a middle-aged woman, elegantly dressed, with a poodle on a lead. She was fumbling in her handbag with one hand while the poodle tugged at the other, as if it wanted to prolong its walk.

'Apricot! Behave!'

In an instant Stewart was out of the car.

'Madame, allow me,' he said, with an extravagant smile.

He took hold of the lead while she found her card and inserted it in the slot by the entryphone. He opened the door and ushered her and the poodle, now resigned to its fate, inside.

'You are most kind,' she said as he handed back the lead.

There were two lifts at the back of the entrance hall. Stewart read the announcements on the notice board until the doors of one had closed behind the woman and her poodle, then took the other to the fourteenth floor. He found himself at the apex of an L-shaped corridor, with light flooding in from the windows at each end. To his right, the carpet had been rolled back so that it lay in an untidy heap. The door of the apartment nearest the lift was wide open. It was 14B.

Stewart looked both ways along the corridor: it was deserted. He stepped over the threshold into what he took to be the living room. His foot sank into a sodden carpet. He took another step, and water oozed over his shoe. There was a door on the far side of the room and he pushed it open, to come face to face with a man gripping a large monkey wrench.

'About time you got here,' the man said.

'The traffic was bad,' Stewart replied.

'You insurance people are always the same. Slow to arrive and slow to pay out. Have you seen the mess downstairs?'

Stewart finessed again. 'In 13B? Not yet.'

'Half the ceiling's fallen in. The tenant's having hysterics.'

'I'll call there next,' said Stewart. 'So what happened?'

'Some kind of malfunction in the dishwasher. The inlet valve jammed open and the water couldn't drain away. The stupid machine must have been pumping out water for three days. The whole place is flooded.'

For three days. No one's been here for three days.

'As long as that?'

'That's when I last saw the tenant.'

'Yves Lavar?'

'No, he's hardly ever here. His son, Olivier. He said he'd be back yesterday but I haven't seen him. I had to use my pass key to get in.'

Stewart's disappointment washed over him like a wave. He realised he had let his hopes build far too high, and reminded himself of his original reason for coming here: to trace Olivier.

'What about his father? Do you know where I can reach him?'

'He lives in Italy most of the time.'

'Where in Italy?'

'I've no idea.'

'Rome? Genoa? What does he do for a living?'

‘Look, I really don’t know anything about him.’ He dropped the wrench into his tool-bag. ‘Now, if you don’t mind, I’ve got to get downstairs.’

‘Of course,’ said Stewart. ‘I’ll close the door when I leave.’

‘You need to check every room. The whole carpet’s ruined. It’s going to cost your company a packet,’ he said, with evident relish.

Stewart waited until the man’s footsteps had died away, then closed the front door.

The apartment could best be described as functional, a reasonable facsimile of a suite at a Holiday Inn. The living room seemed to have no history, devoid of personal touches, apart from a garish abstract painting composed solely of red and black shapes.

The bedroom, by contrast, had all the signs of a teenager in residence: a pile of dirty clothes in one corner, two beer bottles in the waste-bin, half a dozen cigarette butts in an ashtray, a packet of Rizla papers beside it, a poster of Céline Dion in sulky pop-singer pose on the wall.

There was a small cabinet beside the bed. Inside Stewart found a mirror and a wooden box with an elaborate inlaid lid, containing a razor blade and a slim silver tube. So that was Olivier’s thing. He might be dealing heroin, as Fratoni had said, but his own drug of choice had to be cocaine.

On the far side of the bed was a chest of drawers. Stewart pulled out the top one and tipped an array of T-shirts and socks on to the bed. He rummaged through them, then emptied out the second drawer. Among a shower of underclothes, a pair of navy-blue briefs landed with added weight. He picked them up and a revolver fell back on to the bed.

Stewart picked up the gun. There was some finely-engraved writing on the barrel. He looked closely and read: ‘Smith and Wesson .38’. He opened the cylinder to find that each chamber was loaded with a bullet with a copper tip, remembering, from some story long ago, that these were designed to shatter on impact and cause the worst possible injuries. It was all scarcely believable. His daughter, his innocent Fee, was mixed up with a drug dealer who kept a loaded gun hidden in his underwear. Panic was rising, threatening to overwhelm him.

He tipped the contents of the last two drawers on to the bed.

There was nothing more, certainly nothing to tell him how to find Olivier. He was breathing fast and forced himself to walk slowly back to the living room, knowing that he had to find out where Yves Lavar lived. He scanned the dull furniture once again: one sofa, two arm chairs, one table, one television, one hi-fi, one writing desk.

One writing desk. He lifted the lid. Inside was a pile of letters, all addressed to Olivier's father. He ripped one open: it had been sent from Paris, and advertised a share trading scheme. A second was an invitation to a movie premiere long past.

At the back of the desk was a row of drawers. The first contained an address book, decorated on the cover with a cartoon of Mickey Mouse. It had to be Olivier's. He thumbed through the pages but there were only a few, brief entries, most of first names or initials, most with local numbers. There was nothing under 'L' for Lavar or 'Y' for Yves. He slid the address book into his pocket.

Stewart straightened his back. He could hear a succession of dull thuds from below, and supposed the maintenance man was dealing with the ceiling. How much longer before he came back to the Lavars' apartment? He picked up the telephone on the writing desk. There were five buttons for storing pre-set numbers. He lifted the handset and pressed each one in turn.

The first four were dead. When he pressed the fifth he heard a rapid sequence of musical beeps, followed by the squawk of an international connection. There was a repeated single ringing tone. A woman answered in Italian.

'*Pronto?*'

Stewart's Italian was rudimentary at best. '*Possibile parlare Signore Lavar?*'

'*Cosa? Scusi, cosa mi sta dicendo?*'

She couldn't understand.

'*Parla inglese? Francese?*' Stewart asked.

'*No. Mi dispiace, parlo solo Italiano.*'

'*Signore Lavar, per favore. E importante.*'

'*Non c'é. E in Polonia. Chi parla?*'

Polonia? Did that mean Poland? Stewart tried to imagine what a Frenchman who lived in Italy could be doing in Eastern Europe. He switched tack.

'*Signora, per favore, che suo numero telefono?*'

'*Scusi, ma non capisco: lei sta chiamando, lei c'è l'a il numero*!'

She was asking why he needed her phone number if he had already called it. The task of explaining this conundrum in Italian defeated him.

'*Okay, non importante, signora. Grazie.*'

'*Va bene. Buon giorno.*'

He replaced the receiver. A memory stirred, of a Customs investigator explaining how it was possible to decipher telephone numbers from the rising scale of beeps made by the individual digits. He picked up the receiver and pressed the memory button again, listening to the sequence of tones, then cutting the call before it was connected. He did it again and again. Then he began to experiment, pressing the dialling buttons and matching them with the tones in his head. As he identified each digit, he jotted it on a piece of paper, until he had what he hoped was the number for Yves Lavar. It began with 00392 – the code for Milan.

He dialled it again, this time by hand.

'*Pronto?*'

It sounded like the same woman but he had to be sure. He told her he was the one who had called before.

'*Ah, si, vedo.*'

'*Possibile parlare Signore Lavar, per favore?*'

'*Ma signore, ho già detto che non c'è in casa, che è in Polonia. Ma cosa vuole lei?*'

Now he was certain? '*No importante. Grazie, signora.*'

'*Prego.*'

Stewart was closing the apartment door behind him just as the lift arrived.

'All done?' said the maintenance man.

'You were right. It's a complete mess,' Stewart said.

'Wait till you see downstairs.'

'On my way.'

Stewart took the stairs, carrying on past the thirteenth floor until he reached the street. As he crossed towards his car, he felt that he was making progress at last. He had a number for Yves Lavar. And he had a shrewd idea that he knew someone who spoke fluent Italian.

As he unlocked the car, Stewart felt a hand on his shoulder. He turned around to see a police warrant card, held by a man wearing a blue suit. The card said his name was Inspector Emile Desiry. Two other men, balanced a little too obviously on the balls of their feet, were watching from a short distance away.

'Your papers,' Desiry said.

The first thing Stewart touched when he reached into his pocket was Olivier's address book. He felt his face burning. He took out his passport and handed it to Desiry, who looked briefly at the page showing his name.

'Give me your car key.'

'What is this about?'

Desiry took the key out of Stewart's hand and tossed it to one of his colleagues.

'He'll bring your car. You're coming with me.'

Part Two

7

It was still dark when Brady left Indian Point. As he pulled the front door tight behind him, then doubled-locked it with his keys, he sensed – more strongly than on any previous occasion – that he had no idea when he would be back. Zola was uneasy too, and had to be coaxed into the Plymouth, where he sat mutely on the back seat. Brady steered cautiously along the winding road away from his house, as his headlights cut through the night mist drifting up from the Potomac. When they reached Riverside, Brady stopped at the kennels from where he had collected Zola less than twenty-four hours before. The labrador looked up at Brady as he handed him over to the night attendant.

'Sorry, feller,' said Brady. 'Not much of a vacation, was it?'

By the time he reached the fork at Doncaster, where the sign for Washington showed he had fifty-nine miles to go, the first light of dawn was glimmering on the asphalt. He eased his finger into the collar of the white shirt he had broken out of its cellophane that morning. Why did new shirts always chafe your neck, he wondered? And just what was so important about one missing American boy that could have him hauled back to Washington so summarily?

It was a question he and Dominique Halard had pondered the night before. She had begun by laughing, when he'd told her he was calling to see if she knew who was handling the case.

'What's so funny?'

'Because it's me. I've just got back from seeing the minister. I was called to his residence an hour ago. He told me it was something to do with "the Americans". But when I asked for more details, he told me to leave the politics to him. "Just find the children," he said. I've got to leave for Orly in five minutes.

There's a government jet waiting to take me to Nice. Have you any idea what's going on?'

'Not really. All I know is that there's a senator over here who took it to the Oval Office. Presumably, the State Department has been hitting the phones to France.'

'Why is this boy so special?'

'That's what I aim to find out. What you do suppose has happened to him?'

'Hard to say. There's an English girl staying at the same hotel who's missing as well. Could be anything, could be nothing. What's your feeling?'

'The same. We'll know more when you get to Nice. I'll be in the office first thing. Let me know as soon as you get anything.'

'Of course I will. Phil, I have to go.'

'Take care.'

'You too.'

Brady reached FBI headquarters shortly before seven. With the Washington rush-hour not yet underway, the empty expanse of Pennsylvania Avenue made the building look more monolithic than ever. Brady had been delighted when a Washington tourist guide cited it as the ugliest building in western civilisation – a richly deserved prize, he thought. He took the lift to the sixth floor and walked down the deserted corridor to his office.

As soon as he unlocked the door and turned on the lights he sensed himself returning to that timeless ambiance that being at headquarters seemed to inspire. He hung his jacket on the stand by the door, undid his collar button and loosened the staid blue tie he had grabbed that morning.

There were several sheets of paper, stirring in the draught of the air conditioning, sitting in the tray beneath the fax machine. From the header sheet – *POLICE NATIONALE DE FRANCE* – Brady saw immediately that they came from Halard. She'd clearly been busy. He took the pages to his desk, which was closeted from the rest of the office by glass partitions, and started to read.

FROM COMMISSAIRE HALARD
TO SPECIAL AGENT BRADY, FBI HQ, WASH. D.C.

Item one: The disappeared
1. Joshua ('Josh') Walter BEAUMONT, born – Austin, Texas, 16/08/78, height – approx 1.7m, weight – approx 70kg, eyes – brown, hair – brown, complexion – fair. No distinguishing marks.
2. Fiona ('Fee') Sarah STEWART, born – London, England, 09/07/78, height – approx 1.55m, weight – approx 55kg, eyes – hazel, hair – auburn, complexion – fair. No distinguishing marks.

Halard had followed her terse introduction with a mass of procedural detail which, they both knew, was intended for the filing cabinet, or rather for the time when – if something went wrong – some suit somewhere would feel an overwhelming need to review the case. Then came the interesting stuff.

At the time of his disappearance, Joshua was staying at the hotel with his mother, Suzanne Janice BEAUMONT (nee WILLIAMS, born – El Paso, Texas, 17/05/56). She is a director of BioGenius Incorporated, of Austin, Texas, a prosperous biotechnology company that specialises in medical products. His father, Lawrence James BEAUMONT, was killed in a flying accident five years ago. According to Mrs Beaumont, who I interviewed at the hotel this morning, his grandfather, Jesse Earl BEAUMONT, acts as the boy's quasi-guardian. Mr Beaumont is president of BioGenius. According to his daughter-in-law, he is active in Republican politics and an influential supporter of the GOP at state and federal level.

Brady smiled to himself. So that was the connection to the good Senator Bates.

Fiona was staying at Le Bosquet, with her father Thomas Prentice STEWART (born – London, England, 18/12/52), a writer. We have not yet been able to interview Mr Stewart, who left the hotel early this morning, apparently to search for his daughter. According to Mrs Beaumont, he is divorced from his wife, who is an American national at present in the United States. Mrs Beaumont describes Stewart's relationship with his daughter as problematic, but there is no doubt in Mrs Beaumont's mind that the relationship is close and affectionate. I will advise when I have interviewed Mr Stewart.

There were 34 guests staying at the hotel when Joshua and Fiona disappeared. Five of those have since checked out. Two were couples who we are still trying to trace, but, at this stage, there is no reason to believe they have any involvement in this matter.

The fifth guest, however, is a potential suspect. He registered under the name of Mark CARLSON, and I attach copies of the relevant pages of his passport. According to the hotel manager, Carlson had reserved a room for seven nights, but stayed only five, checking out the morning after the children disappeared. His explanation for his early departure was that he had urgent business in Paris. He asked the hotel receptionist to book him on Air Inter flight 8082, departing Nice for Paris at 12.45 hours, and he ordered a taxi from Voyages Orange in Villefranche. We have interviewed the driver, who confirms that he took Carlson to Terminal Two, from where the flight departed. However Air Inter has reported that Carlson did *not* check in for the flight, and was listed as a 'no show'. We are currently checking with all other airlines operating out of Nice to establish if he took a different flight. Will forward all further information soonest.

Brady read the key passages again. It remained entirely possible that the two teenagers had merely taken off by themselves for a couple of days – teenagers did that everywhere. But their backgrounds were certainly intriguing. No less intriguing was this Carlson, who seemed to have changed his plans not once, but twice. And if Halard thought he was 'a potential suspect', Brady was more than ready to trust her instincts.

He studied the page from Carlson's passport. It was hard to tell anything from the photograph: the photocopy had been further degraded by the fax transmission, so that he could discern nothing more than the shape of a face through a screen of grey sludge. And the remaining details were distinctly thin. All that they revealed was that Carlson was born in Baltimore,

Maryland, on September 26, 1947. But it was enough to give him a start.

He dialled the number of the State Department, identified himself to a duty officer, and left a message for Chuck Adams to call him as soon as he arrived at his desk.

'Tell him it's urgent,' Brady said before ending the call.

He yawned, and realised that he was missing the morning's vital first cup of coffee. He crossed to his secretary's desk and was spooning grains of best Colombian into the filter when the door opened.

'I'll do that.'

Betsy Silverman showed no surprise on seeing her boss back at work just thirty-six hours after starting his vacation. In her ten years as his secretary, she had become accustomed to his abrupt changes of plan, and to his inexhaustible allegiance to the agency. She was afraid the strain would tell on him – with his time-worn face, she thought he looked more like Harvey Keitel every day – and was fiercely loyal whenever she heard a hint of criticism, particularly of his tendency to become obsessed by his cases. She took the tin of coffee from his hand and said: 'You're supposed to be on vacation.' The rebuke was little more than a ritual.

'I was – until last night.'

'How did Zola take it?'

'He wasn't too pleased.'

'I'll call the kennels and see how he's doing. So, what's to be done?'

The phone rang. She held out the receiver. 'It's Chuck Adams.'

'Thanks, Betsy.' He handed her Halard's fax. 'Take a look at this.'

'You looking for me?' said Adams.

'You're in early,' said Brady.

'I'm still at home. I got a call from the duty officer saying you needed something urgently.'

'That's right. I've got some passport details here. I need to know if the passport's genuine, whether it's been reported lost or stolen – anything you've got.'

'Do you have the name and passport number?'

'That's about all I have.'

'Read them out.'
Brady did so, adding the other details about Carlson that Halard had sent him.
'Phil, there should be a code in the bottom left-hand corner of the page.'
'Got it.'
'Give me the first seven digits.'
Brady did as he was asked.
'Okay. That tells me it was issued in Baltimore, so that fits. For anything more, I'll have to get on the computer. I should be in the office in about thirty minutes. I'll get back to you as soon as I can.'
Betsy came into Brady's inner sanctum with his coffee – no milk or sugar – and a writing pad. 'What's next?'
'Let's see if Carlson has a criminal record.'
'You want me to call NCIC?'
She meant the FBI's National Criminal Intelligence Centre, whose computer stored details of more than one hundred million known and suspected offenders.
'Right. Ask them to run a check on every Carlson of any first name born between 1945 and 1955.'
'They won't like that,' Betsy warned.
'I know they won't. They haven't got the White House on their back.'
'Next?'
'We'd better see what we can find out about the Beaumonts.'
'Through the Texas office?'
'Right. Is Harry Gonzales still running it?'
'I'll check.'
'If so, send him copies of the fax and ask him to start a full background check on the Beaumont family. We need to make contact with the grandfather. Give Harry all the background. You'd better fill him in on the politics too.'
'You'll need to fill me in first. What's going on?'
'That's what I'm trying to figure out,' Brady replied. 'But it's gotten pretty heavy. It's coming from down the street.' He cocked his head in the general direction of the White House. 'Tell Harry that, and tell him to mind his manners.'
'What else?'
'Baltimore. Who's the SAC?'

Betsy crossed to her desk and thumbed through a list of the Special Agents in Charge at the FBI's fifty-six field offices. 'It is still Harry in Houston, by the way,' she called. 'Baltimore is Steve Petrowski.'

Brady suppressed a groan. It was not the name he most wanted to hear. Petrowski could be awkward at times, especially when he suspected that the Washington brass were about to enter his patch. The phone rang and Brady picked up it.

'I've got something for you.' It was Adams, calling from his office.

'That was quick.'

'You said it was urgent.'

'Appreciate it. Now, please don't tell me the passport's been reported missing. That gets us nowhere.'

'It's not the passport that's missing. It's Carlson.'

'What have you got?'

'Carlson has a business partner in Baltimore, name of Gerard Railton. Carlson went to Europe on a selling trip last month. He hasn't been in touch for almost two weeks, and his partner asked for State's help in reporting him missing to the Dutch police, because he was last heard from in Amsterdam. According to the computer, our embassy in The Hague informed the Dutch authorities three days ago.'

'Two weeks doesn't sound too long.'

'It does when Carlson had been checking in with his partner every day. There's been nothing back from the Dutch so far.'

'Have you got anything else on Carlson?'

'Afraid not, Phil. There will be some detail on his application form but Carlson's passport was issued as a renewal. Passport Services doesn't normally input the data from renewal forms. They just get shoved into a warehouse.'

'And where's that?'

'Roanoke.'

This time Brady's groan was audible. 'I need that form badly, Chuck. An American kid's gone missing from a hotel in France, and it looks like Carlson could be involved. Certainly he, or someone using his passport, disappeared from the hotel at about the same time.'

'I'm on to it. I've already asked the guys at Roanoke to start looking. But it could take some time.'

'How long are we talking?'

'Could be tomorrow. Best would be this afternoon.'

'Best is what I need, Chuck.'

Betsy came back into Brady's office.

'I've got Steve Petrowski's home number for you.'

Brady dialled Petrowski himself. Even before Petrowski answered, in his irritatingly downbeat voice, Brady had decided to pull rank: too much was riding on this for diplomatic niceties. He gave Petrowski the bare details of the case.

'What do you need?'

'Anything and everything you can give me on both Carlson and his partner.'

'I'll see what I can do,' Petrowski said.

'Good,' said Brady. 'You can give me the results when I get there.'

'Get where?'

'Baltimore. I'm on my way.'

Inspector Desiry drove fast, overtaking at will. From the back seat, Stewart saw the speedometer flicker past 150 kph, even when the traffic thickened on the approach to Nice. The Peugeot swept round the port on the crest of the bend, forcing oncoming drivers to make way. A black BMW loomed in the windscreen and Stewart closed his eyes and waited for the impact. His surprise that it did not come merged with gratitude that he was still alive. The carphone rang and Desiry picked it up, steering with his left hand. He listened, then said: 'Got it. Tell Halard.'

Stewart had given up asking Desiry what was happening.

'Have you found my daughter?' had been his first question after he was bundled into the police car.

'No,' Desiry said.

'Where are you taking me?'

'You'll find out soon enough.'

A little later he asked Desiry why he was driving like a lunatic. Without turning his head, Desiry replied: 'No more questions.'

As they passed under the portcullis that served as a gateway to Nice's old town, Stewart supposed that they were heading for the police headquarters where he and Suzanne had reported the children missing the day before. Instead, they swung down a steep ramp into an underground garage, where a uniformed officer hastily raised the entrance barrier. The revolving light on the dashboard swept a blue mosaic around the walls as the Peugeot came to a halt.

'This way,' said Desiry. He led Stewart along a corridor and up a narrow flight of concrete steps to a door which Desiry unlocked. They plunged into a labyrinth of corridors, finally reaching a pair of imposing double doors, where a scrawled note had been pinned up. It read: 'Beaumont Case Room.'

When Desiry pushed open the doors, Stewart found himself in a high-ceilinged room with a line of tall windows along one side. But what was clearly a chamber intended for formal receptions looked as if it was being converted into a war room. There were two rows of trestle tables, some laden with computers and monitor screens, connected by cables snaking across the tiled floor and held down by patches of silver tape. A dozen or more canteen tables were scattered between them. Two men in overalls were manoeuvring a copying machine on to one of the tables, another was feeding telephone cables through the window. At the far end of the room was a smaller table, and behind it a white marker board where the words 'Joshua Beaumont' had been inscribed, in large capitals, with a red felt pen. Seated behind a desk in front of the board was a woman with dark curly hair.

Stewart followed Desiry across the room. The woman was making notes in a file. 'Sit down, please,' she said, without looking up.

One of the canteen chairs had been placed in front of the desk. When Stewart sat on it, he found it had a straight and unyielding back. He sensed Desiry hovering somewhere behind.

'Mr Stewart, what were you doing in the Lavar apartment?' the woman asked.

'I was looking for my daughter, of course. What do you think I was doing?'

'And how did you get in?'

'The door was wide open. The place was flooded and the maintenance man was trying to repair the leak. I just walked in.'

'Why did he leave you alone in the apartment?'

'He said he had to go downstairs.'

'Did you tell him who you were?'

'He never asked.'

She looked up at last. 'That's not true, is it?'

'I don't know what you mean.'

'You posed as an insurance assessor.'

'I didn't pose as anybody. That's what he assumed.'

'So, you got in by deception,' she said. 'That's the same as using a crowbar.'

'Can we just hold on for a moment?' said Stewart. 'Before we go any further, who the hell are you?'

'Plus you were trampling all over a possible crime scene and tampering with evidence,' said Desiry from over Stewart's shoulder. Stewart felt a surge of anger. He stood up and the chair crashed behind him.

'Well, at least I was doing something, while you were sitting on your backside.' He turned back to the woman. 'I want to know who you are.'

'I am Commissaire Halard of the *Police Nationale*. I am attached to the Ministry of the Interior in Paris. Would you kindly sit down?'

Some pieces were falling into place. Suzanne clearly meant it when she said her father-in-law could get things done. Stewart picked up the chair and told himself to stay calm.

'What happened in the apartment?' Halard asked.

'What do you mean, what happened? Nothing happened. My daughter wasn't there.'

'So did you search the apartment?'

'Yes, I did.'

'Why did you do that?'

'I was looking for any sign that she might have been there. Or some clue as to how I could find Lavar.'

'Did you find anything?'

Stewart felt the weight of Olivier's address book in his pocket. He heard Desiry light a cigarette.

'I found a gun.'

'Where?'

'In the bedroom. It was in a drawer, wrapped up in some underwear.'

'What kind was it?'

For a moment, Stewart could not remember. Then he recalled the writing on the barrel. 'A Smith and Wesson,' he said confidently. 'A thirty-eight.'

'Was it loaded?'
'Yes.'
'You handled it?'
'I opened the cylinder, yes.'
'So the fingerprints we found on it are yours?'
Stewart remembered the phone call Desiry had taken in the car: his squad must have gone into the apartment and found the revolver. But why were the police playing these games? He felt his anger rising again, like bile in his throat.
'This is just incredible,' he said. 'Yesterday, when I report my daughter missing, you people say there's absolutely nothing you can do. It won't even become official for a week. Then, perhaps – *perhaps* – some investigating magistrate may decide this is serious. Well, I wasn't willing to wait a week, so I went looking for her myself. Then I'm grabbed in the street without a word of explanation and brought here in a car driven by a madman who thinks he's Jacques Villeneuve. And now you have the cheek to accuse me of breaking in, tampering with evidence, and God knows what else. I don't know what you think you're doing.'
'I'm trying to find your daughter, Mr Stewart.'
'You could have fooled me,' Stewart replied. 'What do you take me for? Do you think I don't know what's going on? Josh's grandfather starts pulling political levers in the States and all of a sudden the French authorities show an interest. We both know that this has nothing to do with my daughter.'
He pointed at the board behind Halard. 'Do you think I can't read? You're here because of Josh. So far as you're concerned, Fiona doesn't even exist.'
Halard's face was flushed. 'You shouldn't be misled by what's on that board,' she said. 'The point is, we know a lot about Joshua because we were able to talk to his mother this morning. We know very little about Fiona, because we weren't able to talk to you. Until now. Which is why you were brought here.'
'I can understand that,' said Stewart. 'But we might get along better if you stopped treating me as a criminal. Unless you think I had something to do with my daughter's disappearance, of course.'
'We don't think anything yet, Mr Stewart. I want to know why you thought Fiona might have been with Lavar.'
'Because I know she and Josh were with him.'

'How do you know that?'

'Because I talked to a woman in Villefranche who saw them together just before two o'clock.'

Halard looked sharply towards Desiry. 'What woman?'

Stewart described his encounter with Madame Robert in the *bar-tabac*, and how her son had provided a description of Olivier's car. As he read the details from his notebook, he heard Desiry repeat them into a phone. Desiry cupped the receiver and asked: 'Do you have the licence number?'

'No,' Stewart told him.

'That's a pity,' said Desiry.

'Well, it gives you something to do.'

Desiry gave him a cold look and turned his back.

Halard waited until the inspector put down the phone. 'Mr Stewart, do you want something to drink?' Her tone had softened.

'Coffee would be nice,' Stewart said.

'Inspector Desiry – if you would?'

With not entirely good grace, Stewart thought, Desiry headed for the percolator across the room.

'We need to go back to the beginning,' Halard said. 'In cases like this, we need to know everything, because at this stage we don't know what's important and what isn't.'

'Where shall I start?' Stewart asked, as Desiry placed a polystyrene cup in front of him.

The next hour was one of the most uncomfortable Stewart had spent, as Halard picked away remorselessly at the most vulnerable aspects of his life.

'I understand you were divorced when Fiona was quite young,' Halard said. 'Tell me about that.'

Long before, Stewart had rehearsed an innocuous version of events which he related to anyone who asked about his divorce. He saw no reason to depart from his script now. He recited how the demands of his work had created increasing strains between him and Rachel; how they'd decided it was sensible to separate for all their sakes; how they'd sat down and explained all of this to Fee – well, as best it could be explained to an eleven-year-old girl. They told her she would live with her mother, while her father would see her often – almost as often as he had before. In the circumstances, Fiona had adjusted very well, Stewart said.

Halard nodded sagely. Then she began probing his bland account. How had Fiona really coped with this catastrophe in her life? Was she angry? Did she feel rejected? Who did she blame? Her mother, or him? Did she play them off against each other?

Stewart protested that all this was irrelevant, but Halard pressed on. How much time had he really spent with Fiona after the divorce? Did he see her every time he was in London? How often? For how long? What did they do when they were together? What did they talk about? How much did he know about her life? Finally she homed in on the most recent events: How had their holiday come about?

Stewart explained that he had been in Southeast Asia, working on a book, when Rachel's mother, who lived in Maryland, had suffered a stroke. Rachel had called him in Bangkok and asked him to come back. He had readily agreed, as he had reached an impasse in his research. Since the school holidays were about to begin, he'd decided to bring Fee to the Riviera. When they arrived in Nice they'd hired a car, and driven to Le Bosquet.

'That's how we met the Beaumonts,' he said. 'We'd come on the same flight from London and got chatting to them while we were waiting for our luggage. We discovered we were all staying at the same hotel and I offered them a lift.'

They had arrived at the hotel at midday, and he and Fee had a snack for lunch. Stewart had to do some work on his book, so Fee spent the afternoon with the Beaumonts at the pool. 'Lavar was there for some of the time.'

'And there were no problems?'

'Problems?'

'Between you and Fiona?'

'Absolutely not.'

'You had dinner together in the hotel that night?'

'Yes.'

'What went wrong?'

The chair felt hard against Stewart's back. 'Who says anything went wrong?'

'We've talked to most of the guests at the hotel by now, and most of the staff. Anyone who was in the restaurant that night knows that you had an argument. What was it about?'

'It was nothing, really.'

'But she walked out on you.'

'She was a bit upset. But the meal was almost over anyway.'

'So why did you lie to the police about it?'

'What do you mean?'

'You told the police there was no row.'

'I just told you, it wasn't really a row. And anyway, I thought if I told them what had happened, they wouldn't do anything to find her. They'd just put it down to a family quarrel.'

'And that was the last time you saw Fiona? When she walked out of the restaurant?'

'Yes.'

'So you were never able to make it up with her?'

'It wasn't a problem. In the morning, everything was fine. I left a note for her at reception, and she left one for me before she went out. It was very sweet, very affectionate.'

'We have her note,' said Desiry.

'You've searched my room? Without my permission?'

'You weren't around to ask.'

Halard added: 'We've searched Fiona's room as well. We were trying to work out what's missing. But there's no way we can tell. Do you have any idea what she was wearing when she disappeared?'

Stewart's coffee was lukewarm. It tasted bitter too. He thought back to the previous evening, when he had searched through Fee's things himself without knowing what he was looking for.

'I'm afraid I don't,' he said. 'I don't know what clothes she brought with her, so I can't tell what's missing.'

'Of course,' Halard said. 'But let's suppose she intended to stay out that night. What would she have taken with her? Was she taking any medicines?'

He wasn't sure.

'Does she use an oral contraceptive?'

The thought had never occurred to him.

'We couldn't find her passport. Would she normally carry it with her?'

Stewart didn't know.

'Does she have any cash or credit cards?'

'I'm sure her mother would have given her some spending money. I was paying all the bills, of course.'

'Does she usually carry a purse or a bag?'

Stewart tried to recall if she had taken one to dinner.

'I think so,' he said.

'Can you describe it?'

He thought some more. 'No.'

'You don't seem to know much about your daughter, do you Mr Stewart?' Desiry said.

It was a low blow and it struck home.

'There is one thing,' Stewart said. 'I gave her a camera. I left it for her at reception when I went out on Saturday morning. When I looked in her room I couldn't find it. She must have taken it with her. All I found was the empty box.'

'This box?' said Desiry. He placed it on the desk between them.

Stewart thought of Fee's note. *Thanks for the brilliant camera.* She had added two crosses as kisses.

'I think we've taken this as far as we can for now,' Halard was saying. 'There is one thing you can do. Call your ex-wife and see if she can help you work out what Fiona was wearing, and what's missing from her room.'

'I'll try,' said Stewart.

A man in overalls deposited a box full of telephones on the table nearest Halard's desk. Halard stood up. 'As you can see, there is now an intensive inquiry under way. And be clear about this. We are looking for *two* children – Josh *and* Fiona. But please leave the detective work to us. No more playing at Sherlock Holmes.'

'Your car's downstairs,' Desiry said.

'We'll be in touch,' said Halard.

'I very much hope so.'

'Trust us, Mr Stewart,' she said.

Halard waited until a guard had escorted Stewart from the room.

'What do you think?' she asked.

Desiry had been scrutinising one of the telephones which had been dumped on Halard's desk. He returned it to the box and looked up at her.

'He's holding something back,' said Desiry.

8

Laurel Drive, Baltimore, had oaks and birch trees as well as laurels. There were lawns too, fronting detached brick houses with porches and driveways, and gardens behind. Number 4513 wasn't the most grandiose house, but it wasn't the smallest either. Petrowski had parked fifty yards further on. He got out of his car as Brady drew up behind him. He was older than Brady remembered.

'What have you got?'

Petrowski got in beside Brady. 'I'm not sure what we're looking at. Carlson has lived at this address for nearly nine years. So has his friend, name of Gerard Railton. They pay their taxes and their bills. They've had one parking ticket between them. Otherwise no traffic violations, no credit card problems, no rows with their neighbours. Model citizens.'

'What do they do?'

'They've got their own computer software company. They used to run the computer department at Johns Hopkins. Then they went solo and now they're making a bunch of money selling stuff for the Internet.'

'So they work together as well as live together?'

'Yeah,' said Petrowski. 'Cosy, isn't it?'

'Meaning?'

'Faggots.'

'I'll say this just once, Steve.' Although Brady used Petrowski's first name, there was a sudden formality in his tone. 'You can cut that out. That's not what we're about. Have you got that?'

'Got it,' said Petrowski, staring fixedly through the windscreen.

Brady asked: 'Is Railton there now?'

'He was when I called twenty minutes ago.'

Gerard Railton was slim, with an angular nose and a shock of black hair. He was wearing a loose pale blue short-sleeved shirt and black jeans. He accepted the arrival on his doorstep of two FBI agents with apparent composure and led them into a sitting room. It was sparingly furnished and immaculately tidy. There were Turkish kilims on the floor, and a gleaming polished table. The shelves and other surfaces were largely bare, save for a collection of Native American painted bowls, a catalogue for a Cézanne exhibition in New York, and a photograph in an ash-wood frame of two men in tennis clothes, whom Brady took to be Railton and Carlson. Railton gestured to the two agents to sit down on a sofa and took a matching chair facing them. Brady noticed that he was fidgeting with the ring on his finger.

'This is about Mark, I assume. Do you have any news?'

'We're not sure,' Brady told him. 'I need to ask you some questions about him.'

'Go ahead.'

'The last time you heard from Mark he was in Amsterdam?'

'Yes. That was ten – no, eleven – days ago.'

'And he was in Europe on business. Does he make many business trips?'

'Maybe a dozen a year. We design software programmes together but he does the selling while I handle the admin back here.'

'And when he's away, he keeps in regular touch with you?'

'Always. He calls me every other day at least, more often if there's business to sort out.'

'Where was he due to go on this trip?'

'Germany, Belgium and Holland.'

'What about France?'

'No. We haven't tried France yet. It's a tough market to crack.'

'Suppose he wanted to take some time off? Might he go there for the weekend, say?'

'It's possible. But not without telling me.'

'Let's say he did decide to go. Where in France would he choose? Paris?'

'I doubt it. We were there together last year.'

'The south?'

'Well, we both adore Cézanne. He might have wanted to soak up some Provençal landscapes. But it still doesn't make sense.

He would have told me, and he wouldn't have gone for so long. He broke a dozen appointments last week. Can you tell me what all this is about?'

Brady explained how a man calling himself Mark Carlson had stayed in a hotel in the south of France for five days and then checked out at short notice. He was supposedly flying to Paris, but never took the flight. 'We've lost track of him from there.'

Railton opened his hands in disbelief. 'That can't have been Mark.'

'What we know is he was using Mark's passport. Let's try to work out if it could have been Mark.' Brady was looking at a sheaf of notes. 'It says here that he was about six foot one.'

'That's about right.'

'What does he weigh?'

'Hundred and ninety, hundred and ninety-five.'

'What about his hair? Blond?'

'Yes,' said Railton. 'He tints it.'

Brady felt Petrowski shift on the sofa beside him.

'Blue eyes?'

'Blue eyes.'

'Does he take care of himself?'

'He had his spleen removed about two years ago, after it became enlarged, so he's wary of vigorous exercise. But he likes to swim. He keeps himself in shape.'

'What about his luggage? The man at the hotel was carrying a soft brown bag with a zip that padlocked at one end. The hotel said it was a Gucci.'

'I don't believe it,' said Railton. 'I gave him that bag for Christmas.'

Brady looked squarely at Railton. 'There's something else I have to tell you. Two young people went missing from the hotel shortly before Mark checked out and disappeared. Obviously, this may have nothing to do with Mark. But we have to consider all possibilities.'

Railton raised his eyebrows. 'You mean because he's gay. Is that what you're implying?'

'I'm not implying anything. I'm just telling you what's happened. I need the names of everyone Mark was due to see. The quicker we can start checking, the quicker we can sort this out.'

Railton went to a computer in the corner of the room. A small printer whirred into action, and Railton handed Brady several sheets of paper. 'That shows every appointment he made on his trip. When you contact these people, could you please be discreet? You may not be implying anything, but other people might draw the wrong conclusion.'

'We'll be as tactful as we can,' Brady said.

The two agents got up to leave, but Railton blocked their path.

'Something's happened to Mark, hasn't it? He'd never just go off like this. Will you keep me informed?'

'Of course,' Brady said. But he felt distracted. Something about the immaculate sitting-room didn't fit.

'One last thing. Mark smokes Marlboros, doesn't he?'

'Mark?' Railton replied. 'Mark *hates* tobacco. He can't stand cigarette smoke. We don't allow it in the house.'

Now Brady realised what was missing from the room: ash-trays.

Stewart had never liked Sherlock Holmes. Conan Doyle's hero was vain, dogmatic, patronising towards Dr Watson, and had a disturbing drug habit. So he had no problem with Halard's instruction not to play at Sherlock Holmes. But he had no intention of leaving everything to the police either.

'Maria,' he said when he got back to the hotel. 'Do you speak Italian?'

Her smile was broader than ever. 'With a name like Scarletti?'

He gave her the Milan number. Soon, she was chatting away with Yves Lavar's housekeeper as though they were old friends.

Yves was a film director and he was away in Poland working on a movie, she reported to Stewart. If Olivier wasn't at the apartment in Monaco, the housekeeper had no idea where he was. Perhaps his sister would know. Her name was Mica, and she lived in Nice.

Stewart found a local number in Olivier's address book marked with the single letter 'M'.

Stewart thanked her and ran upstairs to his room.

'Hello.'

'Is that Mica?'

'Who is this?'

'Mica, my name is Tom Stewart. I'm calling you about your brother.'

Stewart was used to making difficult phone calls. But not ones his daughter's life could depend on.

'What about my brother?'

There was tension in her voice, as though she was on guard.

'He knows my daughter. They were together two afternoons ago and I haven't seen her since.'

'Your daughter? I don't understand.'

'Her name's Fiona. She's just seventeen. We're here on holiday, and she met Olivier at our hotel. They went off to Villefranche together and didn't come back. I'd like to know if you've seen them, or heard from Olivier since.'

There was silence. Then she said: 'Listen, who are you? What was your name again?

'As I said, my name is Tom Stewart. I'm a writer and I live in London. Fiona and I are here on holiday. We're staying at Le Bosquet on Cap Ferrat. The hotel knows all about this. You can call the manager to check what I'm saying is true. I'll give you the number.'

Another silence. Stewart wondered how much she knew.

'I might call him later,' she said. 'But I don't know anything about your daughter.'

'Mica, tell me something. Why does your brother have a gun?'

'What on earth are you talking about?'

'I went to your father's apartment this morning to see if Olivier was there. The maintenance man let me in. There was no sign of him or Fiona, but I found a revolver in Olivier's bedroom. I'm very concerned at what my daughter's mixed up in.'

'Oh shit,' she said. Her tone was of both anger and resignation. 'Look, I don't know anything about a gun. But I was pretty sure there was something wrong.'

Stewart realised how hard he had been gripping the phone. He transferred it to his other hand.

'Why do you say that?' he asked, sounding as casual as he could.

'Because he was behaving very strangely the last time I saw him.'

'When was that?'

'The day before yesterday. In the morning. He came to the house. I thought it was to borrow money, because that's the usual reason he comes here when papa's away. This time I was wrong.'

She hesitated.

'Go on,' said Stewart.

'He had money. Too much money. He showed it to me, a roll of five hundred franc notes. He was full of it, showing off. I asked him where he got it, but he wouldn't tell me. All he would say was, he'd gone into business with a partner he'd just met. I said, "What is this nonsense? You're a schoolboy. What sort of business makes you this kind of money?" He just laughed and said "Good business, that's what".'

A partner. 'Did he say anything else about this partner?'

'Not really. Only that he was American, that's all.'

'Anything else? His name?'

'Olivier didn't tell me his name.'

'Or where they met?'

'No, nothing like that. I'm sorry.'

'Don't worry. You've told me a lot already. Can you remember what time Olivier left you that morning?'

'Around twelve, I think. The thing is, he was supposed to come back yesterday. Before he left he said he was going to take us all out for lunch. The whole family. I told him he was being ridiculous. "The minute you get money you spend it". He said, "There's plenty more where this came from". But he never showed up.'

'This business he's into. Do you think it could be to do with drugs?'

Stewart held his breath until she asked: 'Have you been to the police?'

'They know Fee has disappeared, of course, and they've got a lot of people out looking. But I don't want to get Olivier into trouble, I just want to find my daughter. If there's anything else you know that might help, please tell me now.'

'My brother's always denied it, but I'm fairly sure he takes drugs.'

'Why do you think that?'
'It's just a feeling I have.'
'What happened last time you asked him about it?'
'He didn't get angry, which surprised me. He just said I was wrong.'
'Do you think he does it with other people? Is there anyone else I can talk to? Anyone who might know where he could have gone?'
'I really don't know. He's never talked to me about his friends.'
Stewart was running a mental check-list. *The gun. Drugs. What about the car?*
'When they left the hotel, they went off in his car. It's a Peugeot 205, right?'
'Yes, but it's not his car. It belongs to my father.'
'I thought your father lived in Milan?'
'He does, most of the time. But he comes to France once a month and he keeps the Peugeot for when he's here. Usually he parks it out by the airport. But he's gone to Poland for three months and he didn't want to leave it there all that time, so he left it with me instead. I said Olivier could use it.'
'Do you know the registration number?'
'Not offhand. But it's registered in Monaco.'
'I knew that already. Is there anything else about it you can remember that would help the police to spot it?'
'Not that I can think of. Except that it's got a parking permit for the airport garage on the windscreen. It's bright yellow.'
Her voice was sounding drained. Stewart wondered if she knew anything else, but she broke in before he could speak.
'He's such an idiot at times,' she said. 'I've done my best to keep him out of trouble. Do you have any idea what could have happened?'
It was Stewart's turn to hesitate. 'Not really. But if I get any news, I'll call you right away. Will you do the same for me?'
'Of course,' Mica said.

On that afternoon, some one hundred and twenty miles due south of Nice, a handsome sailing yacht named *Symphonie* turned head-to-wind on the gentle swell. Olivier Lavar, a black hood covering his head, was dragged up on deck by two men.

They removed the hood so that he could see what they were doing. While one held him from behind, the other bound his ankles with chain taken from the spare anchor.

'No!' he screamed. 'I did what you wanted! I brought you the kid!'

One of the men took his arms, the other his feet, and they carried him towards the rail as though he were a sack.

'Please! Please! Oh God! Why are you doing this?'

His terror gave him strength, but he was no match for these two.

'Time to clean up the boat,' said the first man.

'Thought we'd see how far you can swim,' said the second.

They swung his body back and forth, building a momentum, laughing as they did.

'Too much shit on this boat.'

'Time to lighten the load.'

'Get rid of the smell.'

'Get rid of the shit.'

Olivier screamed as he swung out over the waves.

'You sure fucked up, Olivier,' said the first man. 'One!'

'That's a fact,' said the second.

'Two!'

'Ain't that the fucking truth.'

'Three!'

With a final heave they hurled him over the rail. Olivier sensed a momentary rush of air, followed by the shock of cold as he hit the water. He flailed his arms and struggled to the surface only to feel the remorseless weight of the anchor chain round his ankles. A final scream erupted from his throat.

'See, I told you he couldn't swim,' said the first man.

The second said: 'Ain't that a fucking shame.'

The bow of the yacht swung around. At the wheel was a mountain of a man with a straw-coloured beard. For the past two weeks, the barometer had remained steady, but now, he knew, a change was in the air. He had already seen the mare's-tail wisps of high cirrus to the northwest. He looked at the horizon and spotted an encroaching line of purple cloud behind. As the *Symphonie* completed its turn to resume its voyage, its sails filled in the stiffening wind.

* * *

The fax that arrived at the Prefecture from the FBI field office in Baltimore was marked 'FLASH – MOST URGENT'. It was concise and to the point, Halard noted: typical Brady.

> Carlson is an impostor. The real Mark Carlson is a committed non-smoker.
>
> Carlson is a businessman with no criminal record. He was last heard of in Amsterdam eleven days ago, and must now be regarded as a possible additional victim. Through the State Department, I am requesting the Dutch police begin an immediate probable-homicide investigation.
>
> The fact that the subject closely resembled the description of the real Carlson, and had acquired his passport, credit card AND luggage, suggests a carefully planned operation.
>
> Although his presence at the hotel at the time of the probable crime could still be a coincidence, I recommend that the subject now be considered as the prime suspect in the Beaumont case, unless and until he is traced and eliminated from our inquiries.
>
> I also recommend that an All Points Bulletin is issued, and that a thorough forensic examination is conducted of the hotel room he occupied.

Desiry joined Halard beside the fax machine. She handed him Brady's message and said, 'Get Forensics down there at once. And tell the hotel to seal the room and put a guard on the door.'

'What do you want? The works?'

'What else? Tell them I'll meet them there.'

The room seemed clinically ordinary, unlike the ransacked or bloody crime scenes where the forensic technicians usually performed. The bed had been made, the terrace furniture put in place, the bathroom cleaned and restocked with towels and soap – the work of the hotel chambermaid on the morning Carlson had checked out. One of the technicians read Halard's thoughts. 'Don't worry. We'll find something here for you.'

She occupied one of the seats on the terrace while the two men wearing latex gloves embarked on their long-practised routine of searching for fingerprints, fibres and hairs. They tried the less obvious places first – the drawer knobs and window catches that even the most conscientious chambermaid could be forgiven for overlooking. One came on to the balcony and began applying fingerprint powder with a fine brush to the handles of the French doors, and to the door frame itself.

Most technicians, Halard had noticed, like to maintain a commentary on their work but this one was being unusually reticent. His face set, he brushed his dust across more and more of the frame.

'Talk to me,' she said.

'You don't want to hear this,' he replied. 'There's something wrong. Even if Carlson wiped every surface he touched, there should be latent prints from previous guests.' He dusted another part of the frame, looking for the oil deposited on any hard surface by the lightest touch of the fingers, but none of the powder stuck. 'See what I mean? It looks like the whole door has been scoured with some kind of solvent.'

His colleague emerged from the bathroom. 'I'm getting the same,' he said. 'I've got a couple of prints on the soap dish but it's odds-on they're the chambermaid's. And take a look at this.'

Halard followed him into the bathroom. He knelt under the sink and showed her that he had removed the screw at the bottom of the U-turn in the waste-pipe, where a cache of hair was usually to be found. It was not just that the U-turn was barren of its usual clues. The pipe bore several hairline scratches, where someone had undone the screw to remove the waste material before the police could retrieve it. The same was true of the U-turn traps in both the bath and the bidet.

'Our friend knew what he was doing,' the technician said.

'Keep trying please,' said Halard as she stood up, brushing at grains of fingerprint powder that were clinging to her shirt. 'He may have made a mistake.'

'Of course. But don't get your hopes up.'

Halard left them to it. As she entered the corridor she saw Desiry striding towards her. He seemed in a buoyant mood. She still couldn't tell how far he resented her arrival on his patch, even though he knew full well that she had not chosen to be dragged out of bed in the middle of the night and dispatched to Nice on the minister's jet. Still, he was certainly committed to the case – even if his enthusiasm, fuelled by adrenalin, sometimes got the better of him.

'How's it looking, chief?' he asked.

'Not too good,' she said. 'Forensics aren't getting anything at all. Carlson seems to have wiped the room clean. He's beginning to look like a pro.'

'There's something else I can tell you about him,' Desiry said.

Halard sensed that he was pausing for effect. 'Well?' she said.

'He knows Stewart.'

Halard looked at the inspector coolly. 'Tell me about it.'

'I've been talking to the pool waiter who was on duty the day the kids disappeared. Guess what Stewart was doing when his daughter didn't come back? Swimming in the pool with our Mr Carlson. Drinking by the pool with our Mr Carlson. Chatting and laughing with our Mr Carlson. They drank four beers between them, which Carlson paid for on his room bill. Doesn't exactly add up to the worried father, does it?'

'What does it add up to?'

'They're in it together. Don't say you haven't thought that yourself.'

Halard had thought just that, but she hadn't been ready to say it. 'All right, inspector. Make your case.'

'First, he turns up here supposedly to have a holiday with his daughter, but he spends almost no time with her that afternoon. Next they have a blazing row at dinner – which he denies ever happened when he reports her missing. The next morning, what does he do? Does he try to make it up with his daughter? No, he doesn't. He pisses off into Nice to buy a newspaper, leaving her a note promising to take her to lunch in Monaco. But he doesn't turn up because he takes *three hours* to buy his newspaper. And that's exactly the time-frame when she disappears. He also makes a phone call to the hotel, which gives him a very neat alibi. Then what? He vanishes for another four or five hours. He claims he was in the mountains, looking at the scenery. Does he have any witnesses who saw him there? Does he hell. And then – to cap the lot – he's back here being chummy with Carlson, the same Carlson who's in the frame for whatever's happened to the kids. And that's something else he forgets to mention. So you tell me what you think.'

For Desiry, it was quite a speech. 'The trouble is,' she said, maintaining a proper scepticism, 'everything you've described could have an entirely innocent explanation.'

'I know that, chief. But we both know that when you put it all together, it makes an entirely different picture. Plus I felt all along he was holding things back. He still hasn't really told us what he was doing in Lavar's apartment. "I was looking for my daughter". Yeah, yeah. He was looking for something, that's for sure. My guess is, he found whatever it was and lied to us about it.'

'You're seriously saying that Stewart had some part in the disappearance of his own daughter – and the Beaumont boy too?'

'That's something else. I'm not sold on the Beaumont woman either. She was in the restaurant that night and must have seen the row, like everyone else. How come she doesn't tell us about it? And how come when Stewart lies about it to my desk sergeant in Nice, she doesn't say a word?'

'That's a good question, inspector.' In fact, Halard knew, they were all good questions. She remembered the photograph Stewart had given the police, showing his daughter sitting beside the window of an apartment. She remembered Stewart's erratic behaviour at the Prefecture, his outburst of anger and his sudden calm, and how she had tried to divine what lay behind it. She shared Desiry's unease about him, yet her instincts would not allow her to go quite as far as Desiry in believing that he could have caused his daughter harm. At the same time she knew that instincts could sometimes lead you astray. It was like navigating with a compass: your senses might be pushing you one way, yet you had to follow the needle's implacable logic.

Desiry interrupted her thoughts. 'There's one way to take this forward, of course.'

'I know. I'll talk to Stewart. You take Beaumont. Find out if she knows that Stewart and Carlson are friends. Do you know where Stewart is?'

'I've just checked with reception. He's in his room.'

* * *

Lightning sawed to the horizon, throwing the gathering storm clouds into sudden relief. Stewart saw them reflected in the mirror above the dressing table, just to the right of the chair Halard had commandeered. He was struggling to find a comfortable position on the edge of the bed, as Halard questioned him again in that insistent manner he found so unsettling.

'What did you do when you came back to the hotel on the afternoon Fiona disappeared?'

'I came here to my room and waited for her.'

'Did you stay here?'

'For a while. Then I decided to go for a swim.'

'Alone?'

'Yes.'

Halard brushed a speck of powder off her sleeve then focused on Stewart again.

'How do you know Carlson?'

'Who?'

'Your friend, Mark Carlson.'

A memory stirred. Mark Carlson, the man at the swimming pool. That afternoon.

'He's not my friend,' Stewart said.

'But you went swimming with him.'

Stewart felt flustered. 'Yes I know.'

'You just told me you went swimming by yourself.'

'I was, to start with. He joined me halfway through and turned it into a bit of a race.'

'Then you just got talking, and decided to have a drink together? Is that right?'

'You're trying to make it sound unlikely. It was just one of those holiday conversations. What is this all about?'

'What do you know about him?'

'Not very much. He's an American – from Baltimore, I think. He said he was in computers, something like that.'

'How long have you known him?'

'I've told you, I don't know him. I'd never met him before. Look, what has all this got to do with Fee?'

'What did you talk about?'

Stewart thought back. What had they talked about? Or, rather, what had *he* talked about? Because, on reflection, Carlson had been very good at dodging Stewart's questions.

Because Carlson had asked most of the questions. 'What is this about Carlson? Has he got something to do with this?'

'Carlson isn't Carlson. At least, not the Carlson he claimed to be.'

Stewart knew what it was to be afraid. He had felt it in Belfast and Beirut, as he dodged down shattered streets. Now, as he listened to Halard, he felt it again, like a clamp around his chest that made it hard to breathe. The man he had swum and drank with, Halard said, was not the computer software developer from Baltimore whose passport and credit card he had used. He had checked out of the hotel at short notice, having scoured his room clean of every possible trace or clue, saying that he was going to catch a flight he never took. It was as if he had ceased to exist.

'So what did you talk about?' As Halard pressed him again, Stewart became aware how important every nuance of that casual conversation could be.

'He asked what I was doing here. I told him I was on holiday with Fee and he asked if she was enjoying herself.'

'And you said?'

'I said she was.'

'So he knew her name?'

Stewart dug deep into his memory. 'No, I told him her name was Fiona.'

'What else did he ask?'

'Where we lived. I told him London.'

'Anything else?'

'He asked about Fee's friends.'

'What friends?'

'Josh and Olivier.'

'What else?'

He retrieved another fragment of their conversation: Carlson's undisguised curiosity about Suzanne, and the crude compliment he'd paid her. At the time he'd suspected a sexual motive: now Carlson's questions seemed far more sinister.

'Anything else you can remember? Anything at all?'

'Well, he asked if there was a problem over Fee. I had mentioned she was late getting back from Villefranche.'

'And what did he say?'

'He said he was sure she was okay.'

'That was it?'

'I think so. He said he hoped we enjoyed the rest of our holiday. Then I left.'

Stewart walked over to the window. The storm clouds were merging with the night sky.

'I want you to write down everything you can remember about the conversation,' Halard said. 'Word for word. Then I need you to come to the Prefecture in the morning to make a formal statement about everything that's happened since you arrived in Nice.'

'All right,' Stewart said. 'But if Carlson isn't Carlson, who the hell is he? Do you know?'

'We'll keep you informed.' She stood up, as if to signal that the interview was over, but then she said, 'Don't leave anything out of your statement. Nothing at all.'

'What do you mean?'

'I'm not sure you've told us everything you know. Is there something you're holding back?'

'Nothing I can think of,' he said, without hesitating.

Halard put on a trench coat that seemed to be at least two sizes too large, so that she had to roll back the sleeves. Stewart assumed she had borrowed it in Nice.

'You weren't expecting it to rain down here, then?' he asked.

Halard smiled wanly. 'Don't forget what I told you. Don't meddle in this investigation.'

'I didn't tell you,' he replied. 'I never did have much time for Sherlock Holmes.'

9

The world seemed to be spinning. Stewart was on a flight between Madrid and Tangiers when the DC-9 plunged into a dive. He looked at the cabin attendants for reassurance but there was only panic on their faces as they struggled to hold the food trolley against the steepening incline. It felt both unreal and real: the moment he had dreaded but thought would never happen to him; the crash that always happened to other people. He peered through the window and saw the Mediterranean closing in by the second, so it seemed. At last the plane levelled out and the captain came on the intercom to announce that 'the problem' had been resolved.

It felt that way now. He had lain on his bed and closed his eyes. The wind was squalling through the trees outside, and sleep would not come. It was other people's children who disappeared, and usually in movies. *This cannot be real.* But it was, and it was happening to him and to Fee. She had been with him on the plane. While the other passengers had fallen silent, she had called out, in a seven-year-old's piping voice: 'Are we crashing?'

'Of course not, sweetheart,' Stewart had assured her. He had cherished that moment of innocence in the face of danger ever since. He fought to stop the image of it returning now.

The telephone rang and he heard Suzanne say: 'Are you asleep?' Then she gave an embarrassed half-laugh, as if to acknowledge that it was a redundant question.

'I think we should talk,' she said.

They met in the cocktail lounge. The waiter was the same one who had brought him and Carlson their beer beside the pool a little more than forty-eight hours ago. Except he's not Carlson, Stewart reminded himself. Suzanne's hair was pulled back. She looked different, older. They both asked for coffee.

'So who the hell is he?' she asked him. They sat on a sofa at a table beside the bar's long window. The rain was slanting through the arc lights around the pool. 'What did Halard tell you?'

'She virtually accused me of being in league with him at first. "Your friend, Mark Carlson", she called him. Then, after I'd told her I barely knew him, she said that he wasn't a computer software developer from Baltimore, which is what he told me, and that he seemed to be very professional at covering his traces.'

'It's all so creepy,' said Suzanne.

'I know. Still, at least they've got on to him pretty quickly. It's amazing, isn't it? Yesterday they wouldn't give us the time of day. Now it seems like half the police forces of the western world are on the case. You were right about Jesse getting things done.'

She looked discomfited. 'I'm sorry I gave you such a hard time yesterday,' she said. 'And I really didn't mean to criticise you last night. I was just so damn frustrated.'

'Don't apologise. You were right on both counts. What on earth did Jesse do?'

'My guess is that he called Saul Bates. He's a senator from Texas and he and Jesse go way back. Jesse likes to say that Bates has the keys to the back door of the White House. I don't know about that, but he's certainly got influence.'

'You're not kidding. Though I don't think the good Commissaire is too thrilled at being sent down from Paris in the middle of the night on Washington's say-so.'

'Desiry seems pretty mad about it too.' She pushed some strands of her hair back into place. 'That guy could do with a spell at charm school.'

'Did he tell you anything?'

'Not really. He tried to push me around a bit, but I was no use to him because I didn't know Carlson existed until Desiry told me. But he said you had a drink with him?'

'That's right. While I was waiting for Fee to come back.' He pointed to the far end of the pool, its surface scuffed by the wind. 'Over there.'

'How come?'

He described the encounter again. This time, now that he

had put the pieces together, it sounded far more sinister. Clearly Carlson – he could not stop thinking of him as that – had engineered both the swimming race and the pool-side chat. How long had he been watching and waiting for his chance?

'Looking back, the most disturbing thing is the way he tried to get things out of me.'

'What about?'

'Me and Fee. You and Josh. All of us.'

'What about me and Josh?'

'Who you were. What business you were in. What you were doing here. That sort of thing.'

'And you told him?'

'Well, yes. What little I knew.'

'Thanks a lot.'

'I know,' was all he could think of to say, suddenly aware of how naïve he had been.

'It's okay,' she said. 'There's no point in blaming ourselves. It's not going to change anything.' He looked at her and smiled.

'So,' she said after a moment. 'Why was he asking questions about us?'

'I don't know.'

'What has Carlson got to do with the disappearance of our children?'

'We don't know for sure that he has. It could just be a coincidence.'

'And if it isn't?' She was watching his eyes.

'What's the first thing that comes to mind?'

'You say it,' Suzanne answered.

'Kidnapping,' said Stewart.

'I know we have to face up to this. But why? Why would Carlson kidnap them?'

'Money's the usual reason.'

'Yes,' she said.

'And you're the obvious target.'

'But I'm not rich, Tom.'

'Really? I thought you were. From everything you told me about the company – your success with new therapies, that kind of thing.'

She gave a worried sigh. 'It's like a lot of these things,' Suzanne told him. 'It's only true on paper. Most everything I have is invested in the company, and all of Larry's stock is now in trust for Josh. Sure, I get the income, but the stock belongs to Josh – or will do one day. The same goes for Jesse.'

'Trouble is, the kidnappers wouldn't know that. They'd have no reason to believe you didn't own the stock.'

'You said kidnappers,' said Suzanne.

'Yes, I did,' Stewart admitted.

'So you think it's not just Carlson?'

'I don't see how it can be. He can't have been acting alone, because he was talking to me here at the hotel after they disappeared.'

'I don't think that follows,' said Suzanne. 'They could still have been hanging out in Villefranche while he was with you. And if he'd already taken them, why did he need to ask you about them?'

'Fair point. But if he did have them by then, he must have known where to find them after he left me. That means someone else must have been watching them. Remember, Carlson was still around the hotel until yesterday morning. That's at least eighteen hours after Fee and Josh definitely went missing. He must have had help.'

'What about you?' Suzanne asked.

Stewart was startled. 'What about me?'

'Sorry,' she said. 'I mean money. Couldn't you be the target?'

Despite himself, Stewart could not help laughing. 'Hardly,' he said. 'I owe money all over the place, and I owe my publishers a book.'

'Didn't you get an advance?'

'Sure. But I spent it long ago. Plus I've got an ex-wife and a daughter with expensive tastes to maintain. It couldn't possibly be me.'

Suzanne reflected a moment. 'And I don't see it could be me either. If anyone's done this for money, why haven't we had a ransom demand? From what I remember about these things, isn't there supposed to be a ransom note? Or a phone call, telling us where to take the money? We've had none of that.'

It didn't make sense to Stewart and he said so.

'So where does that leave us? If Carlson hasn't kidnapped them for money, why else would he take them?'

Stewart stared at his watch, once again flicking through its modes in a bid to fathom its controls.

'I still can't get the hang of this,' he said. 'It's multi-functional, and when I want to know the time it tells me the altitude.'

'Tom?'

'Now it says we're at three hundred metres.' He gave a small laugh. 'It must be the pressure of the storm.'

'Come on, Tom,' she persisted. 'Why else would Carlson take them?'

'I'm not sure,' he said.

'We have to face this, Tom. You're a journalist, you've been around. You must know about these things. He could be some kind of pervert, couldn't he? One of those creeps who preys on children. You hear about it all the time. You just never believe it'll happen to you.'

Stewart took off his watch and laid it on the table.

'Come on, Tom. This is where you're supposed to tell me that I'm wrong. That it couldn't possibly be that way.'

He looked at her levelly. 'That's just what I can't do, Suzanne. I've worked on stories about serial killers and rapists and I know what can happen. Sure, I can make the case against it happening. These people don't go around introducing themselves to their victims' families. They're supposed to be loners, people who live in the shadows. They can only connect with others by establishing what's called a "false self", and they can't do that when they're hunting. That's because it's impossible for them to maintain both personas, and if they try, they often give themselves away.'

'So you're saying Carlson doesn't fit the picture?'

'That's right. These people can behave normally, but only until the real self takes over. So if Carlson was in hunting mode, he couldn't have switched into his false self. He simply couldn't have sat chatting to me by the pool the way he did.'

'So do you believe all this stuff?'

'As I say, that's the theory.'

'It all sounds too neat to me,' Suzanne said. 'Too glib. The kind of stuff you get in books cashing in on some outrage or other. Supposing Carlson doesn't fit the pattern? Supposing he gets extra kicks from talking to the victims' parents after the kidnap? Or whatever it is he's done?'

'It's possible,' Stewart agreed. 'But there is something else. It's supposed to be very rare for these people to go hunting with someone else. Yet we know Carlson had help. That makes two strikes against the theory.'

She was looking a little more reassured, but then she said: 'Two strikes doesn't add up to out. What else is there?'

Stewart hesitated.

'Tell me,' she insisted.

'It's just that two of the worst cases of this kind in Britain involved two sadists working together. One was Myra Hindley and Ian Brady. That was thirty years ago. The other was Fred and Rosemary West. Do you know about them?'

'Yes, I do,' said Suzanne.

Above the thudding of the wind, Stewart heard a crash. He looked out and saw one of the poolside tables on its side. He had hoped that this conversation would bring a measure of reassurance. All it had done was to confirm their own worse fears. He gestured to Suzanne's empty cup.

'Do you want something stronger?' he said.

'No, in case we have to drive somewhere.'

'What do you mean, drive somewhere?'

'I keep thinking we're about to get a call from the police saying, "Your kids are fine, come and pick them up".'

It wasn't quite the answer he was looking for, but he couldn't work out why.

'More coffee, then?'

She nodded. Stewart caught the waiter's eye and pointed to the cups.

'Is there anything else?' Suzanne asked.

'There's something I haven't told you,' he admitted. 'Something I haven't told the police. You may think I'm crazy not to have done so, but at least hear me out.'

The waiter refilled their cups. Stewart broke an oblong piece of sugar and doused one half in the coffee.

'I'm listening,' Suzanne said.

'I think Olivier is mixed up in all this. I don't know how or why, but I think he was working with Carlson.'

'You'd better explain.'

The details were vivid in his mind as he described what he had done since that morning. First to Villefranche, and the *bar-tabac*. Then finding Fratoni, and prising out Olivier's address. Then the apartment, and the phone call to Italy, and being hauled back to face Halard. And, finally, his call to Mica, and her revelation about Olivier's American partner.

'I'm convinced his partner is Carlson. It was Carlson who gave him the money. At least, that's what my instincts are shouting. If I'm right then Carlson must have recruited him days ago. At least that doesn't fit the *modus operandi* of a pervert.'

'I suppose not,' she said. 'But what do you think it was that Olivier did for him?'

'One possibility is that Carlson needed someone to lure Fee and Josh away from the hotel, someone they would trust. Or he needed someone to follow them while he was talking to me, so that he'd know where to find them afterwards. Maybe he needed somebody to keep an eye on them overnight until he was ready to leave the hotel. If Olivier was part of it, Fee and Josh may not even have realised they'd been abducted.'

'Aren't you missing something?' she said.

'You tell me.'

'Think about it. You say that Carlson was pumping you for information about all of us. Why would he need to do that if Olivier was working for him? Olivier could tell him anything he needed to know. Certainly about me and Josh.'

'You're right, and I can't explain it.'

'In fact there's hardly anything we can explain, is there?'

It's true,' Stewart said. 'All I know is that we have to cling to the very few facts we have. When I worked on newspaper investigations, we used to say: "It's only when you get to the end that you know where you should have started." Of course, there is no magic formula so you have to do all the bits in the middle. The only way we ever got anywhere was by following our instincts and taking it step by step. That's what we've got to do now.'

Stewart saw the barman and the waiter talking together, looking in their direction.

'What we know for sure is that Fee and Josh are missing.

They were last seen with Olivier, who is also missing. Before that happened, Olivier was given money by his so-called American partner. Carlson's American, and he's missing too, except he isn't Carlson. That's what we have to work with.'

He had been waiting for her next question long before he finished.

'Why haven't you told the police any of this?'

'I have. Some of it. But not about Mica.'

'Why not?'

'I don't really know.'

'You're right. You *are* crazy.' She began to stand up. 'I'm going to call them now.'

'No, please.' He reached out and held her wrist. 'Please wait.' It was true – he didn't really know why. Only that it was his instincts again.

'I've just got a feeling there's something else Mica knows that could help us. Maybe even she doesn't know what it is. What worries me is that if I tell the police about her, they'll go in mob-handed. If they treat her the way they treated me, they'll frighten her half to death, and she'll just clam up.'

Suzanne seemed to have suspended judgement. She sank back down on the sofa. He took his hand away and she drank the last of her coffee.

'It's *why* he needed Olivier,' she said. 'That's the key, isn't it?'

'I think so.'

'It's got to be because Carlson wanted them lured away from here. Olivier could easily do that. Just invite them to go somewhere in his car.'

'Right, but then what? I mean, Josh and Olivier are friends, aren't they? Would Olivier really do something to hurt his friend?'

He could see the anger in Suzanne's eyes.

'Maybe he didn't know what was going to happen,' she said. 'Maybe Carlson spun him a story about why he wanted to get Josh and Fee away from the hotel.'

'Well, that fits,' Stewart said. 'Olivier told the maintenance man at the apartment block he would be back yesterday, and he also had a lunch date with Mica's family. So he only expected to be away for the night.'

'So let's say he drove Josh and Fee to wherever Carlson told him to take them. Then what?'

Stewart picked up his watch and looked at it, fighting the impulse to work through the modes again. 'The question is, what's happened to Olivier's car?'

'Carlson's got it?'

'I don't think so. From what the police say, he goes to a lot of trouble to cover his traces. Whether Olivier was duped, or whether he's in this up to his neck, Carlson would want to get rid of the car. They would dump it somewhere. Somewhere it wouldn't be found too quickly.'

'It could be anywhere.'

'Yes, but we know Carlson's a professional. He would know that some places are better than others. He wouldn't leave it on the street, because he'd know that if the police were looking for it, they'd be likely to spot it very quickly. No, the best place is . . .'

Stewart suddenly knew what was wrong with Suzanne's answer about 'driving somewhere'. He pounded his fist on the table, clattering the cups. 'What on earth was that for?' Suzanne asked.

'*I know where the car is!* Mica told me, didn't she? It's at the airport. Why didn't I see it?'

She was still staring at him when a man said: 'Madame Beaumont?'

The barman was standing by their table, holding something in his hand. 'Your son left this in the bar.'

He handed her a pen.

'My son?'

'Yes, when he signed his bill on Friday. Before he was joined by Mr Carlson.'

It was black, made by Mont Blanc, and on the cap, finely engraved, were the initials 'OL'.

In that part of the western Mediterranean notorious for its short, steep seas, the yacht *Symphonie* rode the mountainous black swells. Its bow lifted as it rose to the top of each crest, then dipped as it plunged into the trough on the far side. The noise was overwhelming: the hammering of the rigging, the shriek of the wind, the hiss of the advancing seas.

In keeping with the portents of the previous day, the forecast had predicted moderate winds and seas of no more than two feet. But in the late afternoon the wind had backed to the east and the barometer began to plummet. The cover of purple cloud had spread across the sky like an inkstain, turning the sun acid yellow. The first squall struck, whipping stinging spray across the deck. The storm's leading edge brought with it pelting rain that turned the sea white, then gusts that registered fifty-five knots on the wind gauge before it was ripped from the mast. By nightfall, the sky became as black as the seas. It was impossible to distinguish between the two, save for the gleam of the breaking crests as they raced towards the yacht.

It was the height of the breakers that most alarmed them. It is a sailor's rule of thumb that breaking waves only a third as high as the hull is long can capsize any yacht. *Symphonie* had a steel hull fifty feet long. These breakers were thirty feet high from trough to crest, and building fast.

Turning the yacht into the wind, Jesus Fairley had chosen to face his adversary head on. He had lashed the wheel with rope to hold the rudder steady, and ordered his two crewmates, Katz and Pelican, to follow him below. They waited for the interval between one deluge and the next before opening the hatch and stumbling down the companionway. Now they intended to stay in the main cabin while the storm took its course. Katz, pale-faced from motion sickness, sat at the salon table wrapped in a blanket. Pelican, eyes closed, lay in his bunk. Beside the radio, Fairley worked his way through the wavelengths until he found a weather report in English, broadcast from Monaco. Through the static, it confirmed that a 'very severe storm' was moving steadily east towards the Gulf of Genoa. They sat squarely in its path.

It was an hour later when *Symphonie* shuddered and fell on its side as though it had been pushed by a giant hand. Instantly alert, the three men waited for the yacht to right itself. It did so sluggishly, barely before the next breaker hit. The cabin was a shambles: provisions, clothing, charts, everything that was loose, lay on the floor, awash in the water that had surged up from the bilge.

'Fuck this,' Katz shouted. There was an edge of panic in his voice.

'Shut up,' said Fairley. 'Go and put the boy with the girl. I want them together.'

By the time Katz returned, two new notes had joined the gale's chorus: the constant flogging of the mizzen sail, and an ominous creaking in the superstructure as the mast took the strain. There was a crack like a rifle shot as one of the supports holding the mast gave way.

Pelican swore. 'The sail's got loose. The mast's going to tear this mother apart.'

'Let's get out there,' Fairley yelled.

They donned their waterproofs and safety harnesses. Fairley threw open the hatch and they clambered out just as the next wall of water broke over the bow, smashing into the cockpit and punching them to their knees. It took the combined strength of Fairley and Pelican to close the hatch.

The mizzen sail, which they had reefed when the storm arrived, had unfurled, pulling and tugging at the sagging mast while the broken stay whipped above the cockpit. Fairley pressed his lips against Pelican's ear. 'Get the mizzen down. We'll have to run for it.'

While Pelican and Katz fought to lower the canvas, Fairley unleashed the wheel. As *Symphonie* was lifted by the next swell, he waited for the moment when he must try to turn the yacht around. He knew that if he judged the moment wrong – a fraction too soon, a moment too late – they were doomed. The bow broke through the top of the wave and Fairley spun the wheel hard to port. The yacht swung until it sat broadside on the foaming crest and then – slowly, agonisingly slowly – the bow came round. *Symphonie* leapt forward, planing down the slope of the swell, easily out-running the crest.

Until it reached the trough. As its momentum slowed, the breaker overtook the yacht, falling on it with such force it seemed *Symphonie* must founder. Every beam and joint shuddered and Fairley wondered how much more it could take. He turned and looked out over the stern. A black wall of water towered above them, bearing down.

10

AEROPORT DE NICE. The pale blue neon lettering shimmered through the windscreen, where the wipers were barely holding the torrent at bay. The Renault shuddered under the impact of a gust of wind.

'This place is like a maze,' Stewart said.

'Which parking lot are we looking for?' asked Suzanne.

'The long-term one, I guess. Watch out for any signs.'

He slowed to allow a lone Air France stewardess to cross the road.

'How can they be so stupid?' said Suzanne.

'The people who designed this place?'

'No. The police. How did they miss the connection between Olivier and Carlson?'

'They've got one-track minds. Desiry's the worst. As soon as the waiter told him he'd seen me chatting to Carlson, he jumped to the conclusion that I was somehow involved in this, and didn't bother asking any more questions. I can't stand the man.'

'I'm sure it's mutual.'

'I'm sure you're right.'

Stewart came to a roundabout that looked exactly the same as three others he had already negotiated. There were no signs for the car park. He guessed and took the first exit.

Suzanne said, 'And can you believe Olivier, pretending to be Josh so he could charge his drinks to the room?'

'Right now I'm ready to believe almost anything of Olivier.'

'There it is,' Suzanne said. 'Over there, to the right.'

Stewart took the turning. The entrance came up suddenly and he braked hard.

'Sorry,' he said, but Suzanne was already studying the lines of cars.

'It shouldn't be too hard to spot,' said Stewart, as he described the Peugeot. 'It's black. Look out for wide tyres, tinted windows and Monaco plates. There can't be too many like that.'

He was wrong. As they drove slowly up and down the rows, it seemed that every fourth or fifth car fitted the description. The rain and the orange sodium lights combined to make any dark-coloured paintwork look black.

Time and again Stewart dashed out into the rain to scrutinise a likely Peugeot 205; time and again it proved to be the wrong model, or the wrong colour, or not to have tinted glass. After an hour they had checked every row. His hair was plastered across his face, his clothing was sodden, and his feet were numb with cold.

'It's not here,' said Suzanne.

'I must have got something wrong. Hell, I'm going to call Mica.'

'It's the middle of the night.'

'She won't mind. She's as worried as we are. Stay here.'

'You'll get soaked.'

'I can't get any wetter than I am already.'

Suzanne watched Stewart hunch into the wind as he beat his way towards the terminal. *What in God's name am I doing here?* Three days ago, everything in the world had seemed just fine. She was reunited with Josh in the south of France, a continent away from Jesse's baleful stare, and he was happier than she had remembered in a long time. Her horizons had begun to expand, and she had caught herself thinking more positively about Life After Larry. Now she was trapped inside a car park in Nice in the middle of the night, lashed by the rain, desperately searching for some trace of her son. Doing so, what's more, with an idiosyncratic Englishman with whom she had nothing in common: nothing, that is, apart from the all-dominating fact that both their children had disappeared.

The door opened and Stewart slid in beside her.

'I got it wrong. She said *by* the airport, not at the airport. It's over there, under those hotels.'

Stewart pointed towards a line of dreary modern buildings on the far side of the autoroute. It took them ten minutes to work their way through the labyrinth of flyovers and underpasses before they reached it. The car park had nine floors, all underground. They drove in silence along the parallel lines of cars, concentrating on the search. Now they were under cover, it was at least easier to see.

'Only one floor left,' said Stewart, as he turned down the ramp to the ninth floor. Suzanne looked back over her shoulder.

'Tom, stop. Back there, in the recess. Another Peugeot.'

The Renault's engine raced as Stewart reversed. Then they were looking at it: a Peugeot with wide tyres, tinted glass, a small dent on the driver's side of the bumper, a bright yellow parking permit in the windscreen. There was only one thing wrong. The number plates were French.

'This can't be happening,' said Stewart.

'Let's get out and have a look.'

Suzanne tried the doors: they were locked, as was the boot. She peered inside, but could see almost nothing through the tinted glass. Stewart was on his knees, examining the number plate. The screws which held it in place looked old and dirty but when he brushed one of them with his forefinger his skin was smudged with oil. He drew his fingernail across the adjoining section of the number plate and located a tiny scratch in the metal. He wiped it with his handkerchief: the metal underneath was bright.

'He's switched the plates. This is Lavar's car.'

As Suzanne bent down to look, an image of a child in a foetal position filled her mind. What if the children – their bodies? – were locked inside?

'Tom,' she called, her voice unsteady.

'I know,' he said grimly. 'I've already thought of it.'

He had opened the boot of the Renault and was gripping its jack in both hands, like a battering ram.

'Get out of the way.' The jack smashed into the driver's window, shattering it into fragments. A fraction later a car alarm was wailing around them, the sound reverberating from the walls. The headlights flashed on and off.

He wrenched open the door and leaned inside. Nothing. He groped under the dashboard and found the lever to open the boot. He pulled it and heard the lock open. Suzanne was already at the back, lifting the lid. As he joined her, his eyes took a moment to focus. Then they knew. No bodies. Empty.

There was a squeal of tyres. At the far end of the floor, a security patrol car turned off the ramp and sped towards them.

'Suzanne, search the car.'

The patrol car jerked to a halt a foot from where Stewart stood his ground, doing his best to look as though he was ready to fight. Two stern-looking guards got out and he could see that they were armed with batons.

'Tom.' It came out almost as a scream.

Stewart turned back. Suzanne was holding out her arms to him. In the palms of her hands, offered like a prize, lay a camera. Fee's camera.

The smell hits you first. It's the scent of a disinfectant so powerful and astringent that your nostrils flare and your eyes sting, as if you're swimming in chlorine. It's the same smell you get from an ants' nest, and that's because formaldehyde, which is what they use, is based on formic acid, which ants secrete. Even so, it's not strong enough to override the stench of putrefaction, that sweet smell of physical decay, with its taint of almonds, which adheres to the back of your throat like gas.

Next, the colours. The room is predominantly white – white floor tiles, white walls – relieved only by the dulled silver of the stainless steel sink and draining board, and the trolley set out with its complement of barbarous surgical instruments. The intense overhead light makes everything gleam where it has been scoured clean (with the formaldehyde, of course.) That's another reason the splashes of colour stand out. The evidence tag is a vivid orange. The body bag is a brilliant green, like an English lawn after rain.

Then there are the sounds: rubber surgical boots squeaking on the floor, the clatter of the instruments being selected. And the zip on the body bag.

That was the final piece of advice the young attaché from the American Embassy had received, just before setting off from The Hague for Amsterdam. When you hear the zip, fix your eyes on the wall opposite, just above the sight-line of the bag. That way, you can make the others think you're looking where you should be; that way you can lower your eyes gradually, in your own good time.

The attaché did as he was told. But things did not happen the way they were supposed to. He heard the zip and watched the wall. What he did not expect was the splash of liquid surging out of the bag and on to the tiles, a putrid yellow colour that reminded him of bile and left its imprint on his leg. He reflexed backwards, supporting himself against the tiled wall, and in doing so caught sight of what lay on the stainless steel table. At first it did not make sense, a bloated off-white shape that was supposed to be a body, with the misshapen head at the far end. The legs stretched towards him but the feet did not look like feet at all. He saw a line of dark-red stains, so dark they were almost black. Then he realised what was missing. The toes. These stains were wounds where the toes had been.

'It's the pike,' said the man next to him.

'Excuse me?' he said faintly.

'Pike. They eat everything they can get. They like toes.'

There were five people in the room, grouped around the autopsy table like a tableau. The pathologist and her assistant wore dull green caps and gowns, white masks, translucent latex gloves and green surgical boots. The two detectives from the Amsterdam police had pulled the same uniform over their clothes, but were wearing transparent plastic covers on their street shoes. So was he. It was one of the detectives who had spoken to him.

'I didn't know there were any fish in the canals,' the attaché said, grateful for the distraction.

'More than you would think,' said the detective. 'They had a big clean-up about ten years ago. Reintroduced a dozen different species that had disappeared because of the pollution. A friend of mine caught a salmon on the Heerengracht last month. Not far from where we pulled him out.'

The pathologist started speaking. 'Mature white male,' she said. She was in late middle age, with greying hair and a surprisingly kindly face, so the attaché thought, for someone with such a godawful job. She was talking into a microphone held in front of her mouth by a headband. 'Height?'

'One metre eighty-two,' said her assistant into his microphone.

'Weight?'

'Approximately eighty-five kilogrammes.'

'That's a guess, of course,' the detective whispered. 'With floaters, you can never be sure. First, they're full of water. The flesh gets waterlogged but it's the gas that makes them bloat. Second, they've got parts missing. Because of the fish.'

The attaché lowered his eyes again. He now believed that the cascading liquid had been water caught in the body bag when the corpse was retrieved from the canal. At least, that was the most comforting explanation. What troubled him was that there was still a constant drip from the table: what inner physical regions were these fluids coming from? He had also registered that the corpse appeared to be clothed in rags. He thought he could recognise the remnants of a shirt, but the arms had parted from the shoulders and had split from end to end.

'How long in the water?' This time the assistant asked the question.

'How can they tell?' the attaché said.

'From how bloated they are,' the detective replied. 'They measure how much the body has expanded by comparing the bloated parts with the parts that don't have much flesh – the wrists, ankles, skull. The fatter the person, the harder it is to judge. With this guy – eighty-five kilos – they should get a fair idea.'

The pathologist was squeezing the bloated flesh with a pair of calipers. 'Looks like seven or eight days,' she said eventually. 'Ten, maximum.'

'Jewellery?'

'Gold band on third finger, left hand.'

'Hair?'

'Fair. Maybe blond.'

'Eyes?'

'Can't tell.'

The attaché stole another look. There were no eyes, only sockets. *Out, vile jelly*. The line from *King Lear* surfaced, remembered from his college days. *Where is thy lustre now?*

The attaché got through the next part of the post-mortem

by concentrating on the technique of the pathologist and her assistant. By watching them follow their procedural duet, so precise it could have been choreographed, he found he could avoid focusing too closely on the object of their attentions. Starting from the head, the senior pathologist worked her way down the body, methodically reciting all its bruises, abrasions and other blemishes, including the missing eyes and toes.

'Surgical scar,' she said when she reached his stomach. 'Possibly a gall bladder op.' Her assistant measured each wound with the calipers, dictating the figures into his microphone. Then he photographed them with a Polaroid camera which, the detective helpfully explained, did so to precise life-size, thanks to a measuring device on the front of the camera. Each time the strobe light set around the lens flashed, there was a hiatus of around thirty seconds as they waited for the print to emerge, to ensure it was as clear and precise as it could be.

'Why are they taking so many pictures?' asked the attaché, who was now becoming absorbed in the process.

'Because once they're done and they've released the body, it's the only evidence they've got,' the detective said. 'I've seen bad pathologists screw up that way. These two are good, mind.'

'Give us a hand, boys,' said the pathologist. 'We need to turn him over.' The two detectives stepped forward and stooped to lever their hands under the corpse. The attaché stayed rooted to the spot. To his eternal gratitude, they didn't ask him to help.

As the pathologists resumed their routine, it became clear to the attaché that three aspects of the corpse were attracting most attention. The first was a vivid set of bruises on each side of its neck.

'Should show up well on the Polaroid,' said the pathologist.

The second consisted of scrape-marks on the buttocks and the backs of the thighs. The third was a contorted twist to his head. 'My guess is his vertebral column is broken between the atlas and the epistropheus, meaning the first and second vertebrae,' said the pathologist. 'The X-ray will tell.'

'So what have we got, doc?' asked the second detective.

'Of course I can't be certain yet,' the pathologist replied.

'Of course.' It was the ritual exchange.

'But if you want me to hypothesise . . .'

'I certainly do.'

'Let's start with the bruising. Extreme pressure on the carotid arteries.'

'So someone who knew what they were doing squeezed his neck until he lost consciousness.'

'It's possible. Second, the abrasions on the buttocks and thighs. They suggest he was dragged while unconscious.'

'So whoever put out his lights pulled him across rough ground?'

'Could be cobblestones. There are fragments of grit in the abrasions. Third, the fracture between the first and second vertebrae. Means his neck was broken, severing the vertebral artery. That's what killed him.'

'But did that happen before or after he went into the water?'

'There's only one way to find out. Let's go inside and take a look.'

It was at this point that the attaché's technique for distancing himself from the proceedings failed him. The corpse was lying on its back once more, looking as marooned and vulnerable as a beached whale. Without ceremony, the pathologist took a scalpel from the trolley and made an incision from the sternum to the groin. The attaché caught a glimpse of the insides of the chest cavity and the gut. The room swam and he had to clutch the detective's shoulder to stop himself from falling.

'Happens to us all the first time,' the detective said. 'Try to think of something else.'

The attaché thought of Jodie Foster. Thoughts of her were normally enough to distract him. The image that came to him was of her putting VaporRub around the rim of her nostrils, but he couldn't think when or why. Then it came to him. It was in *The Silence of the Lambs*, in a room not unlike this. *The smell of rotting flesh. Another bloated floater.* The room swam again.

Try again. *Not women. Sport. Baseball. Boston versus the New York Yankees. Red Sox ahead at the bottom of the eighth. Heading for the World Series. Then it rained. Water. Canals.* No good.

There was a cracking sound that he'd last heard while he waited for a butcher to prepare a rack of lamb. He realised the pathologist was breaking open the rib cage with a pair of pliers.

He walked away and sat on a chair beside the door, fixing his eyes on the floor. He could still hear every sound.

'Making an incision into the left lung. Inserting syringe. Some liquid present.' There was the sound of liquid being squirted into a measuring beaker.

'Water in the lungs, doc?'

'Some. Repeating the procedure on the right lung.'

That squirting sound again.

'How much have we got?'

'Not enough for a decent cup of coffee.'

'What do you think?'

'We need to check the stomach, but I'd say he was dead when he went into the canal, or as near as makes no difference.'

'So what we've got is a cast-iron homicide?'

'That's very likely to be my opinion.'

'Somebody who knows how to kill?'

'I would say so.'

'A pro?'

'You've got it.'

The attaché said: 'Can I ask a question?' He stayed where he was, looking deathly pale.

'Go ahead,' said the pathologist.

He consulted the notes that the FBI had faxed from Washington. 'I need to know if there is a purple mark, like a birth mark, on the inside of the left thigh. At the very top.'

'Wait one. I didn't see it but we'll have a look . . .

'Yes. It's in the crease between the thigh and the genitalia. Star-shaped, about four centimetres in circumference.'

'And you said that he'd had a gall bladder operation?'

The pathologist said she was wrong about that. What the corpse was missing was its spleen.

A vein was pulsing in Halard's neck. Her voice was glacially calm but Stewart suspected her anger was barely under control.

'You idiots,' she was saying. 'Do you realise what you've done? Your fingerprints are all over the car. You've probably destroyed any forensic evidence that was there. I could charge both of you. Obstructing the police, criminal damage – that's the least you've done. Apart from making it harder for us to find your children, of course. What in God's name did you think you were doing?'

They were at the Prefecture, facing Halard at her desk. Suzanne had said nothing since they'd been arrested at the car park. Stewart found it baffling that Halard should have so little imagination. He thought of saying: 'What the fuck do you think we were doing? We were looking for our children.' He decided to be more diplomatic.

'We knew what we were doing,' he said, with studied calm. 'The children could have been inside the car, or in the boot, and on the point of suffocating. Surely you can see that?'

Inspector Desiry, his arms folded, was perched on the corner of the nearest table. 'And just how did you find the car?'

'Sheer perseverance,' Stewart said, keeping his eyes on Halard. 'Perhaps there's a lesson in that for you.'

'You should have called us,' she insisted. 'We'd have been there in five minutes.' The throbbing in her neck was subsiding.

Suzanne shifted on her chair. 'When will we know what's on the film?'

'Any moment now,' said Halard. 'But Mrs Beaumont,' she warned, 'don't get your hopes too high. There may be nothing on the film to help us.'

'At least we know Lavar's mixed up with Carlson,' Stewart said.

'Not necessarily. Finding Fiona's camera in the car doesn't prove anything.'

'I wasn't thinking of the camera.' Stewart retrieved the Mont Blanc pen from inside his jacket and handed it to Halard. 'Do you see the initials, O.L.?' he asked. 'That's O.L., as in Olivier Lavar.'

She scrutinised the initials, then looked at Stewart.

'Olivier left it in the bar at Le Bosquet on Friday night after he'd signed for two drinks, pretending he was Josh,' he said.

'Go on.'

'That was just before Carlson joined him and bought him another drink. They were there for about twenty minutes, and then they left together. They seemed to be very friendly.'

'How do you know all this?'

'The barman told us. I'm sure he would have told Inspector Desiry too, if the inspector hadn't jumped to conclusions the minute he heard I'd had a drink with Carlson.'

He looked to see if his jab had landed, but Desiry had gone to meet his sergeant who was carrying a pile of photographic prints still damp with fixing fluid. Desiry started to peel them apart, laying them out one by one on the nearest table. When Stewart and Suzanne reached him, six pictures already formed an orderly row. Fee's pictures.

She was gazing at him from above a pair of sunglasses that were poised on the end of her nose. Her hazel eyes shone, combining the air of disdain she liked to display with the vulnerability he knew lay underneath. Her face filled the entire frame. There was a similar shot alongside, and then a third, taken from a wider angle, showing her looking into camera from beneath one of Le Bosquet's pool-side sunshades. Stewart's head swam.

'Oh Fee,' he said. 'You heart-breaker.'

Tears were welling in Suzanne's eyes. She was staring at two pictures of Josh posing for Fee beside the pool.

'Trust him,' she said valiantly. 'Playing to the camera as usual.'

Desiry continued laying out the pictures. There was a view of Le Bosquet's driveway, winding through trees, then one of a line of balconies, overlooking the pool, framed by the foliage of two eucalyptus trees. Then came two pictures of a man in long-shot inside one of the bedrooms.

'Either of you recognise him?' Halard asked.

They shook their heads.

Fee's next shot was of a woman drying her hair. Then came a picture which took Stewart a moment to work out, for part of the frame was filled by an out-of-focus frond of eucalyptus. Beyond it, a man sat at a table on a balcony, lifting a cup to his mouth. Stewart recognised him at once.

'That's Carlson,' he said.

‘Are you sure?’ Halard asked.

‘No question. It’s him.’

Halard picked up the nearest phone and asked for the police laboratory. Then she asked Desiry if there were any more shots of Carlson. Desiry rapidly peeled apart the remaining prints.

‘None,’ he said.

‘What number is the Carlson shot?’

‘Frame ten,’ said Desiry.

Halard briskly instructed the lab to make fifty copies of the picture, with Carlson’s face enlarged as much as possible. ‘I need them in an hour. If anyone has a problem with that, refer them to me.’

She told Desiry to organise a fresh search for anyone who could have seen Carlson after he had disappeared from the airport. ‘Airline desks, car rentals, bus drivers, taxi drivers. Do the same at the railway station, the bus station. I want every hotel checked. Get copies of the photograph to every other department. Don’t forget the *Sûreté* and the CRS. And transmit a copy to Brady in Washington.’

Suzanne had recovered her composure and was looking at the picture of Carlson. ‘So that’s him,’ she said. ‘It’s not how I imagined him. I didn’t expect him to look so . . .’ She couldn’t find the word.

‘So normal?’ Stewart suggested.

‘That’s it. Why do you think Fee took his photograph?’

‘Luck, probably. I’d put a roll of film in the camera, and I expect she was shooting everything in sight.’ He was seized by the irony that his peace offering to Fee had provided their first solid lead.

Stewart began looking at the remaining prints Desiry had left on the table. Two small children on another balcony; patterns of light on the surface of the swimming pool; a scowling young man walking into the frame. ‘That’s Olivier,’ said Suzanne.

Halard heard her and returned to the table. She took the photograph from Suzanne and made a note of the frame number. Then the ambiance of the pictures changed. The three teenagers had clearly left the hotel, for there was a shot across water of a wooded promontory, with a line of rocks in the foreground.

'That's looking back at Cap Ferrat, isn't it?' Stewart asked. 'Taken from the road into Villefranche?'

'I think you're right,' said Suzanne.

Then came a bay, with a line of buildings along a waterfront.

'And that's Villefranche, as you approach the old town.'

The next shot showed Madame Robert's *bar-tabac*, with Josh emerging from the doorway. Then Fee was coming out of the same door, waving at the camera. To Stewart, it looked as if she was beckoning to him, like the figure on the ridge in his dream. *I've left these pictures for you*, she seemed to be saying. *Now come and find me.*

'You realise what she's done, don't you, my clever daughter?' he said. 'She's documented their journey.'

The next photograph was taken inside the car, and showed Josh grinning from the front passenger seat, a bottle of Kronenberg beer in his hand. Part of Olivier's head was visible at the left-hand edge of the frame. The next showed Fee, all pretensions to adulthood abandoned, poking out her tongue. Then came another landscape, showing Cap Ferrat again, this time as an undulating line across the horizon.

'That looks like Beaulieu,' Stewart said.

Desiry had joined then at the table. 'Just going into the town,' he said. 'Where the road swings right up the hill.'

The next – a rocky promontory – was of Cap d'Ail. 'They're heading towards Monaco,' Desiry said. Then came a shot of a steep slope descending to the sea, with a cliff in the background. 'Looks like they've come off the main road. They're looking west and that headland is Cap Ferrat, so I'd say they're heading down into one of the inlets.'

'How many shots left?' Halard asked.

'Three,' said Stewart.

The first of the three showed Josh and Olivier side by side, leaning against the Peugeot, an arm across the other's shoulders. The car had stopped on a rough gravel track, with gorse bushes in the background. Two pictures left.

The next was a bitter disappointment, showing only a uniform expanse of scrub, photographed from directly above. Either Fee had been experimenting, Stewart guessed, or she had pressed the shutter by accident.

Her last picture more than made up for it.

It must have been taken from the top of a cliff, for it looked down to a narrow bay cut into a wooded foreland, with a silvery fringe of sand along the shore. At the heart of the bay, perhaps one hundred metres from the beach, sat a white-hulled yacht with two masts, its sails furled, riding at anchor. Beside it floated a black dinghy. There was a solitary figure on deck, though anything further about him – or her – was impossible to tell.

The photograph was perfectly composed, with the arms of the bay running along the sides of the frame, directing the eyes to the yacht. But its most crucial detail resulted from luck. The yacht was riding parallel to the line of the bay, its stern facing inland. What now preoccupied the four people around the table was the line of black lettering two-thirds of the way up the stern – lettering that, if only they could read it, would tell them the yacht's name.

'We should be able to magnify it,' Desiry said.

'How good is the lens?' Halard asked.

Stewart remembered telling himself that nothing was too good for his daughter, as he handed over his credit card at the Dubai Duty-Free.

'Bloody good. Or it should be,' he said.

Halard seized the nearest phone and asked for the lab.

11

Fiona Stewart lay curled up on her bunk, her knees drawn up to her chest, her hands cupped against her cheek. Although sunlight was filtering through the cabin portholes, and the sea was calm, the cabin still seemed to be tilting and rocking, as if the storm had not yet subsided. At its height she had felt quite helpless, imprisoned in the cabin where there was no fixed horizon, the walls were one moment the roof, the next the floor, and the crashing of the sea and the roaring of the wind merged into an inferno of noise. Fear and nausea had washed over her, draining the strength from her limbs until she was certain she could not survive.

She looked across to the other bunk, where Josh lay asleep, breathing deeply. She gripped the wooden rail of the bunk, reassuring herself that it offered a point of stability. What had happened to her? What had she done to bring all this upon herself? As she struggled to make sense of the past two days, they assumed the quality of a movie, as if she had stepped out of herself and was watching as the scenes were played and replayed on a distant screen.

Sunlight is dancing on the water as she sits beside the pool at Le Bosquet. She is talking and laughing with Josh. They photograph each other with the camera her father has given her, posing for each other, trying out the zoom.

She is in the back seat of Olivier's car and the pine trees are speeding past. Olivier tells them about his friend who has a yacht. He can take them sailing that afternoon. It's moored near Villefranche. They stop at a *bar-tabac* to buy beer and another film for her camera. She photographs the scenery and Josh fooling about. They stop on a clifftop and see a white-hulled yacht in the middle of an aquamarine bay. She photographs the yacht. They drive down a stony track to the water's edge where she pushes the camera under the front seat to keep it safe.

Olivier's friend is pulling a black dinghy on to the shore. He is smiling. 'My name's Mark Carlson,' he says. 'Great to have you guys along.' He has blond hair and a line of perfect teeth. He says he has to borrow Olivier's car to buy cigarettes and tells them to take the dinghy out to his yacht. He'll be back in twenty minutes.

Josh steers the dinghy. He tells Fee that the yacht is a ketch, with two masts, fore and aft. She sees the yacht's name, picked out in black lettering on the stern. *Symphonie*. Like Beethoven's Fifth. They clamber up a short ladder on to the deck, Olivier first, she next, Josh holding the dinghy steady.

They look across at the shimmering view of Villefranche and its fortified castle rising above the port. Olivier descends a short flight of steps into the cabin. They hear a shout from below and follow him. Fee is seized from behind and tied and gagged. She is bundled forward into a narrow cabin and pushed on to a bunk. The door slams. The screen goes dark.

There is the rumble of an engine, the clatter of the anchor being hauled on to deck. The propeller bites, water slaps against the hull, the cabin vibrates as the throb of the engine increases. The air is hot and stifling. She lies on her bunk, unable to move. Perspiration gathers under her arms and trickles across her back. There is a chink of light from the far side of the cabin but she can make out only shadows. She deduces that she is alone. The light fades.

Still darkness. Still moving. The gag has made her mouth furry and rank. She has a burning thirst. The bindings are chafing her wrists and ankles and her shoulders are numb with pain. The door opens and a man enters, looming like a giant in the half-light. She senses his weight as he sits beside her and smells his sweat. She catches a glimmer of metal and feels a cold blade against her ankles. She stiffens in terror but her bindings are cut. Cramps grip her calves. His hands massage her legs. He turns her on to her back and pulls away her gag. She is gripped with a new fear but he does not touch her again.

'Keep quiet,' he says. He is American. 'You can turn on the light when I leave. The switch is on the bulkhead.'

'Where's Josh?' she asks.

'Don't worry about him.'

'What about Olivier?'

The man has gone.

Why? Why, why, why? Is it something she has done? Or Josh? Or their parents? Have they been kidnapped? Where are they being taken? Who is her jailer on the boat? Who is Mark Carlson? Why did he smile? She has no answers. What keeps filling her mind is the row with her father. Shouting at him. Saying the worst things she could think of. Hoping she had hurt him. Standing up, swearing at him, running off. Lying in her room hoping he would come so she could say she was sorry. Falling asleep. Finding his note in the morning saying he has gone into Nice and will see her later. She waits for him to come back, but he doesn't.

It is her idea to go somewhere. Olivier says they should go to Villefranche, she says it's cool. Josh doesn't want to go, he has to read his book. Don't worry about your book, she says. Don't worry about your mother either. Come on, Josh, get a life.

Her father still isn't back. She wants to see him, she doesn't want to see him. She persuades Josh. She persuades herself. They exchange guilty looks as they write notes to their parents saying they are going to Villefranche. They do not mention Olivier, or his car.

They go. It is her father's fault. It is her own fault.

She is dreaming of her mother. They are in a car and, as usual, they are late. It is the start of her holiday and they are speeding down the fast lane of a motorway. She knows she has to meet her father and guesses they are going to Heathrow. Her mother is yelling at the driver, 'Move it – terminal two!' They are running through the departure hall and her mother points and shouts, 'Your father's over there.' She looks and sees only a tide of faces. She screams. She hears the screams but they are Olivier's screams, muffled, from a distance. She can make out some words: 'Please God . . .' – '. . . doing this?' She wakes, but Olivier is not there.

She remembers the storm. As it gathered, there was an ominous stillness. It was broken by a thunderclap, followed by rain beating on the deck above. The wind built to a shriek and the cabin pitched and tumbled like a roller-coaster. The door burst open and Fee thought that the sea would pour through – but it was Josh who was pushed in, slithering across the cabin floor and crashing against her bunk. The cabin seemed to stand on end and Fee was thrown out on top of him. Arms and legs entangled, they were thrown against the far bulkhead.

'Wedge yourself in,' Josh shouted in her ear.

They sat with their backs against one bunk, feet pressed against the other. The cabin tilted in the opposite direction, leaving them perched at the top of a steepening slope. For what seemed an age, they managed to hold themselves steady in this way as the cabin continued its insane pitching. Then came a moment more terrifying than any before. There was a monumental crash and the cabin fell sideways until it was almost upside down, breaking open their grip and slamming them into the wall above the bunk. The impact drove Fee's breath from her body and she saw Josh's head jerk back as he hit the bulkhead. There was a moment of terrible quiet. Then the cabin slowly returned to the vertical and the din resumed.

'Are you okay?' Fee yelled.

'I think so. How about you?'

'I'm all right, now I can breathe again.'

As the cabin righted itself, they had fallen back into the bunk together. They clung to each other, Fee's arms round Josh's neck, his around her waist, as the boat swung round, shot forward then shudderered to a halt. There was another explosion of sound from above and then they were moving again. They held each other more tightly than before, each feeling the rise and fall of the other's breathing, as they braced themselves for the next cataclysm. But the boat was moving more evenly now, and eventually they eased their grip.

'What's happened?' Fee shouted.

'I think we must have capsized,' Josh yelled back. 'But we're back the right way up.'

Still they lay together, waiting for the storm to subside, waiting for this nightmare to end.

The door opens and a man enters. He is wearing a loose black hood with slits for his eyes that reaches his shoulders. He is a giant, and sounds and smells like the man who cut her free.

'You two okay?'

He does not wait for an answer. He places a tray on the cabin floor. There is bread, cheese, fruit and a bottle of mineral water.

'Where are you taking us?' Fee asks. He ignores her and goes out. Fee looks down at the food, then across to Josh, who has fallen asleep in the other bunk. Although she has not eaten since before the storm, she is not hungry. She tightens her grip on the rail of her bunk, finding reassurance in its solidity. She is a child again, back in her own bed, hearing her parents move around the house downstairs as she waits to fall asleep. She thinks of her father, remembering him then, remembering him now. When would he come to take her home?

12

First came the neck, three-quarter view, the Adam's apple prominent. Then the tip of the chin that built gradually into the jaw; jutting, determined arrogant. Next, the bottom lip, and with it the start of the cheeks and the lobe of one ear. As the mouth took shape, Special Agent Virgil Tanner of the FBI felt the first flicker of recognition.

Even at 7 a.m. Tanner's cramped office at the American Embassy in Bangkok was stifling. The air conditioning in his part of the building had broken down – *again* – and the fan that Maintenance had provided merely shifted the hot, heavy air around the room. The humidity of Thailand that he'd never grown accustomed to, combined with a bout of indigestion from the noodles he'd eaten the night before, were making him irritable. With little enthusiasm, he had begun reading through his schedule for the day when the drum of the Photofax machine began spinning.

Now the top lip was coming, thin and straight, except where it turned down at the corners. The nostrils were flared, the tip of the nose slightly blunted, the cheekbones high. The ear, now that Tanner could see most of it, seemed small, out of proportion to the rest of the features.

Tanner's other fax machine came to life. It was much faster than the Photofax, and Tanner went over to inspect the incoming message. It was a Look Out Request, marked 'All Points', which meant that other fax machines in Bureau offices across America, and in all twenty-three of the FBI's liaison offices overseas, were receiving the same bulletin and picture. So was every outpost, domestic and foreign, of US Customs and the Immigration service and, for good measure, the cowboys of the Drug Enforcement Administration, and the US Marshals, and – Tanner would bet on it – the CIA.

State and local law enforcement agencies would also be on the distribution list, and soon just about every police precinct in America and every sheriff's office would see the picture and the appeal that went with it: Do you know this man?

The LOR came from FBI headquarters and was signed by the Director himself. But it was no surprise to Tanner that the Case Agent was listed as 'S.A. Brady', for the precision of the message bore all the hallmarks of Phil Brady's spare and analytical approach.

It described the disappearance of two young people from Nice, the ambiguous role of one Olivier Lavar, and the strong suspicion that had fallen on an unknown American using the name and the passport of Mark Carlson. The fate of the real Mark Carlson was also described. In the light of the preliminary autopsy findings provided by the Dutch authorities, his death was classified by the Bureau as 'probable homicide'.

Tanner returned to the Photofax. The eyes were coming now. Even in black and white, the reproduction was remarkably clear.

It was the forehead that settled the matter, leaving Tanner in no doubt that he knew this face. Broad, unlined, the arc it travelled between the eyebrows and the hairline was so long that the spinning drum took more than a minute to depict its full sweep.

'Well, well, well,' Tanner said to the completed portrait he held in his hands. 'You bad-assed sonofabitch.'

He spun the combination dial of the office filing cabinet and removed a blue document folder from the top drawer. It contained a series of reports that Tanner had submitted to Washington over the last two years, together with a set of grainy colour photographs that had clearly been enlarged from pictures shot in difficult circumstances.

He removed one that showed a man sitting on a barstool, next to a unsmiling young Thai woman. She was wearing shorts cut off just below her crotch and the man's hand nestled between her thighs as though he owned her. He placed it alongside the picture sent from Washington. The man's hair was quite different: in the bar photograph he wore a copper-coloured ponytail, which had been replaced by a short-cut thatch that appeared white in the facsimile. Tanner's expert eye was not deceived so easily.

'Red Kain,' he said. 'Meet Red Kain.'

The unsmiling girl's name was Kop, and Red Kain didn't own her – though he thought he did. If anybody owned Kop, it was Virgil Tanner.

She had been his informant for more than two years, enabling him to keep track of Red Kain; chivvy him, spy on him, make him the focus of the highly incriminating reports that Tanner had been sending to Washington.

The reports described Kop as 'C.I.1' – Confidential Informant number one. Tanner called her his 'one-woman Trojan horse'. Kop shared Kain's house, and his bed when he demanded it. Everything she saw, everything she heard, was faithfully reported back to Tanner.

When he first recruited Kop, Tanner had intended to persuade her to place a listening device in Kain's house, even though he knew it was risky. But as he trained and nurtured her, he realised that she had a remarkable talent for memorising passages of conversations, even in other languages.

In another time or place, with the privileges of a western education, there was no telling what she might have become. In Bangkok, Tanner nurtured her natural intelligence, training her to mentally repeat what she heard, over and over until it stuck, and then replay the fragments word for word.

The sweetest thing of all was why she did it. It was not for the ten or twenty dollars Tanner gave her each time they met, to keep her father in gin. She did it for revenge, for the sheer hatred she felt for the man who called her his brown bunny; who boasted that she 'came with the house', as though she was a piece of furniture.

Of course, Kain guarded his secrets. He never talked to Kop about his business, which Tanner was convinced consisted of trafficking in heroin and morphine base. But Kop garnered scraps and details that were priceless to Tanner, memorising them until their next rendezvous.

Every second Sunday morning, Tanner would stroll from his apartment to the jetty of the Oriental Hotel. If he found a red paper flower tied to the third stanchion, he would take a water taxi up the Chao Phraya river to the floating market, where Kop would be waiting for him. They would stroll along the river bank and Kop would replay for Tanner every image and word of Red Kain she had managed to retain. It was thanks to Kop that Tanner knew Kain had left town, and that something special was up.

'He not coming back,' she had said at their last rendezvous.

'He tell you that?' asked Tanner.

'No, but he lock up the house when he go. He never done that before. Tell me to clear off. Then he give me two thousand baht. He never did that before either.'

About eighty dollars: not much in the way of severance pay, thought Tanner.

'What did he say?'

'He tell me he find me when he come back. But I don't believe him.'

'Anybody come out to the house before this happened? Fairley? Katz? Pelican?'

'Not them. Stranger came. Three days before Red go. We fetch him from the Oriental. Take him to the house.'

'Describe him.'

'Fatter than you but not as tall. He sweat like you. Dark hair. He speak English but I think it not his language. He say strange words I not understand.'

'Like what?'

'*Merde. Calmes-toi.*'

So the stranger spoke French. Tanner's interest quickened, for he believed that France was where most of Red Kain's morphine base was turned into heroin; heroin that killed kids in the back alleyways of America.

'Do you know his name?'

'Red told me his name was Cabrini.'

There was a name for any cop to conjure with. It came right out of the dopers' Hall of Fame.

He asked her if Cabrini's first name was Antoine, but she didn't know.

'How long did Cabrini stay at the house?'

'Two hours. Maybe less. Then we take him back to the Oriental.'

'And what did they talk about, Cabrini and Kain?'

Kop told him what she'd heard. One of the things that made her a priceless informant was that she did not elaborate or try to fill in the gaps. The snippets, the phrases, flowed out like a river.

Take a look. Where is she now? Palma de Mallorca. Spain, for fuck's sake. I told you day one. Risky if she stays in France. Tell them to bring her to you. Two hours, three at most. Puff, she's gone. No-one will notice her.

'Okay, she's fine,' Kain had said, then asked her for more beer.

Pictures? It's done. They'll be waiting when I get back. Done where? In England of course. How do I get them? On the computer. No meetings. No phone calls. Your cousin, Sanpiero. You're sure his place is safe. What about the police? No problem. How long do you need it for? How much he wants the kid back. Sanpiero is a patient man. What about you? It depends. Whether I get what I want.

'And if not?' the visitor asked.

The rain had drowned Kain's answer.

Although he paid Kop her dollars, Tanner was disappointed. He'd been hoping for more: talk of consignments, dates, routes, names.

But Tanner was in little doubt that Kain and this Cabrini were plotting an abduction, or worse; something illegal, something that could put Red Kain in jail. So Tanner had sent a 'flash' to the Bureau in Washington reporting the conversation, and recommending that the French and British be advised.

'Advised of what, exactly?' the suits in Washington had responded. Who is the potential victim? Who is the woman in Palma? When and where will the supposed abduction take place? Is Kain travelling on his own passport or under an assumed identity? If so, what name is he using? If so, has he changed his appearance? If so, please provide a description.

What? When? How? Where? Firm it up, Tanner.

Tanner had tried. For more than a month, he had combed Bangkok, tapping every one of his sources, seeking any whisper of what Kain was up to. He had drawn a blank. Nobody knew.

Now Tanner knew.

Sitting at his desk in the embassy, he studied the final section of Brady's LOR.

A camera belonging to the victim Fiona STEWART has been recovered. The film it contained apparently documents the victims' movements from the hotel to the point of their abduction. The last frame depicts a sailing vessel that has been identified as a French-registered ketch, SYMPHONIE, which is based in the Spanish port of Palma, Majorca. Inquiries by the Guardia Civil have established that the boat was chartered by a Dutch corporation, ABEL Holdings N.V., for a period of two months, commencing June 20. ABEL Holdings is a bearer-bond company registered in the Dutch Antilles and it is therefore not possible to identify the beneficial owners.

The charter fee and deposit, totalling $125,000, was paid in cash, in US currency, on June 18 by an American using the name Harold FOSTER. He established his identity using a New York driver's license. Both the license, and the address given on it, are fake. The Spanish authorities have no record of Foster entering or leaving the country.

The following partial description of Foster has been received:

White male
AGE: Approximately 45 years
HEIGHT: Approximately 6ft 4ins
WEIGHT: Approximately 220lbs
BUILD: Muscular
DISTINGUISHING FEATURES: Suspect has a scar running from below his left earlobe to the nape of his neck . . .

Tanner had no need to read any further.

Fairley. Jacob Joseph Fairley, known from his biblical forenames as Jesus. Former grunt, white trash, too poor to dodge the draft; a Known Associate of Red Kain. They were fellow Marines, peas from the same pod: Vietnam vets who never went home. Now he was a bum, shacked up in Bangkok with his own little brown bunny; a hand-for-hire for any dirty business Red Kain required.

Tanner switched on his personal computer, an innovation

at the Bureau which he was still struggling to master. He brought up a blank Field Report form and began laboriously typing the header. As he filled in the Case Name – 'Beaumont/Stewart' – he paused.

Stewart. Why was that name familiar?

He rummaged through the top drawer of his desk until he found a business card bearing an address and a telephone number in London. At the centre was the name 'Tom Stewart'; underneath, in smaller type, the word: 'Writer'.

Tanner had been handed the card three weeks before, when he was trawling the sleazy clubs of Patpong for any word of Red Kain. He was not the only one looking for Kain, apparently. On the back of the card Stewart had written: 'Mr Kain, Please call me at the Montien Hotel, telephone 254-0023. Urgent.'

Tom Stewart, Fiona Stewart – both linked to Red Kain. Coincidence? Tanner doubted it. As a general rule, he didn't believe in coincidences.

It was still evening in Washington, twelve hours behind Bangkok, and outside normal office hours at FBI headquarters. But the gossip around the Bureau, even in its most distant outposts, was that when Phil Brady ran a case he slept on the sofa by his desk. Tanner picked up the phone.

The rumour was not true, evidently, for what he heard when the phone answered was the voice-mail announcement of Brady's formidable secretary, Betsy Silverman. 'There is nobody in the office at the moment,' she said in clear tones. 'If you want to leave a message, press one. If you want to speak to an agent, press two. If this is an emergency, press zero, one, zero.'

An emergency? You could say that, thought Tanner. He pressed three buttons and waited for several million dollars' worth of new technology to perform one of its miracles.

A synthesised voice replaced Silverman's: 'If you are Bureau personnel press one now, otherwise hold for an operator.'

Tanner did as he was told.

'Enter your Bureau ID number now.'

'If you are calling about an active case, enter the last four digits of the case reference number now.'

'Paging the agent. Please hold the line.'

Less than two minutes after Tanner had picked up the phone, he heard a high-pitched tone, followed by a voice coming from God-knows-where.

'Brady.'

Inspector Desiry was driving too fast again, but Stewart barely noticed. As they left Villefranche behind and began the steep descent towards Nice, segments of their conversation replayed in his mind.

'You've found her?' he'd blurted out when the phone jangled him awake, and he heard Desiry urging him to get up.

'No,' Desiry had said, without ceremony. 'But there's been a development. I'm waiting for you downstairs.'

Barely daring to wonder what Desiry meant, Stewart had pulled on his chinos and a T-shirt and raced down to Le Bosquet's lobby. The clock above the reception desk showed three minutes past two.

'What's happened?'

'We've found out who Carlson really is,' Desiry said,

'Who is he?'

'The Commissaire will tell you,' he said as he steered Stewart into his car. 'She's at the Prefecture now.'

They drove in silence, Desiry concentrating on the curves, Stewart bracing himself in the back seat. He pictured the man who had taken not only Carlson's identity but, apparently, his life. Stewart could see the jut of his jaw, the too-perfect smile, the broad forehead, as clearly as if he was sitting in the car beside him.

Most of the lights at the Prefecture were off. Halard was at her desk, looking ghostly in the glow from her anglepoise lamp, the shadows underscoring the blue lines of fatigue beneath her eyes. She was wearing a fresh, tailored charcoal suit but although her manner was still brisk it had lost some of its edge.

She watched Stewart walk towards her: 'We need to have another talk.'

'You know who Carlson is?' Stewart could hardly contain his impatience as he sat on the familiar straight-backed chair.

Halard consulted her notepad. 'The man who posed as Mark Carlson is Robert Michael Kain,' she said, and Stewart's world disintegrated.

At first he felt empty; then a tumult of emotions engulfed him. Fear struck to his core, fear such as he had never known before. Next came anger, at the terror this man must have caused his daughter. Finally – although for a moment he hoped he had escaped it – came remorse over his own role in precipitating this catastrophe. He remained motionless, unable to speak. The details of Kain's life resounded in his head like a mantra.

Kain. Robert Michael Kain. Born Akron, Ohio, May 17, 1947. Known as Red Kain, because of his copper-coloured hair. Former US Marine, Vietnam veteran, holder of the Bronze Star. Now brothel owner, suspected con artist, and – long before Mark Carlson's body was pulled out of an Amsterdam canal – suspected killer. Suspected, that is, by Tom Stewart, who had done all he knew to find him.

Please call me, Stewart had written on the back of business cards he had handed out in every sleazy club and bar in Bangkok.

He'd never found Red Kain. Red Kain had found him.

Stewart felt Halard watching him, trying to gauge his emotions. Desiry pushed a beaker of coffee into his hand. Finally Halard spoke, inquiring, probing, as always.

'Tell me about Kain,' she said, turning to a fresh page in her notebook. 'Tell me why you were looking for him in Bangkok.'

Questions flooded into Stewart's mind. How did they know about Kain? What did they know about Kain? Did they know where Kain was? There was too much for him to sort out. Stewart heard himself reply, in a flattened, weary voice. 'It's a very long story.'

She said something he did not catch.

'I'm sorry?'

She said it was just an expression. It meant time was all they had.

13

Four years ago – was it really that long? – Stewart had sat in the offices of his New York publishers, listening to his editor who was framed in the window of his twenty-first-floor office with the Chrysler Building gleaming behind him.

'We're too close to it here, Tom,' he was saying. 'This book needs a writer who can stand back and see the whole picture. Someone who's been there, knows the territory and the history, but is free to make his own judgments. Someone without any baggage. We thought of you.'

Stewart was flattered, as he was meant to be. The proposal was immensely tempting: succoured by a generous advance, he should research and write the definitive account of the American servicemen lost in the Vietnam war whose fate had never been determined. Known as the MIAs – the Missing in Action – there were more than two thousand of them, who, a quarter of a century on, remained a national obsession.

Over the next month, Stewart read all the news reports, articles and books he could find, and talked to friends and contacts in the worlds of journalism, politics and the military. What came to intrigue him was that while most of the families of the missing accepted that the MIAs had died, others remained convinced that at least some were still alive. They insisted that their loved ones were being held prisoner in Vietnam, or Laos, or Cambodia, or had been brainwashed and assimilated into their former enemy's society. It was all so simple: trace them, rescue them, bring them home.

Tenuous though their arguments might have seemed, the families found no shortage of vociferous supporters. They included politicians and lobbyists who protested that the US government was far too gullible in accepting Vietnam's insistence that no MIAs were left alive. Then there were groups, often Vietnam veterans themselves, who claimed to have proof that individual MIAs were still prisoners. There was talk of organising rescue missions to search for them, usually at a high price.

'What do you say, Tom?' his editor asked when he said he would accept the commission. 'Are these people deluding themselves? Or is there any chance some of these men are alive?'

That was exactly what Stewart intended to find out. He signed the contract, paid the advance into his bank account and embarked on his research with both enthusiasm and a clear view of the shape of his book. But as the months passed his enthusiasm and his clarity dimmed. While he was moved by the tenacity with which the relatives clung to their belief, he was troubled by the motives of those who supported them. Were the politicians idealists – or opportunists exploiting the grief and rancour of a lost war? Were the mercenaries who offered to mount rescue operations genuine patriots – or con-men? And never before, when researching a story, had he encountered so many myths, lies, unprovable claims and dead-ends.

'It got to the point where I'd almost decided to give up, even though that meant repaying the advance.'

'What changed your mind?' Halard asked.

Stewart placed the empty beaker on the edge of her desk. 'I met Luke Lewis.'

It was in Washington almost two years before, on a flawless Friday evening in late summer. Stewart had spent the day in the reading room of the Veterans' Administration on Vermont Avenue, poring through the records of some long-forgotten skirmish, finding nothing to inspire him. Afterwards, he took a cab to Constitution Avenue and walked down the Mall – as he had a dozen times before – until he came to the sloping path where the black marble wall rises, with the names of the dead etched on its face. It was one of the saddest places Stewart knew, yet he was irresistibly drawn to it.

He wasn't sure how long he'd been there before he spotted Luke Lewis maintaining his solitary vigil before the wall. It was only when Stewart saw Luke reach out and run the tips of his fingers along one of the names that he decided to approach him. He introduced himself and explained about his book, and

Luke responded by beginning to tell his own story. Stewart soon sensed that this open, articulate young lawyer had a firmer grasp than most of the complexities of the tragedy he was part of, and a clearer view of his own ambivalent feelings, where reason was at war with hope.

They sat on the grass and talked until dusk, when the lights of others who had come to search for names flickered darkly against the ebony marble of the memorial. Luke invited Stewart back to his sprawling apartment near Dupont Circle, and they'd stayed up half the night. By the morning, Stewart knew how to write his book. He would focus it on Luke Lewis, whose quest for his father would serve as the paradigm of both the personal story and its broader canvas: to explain why belief in the MIAs had taken such a hold on the nation.

Luke had been five years old when two men in uniform had knocked on the door of the family's farmhouse in Kansas and told his mother that his father was 'missing in action' in a place called Khe Sanh.

As Luke later learned, it was a steep mountain valley close to the Laos border, where Luke's father had led a company of Marines into an ambush. The North Vietnamese army had taken advantage of the monsoon season, when rainclouds shroud the landscape, to honeycomb the mountains with bunkers and foxholes extensive enough to hide an entire division. The patrol, led by Captain Barney Lewis, had been close to the crest of one of those mountains – codenamed Hill 861 – when they were raked by ferocious machine gun fire from a distance of barely twenty yards.

Trapped, unable to go forward or back, the survivors dug themselves in, and Lewis called up artillery and air support which pounded at the North Vietnamese positions for the next three days. But the enemy defences were almost impenetrable and it was the Marines who suffered most. When Lewis was ordered by his commanders to retreat, he radioed back that he did not have enough fit men to carry the wounded, let alone the dead. He said he was pulling his men back into the cover of a bank of fog, to 'fight until it's over'.

'Those were the last words his commanders ever heard him speak,' Stewart said.

Halard's note-taking had slowed. She stretched out her right arm and made a fist, then opened and closed it several times to ease the cramp in her fingers.

'And what has Kain got to do with all of this?' she asked.

'I warned you it was a long story,' Stewart said.

Kain, he explained, was a platoon sergeant in Lewis's company and the second most senior man still able to fight. It was Kain who supervised the ferrying of both the wounded and the dead into the fog, while Lewis and a handful of other survivors held the Vietnamese at bay from the edge of a clearing. Then Lewis told the others to retreat while he gave covering fire. He said he would be right behind them.

At this juncture, the official history of Khe Sanh depended on the testimony of just one man: Red Kain. As he told it, when Lewis did not show up, he went back to look for him. He was too late. As he neared the clearing, he saw Lewis surrounded by North Vietnamese with his arms raised. They were pushing him across the clearing with the butts of their guns. Then they disappeared into the trees.

'Kain said there was nothing he could do,' Stewart told Halard. 'He was completely outnumbered, and if he'd tried to rescue Lewis, they would have both ended up dead. So he returned to join the rest of his men.'

There were plenty of witnesses to what happened next. That night, with Kain in charge, the company made a break for it under cover of torrential rain, which reduced visibility to a few yards.

Ignoring orders to leave the dead, Kain resolved to bring back every marine. The bodies, as well as the wounded, were loaded onto makeshift stretchers, and the group set off down trails turned into quagmire. The men slipped and slithered, repeatedly dropping their cargo. Kain was the driving force, ordering them to retrieve their loads, pushing them to their physical limits and beyond.

'It took them all night to reach safety but, thanks to Kain, they made it. Not a single marine was left on the hill – except Barney Lewis.'

Halard paused again from her note-taking. 'So, Captain Lewis was thought to be still alive?' she asked.

'Officially he was listed as MIA. But, yes, based on what Kain said, the Marines believed he'd been taken prisoner. That's what they told the family.'

At first, this had meant nothing to Luke: all that had happened was that his father had gone away and had not yet come back. His faith that he would do so was buttressed by his mother's conviction that her husband was still alive. But when the war ended, and the American prisoners came home, his father was not among them.

While Luke's mother had never given up hope, Luke's emotions had followed a different trajectory. At first he had shared his mother's implicit faith. Then he had become sceptical, without ever daring to confide his doubts to her. By the time he was twenty-two, and going to law school, he was sure his father was dead. Then, just two months before Stewart met him, Luke had dared to believe his father might be alive after all.

First had come garbled reports of a prison camp just over the Vietnam border in Laos, less than ten miles from Khe Sanh. The reports were strengthened when a Laotian farmer claimed he had seen chained westerners working in the forest. Luke had remained cautious – until he was shown a photograph of his father.

'At least, that's who he thinks it is.'

'Did you see the photograph?' asked Halard.

'He showed it to me at his apartment that first night.'

'What did you think?'

Stewart had been dubious. It was grainy picture, taken with a long lens, of a ragged-looking man in his early fifties. It was the right age. Judging from the portrait Luke showed him of his father, taken shortly before he left for Vietnam, the head and nose were the right shape too. But it was still frustratingly indistinct.

'It didn't convince me,' Stewart said, 'but that wasn't the point.'

The point was that the photograph had persuaded a group of wealthy Texas businessmen to pay a group of mercenaries based in Thailand to mount a full-scale reconnaissance. Although there had been similar operations before, this was by far the best equipped. The mercenaries were heavily armed and flew into Laos in helicopters. They returned with two more pieces of evidence. The first was a videotape of what looked like a prison compound only recently abandoned.

'Luke played it for me, and he agreed that it still wasn't

conclusive. It was the second item which clinched it, at least for him.'

'Tell me about it.' Halard clenched her fist again.

Stewart sensed that the caffeine from the coffee was waning; his eyes were narrowing, warning him that fatigue was taking over.

'It was part of a page torn from a King James bible,' he said. 'That's the version Luke's father always carried. John, Chapter Sixteen. It went something like: "And in a little while you will see mine, and your sorrow shall be turned to joy." The mercenaries said it had been found under a stone in the compound, and Luke was convinced his father had left it behind as a sign that he was alive.'

Reverentially, Luke had handed Stewart the printed fragment, shielded in a plastic case. Stewart had been moved by the strength of Luke's belief in this relic, and it was that, as much as anything, which had restored his own dedication to his task.

'That's what I had: what seemed like a cast-iron case of an MIA taken prisoner, who had never returned, together with evidence suggesting that he was still alive. It all seemed straightforward.'

'Until?' Halard looked at him expectantly.

'Until I started looking for Red Kain.'

Stewart felt a cramp at the base of his spine. He realised he had been hunched in the same position on the unyielding canteen chair for almost an hour.

'I need a break,' he said.

She nodded. He stood up and arched his back, then walked over to one of the Prefecture's tall windows. Amber pools of light dwindled down the deserted street; the night sky was a uniform grey. His story had even more of a ring of doom about it, now that he knew how it ended.

'How did you try to find him?' she asked when he returned to the chair.

While the other survivors of Hill 861 were easy to track down, mostly through the Veterans' Administration, Kain had remained utterly elusive. Letters to old addresses came back marked return to sender, telephone numbers proved hopelessly out of date. Then Stewart began to hear conflicting stories. Kain had gone to Canada. Kain was in Europe. Kain had never returned from Southeast Asia. Kain had been killed in a road accident. Kain had survived the accident, but died later. There had never been an accident, and Kain was very much alive.

Whatever the truth, the picture that began to emerge of him was at odds with the heroic figure Stewart had read about in the official account of Khe Sanh. Other members of the company made no secret of their dislike for Kain. He relished combat and took a sadistic pleasure in killing. Some said he had sold heroin to enlisted men. There were tales of bitter hostility between Kain and Lewis: a shouting match, a fist-fight, rumours of a threatened court-martial.

'Then I heard something that completely threw me.'

Halard looked at him again. So far, she had shown no surprise at anything he'd told her. Stewart was beginning to wonder just how much she already knew.

'I was in Chiang Mai, in northern Thailand, looking for the mercenaries who'd carried out the reconnaissance. I didn't find them but somebody told me that Kain had been the organiser. I couldn't believe it. I called Luke in Washington and asked him to find out exactly who had raised the money in Texas. Sure enough, the trail led back to Kain.'

'When was this?'

'About six months ago.'

'What did you do then?'

'Luke came up with a contact address that turned out to be a guest house in Chiang Mai. But Kain hadn't been there for more than two years. Nobody in Chiang Mai knew anything about him.'

In the darkness beyond Halard's desk, a cigarette lighter flared. Desiry had remained so still that Stewart had almost forgotten he was there.

'Tell me something,' he said. 'Why would Kain want to rescue Lewis if they hated each other's guts?'

'The obvious reason was money. There was talk that the Texans put up more than a million dollars for the operation, though I could never confirm that. Even so, it didn't make any sense to me. I was even beginning to doubt Kain's story of what had happened on the hill.'

'Why?' Halard asked.

'Because by this time, the Vietnamese were doing their utmost to account for all the MIAs, so that the Americans would restore normal relations. If they had taken Lewis prisoner, why didn't they say so, even if he had died later on? They had nothing to lose, everything to gain. But they kept insisting they knew nothing about Lewis. They even produced the division commander at Khe Sanh who swore as a matter of military honour that no prisoners were taken on the hill.'

'So you believed that Kain lied about what he saw?'

'I was coming to believe it, yes.'

'Why would he do that?' Her questions were suddenly staccato.

'That's what I'm about to tell you.'

Three weeks before, Stewart had sat on a boulder on the edge of a clearing on Hill 861 – the same clearing where, by Kain's account, Barney Lewis was taken prisoner. The clearing was some one hundred metres across, lit by shafts of sunlight piercing the trees. A dozen figures were stooped over the dusty soil, sifting it with trowels, heaping it into sieves, watching intently as it fell back to earth. They were members of a Joint Task Force, established by President Bush in January 1992, and charged with providing a 'full accounting' of every MIA in Vietnam, Laos and Cambodia. As they readily told Stewart, it was a 'mission impossible', for the standards of proof were absurdly high. It was not enough that eye-witnesses had seen a plane crash, the wreckage had been located, or fragments of human bone had been unearthed from the cockpit. Nothing short of a DNA match between those fragments and a living progeny would convince Washington to close the file on that particular MIA, confirming that he was no longer missing, but dead.

Rarely did the searchers find bone fragments large enough to reach that degree of certainty. But sometimes they did.

'There's no doubt in your mind?' Stewart had said to the tall man with silvery hair standing beside him. The name on the jacket of his brown and green combat fatigues announced him as Brigadier General 'Bull' Jordan.

'We'll have to wait for the DNA tests. But no, there's no doubt.'

Jordan led Stewart to a green tarpaulin pegged down from the branch of a tree. Beneath it was a small wooden packing case, draped with white plastic sheeting so that it resembled a cot. Inside were the items that had been unearthed from the clearing. There were fragments of faded green cloth from a marine's combat fatigues, and a punctured water bottle, blackened with corrosion. There were also large fragments of bone, stained brown by 25 years in the soil: part of a clavicle, a six-inch length of femur, and the rear half of a human skull. Barney Lewis's skull.

There was more. Jordan held the skull in his hand and pointed to the neat, round hole that had been drilled in it by a bullet.

'This bullet,' said Jordan. He removed a transparent Ziplock bag from the bottom of the packing case. Inside was a slug, misshapen after its passage through bone, but still bright and hard.

Jordan took it out of the bag and held it between his fingers. 'This is forty-five calibre. That's not what the enemy used. I'm no ballistics expert, but I'd bet my pension this was fired from a Colt automatic. That's what Lewis was carrying as his sidearm. If you want my opinion, Lewis was lying face down on the ground when somebody shot him through the back of his head with his own gun.'

Afterwards, Stewart supposed that his senses must have been dulled by the heat and the exertion of the climb up to the clearing. Almost mechanically, he took out his camera and asked Jordan if he could photograph the skull and the slug in the shallow depression where they'd been found. He framed his shot so that the searchers, still preoccupied with their work, could be seen in the background.

Then as the implications sunk in, he felt chilled, despite the overhead sun. By the time he asked Jordan his next questions, he was already framing the answers.

'Are you saying that after the Vietnamese captured Lewis and led him away from the clearing, they brought him all the way back here and executed him?'

'It's possible.'

'But you don't believe it?'

Jordan had not replied.

'Why don't you believe it, general?'

'Have you ever seen what howitzers can do? Throughout that night, while the company withdrew, we laid down a barrage on this hill you would not believe. No man in his right mind would have walked across this clearing just to shoot an American prisoner. Hell, if they wanted to kill Lewis, they could have shot him anywhere. They didn't have to walk into a firestorm to do it.'

'So what's the explanation?'

'Captain Lewis wasn't murdered by the enemy.'

Halard had long since pushed her notebook to one side.

'Did Jordan say Kain shot him?' she asked

'He didn't go as far as that,' Stewart replied. 'But by Kain's own admission, he was the last American to see Lewis alive. If it wasn't the Vietnamese, who else could have done it?'

Stewart was certain Halard was hearing something new. Her eyes held his, and she pursed her lips. This time, it was she who proposed a break. As she slipped out of the room, Stewart stood at the window again. There was a solitary figure in the street, merging with the darkness then stepping into the pools of light. He had dulled the nag of anxiety by reciting his story, but now it was becoming strong again. He looked back into the room. Desiry was making a phone call, whispering into the receiver as though he was talking to a lover. He felt relief when he saw Halard return. She'd brushed her hair; there was a fresh touch of red on her lips.

'Are you going to tell us you decided to confront Kain?' she said. 'To accuse him of murder?'

'More or less.'

He heard Desiry suck in his breath.

'I know what you're thinking,' Stewart said. 'I was meddling in police business again.'

'You're right,' said Desiry. 'Murder *is* police business.'

'I had no choice,' Stewart said. 'I owed it to Luke.'

'Tell us what happened when you went to Bangkok,' said Halard. 'How did you know Kain was there?'

'Before I left for Vietnam, Luke had passed on a rumour he'd heard that Kain had been seen in a club in Patpong, which he was supposed to own. It's called the Last Chance Saloon.'

Stewart had gone there the first night, after flying in from Hanoi. For what seemed like hours, he sat with a girl perched on his lap, buying her drinks at three dollars a time. When her glass was empty, she would massage his groin with her buttocks, and try to persuade him to take her back to his hotel – 'only $20 for the night,' she implored, in vain.

He had stayed until the club closed, and the obscenely fat *mammasan* who ran the place had tucked the takings into her capacious bosom. There was still no sign of Red Kain, but by then he'd spotted the gun. It was silver, a Colt automatic, hanging with other trophies on the wall behind the bar. A Colt automatic like the one Barney Lewis carried as his sidearm, like the one he was shot with, in the back of the head.

He did not mention the gun to Halard.

'Did you go back?' she asked.

'Every night that week. On the second night I asked the *mammasan* if she was expecting Kain. She was wary at first, but later on she opened up. By then I was getting to be a pretty good customer.'

In more ways than one. 'How much for the Colt?' he'd asked her on the third night. She said it wasn't for sale but the way she said it he didn't believe her. Everything was for sale in the Last Chance saloon.

'What did she tell you?'

'She confirmed that Kain owned the club but said he only came in from time to time. She claimed not to know where he lived, or how to get hold of him. But she offered to take a message.'

The first note Stewart left had been innocuous: simply 'Please call me', with the name and number of his hotel, scrawled on the back of his business card. When that produced no result – the *mammasan* had merely shrugged when he returned to the club the following night – he decided to be more explicit.

'In my second message I told him I was writing a book about Khe Sahn and Barney Lewis, and I wanted to go over his account of what happened on the hill.'

'And you gave that to the *mammasan*?'

And $400. For the Colt.

'Not only her. During that week, I looked for Kain in every other dive in Patpong. I found plenty of people who knew him, and I left the same message with all of them.'

'What would you have done if Kain had contacted you?' asked Desiry.

'I would have told him what I knew. And what I believed.'

'What did you imagine he would say then?' Desiry sounded incredulous.

Stewart shrugged. 'It didn't really matter what he said. I just had to be able to describe the end of my quest in the final chapter.'

'Did you make any other attempts to reach him?' Halard asked.

'On my last night in Bangkok, when I still hadn't heard from him, I decided to write him a letter.'

Stewart had lifted the girl from his lap and given her twenty dollars just to leave him alone. He asked the *mammasan* for some paper and a candle, and wondered just how far to increase the pressure. Finally, in the guttering light of the candle, he wrote:

Dear Mr Kain,
I have to return to London tomorrow, but it is vital that I see you. During my research into Khe Sanh, some curious contradictions and questions have arisen. I will write my book whether you agree to see me or not, but it is only fair that I give you the chance to answer these queries; to tell your side of the story.

I am willing to come back to Bangkok, or I'll meet you anywhere else you nominate.

Please write to me in London, or call. I will be in France for the next couple of weeks, but I'll check my answering service regularly, so please leave a message. Or, if you prefer not to make direct contact, put a personal ad in the International Herald Tribune, addressed to TS. Just suggest a time and place. The Tribune is readily available in the south of France, and I'll check for your ad each day.

Tom Stewart

'You didn't exactly make it hard for him to find you, did you?' said Desiry.

That was the whole point, Stewart replied.

14

The bar at Le Bosquet was deserted, except for the waiter polishing glasses. He asked for a coffee and sat at the table where, the waiter told him, the man who called himself Carlson had drunk bourbon with Olivier Lavar; and where, Stewart was convinced, Red Kain had arranged Fee's abduction. Though Stewart knew it was irrational, he hoped that by revisiting the scene he might gain some insight into how Kain and Lavar had planned their crime. He also knew he was putting off the moment when he must go upstairs and admit to Suzanne that their children had been kidnapped, and possibly worse, because of *him*, because of what *he* had done. And then he must call his former wife and tell her the same.

'Tom, old chap,' said a fruity voice. 'How are you? Not so hot, I imagine.'

He looked up to see a short rotund man standing over him, a mask of concern on his florid face. His navy blue, double-breasted blazer almost concealed his paunch. His maroon tie was patterned with small motifs of a classical figure, holding scales and a sword. Stewart thought he looked like a plain-clothes policeman, if somewhat gone to seed.

'Awfully sorry to hear about this mess.'

'I'm sorry, do I know you?' Stewart said guardedly.

'It's Sail, Tom, Johnny Sail. Good Lord, you must remember. Last saw you in . . . Cyprus, wasn't it? Remember that night we got pissed together? Or perhaps not – you were pretty paralytic. I had to pour you into a taxi as I recall.'

Not a cop, then. And Stewart had never been to Cyprus.

'Look, Mr Sail . . .'

'Come on, Tom. It's Johnny.'

'All right then, Johnny. But you've got the wrong man. We've never met, in Cyprus or anywhere else, and you know it. What do you want?'

'I don't want anything, old chap. I've come to see if I can help. About your daughter. Fiona, isn't it? See if there's anything I can do. We Brits have to stick together.'

Now Stewart knew who he was – or rather, what he was.

'Don't give me that crap. You're a hack, aren't you? Which paper?'

'Freelance. I prefer to be my own master – like you, Tom.'

'Okay, but who do you write for? Who sent you here?'

'Nobody sent me, Tom. Came off my own bat. Heard about Fiona, and thought I'd drop by and have a word with you.'

'How did you hear about Fiona?'

Sail tapped the side of his nose with a finger. 'Mum's the word. We live or die by our contacts. Right, Tom?'

'Yes, well I've got nothing to say to you. I'm not a fool, Sail. I know what you're up to, and you can just piss off.'

Sail looked contrite. 'Wish I could old chap, really do. But what with the Beaumont boy missing as well, and the FBI involved, and the White House up in arms – well, you know how it is. Doesn't matter whether I write it or not. Won't be long before the story's on Reuters, will it?'

He spoke with all-knowing confidence, but Stewart wasn't taken in. He knew how tabloid reporters worked, finessing one or two facts with rumour and guesswork, pretending that since they knew the whole story anyway, 'you may as well tell me your side'. He had done it himself, not so long ago.

'So just what have your contacts told you?' Stewart asked, contriving to make 'contacts' sound like a profanity.

'Mind if I sit down?' said Sail. Without waiting for an answer, he settled into the chair next to Stewart. 'Fancy a snifter? You look as if you could do with one.'

Stewart watched him in silence. Sail seemed to abandon the idea of a drink.

'Halard's pretty good, so that's some comfort for you,' he said. 'It's not every day that you get Supercop on a case like this. Supercop's what the papers call her here, by the way. Youngest Commissaire on the force, a nose like a bloodhound. And she's got the clout to get things done.' He looked around the restaurant with a conspiratorial air, as if to make sure he couldn't be overheard. 'The word is, she's *very* close to the interior minister, if you get my meaning.' Sail winked.

'I asked you a question. What have you been told?'

Sail folded his arms and closed his eyes in apparent concentration, as he wondered how much he should reveal.

He had spent years cultivating his police contacts the length of the Riviera, and had learned about the disappearance of Fiona Stewart within hours of her father reporting it. One British kid missing on the Riviera for less than a day wasn't worth even a paragraph in the London newspapers Sail served, but the next day he had been tipped off that Halard had flown into town in the Interior Minister's Dassault jet to set up a war room in the Prefecture. Twelve detectives from the *Police Nationale* had been assigned to her, including one of Sail's most productive contacts.

Why? he pressed his source when they met for a drink that evening. Why have they sent Halard?

Because an American kid has also gone missing, the detective said, and he's got a billionaire grandfather with a direct line to the White House. (He was talking in French francs, but Sail was not troubled by such semantic niceties.) The White House had called the Elysée, and Halard was packing her bags. Get the picture?

Indeed Sail had – in more ways than one. The police were circulating photographs of the missing kids – and by the time he and his detective contact parted, Sail had acquired high-grade copies for the entirely reasonable price of one thousand francs.

It was not until the next morning, after he'd received a further titbit from his source, that Sail telephoned the news editor of the *Daily Express*. The immediate response, when he outlined his 'exclusive', was not overly enthusiastic. 'They've probably gone off bonking, Johnny,' said the editor in a voice that implied he'd heard it all before.

'What, all four of them?' said Sail.

'Four?'

Yes, said Sail, because there had been further developments. A French movie producer's son was also missing, *and* an American named Carlson, who may or may not have connections to the CIA – 'that last bit yet to be confirmed,' said Sail prudently. Now the FBI was involved – and, the latest twist, Dutch police had just pulled a body out of an Amsterdam canal.

'No confirmation yet, but my man thinks it's Carlson,' Sail said.

'Brit Girl Missing In Riviera Riddle,' said the editor, displaying his genius for reducing the most complex and potentially tragic events to tabloid essentials.

But the editor wasn't yet sold. He pointed out that all Sail's information depended on one anonymous source. 'You need to firm it up, old boy.'

One more thing. 'Get the human angle,' the news editor added. 'Get to the girl's father.'

Sail opened his eyes. 'Let's see. Fiona Stewart, schoolgirl, and her father, Tom, former practitioner of my humble trade, now distinguished writer, come to fashionable Cap Ferrat on holiday, while Fiona's mother – Tom's ex-wife – goes to the States to take care of an illness in the family. Two days before her seventeenth birthday, Fiona . . . She's a pretty girl, by the way. Did you take that photograph of her?'

Stewart gritted himself to show no reaction.

'As I was saying, two days before her seventeenth birthday, Fiona vanishes off the face of the earth together with one Joshua Beaumont, also sixteen, son of Suzanne, scion of Jesse Beaumont – who, rumour has it, is not short of a shilling or two. Also missing, one Olivier Lavar, school chum of Josh, and one Mark Carlson, American, fortysomething, into computers – and very much under suspicion. Except his real name isn't Mark Carlson. How am I doing?'

Stewart was appalled. 'Go on,' he said.

'No clues, no ransom demand, no nothing,' Sail continued. 'All *les flics* know for certain is that the night before Fiona disappeared, she had a blazing row with her father, and . . .'

Stewart sprang from his chair. His fist tightened but he managed to suppress his urge to punch Sail in the face. 'Jesus Christ!' he said. 'Who the hell have you been talking to?'

'Steady on old boy,' said Sail, struggling to his feet.

'Desiry's your source, isn't he? Inspector fucking Desiry.'

Sail gave him a wide-eyed look. 'Who?'

Stewart kept his face close to Sail's. 'Listen to me. If you write anything that even hints I've got anything to do with my daughter's disappearance, I'll sue you, and whichever bloody rag prints it. Do you understand? I'll come after you, I swear to God.'

'Dear chap, you've got it totally, totally wrong. I was telling you what I was told, that's all. I knew from the start it was bollocks. Told them so, in fact. I said to my man, "You're barking up the wrong tree there". And, of course, as soon as Carlson turned up dead, my man admitted I was right.'

Sail might as well have punched Stewart in the gut. 'What did you say?'

Sail's instincts were highly tuned. 'They haven't told you, have they? About Carlson? They pulled him out of a canal in Amsterdam.'

'When, for God's sake?'

'Last night or this morning. They're still waiting for confirmation of his identity, but it's ninety per cent certain. The word is, he didn't drown. You'd better sit down.'

Stewart slumped back into his chair. For the second time that day he felt stunned, as he tried to absorb the implications of what he had just been told.

'Look, in the circumstances, you can see I've got to write something, can't you?' Sail made it sound as if he had no choice in the matter. 'The thing is, can I do anything to help you? Reading between the lines, I'd say you're not entirely enamoured of Nice's finest – the presence of Supercop notwithstanding – and who can blame you? Now, as I see it, if the White House can get the French moving, why can't Number Ten give them a prod as well? What I'm suggesting is this: If you and I work together, I can write a piece about your experiences that will have the back benches in uproar. I'll guarantee you the PM will be on to the Elysée before you can count to ten. It's up to you, Tom. If you want me to help you, just say the word.'

Stewart knew that he was being manipulated. There was even a distant part of him that admired Sail's shameless technique and sheer nerve. But Stewart's anger and fear and confusion had fatally reduced his resistance. What Sail warned him was true: he would write his story regardless, so Stewart might as well try to shape what it said. Sail was probably right in another way. Any pressure that could be brought to bear on the French authorities could only be of help.

And so Stewart submitted to Sail's questioning. Its intensity reminded him of Halard's interrogations, though without the edge of her innate suspicion, for Sail was an expert listener. By the time the session was over, Stewart had told Sail most of how it felt to be caught up in what the *Daily Express* would herald, on the next day's front page, as 'EVERY FATHER'S NIGHTMARE'.

Most but not all. Stewart did not reveal that he knew the real identity of the man who posed as Mark Carlson, nor why he believed that man had taken his daughter. He knew that, sooner or later, Sail would find that out. He'd face that when it happened. For now, some things were too horrific to confess to a total stranger. Bad enough that he must confess them to a friend.

Suzanne plucked a eucalyptus leaf, savouring its rich, clean perfume as she crushed it in her palm. A pair of magpies strutted among the scattered flakes of bark. Stewart was walking towards her, looking as if he had hardly slept. She wondered how she looked to him, in the aftermath of seeing Josh so carefree in Fee's pictures; and of a whole day spent listlessly waiting for news of the search for *Symphonie*, news which hadn't come. She had slept badly, woken early and come into Le Bosquet's gardens partly in a bid to clear her mind, partly because she couldn't face jostling for the hotel's lavish morning buffet.

'Have you had breakfast?' he asked, chiming with her thoughts.

'Not yet. I'm not sure I want any.'

'How about coffee?'

'You seem very sociable this morning.'

'I don't feel it. I've been up most of the night.' He seemed embarrassed, avoiding her eye at first, then looking directly at her.

'There's something I need to sort out with you. Something I have to tell you,' he said.

It seemed a momentous announcement. 'You sound very mysterious,' she said.

'It's something I only found out a few hours ago.'

'In the middle of the night?'

'Around dawn, more like.'

They decided to risk the buffet, and emerged with fresh-squeezed orange juice and coffee, which they set on an ornate white table beneath the eucalyptus. The magpies were remarkably bold, continuing their foraging just a few feet away. Stewart seemed reluctant to begin.

'Well?' she asked. 'You might as well tell me.'

He sipped his coffee and put down the cup. 'There's no easy way to say this, so I'll just say it. I'm the reason our children were kidnapped.'

She looked at him without comprehending, the words not striking home. Before she could respond, he added: 'I'll tell you why.'

Although it was all fresh in his mind, from his marathon session at the Prefecture, he had an immense sense of weariness as he repeated the story, now that he knew what it truly portended. Even the edited version, the curtain-call of the epic he had related to Halard and Desiry, took him three or four refills of coffee to relate, with the magpies long since adjourned to the far side of the garden.

The story was so convoluted that Suzanne found it hard to follow. Yet she absorbed enough to indulge in a sense of relief, knowing it was his fault, not hers, that the children had disappeared; and discovering some of the answers that had eluded them as they were agonising in the cocktail lounge. With the relief came guilt that she should have such feelings; and then the guilt became anger, as she listened to his *mea culpas*, his excuses for the wanton risks he had taken, all for the sake of a book. He came to an end, and there was a silence, a vacuum, that her anger flooded into.

'You must be crazy,' she said, 'messing with someone like that. A drug pusher, a killer, a psychopath. You go looking for him in the worst bars in Bangkok, begging him to come after you. And you weren't just putting yourself at risk, but your daughter too. And my son, come to that.'

He had no answer.

'What else did the police tell you?'

'None of it's good news. It's not just Kain we have to worry about. He has some very unpleasant friends.'

Suzanne's anger was merging into fear. 'You'd better tell me everything.'

Kain, he related, was a key player in an international heroin-smuggling operation, a network with staging posts in Thailand and Marseille and markets throughout the industrialised west. Kain operated out of Bangkok, roaming through the so-called Golden Triangle, an area embracing Burma, Laos and northern Thailand, buying, selling, making his mark-ups in a trade worth billions of dollars. It was a business where only the most ruthless survived. And Kain, above all, was a survivor.

Suzanne could scarcely believe what she was hearing. Less than a week before, she had come to attend a conference in Nice, looking forward to enjoying a precious few days with her son. Now she was learning about heroin-traders and killers who seemed like characters out of half-remembered novels. Not just learning about them, either, but becoming part of their grotesque world.

'Anything else?' she asked; having gone this far, she might as well hear the rest.

She was not a bit surprised when he said there was more. He told her about the gun he had bought in Bangkok, the Colt automatic secured from the trophies on the wall of Kain's bar.

'Do the police know about this?'

No, Stewart admitted.

'You're insane.'

He thought she was going to stand up, knock the table, spill the coffee dregs; threaten to call the police 'right now', as she had in the cocktail lounge. She stayed where she was, watching him warily, waiting for his explanation.

'The point is, I think Kain wants the gun very badly. If he did kill Barney Lewis, the gun can prove it, because the police can match it to the bullet. Don't you see? If they get hold of the gun, we've lost our biggest bargaining chip.'

'Bargaining chip?'

'I'm going to trade with Kain. He can have the gun back. I don't want it any more, or my book, my research notes and tapes either – or anything else to do with Kain and Hill 861. I'm willing to hand it all over, destroy everything, if he gives us back our children.'

He watched her absorb what he'd said, saw her grasp the logic, saw her relief. He felt that he had drawn her back from a precipice, and that they were acting together again.

'You still need to explain how we reach Kain,' she said.

'The police are convinced that Kain had local help, almost certainly from his friends in the heroin business in Marseille. We need to find his friends and give them the message that we're ready to deal.'

'Deal? For the lives of our children?' She did not wait for an answer, as she realised that dealing was what they had come to. She asked the next question herself: 'How?'

'When I got back from the Prefecture this morning, I was ambushed in the hotel by a hack who sells stories to the British tabloids. He'd heard about Fee and Josh from one of his police contacts.'

'We don't need this,' she said wearily.

'It was bound to happen. The point is he knew a hell of a lot already. He must have excellent police contacts and my bet is they can tell him everything we want to know.'

'Will he help?'

'I don't see why not,' he said. 'I'll try to get hold of him now.'

He stood up. 'First I've got another call I have to make.'

Suzanne knew he meant Rachel, and watched him walk back into the hotel.

15

When Commissaire Halard began the quest to establish Red Kain's movements after he vanished at Nice airport, she was back on familiar territory. Her fame as 'Supercop' depended, in part, on her success in tracking down every member of an international gang that had stolen treasures from the Louvre and shipped them via Corsica to Japan. With both the political clout and unlimited resources at her disposal, she felt reasonably confident she could track down Red Kain.

She woke the minister in Paris with a call early on Tuesday morning. At 7 a.m. one of his senior officials telephoned a *juge d'instruction* in Nice and persuaded him to issue a search warrant authorising Inspector Desiry to open every luggage locker in the airport terminal. It took Desiry and his team just forty-five minutes to find Mark Carlson's Gucci bag. The handle had been neatly removed with a knife, to ensure there were no fingerprints, and the clothes inside – which belonged to the real Mark Carlson – had all been freshly laundered at Le Bosquet. Halard sent them to Forensics but correctly assumed they would yield no traces of the impostor who had worn them.

Halard's next assumption was that Kain had altered his appearance at the airport, and so she instructed the officers who were searching for witnesses to emphasise physical characteristics that cannot be changed in a hurry: height rather than weight; the shape of the face, nose and chin, rather than eye-colour or length of hair. The police artist embellished Fee's photograph of Kain by computer to show a range of ready disguises he could have used – hats, wigs, facial hair, contact lenses of different colours, spectacles of different styles. A picture of Kain wearing granny glasses struck a chord with an airport bus driver who felt 'reasonably sure' he was a passenger he had taken into Nice, dropping him off 'near the big hotels' on the Promenade des Anglais.

The clerk at the Avis car rental desk in the lobby of the Aston Concorde hotel was more definite. When one of Desiry's officers showed him the same picture of Kain, he was 'almost certain' he recognised an American, Edgar Bartlett, who had come into the hotel and rented a Renault Clio for two weeks. Thus another alias for Red Kain was added to the All Points Bulletin – and in Trenton, New Jersey, another missing man's worried partner would receive a visit from the FBI.

'He told the Avis clerk he was going to Spain,' Halard told Brady when she called Washington to bring him up to date. She found him dependably reassuring to talk to, and did not object to his habit of leading her through a check-list of questions to ensure there was nothing she had missed. Although he let slip the occasional barbed remark, she preferred to think that this was nothing personal, merely that it reflected his insistence on maintaining the highest standards. 'I've alerted the Italians as well,' she added. 'We're up against a professional, Phil.'

She wondered if Brady might say 'so is he', but he was evidently in one of his hardball moods. 'What's your guess on the children?' he asked.

'I'm assuming they're still on the boat. I've got an alert out for *Symphonie* in every port from Gibraltar to Sicily. The gendarmes are checking creeks and inlets, and the Spanish and Italians are doing the same.'

'How far do you think they could have got?'

'The problem is, we don't know what effect the storm might have had on them, and that makes the calculations very difficult. But we have assumed a maximum sustained speed of eight knots, and extended the search area to a radius fifty miles beyond that, which could take us to North Africa. I've got Navy aircraft doing a sea search as far as the coast of Algeria.'

To anyone but Brady, Halard thought, it would sound an impressive effort. 'The truth is, I'd have hoped for a sighting by now. But we've not had a glimmer.'

'What about the lead from Tanner? Have you worked out what Kain meant by Sanpiero's place?'

'We're working on that. But we have to identify which cousin

Cabrini was referring to. Antoine's got cousins everywhere, and at least half of them seem to be called Sanpiero. So far we know for certain there are two in Marseille, one in Bordeaux, one in Lyon and another in Corsica. There may be others in Sicily and Algiers. It's a mess.'

'What are you doing about Stewart?' Brady asked. 'Have you tackled him yet about the gun?'

'No. I figure he didn't tell us about it because he thinks the gun is what Kain wants from him – that plus all the research material, and his silence about Vietnam. He could be right, so I've decided to wait and see if Kain makes contact. I've got watchers on Stewart and Mrs Beaumont, and their phones at the hotel are being monitored. But the surveillance has to be discreet, otherwise Kain won't make contact.'

'Stewart's one pig-headed so-and-so, isn't he? You'd think he'd know we'd find out about the Colt.'

'Perhaps he doesn't know how efficient the FBI is,' said Halard.

'Touché,' said Brady. 'When do you think Kain will get in touch?'

'Not until the children are stashed away and Kain feels he's somewhere safe.'

Halard was beginning to feel at the wrong end of an interrogation. 'What's your take on Kain?' she asked. 'You know more about him than me. What do you think he's got in mind?'

'My assumption is he's going to tell Stewart that if doesn't give the gun back, and if he goes ahead and publishes his book, his child dies. Or something like that.'

It was Halard's turn to persist. 'But what's to prevent Stewart publishing after he's got his daughter back? How's Kain going to stop him then?'

'Look at it from Stewart's point of view. If he gets her back from Kain, does he really want to put her at risk again? Take a look at the background report I've just had from Tanner. I'm about to send it to you. Looks like at least three homicides in Thailand are down to him, including a fourteen-year-old kid whose father crossed him in a heroin deal. He's a grade-one asshole. I wouldn't like to be in Stewart's shoes right now.'

He's only got himself to blame, Halard thought, though she stopped herself from saying it.

'What about the Beaumont boy?' Brady asked. 'Why do you think they're holding him as well?'

'We don't know that they are – at least not any more. The assumption has to be that since he and Fee were together, Kain's people had to snatch them both. But that doesn't mean they have to keep him.'

'You think they've got rid of him?'

'You tell me, Phil. You're the Kain specialist. Do you have any more on his associates?'

'We've got three in the frame so far. Tanner is as sure as he can be that the guy who picked up the boat in Majorca was Jesus Fairley. His file and picture should be with you within the hour. The other two are guesswork, but Tanner's pretty confident. He says they're close buddies of Kain and Fairley, and neither's been seen in Bangkok for the last two weeks. The first one is James Francis Pelican, as in the bird. He's another ex-marine, same unit as Kain and Fairley. The second one is a Brit, name of Peter William Katz. Tanner says the word in Bangkok is that he's a former paratrooper who got into some kind of trouble in Northern Ireland – he was either charged with raping a young girl, or at least suspected of it. He got kicked out of the forces and became a mercenary – first in Africa, then he turned up in Southeast Asia about five years ago. I've asked our liaison office in London to talk to Scotland Yard about him.'

Halard stayed silent as she absorbed Brady's information.

'Of course, the quickest way would be to find Kain,' said Brady.

For the first time, Halard felt irritated by his implied criticisms. 'What do you think I'm trying to do?' she asked.

Brady ignored her sarcasm. 'My bet is he's in Italy.'

'I don't think so. Even if the car's there, he won't be. He lays trails to confuse us, Phil. It wouldn't surprise me if he were sitting somewhere in Nice, laughing at us. Or just down the block from you in Washington. Do you want to bet on it?'

'I'll save my money,' Brady laughed.

It proved a wise decision. Halard had asked the Italian police to search public parking garages, particularly at airports, for the Renault Clio Kain had rented. The Italians found it at Milan airport. Soon afterwards they reported to Halard that an American using the passport of one Edgar Bartlett had taken a Swissair flight from Milan to Geneva, paying for his ticket in cash.

Within two hours, the Swiss police reported that Bartlett had left from Geneva the following morning, taking Lufthansa's 7.20 a.m. flight to Frankfurt.

But the German police had no record of Bartlett's arrival.

It was at this point that Halard's faith she would find Red Kain began to weaken. 'What if he was in transit, and flew on somewhere else?' she asked.

Then there would be no immigration record, the Germans told her, since he had never officially entered the country. It took further calls to the minister's office before the German authorities agreed to obtain the passenger manifests for every international flight out of Frankfurt that day.

No record of any Bartlett, the Germans reported.

'So, he arrived but he never left,' Halard countered. 'Then he must have switched passports.'

Apparently.

Galvanised at last, the German police obtained the manifests for every incoming flight to Frankfurt and compared them with the outgoing lists. They checked them name by name until they found what they were looking for: a departing passenger who had materialised from nowhere.

'Herbert Kramer,' they reported to Halard. 'He called ahead and booked a seat on a KLM flight to Amsterdam. Picked up his ticket at the KLM desk in the transit lounge, paying cash.'

Carlson, Bartlett, now Kramer. One dead, one missing, one God-knows-what. Halard felt chilled as she called Brady and asked him to check with the State Department if a Herbert Kramer had been reported missing.

'Nothing so far,' Brady said when he called back an hour later. 'State's still checking, but it looks like Kramer's passport is fake. The question is, what's the Amsterdam connection? It all leads back to there.'

Halard had no answer. The Dutch police confirmed that Herbert Kramer had arrived at Amsterdam's Schipol airport, and passed through Immigration on an American passport. On his landing card he had written that he would be staying at the Hotel Pulitzer, but the Pulitzer had no record of him. Nor did any other hotel in the city. There was no record of him leaving Holland either.

Herbert Kramer, as she reported to Brady, had vanished.

'We'll find him,' Brady told her.

She knew he was not as confident as he tried to sound.

On a half-moon night *Symphonie* slipped into a deserted bay where Sanpiero Cabrini was waiting, his ancient truck hidden in the darkness.

'A girl?' he said when he saw Fiona, blindfolded, her hands tied, being led along the tiny landing stage. Antoine had said nothing about a girl. He thought of the journey ahead, along tracks where nothing else could pass, ending at a cliff path best suited to goats and men as sure-footed as he, which they would descend to where the next boat was waiting. Cabrini could not explain this to the three men who had come ashore for they would understand little of the patois he spoke. He shrugged: they would have to make the best of it. Perhaps the big one, the one the others called Jesus, would carry the girl down the steepest parts.

Jesus Fairley did indeed lift Fiona into the back of the truck, then did the same for Josh. He covered them with the sacking Cabrini had left there and warned them to be quiet, though they had not uttered a sound. Then he was speaking to the other men. One walked back to the dinghy that had ferried them to the landing stage and pushed off, rowing back towards the *Symphonie*, the white of its hull a glimmer in the light of the moon. Good, thought Cabrini; one less mouth to feed.

'Let's go.'

Cabrini was anxious to be moving. A difficult drive lay ahead, and afterwards he must report to Antoine that all had gone well: 'You must phone before dawn,' his cousin had said. Fairley nodded. 'Come on, Katz,' he said, and they climbed aboard the truck, the three of them wedged into the cabin, the boy and the girl behind. Cabrini's truck spluttered into life. Driving on his side-lights, he set off up the twisting track that climbed away from the shore and into the night.

The guileless face of Fiona Stewart stared up at Victor Canning, her expression caught somewhere between surprise and amusement. Her mouth was slightly parted and her hair was pulled back behind her ears, though wisps of it had escaped to catch the light. She looked younger than seventeen, Canning thought.

'Let me speak to Antony Palmer,' he said into the telephone.

British girl missing in Riviera riddle

Alongside the headline, the girl's picture occupied at least one third of the front page of the *Daily Express*.

'Mr Palmer's office,' a woman said.

'This is Victor Canning. Let me talk to him.'

'Ah, Mr Canning. I'm afraid Mr Palmer's in a meeting with a client. Shall I ask him to call you back?'

'Tell him it's important,' Canning said.

She hesitated before saying, 'Please hold the line, Mr Canning. I'll see what I can do.'

As he waited, Canning read the report again.

WORLD EXCLUSIVE
by JOHN SAIL
On the French Riviera

A BRITISH teenage girl, missing from a plush holiday hotel on the French Riviera for four days, is believed to have been kidnapped. Schoolgirl Fiona Stewart, from Islington, north London, was on holiday with her father when she vanished two days before her seventeenth birthday.

Also missing from the Hotel Le Bosquet on Cap Ferrat is Joshua Beaumont, the 16-year-old grandson of a Texas billionaire.

At first French police believed that the teenagers had run off together.

But then detectives learned that an American who suddenly checked out of the hotel on Sunday saying he had 'urgent business' in Paris, did not catch the flight he had booked.

The man, who used the name Mark Carlson, took a

taxi to Nice airport – and disappeared. And yesterday the mystery deepened when a body pulled from a canal in Amsterdam was identified as Mark Carlson, a computer software developer from Baltimore, Maryland.

Police believe that he was murdered two weeks ago, and that his passport was used by the 'Mark Carlson' who stayed at the hotel.

Last night, Fiona's frantic father, Tom Stewart, a 43-year-old writer, said: 'I'm convinced this man has taken my daughter. I don't know why, but I'll do whatever he wants to get her back.'

Full story – turn to pages 4–5

'Victor,' said a plummy voice. 'What can I do for you?'

'We need to meet.'

'Of course. Let me just get my diary.'

'This afternoon. Three thirty.'

'Victor, I'm sorry, but that's impossible. You see, I have this . . .'

'Outside Temple tube station on the Embankment. I'll pick you up.'

'How are you today?'

The stone-faced official at Washington's Dulles International airport ignored the question. He looked briefly at the man standing at his booth, then at the photograph in the well-worn passport he had proffered. He turned the passport face-down and passed it over the eye of an electronic scanner. Still tight-mouthed he watched his monitor while the computer of the US Immigration and Naturalization Service checked the passport's details against the 'Stop List' that was updated several times each day.

Thousands of names, furnished by a score of US government agencies, were on the INS 'Stop List'. On this particular day, they included Mark Carlson, Edgar Bartlett, Herbert Kramer, and Robert Michael Kain – all of them flagged with the Grade 1 instruction: 'Detain and inform FBI'.

But no agency had posted an alert for David Hinson, who – had he been asked – would have described himself as an expatriate geologist, resident in the Netherlands, and working as a consultant in the exploration for North Sea oil. He was tall, with sandy hair that fell over his forehead. There was a spot of gravy on his red tie. The left lapel of his crumpled beige suit sported a small pin that indicated he was a veteran of the US Marines.

'NO MATCH' appeared on the computer screen.

The official looked at the Amsterdam address Hinson had written on his Customs declaration form, where it asked for details of his permanent residence.

'Coming home, or visiting?' he asked.

'Just a visit.'

'Were you in Nam?'

'Four tours. Marines. Third Amphibious Force. You too?'

'Don't compare,' said the official, handing back the passport. 'Have a good day.'

Red Kain passed through Customs without hindrance.

In the arrivals terminal he found a bank of telephones and waited patiently for one to become free. He dialled a toll-free 1–800 number that answered with a bleep and he spoke four words.

In Los Angeles an unattended computer converted his words into a digital signal that was encrypted, then flashed by satellite to Zurich.

In seconds, a written message was waiting for collection in the electronic mailbox of RAVEN.

It said: RED BIRD HAS LANDED.

Part Three

16

Suzanne Beaumont was sitting on a stone wall on the edge of the main square in Le Cannet. Behind her, far below, Cannes was spread out like a map, with an abrupt transition from the gleaming white of its luxurious promenade hotels to the mirrored blue of the Mediterranean. The wall was crumbling and Le Cannet was grey and dusty, its shop-fronts fading like watercolours from another era. She stood up to meet Stewart as he crossed the square, moving through the green shadows cast by the plane tree that stood like a pillar at its centre. The sun was behind her, high above the glinting sea, silhouetting her body against her dress.

'Any luck?' she asked

'This place is a maze,' he told her. 'A bit like Villefranche. But I've found the street. I didn't go all the way down, but it looks as though he lives above a bicycle shop.' She smoothed her dress and brushed her fingers through her hair, so that it briefly flared as it caught the sun.

'You really think this is going to work?'

'Remember, he did offer to help,' Stewart replied.

'That was when he was trying to get a story out of you,' she said, archly. 'You of all people should know what journalists are like.'

'Except that now the story's even better.'

'Yes, but he can't write it. At least not while Kain's alive.'

'Unless . . .' He suppressed his thoughts long before he could put them into words.

'Unless what?' she said.

'Unless things don't work out,' he finally said.

He was relieved that she did not press him to spell out what he meant.

The street was lined with tall, narrow houses. The window of the cycle shop contained a parade of multi-coloured singlets and Spandex shorts. On an adjoining door-jamb, displayed in a neat brass frame with a perspex cover, was a business card that read: '*John Sail, Journaliste*.' There was no bell. The door swung open at Stewart's touch to reveal a steep flight of stairs covered in worn linoleum. At the top was a more substantial door with a bell-push to the side. The distant strains of a violin – Vivaldi? Albinoni? – came from within.

'Ready?' Stewart asked.

Suzanne nodded and he pressed the bell.

Sail displayed only a moment's surprise. 'What an unexpected pleasure,' he said, as he opened the door. 'Were you just passing?'

'In a way,' said Stewart. 'I tried calling but you were out.'

'Mrs Beaumont, I presume?'

Suzanne offered her hand. Sail lifted it to his lips and applied a light kiss. 'Your timing is immaculate,' he said. 'I'm about to make coffee.'

With an elaborate flourish, Sail beckoned them inside. The apartment – they were evidently in his living room – was larger than Stewart had expected. In one corner, the equipment of a busy overseas stringer – a small early-model computer, a fax machine and two telephones – sat on a large walnut desk. Another corner had been converted into a kitchen, with glass-fronted cupboards, a rack of herbs and spices, and a line of cooking pans hanging from a beam, ordered according to their size. At one end of a countertop stood a chrome Italian coffee-maker.

In a third corner was a hi-fi with an opalescent display screen that flickered in step with the cadences of what proved to be Vivaldi. The wall alongside was lined with books: dictionaries, atlases, directories, an array of hardbacks in English and French. Stewart saw his photograph of Fee, occupying almost half the front page of the *Daily Express*, resting on a filing cabinet. Already neatly clipped, it was evidently waiting to be mounted in Sail's cuttings-book. Sail caught Stewart's glance.

'Any news?'

'Nothing,' said Stewart.

'On either of them?'

'No,' said Suzanne.

'I'm sorry to hear that,' said Sail. 'Look, won't you sit down?'

He pulled back a rattan chair beside his dining table and held it for Suzanne before attending to the coffee machine. Stewart looked along Sail's shelves and found one of his own books: an account of an American climbing expedition which, at the behest of the CIA, had attempted to install surveillance equipment directed at China on a Himalayan summit. Neither the attempt, nor his book, had been particularly successful. He held the book up for Sail to see.

'I'm flattered,' he said.

'I enjoyed it, Tom. You must be sure to sign it before you leave.' The coffee was under way and Sail joined Suzanne at the table.

'To what do I owe this pleasure?'

Stewart sat down next to Suzanne. 'The last time we met, you offered me your help. We'd like to take up your offer. If you meant it, of course.'

'Of course I meant it, old boy. Man of my word, and all that. What can I do?'

'First we have to get some things straight. I'm going to tell you everything we know about our children's kidnapping. But you can't use any of it until we say so. And you may never be able to use it at all. Exactly why will become clear. Is that a deal? We can only go ahead if we're sure we can trust you.'

'Glad you mentioned trust, Tom. Because you weren't exactly straight with me last time, were you? Only told me the bits you wanted me to know. I won't say you lied, exactly, but you were pretty economical with the truth, as the noble Lord Armstrong put it. You forgot to mention this chap Kain. You said nothing about your book. And you said you didn't know why your children had been kidnapped.'

'You've been talking to your police source again,' said Stewart wearily. 'You probably know more about all this than I do.'

'Come, come, Tom. You're exaggerating. But one does try to stay informed. The point is, I'm ready to help, just so long as you level with me. I could have got egg all over my face last time. I can't afford to take that risk again.'

'I am going to level with you. But you must agree to our terms.

You can't use anything we tell you until we say so, even if that means never at all. It all depends how things work out.' Stewart paused. 'Let's be clear what's at stake here. We're talking about our children's lives.'

From behind Sail, there was a hiss. 'Coffee time,' he said. 'Espresso okay?' He busied himself at the counter before returning with a tray bearing three steaming porcelain cups.

'Do we have a deal?' persisted Stewart.

'Yes we do. Nothing in print until you give the word. Now tell me how I can help.'

Stewart did not tell Sail everything. But he found Sail's listening mode so beguiling – relaxed in his chair, eyes moving from his to Suzanne's – that, even though he recognised a fellow-journalist's tricks, he revealed more than he had intended. He began by saying that no longer did this appear to be a straightforward kidnapping. Six days had passed since the children had vanished, and still there was no ransom demand.

'That's why we think it must be to do with my book' – Sail nodded in encouragement – 'and Kain must want it stopped. I'm ready to give him what he wants' – Sail nodded again – 'and we want to get a message to him to that effect.'

'Saying what, precisely?' asked Sail.

'I'll abandon the book and give him all my files, film and research notes. Just so long as we get the children back.'

'Are you serious?'

'Absolutely.'

'Would I be right in thinking that the good Commissaire Halard is not entirely *au fait* with what you have in mind?'

'You would.'

'Meaning that you intend to go it alone from now on?'

'Exactly. So you can see how much trust we are placing in you.'

'But I still don't see how I can help. What is it you want me to do?'

'We want your help in reaching Kain.'

Sail pursed his lips. 'Well, I do pride myself on my contacts. But I don't have an inside track to kidnappers. Not as far as I know.'

Stewart leaned forward. 'Johnny, you just might have, at least if what the police told us is correct. What Halard said, and she told us it came from the FBI, is that Kain works the Golden Triangle. He's up to his neck in heroin.'

There was a long exhalation from Sail, as if a mystery had been unveiled.

'To get right down to it,' Stewart continued, 'Kain is supposedly a major dealer in morphine base, and he works with a group of traffickers in Marseille. The police are convinced the only way he could have staged the kidnap here is with local help. And who could have provided that, other than the people he already knew? That's why we came to see you. With all your contacts, can you suggest some names? Who are the players here? Who could have given Kain the help he needed?'

Sail leaned back in his chair. 'I have to say it all makes sense.'

'And you can help us?' asked Suzanne.

'Let's take a look.'

He crossed to a bank of filing cabinets next to his work-desk. Taking a bunch of keys from his pocket, he unlocked one of the cabinets and eased open the top drawer. It was bulging with folders. 'They're all here,' said Sail. 'The suppliers, the dealers, the traders, the mules.'

He pulled open the second drawer. 'This one's got the lawyers, prosecutors and defenders, some of them straight, some of them bent. It's got the cops, in the same categories, and the politicians too. There's no lack of those.'

'It looks like a life's work,' said Suzanne.

'I've been on their trail for years. I've been writing about them, too. The odd piece here and there, keep the story moving, but nothing too risky yet. When I'm ready to write the big one, I'll go for it. Then it'll be time to leave.'

'You mean leave Le Cannet?' asked Stewart.

'France, more like.'

'If you had to take a punt on Kain's French connection, who would you choose?'

Sail pulled the thickest file from the top drawer. 'If you're talking about heroin from the Golden Triangle, there's one man at the top of the heap.' He laid the file on the walnut desk. 'Go on, take a look.'

The first item in the file was a photograph of a thick-set man in his late fifties, with heavy features, a bulbous nose, and hair which had receded on each side, leaving a quiff marooned in the centre of his head.

'Meet Antoine Cabrini,' Sail said.

'Tell us about him,' Suzanne said.

'How much do you want to know?'

'The headlines will do to start with,' said Stewart. 'You're good at those.'

'I'll do my best,' said Sail. 'Antoine Cabrini controls the heroin trade in Marseille, or most of it. His family is old Corsican *milieu*, who arrived here two generations ago and were still fresh off the boat when they started running whores on the Marseille waterfront. In those days it was fixing, enforcing, loan-sharking, all the usual stuff. After the war the Cabrinis won themselves brownie points by red-bashing – busting strikes, beating up Communist dock workers, that sort of thing. Then they got respectable, or appeared to, by starting an international freight company. It's called Cabrini et Fils. It's the perfect front.'

'Where's it based?' asked Stewart.

'Marseille, down by the docks. Cabrini's got a huge depot there. You should take a look. The set-up's ideal. It enables Cabrini to launder money through the business. It puts a lot of dirty business his way too.'

'How so?' asked Suzanne.

'Cabrini goes in for a lot of load-sharing. I'll tell you how it's done. Let's say we're both running freight companies. You've got lorries, I've got lorries. You're in Marseille, I'm in Hamburg. I've got a load for the south of France but nothing to take back, so you find me a load. I do the same for you in Germany. Cabrini does it with at least a hundred other companies from all over Europe. It's called consolidating. That's the legitimate part.'

Sail was pacing the room as if the caffeine had shot him full of energy.

'Cabrini's got huge lorries coming into his depot twenty-four hours a day, seven days a week. Now and again his crew select a lorry that's been parked up overnight and do a little engineering work. They weld an extra panel inside the trailer, slap on some paint, and knock in a few dents so that it matches the rest of the interior. That gives them a secret compartment that's virtually undetectable, short of tearing the lorry to pieces. And before welding it shut, they pack it with heroin. Maybe the driver knows, maybe he doesn't. What matters is that Cabrini never does it to one of his own trucks. They're all clean. But he's still shipping heroin all over Europe.'

'Including Britain?'

'No question. In fact, it's my belief that Cabrini's main partner is a Brit. Of course, we've still got border controls on our side of the Channel, but with thousands of lorries pouring across every day, those poor saps in Customs haven't got a chance of spotting the dodgy ones. It's needle-in-haystack time.'

'Don't the police know all this?' Suzanne asked.

'Of course they do. But Cabrini's a ruthless bastard who doesn't mind shutting people up, one way or another, if they're a threat. He's also good at covering his tracks, and the police have never been able to come up with enough evidence to put him away. But you can take it from me that there's no doubt what he's up to. If Kain really is a major player in the business, the chances are Cabrini's your man.'

'How do we meet him?' Suzanne asked.

'I wouldn't say Cabrini was a creature of habit,' said Sail. 'But for a mafia boss he can be surprisingly predictable – which probably shows how secure he feels. He has a weakness for lunch by the Old Port – especially when it's the oyster season, like now. If we're to find him anywhere, it'll be there.'

'You mean you'll take us to him?' Stewart asked.

'Well, I've got to be a bit careful, old boy. Cabrini's getting rather sensitive to my poking about in places he doesn't want me to look. But you'll need me to point him out.'

There was a gold-and-glass carriage clock on Sail's desk. 'Just coming up to ten,' he said as he locked the file back in the cabinet. 'We should make it there by one, provided the old girl doesn't play up on me.'

'Old girl?' asked Suzanne.

'The Jaguar.'

'We've got a hire car,' said Suzanne. 'We can go in that.'

'I insist,' said Sail. 'It won't take a moment to fetch her. It does her good to get the cobwebs out of the system. About time she went for a spin.'

* * *

Suzanne settled back against the tan leather upholstery of Sail's Jaguar as it joined the Nice – Marseille autoroute. There was a battered Panama hat with a diagonal pink and green band on the back shelf. 'Great car,' she said. 'You must take good care of it.'

'Not bad, is she?' Sail turned his head so he spoke from the side of his mouth. Suzanne, who was in the back seat, had warmed to him, once she had decoded his elaborate linguistic mannerisms and decided to accept his dated courtesies at face value: there was clearly more to this seemingly mercenary British hack than he cared, at first, to convey.

'Weber carbs,' said Sail.

'Excuse me?'

Sail chuckled. 'Weber carburettors. Twelve of them. I had the engine rebuilt at a little place near Goodwood. Twin overhead cams, hand-forged high-compression pistons, 160 brake horsepower.'

'I'm impressed,' said Stewart.

'I've no idea what you're talking about,' said Suzanne.

She saw Sail's gloved hands ease the steering wheel as he pulled out to overtake a line of trucks. The engine surged as the speedometer on the walnut fascia flickered close to 100 mph. 'What a trouper,' said Sail. 'Thirty years old, and still one of the best.'

Some two hundred metres behind, an anonymous grey Peugeot joined the Jaguar in the outside lane. When Sail crossed back to the centre lane, the Peugeot followed suit.

17

Stewart's eyes were watering as he climbed out of the Jaguar. There was no air conditioning in the car park and blue exhaust fumes were mingling with the clammy heat. He was first up the stairs, breathing heavily by the time he reached the street. A pair of motor scooters surged past him, their engines racing. On the far side was an array of masts, rising from the yachts and launches moored in the harbour.

'I don't think we should rush this,' said Sail, as he emerged from the exit. He was wearing the Panama hat, and Suzanne was a step or two behind. 'I'm rather keen that Cabrini doesn't spot me. We'll try Le Mistral first.'

He steered them into a lane between high buildings that was lined on both sides with restaurants. Each had a narrow terrace marked out with tables and awnings, and a menu mounted on a stand at the entrance. Stewart spotted the name 'Le Mistral' on a sign ahead.

'I wonder if they've got *belons*,' said Sail.

'What are they?' asked Suzanne.

'The finest oysters in Europe, my dear. They're harvested in Brittany and they're down here six hours later, thanks to the TGV. Tell you what, Tom. Why don't you go past first and see if you can spot him?'

Stewart recalled the bulbous nose and quiff of hair from the photograph Sail had shown him. There was no one like that at the tables outside Le Mistral but inside, with his back to the window, sat a man alone with a balding head. Stewart stopped to peruse the menu.

'A table, monsieur?' A waiter was smiling effusively.

'Do you have one inside?' Stewart asked.

'Of course, monsieur.'

He followed the waiter until he got a better look at the lone eater. His nose was slim and the front of his head was devoid of hair.

'Sorry,' said Stewart to the waiter. 'I've changed my mind.'

Sail and Suzanne were waiting beyond the restaurant. 'Nothing doing,' said Stewart. Further along the lane was a mustard-coloured awning bearing the emblem 'Chez Paul'. 'Can you see what I can see?' Sail asked.

A blackboard positioned beside the entrance was chalked: '*Belons*'. 'Let's stroll past together,' Sail proposed. As they did so, Stewart glimpsed a middle-aged man sitting in a corner of the terrace, his back against the wall. When he tried to see the man's face, his view was blocked by a young man in a loose-cut linen suit.

'Keep going,' hissed Sail. 'Turn right at the top.'

Another waiter beckoned as they turned the corner. 'Table for three? Are you English? We have very good bouillabaisse.'

'*Non merci*,' said Sail, taking a step away. 'It's him.'

'At the back of the terrace?' asked Stewart.

'The very same. Are you sure you want to go through with this?'

Stewart looked at Suzanne who nodded.

'We're sure.'

'I'm going to take my leave of you,' Sail said. 'I think one of Cabrini's goons may have spotted me and it won't do you any good if he sees you with me. When you've finished here, why not make your way to the Café de Rome? It's on the other side of the harbour and the grub's decent enough. I'll look for you there in a couple of hours. I'll be in the old girl. Keep an eye out for me as I won't be able to park.'

'Are you sure you don't mind hanging around?'

'Don't worry, I've plenty to do. See a man about a dog, that sort of thing. One final piece of advice – don't push Cabrini too hard. He's on a short fuse at the best of times.'

Sail shook hands with Stewart and Suzanne. Stewart saw his Panama bobbing down the street in the direction of the car park.

'What a character,' said Suzanne.

'He's certainly a one-off,' said Stewart.

Cabrini was at a circular table, his back to the wall. An oval platter had been placed before him, fringed with seaweed and containing a dozen oyster shells, some already emptied, others awaiting his attention. There was a bottle of Chablis alongside. Two young men occupied the next table, which was bare but for a bottle of mineral water and two glasses. One was wearing a cream linen suit. As Stewart and Suzanne approached, he stood and blocked their path.

'Mr Cabrini,' said Stewart, over the guard's shoulder. 'Could we talk to you?'

Cabrini looked at Stewart, then at the bodyguard, making a sideways motion with his head. The bodyguard ran his hands down Stewart's jacket, patting the sleeves and pockets, and felt his legs, from his crotch to his ankles. He pointed to Suzanne's shoulder bag. She handed it to him and he placed it on the table. The guard stood aside.

Cabrini was squeezing a lemon over an oyster, which contracted as the juice hit. He eased it out of its shell with a fork and slurped it into his mouth. He savoured it before swallowing, then wiped his lips with a white linen napkin.

'Do I know you?' he asked.

'You don't. But I believe we have a mutual acquaintance. In Bangkok.'

Cabrini's eyes roamed over the platter. 'I don't know anyone in Bangkok.' His fork was poised as he contemplated his next choice.

'I'm talking about Red Kain,' said Stewart.

Cabrini's fork was descending on the platter. It seemed to hesitate as Stewart spoke, before plunging towards Cabrini's selection.

'Who?'

'Kain,' said Stewart. 'Red Kain.'

'I don't know any Kain.' Another oyster was on its way towards Cabrini's mouth.

'Perhaps you know him under another name,' said Stewart. 'I need to get a message to him. Can you help?'

Cabrini swallowed and looked briefly at Stewart before returning his attention to the platter.

'You see, Monsieur Cabrini, I have something which belongs to him, and he has something which belongs to us.'

Another oyster was liberated from its shell.

'What I'd like you to tell him is that I have no further interest in his property. I just want to make sure he gets it back.'

Another slurp, another swallow.

'I can guarantee that it reaches him safely. In return, we want our property back. All we're proposing is an exchange of goods. It's as simple as that.'

Cabrini wiped his lips again and took a mouthful of Chablis. 'Who are you?'

'My name is Stewart, Tom Stewart. This is Mrs Beaumont.'

'You're speaking in riddles,' Cabrini said. 'I have no idea what you're talking about and I don't know this Red Kain.'

'What about Carlson?' asked Suzanne. 'Does that name ring a bell?'

There was one oyster left. Cabrini readied his fork.

'Please,' said Suzanne. 'Whatever he calls himself. All we're asking is that you pass on our message.'

'I am sorry, madame, you're wasting your time. And mine.'

'One more thing,' said Stewart. 'Just tell him that I'm no longer interested in Vietnam. I don't care what happened and I'm not going to write the book.'

Despite himself, Stewart could sense his voice rising. Cabrini's fork was descending towards the platter. 'They're leaving now,' he said. There was the scraping of chairs as the two bodyguards stood up. The final oyster disappeared into Cabrini's mouth.

'Just tell him it's over,' said Stewart. 'He's won. He doesn't need to do anything more.'

The man in the linen suit handed Suzanne her shoulder bag. As he stood aside, the waiter arrived with a second platter of oysters. Cabrini took another swallow of Chablis and asked for more lemons.

'Six, this is One. What's going on?'

'Nothing, One. I think Owl's ordered something to eat. We could be here for the duration.'

'Don't fall asleep.'

'Roger, One.'

Inspector Desiry placed the short-wave radio on the passenger seat of his car, then picked it up again. 'All units, that applies to you lot too. Stay alert.'

One by one the units briefly acknowledged the order. Desiry settled back in his seat and forced himself to concentrate on the flow of traffic grinding along the Quai du Port.

On his instructions, the surveillance was mostly blind. Only one detective from Unit Six, equipped with a camera and a telephoto lens, could see the targets and anyone who might approach. The other units had been placed out of sight around the area, ready to pick up the targets no matter which direction they headed.

'One, this is Six. Tomcat's having a beer.'

Now there was a good idea. Desiry could do with one himself. His eyes drifted from the road to the harbour. The day had lost its sheen under the relentless assault of traffic fumes, and the water was a flat, grey calm, with patches of oil spreading rainbows across its surface. His mobile phone warbled. It was Halard, as brisk as ever.

'Any developments, inspector?'

'Nothing so far. They're still at the café. We're taking pictures but nobody's gone near them except the waiter.'

'I've got some more information on Sail.'

'Go ahead.'

'He's accredited by the Ministry of the Interior as a correspondent for the British *Daily Express*. He's been here for the last seven years. Nothing against him on file.'

'Hardly likely to be one of Kain's people, then?'

'Probably not. But he did lead them to Cabrini – so long as you're absolutely sure it was Cabrini they met.'

'No question. I'd know that face anywhere.'

'So, Sail knows Cabrini, and Cabrini certainly knows Kain. It looks to me as if Stewart is trying to cut a deal with Kain.'

'Could be, but I'll tell you something else. He's wearing chinos and a short-sleeved shirt. There's no way he's packing a Colt .45. Unless it's in the woman's bag.'

'Inspector, I doubt very much that he's brought the gun into France.'

'Then how's he going to give it back to Kain?'
'That's one of the things you're there to find out.'
The radio crackled. 'This is Six. Owl's gone inside. I think she's gone to the toilet, but I'm just going to wander over and make sure she's not chatting to anyone.'
'Roger, One. Make it casual.'
'Will do.'
'Owl?' queried Halard.
'Owl and Tomcat,' said Desiry. 'Their codenames. Seemed to fit, especially him. What a prick. What did he think Kain was going to do when he found out about the gun? Give him an interview? "You've got me cold. What would you like to know?" Jesus!'
'Mr Stewart is a risk-taker, apparently.'
'He's an idiot is what he is. Why didn't he tell us?'
'He thinks the gun is what he can trade for his daughter's life.'
The radio crackled again. 'This is Six. Everything's cool.'
'I'll let you get on, inspector,' Halard said. 'Keep me informed of any developments.'
'Count on it. Where are you Six?'
'Heading back for my O.P. She didn't make contact with anybody. And I was right. It's feeding time for Owl.'
'Lucky for some,' said Desiry.

Without enthusiasm, Suzanne contemplated an *andouillette* that had burst from its skin, spilling its innards among the *pommes frites*. 'Is that what you ordered?' asked Stewart.
'I'm not sure.'
Stewart turned in his chair to search for the waiter.
'Don't bother, Tom. I'm not hungry, anyway.' She pushed the plate to one side and took a mouthful of orange juice. 'At least this is fresh. And cold.'
Stewart smiled and sipped his beer.
'Don't you think . . . ?'
She left the question unfinished. Since leaving Chez Paul, they had endlessly reviewed their audience with Cabrini, trying to make sense of what he had and hadn't said; reading into it what they hoped it might have meant, or feared it didn't. Did Cabrini really not know Kain? Or was he just protecting

himself? And if he did know Kain, had he understood the message? And would he pass it on? Always, it came down to the same thing: They didn't know. They had no way of knowing.

She tried again. 'It was the way he hesitated when you first mentioned Kain's name. Just for a second. Like he was . . . I don't know, surprised?'

'Or bewildered,' said Stewart.

'We're nowhere, aren't we?' she said. 'There's nothing we can do but wait.'

Stewart was silent for a moment. 'I was thinking,' he said. 'There is one thing.'

'Go on.'

'It's the British connection. Remember what Sail said. He hadn't quite pinned it down, but he knew Cabrini had a partner in London, and he thought he knew who it was. If I've got Sail right, he's probably closer than that, otherwise he wouldn't have mentioned it at all.'

'Maybe,' Suzanne said, without sounding convinced.

'Remember, I know the Johnny Sails of this world. When we meet up I think I should push him hard for the name of the British connection.'

'Then what?'

'I'll go to London and see him.'

'What's the point? If Cabrini doesn't know Kain, there's even less reason anyone in London should know him.'

'I know it's a long shot. But my instincts are saying London, London. I could get a plane this evening. Depending on what I find, I'll be back tomorrow night.'

Suzanne reached across the table. 'Oh Tom,' she said, taking his hand. 'It all seems so hopeless. It's like being on a desert island and sending off messages in bottles, and knowing that the chance of anyone finding them is non-existent. Or as good as.'

He squeezed her hand. 'I think the odds are better than that. Anyway, we've got nothing to lose.'

'What happens if Kain gets in touch while you're away?'

'I've got a mobile in London. You can call me any time and I'll be back on the next flight.'

She took away her hand.

'Do you really think Sail will give you the name?'

'We're about to find out.'

Sail's Jaguar was easy to spot as it edged along the quayside. The traffic had thickened, and he was making slow progress. 'Let's go,' said Stewart, depositing a two hundred franc note on the table. 'He won't be able to park.'

The Jaguar was less than fifty yards away on the far side of the road. Stewart saw Sail's anxious look as he searched for them among the pedestrians. He waved both arms above his head until Sail noticed him and drew to a halt, his emergency lights flashing as he signalled other cars to pass.

'He's seen us,' said Stewart. 'We can cross further up.' As they approached the Jaguar, Sail gave the thumbs-up sign. 'He looks in a good mood,' said Suzanne.

They were almost opposite the car, watching for a gap in the traffic. A space materialised as a lorry piled with fruit lumbered towards them, the cars behind fidgeting to pass.

'We can make it if we're quick,' said Stewart. As Sail reached across to open the front passenger door, Stewart saw he was wearing a yellow rose on his lapel he had acquired since they parted at Chez Paul.

A dark shape, little more than a silhouette, appeared in front of the lorry. There was a sudden, brittle roar. There was a rider wearing a smoked-glass visor, and another, his passenger, with a black, stumpy stick in his hand. There was a second roar, angry and staccato; a spurt of flame, the shattering of glass. There was a flash of colour, of yellow and red, of a rose and of blood, as Sail's smiling face slid from Stewart's view. Stewart felt paralysed, frozen, as his senses struggled to impose order on these tumultuous events.

'Suzanne . . . !'

The cry died in his throat as he was engulfed by a third roar, louder than the rest. A sheet of light seared across his retinas, a wall of sound slammed into him, reverberating through every limb.

Suzanne . . . He tried to shout again but the sound would not come. He was falling into space, a void with no beginning and no end.

* * *

Among the surveillance team, it was Desiry who had seen the Jaguar first.

'Six, this is One. He's eastbound on the quay. He's just passed my position, and you should have him any minute now. Could be he's going to pick them up.'

'Roger, One. Don't see him yet . . . Okay, they've seen something, they're getting up. Looks like Tomcat's paying the bill.'

'Heads up all units.' Desiry spoke urgently into his radio. 'Be ready to move.'

As the other units acknowledged his order, Desiry started his engine and watched in his mirror for the chance to make a U-turn.

'Got him, One. He's slowing down. Tomcat and Owl are up and moving, about to cross the road . . . I can't see them now, too many people, but he's definitely stopping for them . . . He's stopped . . . There's a lorry trying to get by . . . What the fuck! There's shooting! Someone's firing at them! From a motorbike!'

Desiry was halfway out of the car. 'All units, move in now. Move it!'

Two hundred metres ahead he could see the shape of a crouching man, with a stumpy stick in his hand. The stick was spurting flame at the Jaguar. An orange fireball laced with black smoke grew out of the back of the car and there was a dull thud.

'Oh, Jesus,' said Six. 'The car's gone up. They must have hit the tank.'

Desiry was running down the road. 'Owl and Tomcat,' he shouted into the radio. 'Where are they?'

'I can't see them.'

'Are they in the car?'

'I don't know. There are people down all over the place.'

Desiry could see that for himself. He had almost reached the wreckage when the Jaguar's second petrol tank exploded.

Even though the *pompiers* had doused the last of the flames, the wreckage of Sail's Jaguar radiated a heat that made Desiry, waiting at the harbour's edge, feel he was standing too close to a barbecue. The road surface around the Jaguar's skeleton had fused into ugly corrugations where it had first turned molten in the intensity of the blaze, and had then been cooled by the *pompiers'* hoses.

'Best give it another few minutes to cool down,' said one of the firemen, and Desiry nodded.

A siren wailed as an ambulance took the last of the casualties to hospital. The count, Desiry had reported to Halard, was seventeen injured. Mostly shock, cuts and bruises, but one woman had lost an arm, severed by flying glass. He dropped a half-smoked cigarette into the water and pulled the radio from his pocket.

'Five, this is One. What have you got?'

'Nothing so far. Still checking.'

Desiry grunted in response. Judging by the din of car horns the gridlock in the surrounding streets was becoming thicker – as was the crowd held behind the lines of yellow tape that cordoned off two hundred metres of the Quai du Port. He had never ceased to be amazed by the voyeurs who flocked to the scene of any disaster. 'Fucking ghouls,' he said.

'Say again?' said Unit Five.

'Nothing, Five. Four, any news?'

'We've checked every shop along the Canebière, and there's no sign of them. Nobody's reported seeing them, either. Doesn't look like they came this way – if they went anywhere. What do you want us to do?'

'Keep going.'

'How far?'

'Until I tell you to stop.'

'What about the car? Have you checked it yet?'

'Not yet.'

Not yet, but soon. Two firemen in silver protective suits were levering at the driver's door with a metal bar. The door gave way, and one peered inside. He beckoned to Desiry.

'One, this is Three.'

'Go ahead,' said Desiry, grateful for the excuse to delay.

'We're in the Place Sadi-Carnot. We've found a witness who saw a couple getting into a taxi a few minutes after the explosion. Could be them. Their clothes were scorched and the woman was limping. Sounds like they were pretty close to the car when it went up.'

The fireman was holding up the finger of one hand. One finger, one corpse – not two, not three.

'Any description of the taxi?' Desiry asked. 'The number?'

'You're joking, chief. White Mercedes, or maybe a BMW, is the best the witness can do.'

'Well, fucking find it. Get more witnesses. Find that taxi. Find out where they've gone.'

18

Their three coffee cups were still sitting on Sail's countertop. Funny of Sail, Stewart reflected. He was so meticulous, why didn't he wash them up? The banality of his thought caught him unawares. There is no Sail, only what was left in the wreckage on the quayside in Marseille. His hand was trembling as he pulled open a drawer beside Sail's sink.

'No knives in here,' he said to Suzanne. 'Where do you think he keeps them? Kept them?'

She opened Sail's fridge. 'We should drink something sweet. Juice, cola, anything.' Her hair was dishevelled, her face grimy, there was an ugly reddening on her arm and a livid graze on her knee. 'For the shock.'

'I can feel it taking hold.'

At first, as they headed out of Marseille in a taxi, they had been possessed by a supernatural calm, as if they were still in the eye of the storm.

'How did we get away?' Suzanne had asked.

He'd said his first fear was that she had been engulfed by the first explosion.

'The first? How many were there?'

'I think there were two. After the second one, I saw you lying on the pavement. How did you get there?'

'When Sail stopped, I couldn't reach the nearside door, so I went round behind a parked van. Pretty lucky, really. I must have been there when the car blew up. What happened to you?'

Stewart found it hard to explain. He had been about to cross the road when some sixth sense made him hesitate. 'I'm not quite sure. I think I knew something bad was about to happen. I must have run, or ducked. I know I heard both the bangs, and there was a monumental flash. I reached you just as you were trying to get up. I grabbed you and we ran until I saw this taxi.'

Their minds had stayed clear as they sped along the autoroute towards Cannes. *Who killed Sail? Was it Cabrini? Or Kain? Whoever it was, were they trying to kill them as well? And why? Because they were too close to the truth? The truth about what? Cabrini's heroin smuggling? Or the kidnapping?* The trouble was, none of it made sense, or took them closer to their children. The logic gradually imploded as the shock seeped through. Even as it did, they retained the clarity to make two key decisions. They had to go to London; but they had to get into Sail's apartment first.

'We must find the name of Cabrini's British connection,' Stewart had said. 'It should be in his files.'

'I don't want to leave here,' Suzanne protested. 'I still feel that Josh is here, or some part of him. I feel I'm deserting him, wherever he is.'

'I'm the same,' said Stewart. 'But we can't stay here. If we really were the targets, whoever did it may want another shot. Once we leave Sail's we'll go straight to the airport.'

'Shouldn't we go the hotel first? What about our things?'

'Too risky. Everyone knows we're staying there. The hotel can always send our stuff on. Have you got your passport?'

Suzanne looked in her shoulder-bag. 'It's here. Thank God you picked it up.'

'I've got my credit cards. We can buy something to wear on the way to the airport.'

The taxi had taken them to the square at Le Cannet. Stewart's rented car was still parked nearby. Breaking into Sail's apartment proved disconcertingly easy: Stewart used the old credit-card trick, sliding it into the lock in the manner once demonstrated by one of his more louche contacts. Sail had closed his filing cabinet before leaving that morning, and the key was presumably still in his pocket, or what remained of it. On top of it was Stewart's book about the CIA-backed mountaineering expedition which, he remembered with a pang of guilt, he had neglected to sign. Stewart found a stout knife in the cupboard above the counter top. He pushed it into the gap above the top drawer of the filing cabinet and levered it back. There was a sharp crack as the blade snapped.

'Bollocks,' he shouted. As he stooped to retrieve the blade, his hand started trembling again. He felt light-headed and sat on the floor.

'Are you okay?'

Suzanne emerged from Sail's bathroom. Her arm was redder than ever.

'I felt dizzy for a moment,' he said. 'You should put something on that.'

'I can't find his medicine cabinet.'

Suzanne went into Sail's bedoom. Stewart climbed to his feet and joined her. There was a three-quarter size bed, with more bookshelves above it. On a chest of drawers stood a photograph of a cricket team posing in their whites, with Sail at the end of the back row, his Panama hat – far less battered then – pushed back jauntily on his head.

'Of long ago,' said Stewart.

'Tom?'

'Sorry. Talking to myself. It's from a poem about cricket.'

'I keep thinking about the rose,' said Suzanne.

'Now you're not making sense either.'

'The one on his lapel. It wasn't there when he said goodbye.'

'I'd forgotten.'

She pulled open a cupboard. 'Got it,' she said, taking out a first-aid kit.

Stewart found a long-handled screwdriver in a tool-box at the back of a walk-in wardrobe. He returned to the filing cabinet, pushed the tip into the gap, and levered the screwdriver back and forth. The edge of the drawer buckled.

Suzanne came to join him. She had bandaged her arm and there was a large sticking-plaster on her knee. 'We'd better get a move on,' she warned.

'We can't leave without those files. Why don't you keep a look out?'

She stood beside the window, which gave her a view almost down to the square. Stewart eased the screwdriver along the drawer towards the lock and pulled it back. The drawer yielded slightly and he levered again, harder this time. He tumbled on to the floor and thought that the screwdriver must have broken. Then he saw the drawer hanging open above him.

'We're in!'

'Make it quick,' she said. 'Two men have just gone into the

bike shop. One had a piece of paper in his hand. It was as if they were looking for somewhere. Or someone.'

Stewart scanned the labels marking Sail's files. There it was: 'Cabrini, the British connection.' He opened the file and found a sheaf of typed notes. The first page began:

> Tel. Int. with RS, NSY, re VC/AC connection: May 19, '94. NOT for attrib.
> RS sd that AC/VC go back at least 15 yrs [79–80 – CHECK which]. VC had money problems due to over-rapid expansion after old man ret. AC supplied first load: Mars. – UK. Told RS word at this end was VC made 50g. from first run. RS said that sounded right. VC did 3 or 4 more runs using own lorries. Never carries stuff now . . .

'Look at this,' he said, going to the window.

She looked over his shoulder. 'What is it?'

'I'm not sure yet. But obviously AC means Antoine Cabrini, and it looks like VC is his British connection. It also looks as though the British cops know something about all this.'

'How can you tell?'

'NSY. Stands for New Scotland Yard. This means we can find him, Suzanne.'

'The cops will talk?'

'I know one who might. We go back a long way.'

'We have to get out of here.'

She had found a hold-all and he stuffed the file inside.

'I'll go first,' Suzanne said.

'When you get downstairs, head up the street away from the shop. The car's parked near the square. We can work our way round from the back.'

She opened the front door carefully, checked the street and beckoned him on. Stewart came down and pulled the door shut behind him. They walked quickly to the top of the street, where they paused to look back. Two men were pushing open Sail's front door.

Antony Palmer sat in the debilitating heat of the Howard Hotel Health Club, watching lines of sweat trickle down his torso.

They followed a switchback path, disappearing into the folds of his flesh, then welling up and emerging as they descended inexorably towards his private parts. There had been a time, at the start of his career, when Palmer had taken care to keep himself in trim. Twenty years on his body was no longer one to inspire proprietorial pride.

Another body settled on the slatted bench beside him. Victor Canning's stomach was flat, his muscles tight. Typical Victor, Palmer thought: maintaining body and mind in their taut, coiled state, a key part of his strategy of remaining in control. As their thighs briefly touched, Palmer shifted uneasily. He had wondered if Victor was homosexual, and concluded that he was not. He sensed instead that Victor liked to maintain this closeness, this almost insolent familiarity, to convey a message of threat.

Palmer waited. There was no greeting from Victor, for theirs was a relationship shorn of niceties. It had been that way almost from the start, when Victor had cut away the pomposities with which lawyers try to cloak themselves. On the first occasion they had sat in Palmer's panelled office in Chancery Lane – a five-minute step from the sauna they now shared – Victor had selected his target. Every man, Victor liked to say, had his price: the only question was where it was pitched. And Victor had found his.

'I need someone who will act for me in a wide variety of circumstances,' Victor had said.

'Of course, Mr Canning,' Palmer confidently responded. 'That is what we are here for.'

'I have a very broad range of business interests, and I want them taken care of.'

'Of course,' Palmer murmured.

'I need someone I can trust absolutely.'

'Mr Canning, trust is our watchword.'

'I am willing to pay the top price once I am certain I have found that person.'

Palmer's pulse quickened. Although he did his best to maintain his show of calm, he later knew that this was the moment he had given himself away. Remorselessly, Canning had homed in. He asked Palmer what hourly fee his firm charged. When Palmer replied that it was £150, Canning offered to pay £500. He also proposed that Palmer's firm should bill him for its official rate of £150. The remaining £350 would be delivered to Palmer in an envelope containing British banknotes – not new ones, Palmer would soon discover, but thumbed and worn, as if they had been used in a dozen or more transactions of varying degrees of propriety. Which was usually how it was.

Once Palmer had agreed, Canning knew he was hooked. That was because from the moment he started to cheat on his partners, he was complicit with Canning and would never be able to reveal what Canning had asked him to do. At first, that required him to set up companies which would help obscure the trail through Victor's labyrinthine affairs. Then it meant setting in motion the transfer of gargantuan sums of money around the globe, their origin long since obscured. In the end it meant doing whatever Victor stipulated, no matter what that entailed. Sometimes Palmer would talk to Canning in terms of receiving his instructions, as if that somehow freed him from responsibility for what Canning wanted him to do.

'Don't give me that shit,' Victor would respond. 'This is illegal. That's what I'm paying you for.'

And Palmer would not deny it, for he knew it was true.

What was it to be today? Palmer knew better than to ask. He had become used to Victor's silences at the sauna. One reason they met there, Victor explained, was so that he could cleanse his body of its poisons: he called it 'sweating out'. Victor's theory accorded with his business philosophy, which also had to be in order, with all dues paid, obligations met, and irritants purged.

'Lunt is cheating,' Canning said at last.

'I'm surprised to hear that. I thought all our wholesalers were on the level.'

Canning laughed. 'No one in this game is on the level. This one's been at it for some time.'

'How can you be sure?'

'I make it my business to be sure. Out of his last six loads, he claimed that four were under – anything between one and two pounds light.'

'It happens, doesn't it?'

'Yes, it happens. That's why I had him checked out. The last load was weighed half an hour before he took delivery. It was spot on. But he still said it was short. I want him taken care of.'

'A warning?'

'No more warnings.'

'An accident?'

'No accidents either. I want this absolutely clear to any other arsehole who thinks he's going to take me for a ride.'

'Are you sure about this? What about the risk?'

'Just do it the usual way. The cut-outs are all in place, aren't they? Just give the word. I want it done this weekend.'

'That soon?'

'He's got to pay for what he's done. I want to hear on Friday night that it's been arranged.'

'I'll call you.'

'No, no phones. I want the details. We'll make a meet.'

'The Rose and Crown?'

'Ten o'clock.'

A vein was throbbing in Palmer's temple. The steam in the sauna had thickened, and the heat had intensified. Palmer did not prolong the discussion: there was no point. Canning stood up, the sweat glistening on his back.

'It's fucking hot in here,' he said.

He was swallowed by the steam as he headed for the cold bath in the adjoining room. Palmer heard the splash as Victor dived in. Even though he felt faint with heat, he stayed where he was.

19

Sweet Thames, thought Suzanne. Sweet Thames, run softly . . . Run softly, as I end my song? From the window of Stewart's flat, beyond the roofs of the unlovely industrial buildings dumped there during the booming British eighties, she glimpsed a grey sliver of London's river, with a warehouse in the background. Was it really *as* Spenser ended his song? Or *till*? She couldn't remember.

She touched the bandage on her right arm: the scorched skin beneath was well-padded now. Tom had dressed it with unexpected expertise that morning. She had cleaned her grazed knee herself and in doing so had found an impressive number of bruises and tender places that were only just making themselves felt. 'Would you like to go to hospital?' Stewart had asked.

'And sit in casualty for hours waiting for an X-ray?'

'I'd forgotten you knew about the National Health Service,' said Stewart.

'I'll leave it for the moment. Let's see how I feel tomorrow.'

He told her he had located his police contact, a detective inspector working in one of the outer London divisions. They had arranged to meet for lunch.

'I'll call you as soon as I've seen him,' he assured her. 'Get as much rest as you can. I think you've been affected worse than me.'

Tom's work-station was set against the wall beside the window. Not much inspiration to be had from the view, Suzanne thought, but at least he could benefit from the natural light. His desk was neatly arranged, suggesting he was better-organised than he sometimes conveyed, and there was a filing cabinet marked 'Missing Project': the Vietnam book, she assumed.

One drawer was half-open: the files were labelled tidily, much like Sail's. She was suddenly assailed with the guilty recollection of how they had rooted through his belongings just two hours after he had died. 'Help yourself to anything you need in the kitchen,' Tom had said before going out. She found a box of tea-bags and turned on the kettle. The view from this side of the apartment was no more inspiring: a deserted railway line, some low terrace houses, and the gaunt shapes of monolithic office blocks. She took her tea back into the living room.

There were three photographs on a mantelpiece. One was the shot of Fee, framed in the same window Suzanne had just been looking from. The second had to be of Tom with his parents. He was around ten at the time, she guessed, wearing shorts, standing with a stern-faced man wearing wire-rimmed glasses and a woman in a floral hat.

The third was somewhat startling. Tom was standing alone on what was evidently a wintry mountaintop, for he was posing beside a cairn of stones that were encrusted with snow, while lines of white-capped peaks receded into the distance. At first she presumed that his climbing partner had taken the photograph, and wondered who he – or she – was. Then she realised he could equally have climbed the mountain by himself, and had set the camera shutter to delayed action while he struck his pose.

There were five books on the mantelpiece too, set between a pair of bookends made of polished black slate. One was the book Tom had spotted in Sail's flat, his tale of the Himalayan expedition suborned by the CIA. The other four were all by Tom too, and she realized that this display must represent his collected works. One was entitled *State of Shame*. She picked it out and read the tag-line on the cover: How the west stood by while a million died during Nigeria's civil war.

Next to it was *Divided they Stand*, about the Northern Ireland conflict in the 1970s. The fourth was called *Days of Rage*, and concerned the war in the Lebanon. The last had the title: *State of Terror: Augusto Pinochet, 1973–1989*. This was an American edition, evidently a second printing, for it carried admiring tributes on the dust jacket, as well as boasting that it had won a non-fiction prize in Britain. 'A searing revelation of US involvement in the downfall of Salvador Allende and the assassination of Chile's exiled dissidents', declared the *New*

York Times. The *Washington Post* called it 'a terrifying saga of murder, conspiracy and deceit'.

Suzanne felt embarrassed that she knew so little about Stewart's past. It was not that he was unduly modest: she had simply failed to enquire what else he had written, the Vietnam book aside. She realised he knew far more about her than vice versa, and wondered if being a writer gave him a shield: an excuse to ask other people about themselves, while not revealing anything of himself. It was at one with the casual charm Tom had deployed when he introduced himself at Nice airport and proposed that they share a taxi to Le Bosquet.

It had crossed her mind at the time that this might be a predatory move, that perhaps he operated on instinct whenever a halfway presentable woman crossed his path. Such musings had been overwhelmed by the astronomical chance – if that is what it was – which had decreed their children should be abducted together. But even now, if someone asked her to compose his *curriculum vitae*, she would be pushed to write more than half a dozen lines.

She still had his last book, the Pinochet investigation, in her hand. She turned it over and saw his photograph on the back. He was sporting the scar on his cheek, which looked fresher than now. She turned inside the back cover, and there it was: the CV she needed.

'Tom Stewart,' the American publisher's blurb declared, 'is one of England's most outstanding writers and investigators. Born in Reading, Berkshire, his father was a doctor, his mother a teacher. After studying at Oxford University, he proceeded via a stint at a regional newspaper on to Fleet Street, focus of Britain's newspaper industry. While a staffer at the London *Sunday Times*, he had assignments in Africa, Northern Ireland, the Middle East and Latin America, while penning acclaimed titles on a diverse array of topics of contemporary global concern. His off-duty activities include trekking and back-packing. He was married in 1973 and has a daughter he adores. This is his fifth book.'

Not much immodesty there, Suzanne thought. Or grammar, come to that. She placed the book on the living-room table, next to the file of papers Stewart had grabbed from Sail's apartment. She picked up the first sheet and took it to the sofa that ran along one wall of the living room, reading again the enigmatic notes Stewart had shown her in Sail's apartment.

> Tel. Int. with RS, NSY, re VC/AC connection: May 19, '94. NOT for attrib.
> RS sd that AC/VC go back at least 15 yrs [79–80 – CHECK which]. VC had money problems due to over-rapid expansion after old man ret. AC supplied first load: Mars. – UK. Told RS word at this end was VC made 50g. from first run. RS said that sounded right. VC did 3 or 4 more runs using own lorries. Never carries stuff now.
> AC was orig. consolidator for C snr. providing legit loads . . .

Suzanne yawned. Her strength seemed to be ebbing and she remembered Tom's advice to take things easy, rest up all day if she liked.

Tel. Int.

Tel for Television? Telegraph? Telephone?

Int for Integrated? Intermediary? Internal?

She felt her eyelids becoming heavy and rested her head on the back of the sofa. The paper fell from her hand.

When the telephone rang, she could have been anywhere: London, Nice, Austin, she had no idea.

'How are you?' enquired Stewart. She remembered she was in London.

'Not too bad,' she said.

'Did I wake you?'

'Sort of. I was only dozing. You weren't to know. How are you making out?'

'Not very well. My man didn't show. I called his station and found he'd had to go out on a job.'

'So where are you, exactly?'

'Harrow. It's miles out of town.'

'And we're no nearer knowing who VC is? Or RS, come to that?'

'That's right.'

'How much longer are you going to wait?'

'I'll stick around for another couple of hours.'

* * *

Detective Chief Superintendent Raymond Skinner, head of the Criminal Intelligence section at Scotland Yard, sat at a desk that was as neat as he was, and said to his sergeant, 'So what have you told the French?'

'I stalled, guvnor. Said we'd check the files and get back to them. She's not happy.'

Sergeant Bert Humphries was considered by some of his superiors at the Yard to be slow-witted, as well as profane, which was why, edging towards retirement, he remained a detective sergeant. But he had other qualities, of which one was absolute loyalty – a virtue much valued and encouraged by Ray Skinner.

Skinner brought together the tips of his manicured fingers to form a steeple under his nose. On his desk lay the 'Most Urgent' fax from Commissaire Dominique Halard that had arrived at Scotland Yard overnight. It had been directed to Skinner because it contained the name and date of birth of Antoine Cabrini. In the central computer of the National Criminal Intelligence Service, Cabrini's name was flagged, which meant that any inquiries about him were to be referred without fail 'to DCS Skinner, CIS'.

The fax was five pages long, written in fluent if Americanised English, and set out succinctly the events surrounding the disappearance and 'probable abduction' of Fiona Stewart and Joshua Beaumont. It described the urgent but so far unsuccessful attempts to locate both a yacht named *Symphonie* and the chief suspect, one Robert Michael Kain. Kain's apparent motive for the kidnapping was also described, as was Halard's belief that Stewart was attempting to contact Kain to negotiate a deal for the safe return of the children – a deal that probably included handing over a gun Kain had used in a murder.

Stewart's possession of the gun, Halard had written, was only one of the items he had failed to mention to the police – and only one of the reasons she described him as a 'non-cooperating witness'. For that reason she had placed him under surveillance in the hope that he would lead the police to Kain. Her fax frankly admitted how that strategy had failed – and in a somewhat dramatic fashion. Here, Halard had described the murder of John Sail, including the gory details that had been omitted from that morning's edition of the

Daily Express, with its headline: 'Express man dies in Riviera blast'.

'Poor bastard,' Humphries had remarked to his boss. 'Still, no one can say you didn't warn him.'

'More than once,' Skinner had replied.

The French team had lost track of Stewart and Mrs Beaumont, finally learning from a check of the passenger lists at Nice airport that they had gone to London. But not before they had broken into Sail's apartment and removed documents – moments before the police arrived – from a section marked 'British Connection' in Sail's filing cabinet.

Halard was therefore as certain as she could be that the couple had flown to England in a continuing attempt to contact Kain, through this British connection.

She had ended her fax with two urgent requests. First, that Scotland Yard make immediate inquiries to establish if Kain and/or Cabrini had criminal associates in the United Kingdom. Second, that Stewart and Mrs Beaumont be located and placed under immediate covert surveillance.

'Is Kain in the computer?' Skinner asked.

'The FBI sent us an advisory on him in '94, and he was put on the immigration watch list, but nothing specific. He's never been here, so far as we know.'

'And nothing to link him to our man?'

'Nothing at all. But there's not much doubt who Stewart is looking for, is there sir?'

Skinner placed Halard's fax in the top drawer of his desk and locked it. 'Keep stalling, sergeant. If she asks, tell her we're still trying to locate Stewart and Beaumont. Then take a run out to his Wapping address, and see if there's any sign of them. Just you. I don't want you mob-handed. See if they go anywhere. But, if they go south of the river, break off. Is that clear?'

'Loud and clear, sir.'

'What's the word on Palmer?'

'He's shitting himself, as per usual. Called me on my beeper twice last night. Wanted reassurance that we're not going to feed him to the lions. I told him, "Tony, it's entirely up to you. You keep your side of the bargain; we'll keep ours." He's a fucking windy bugger.'

'Aren't they all,' said Skinner.

20

Slowly, she was beginning to get the hang of it, beginning to decipher Sail's abbreviations and his convoluted prose style. The second page of his notes began:

> VC definitely major player in the UK, bt. also invlvd. in some of AC's deals. RS mentioned Belg., Holl. and Grmny. as for-examples. And the States.

VC: undoubtedly Cabrini's British connection – but more than that if RS was right. RS seemed very sure of his assertions, and very talkative for a cop. Suzanne wondered if RS always spoke to reporters so freely. And if Tom could find him, would he help?

It was gone five, and there had been no further word from him all afternoon. No news was good news – or just no news? She told herself to concentrate and went back to studying the notes.

> VC's ultra careful – unlike AC. Not extrav. Modest lf. styl.. Lives within legit. income. Pays taxes, etc. Drives same car as RS: Dark blue Ford Mondeo, two yrs. old. Gives to charity: sick kids, hosptls., so forth. Was member of same Rotary Club as RS for 2–3 years in late 80s. [GET DATES!] Comes across as Mr. Ideal Citizen. Vry. convincing front. RS: 'If you met him, you'd never guess what a bastard he really is – never in a thousand years.' Giveaways? RS: 'His eyes. They're dead.'

On a pad she had found on Tom's desk, Suzanne added the details of VC's car.

Askd. if VC/AC ever met in Lndn.
RS: 'From time to time,' but they're ultra careful.

RS said the last time he was aware of was 'about six months ago' [CHECK: SEP. '95? DATES OF PREVIOUS MEETS?] when AC came to Lndn. with his wife. Stayed at Selfridges Hotel for three nights and met VC at Quaglino's [CHECK SPLL!] restaurant [IN SOHO?] for lunch. Sd 'nothing worth listening to'. Went for a walk in Hyde Pk. where the mikes couldn't pick them up.

AC never makes ph. calls to VC's home and has never visited there, so far as RS knows. RS pretty sure about that bec. VC never allows any of his assocs. there: 'His home is his fortress,' and so forth.

Askd. if AC had ever been to VC's airport place?

RS sd yes, 3 or 4 times in past 8 years. Didn't worry VC since he and AC were in the same legit. biz. RS sd they were 'very visible' about their legit. assoc. because it provided perfect cover.

In the margin, there was a tiny three-word handwritten note she could not make out. She took it to the window but even in the natural light all she could read was the last word: 'Rd.'

Another of Johnny's abbreviations? Short for Road? VC's address? If so, the address of his fortress home? Or his airport place?

She was searching for something to magnify the note on Tom's desk when the front door opened. For a moment she froze, then Stewart called: 'Hi, I'm back.' He came into the living room carrying two supermarket bags. Although he smiled she sensed there was something wrong.

'What is it?'

'I've wasted the entire the afternoon in some grotty pub, waiting for my contact to turn up.'

'What happened to him?'

'I've no idea. I'll have to try again tomorrow.'

She knew that wasn't all that was troubling him. He dumped the supermarket bags on the kitchen table and strode to the balcony where he leaned out trying to see the street below.

'What is it?' she asked again.

'Nothing. I'm probably just being paranoid.'

She joined him on the balcony. 'You want to share it with me? You're making me pretty nervous.'

'When I came in just now, there was somebody sitting outside in a car. I walked right past him. When I looked back, he wasn't there.'

'You mean the car had gone?'

'No, just the driver. There was no sign of him. He must have ducked beneath the dashboard.'

She suddenly felt afraid. 'Somebody's watching us?'

'I don't know.'

He leaned further out over the balcony. 'I can't see the car now, either.'

'Please be careful,' she said.

'I think it's gone,' he said, stepping back from the rail. 'Perhaps I'm just imagining things.'

'But you don't think so.'

He put his arm round her shoulder and steered her inside.

'What have you been up to?' he asked, determined to change the subject.

'Not much. Sleeping, mainly. And trying to make sense of Johnny's notes.'

'I know what you mean,' he assured her. 'I tried to read them last night after you'd gone to bed, but my eyes kept glazing over.'

'It's not so bad once you get used to his abbreviations. But what does "Tel Int" stand for?'

'Must be "Telephone Interviews". Did you learn anything useful?'

'I may have done. Take a look.'

She handed him the writing pad.

VC owns a transport company in or near London.
He drives a dark-blue Ford Mondeo.
He deals in heroin in the UK. Also in other parts of Europe, with Cabrini.
VC and Cabrini also do legitimate business deals, and Cabrini visits him in London.
But Cabrini never goes to or calls VC's house.

Does visit VC's transport company, which is at or near a London airport. Sail calls it 'the airport place'.

'This is brilliant, Suzanne,' he said after reading her notes.

'Thanks, but I'm not sure how far it takes us. How many airports are there near London?'

'Too many. Heathrow, Gatwick, Stansted, Luton. And one in the City. God knows how many transport companies there must be around them.'

'We just might have the address.'

She showed him the second page of Sail's notes, with his tiny handwriting in the margin. 'I think the last word is road, but the rest is too small to read. I was looking for a magnifying glass when you came home.'

'I've got a lupe somewhere,' he said. 'One of those things for looking at transparencies.'

Stewart rummaged around in the drawers of his desk until he found it. Magnified eight times, Sail's notation was plain to see: 'Clay. Pk. Rd.'

His mind was racing ahead. 'Pk probably means Park, so it's Clay something Park. Rd means Road, so it's got to be the name of a street. There can't be too many of those.'

He found his London street atlas and ran his finger down the index: Claybridge Road, Claybrook Road, Claygate Lane, Clayhill Crescent, Claymore Road . . .

'Here we are, Claymore Park Road,' announced Stewart. 'There's two of them.'

'What do you think? Is it his house or his depot?'

'Let's see where they are.'

One was in Southall, the other in Croydon.

'Is either near an airport?' she asked.

He looked doubtful. 'Of the two, Southall's nearer. It's in West London, under the Heathrow flight path. Croydon's in Surrey, but it's at least 20 miles from Gatwick.'

'So if it's Southall, that could be "the airport place"?'

'There's one way to find out.'

'Now?'

'No, not today. It's getting too close to rush hour and it would take us hours to get across London. We'll do it first thing in the morning.'

'What about trying again to see your man? To see if he can tell us more about VC? Or get us to RS at Scotland Yard?'

'I think we should go on this,' Stewart said. 'At least it's something concrete.'

It was her turn to look sceptical.

'What's bothering you?' he asked.

'What happens if we *do* find VC? Are we just going to walk right up to him after what happened in Marseille?'

'We're going to have to come up with something,' Stewart conceded.

He busied himself, putting away the lupe and the atlas. 'Do you fancy a walk? There's a pub half a mile away where we can sit by the river. I'll fix supper when we get back. Didn't know I could cook, did you?'

'There's a lot about you I don't know,' said Suzanne.

He was slicing tomatoes in his kitchen when she asked him about Fee.

'What about Fee?'

'That's the point. You've hardly talked about her at all.'

It was true. It was as if they had made a pact, unspoken but none the less powerful, not to discuss their children, in the belief that this was the least painful option. The trouble was, Suzanne had a nag in her belly that returned whenever nothing tangible was happening, sometimes lurching so violently she could feel her stomach contract. She would wonder where Josh was, and what he was doing, and whether he was all right, and her questions always ran into a wall of frustration and anxiety because the answers were beyond reach. Instead she would try to focus on memories of good times they had shared, conjuring images so precious she did not want to talk about them in case they were somehow degraded. They were hers and Josh's, and belonged to no one else, and she wanted to guard them intact.

'It's very painful, isn't it?' he said, echoing her thoughts as he scooped the tomatoes into a bowl. 'Talking about her is more than I can bear.'

'Maybe we should,' Suzanne said. 'Maybe it will help.'

'So what do you want to know?'

'Anything. What was she like when she was small?'

'Adorable. I have these images. Like snapshots. She's a little girl with strawberry blond hair skipping round the garden. She's throwing a ball to me and calling to me to throw it back and clapping her hands in delight when it goes high in the air. Then she's older, and serious, and reading stories to me that I used to read to her. It's all very fragmented, that's the only thing.'

'How come?'

The real answer, he knew, was because he had been a fragmented father, only there when he could free himself from the dictates of his work; when he was not cruising the trouble spots of the world, savouring the taste of danger, the hotels and the expense accounts, joshing and camaraderie with his fellow firefighters, as the travelling newspaper correspondents liked to call themselves. He was slicing the last tomato when the blade slipped and gashed his forefinger, blood welling from the cut.

'Bollocks,' he said, from anger as much as pain. He pushed his finger under the tap and saw pink stains in the water as it swirled into the plughole.

'What have you done?' asked Suzanne.

'Cut myself. It's nothing.'

'Let me see.'

The blood was flowing again as she contemplated the injury. He told her there were plasters in a drawer and she stretched one around his finger.

'I'll do that,' she said, taking the knife and starting to dissect a cucumber. Stewart unwrapped a pack of cannelloni he had bought on his way home. 'Hope you don't mind supermarket pasta,' he said. 'They do a very good sauce to go with it.'

'That's fine by me,' she said. She put the sliced cucumber in the bowl with the tomatoes. 'You know, I've been thinking about you.'

'I'm flattered,' he said. 'I've been thinking about you too.'

She laughed.

'What I'm saying is, we've been living this nightmare for what seems like years, and I hardly know a thing about you. That's why I was asking about Fee.'

'We haven't really had much time for that,' said Stewart, defensively.

'Well, you pretty much know my life story.'

'That's because you're American. You don't seem to mind what you tell virtual strangers.'

'Come on, you don't have to play the uptight Brit with me,' she laughed. 'Anyway, you're not the only one who can do research. I know a lot about you now. *Born in Reading . . .*'

It took Stewart a moment to realise how she knew. 'You've been reading the blurbs, haven't you? They're rather over the top. Especially the American ones. Cool understatement doesn't seem to be their style.'

'What's Reading like?'

'Not very interesting.'

'What about Oscar Wilde? And Reading jail?'

'That's interesting, I agree. But there's not much else.'

'What were your parents like?' She pointed to the picture of the family trio.

'Very straight. Can't you tell?'

'And Oxford? Is that where you studied journalism?'

'You can't study journalism at Oxford. You have to do it in your spare time. Or at least try to. I was supposed to be studying English but I didn't manage it very well. I spent so much time on journalism I got chucked out. Or sent down, as they say.'

'Weren't your parents upset?'

'I think they were, really. But they didn't say much about it.'

'Then to Fleet Street?'

'Yes, via the *Birmingham Mail*. It was the standard career path. The *Sunday Times* was brilliant. And it got me into writing books.'

'How's that been?'

'It's hard work, making a living from writing non-fiction. The big breakthrough was Pinochet. It seemed to hit a chord in the US, when a lot of stuff about the CIA was coming out. It was thanks to that I was asked to do the MIA book.'

'All this stuff about climbing mountains. Isn't that dangerous?'

'It can be, sure. I used to pretend it was safe provided you followed the rules, but I think I was trying to kid myself. And other people.'

'Like Rachel?'

Stewart was adjusting the oven timer. He looked up sharply in response to her question. Suzanne caught his look, and suspected she had gone too far.

'I'm sorry,' she said. 'I was being the American again.'

'It's all right,' he said. 'The cannelloni's cooking. How's the salad?'

'It's fixed.'

'Then let's have a glass of wine, and I'll answer any question you like. Well, within reason.'

Suzanne sat at the kitchen table, which he had already laid. He opened the Chablis he had bought and poured it into gently into their glasses.

'So what would you like to know?'

'Some of the basics? Like where did you meet?'

'It was in a town called Leamington Spa. It's almost as boring as Reading. I was down there on a food-poisoning story. She was working for a local radio station and we agreed to help each other. It all led on from there.'

'But she's American, right?'

'That's right. She was over here on a job-exchange. Two radio stations, one in each country, swap one of their promising young reporters for six months. After that she had a straight choice between going home and staying with me. She chose me.'

'What next?'

'Everything was fine to start with. We moved to London when I moved on to the *Sunday Times* and she got a job at the BBC. Her career was going well, so was mine, and then we had Fee.'

He sipped at the Chablis, its pebble freshness lingering in his throat. He was back in the territory he had reached when he cut his finger. He guessed that Suzanne was wondering whether to ask her next question.

'So what went wrong? If you don't mind my asking?'

He did and he didn't. He took another swallow of Chablis.

'No, that's okay. Looking back, I guess it was mostly my fault. I was in love with journalism – the deadlines, the by-lines, the adrenalin, the buzz. When she had Fee, I never shared the load. I changed my share of nappies, sure. But that's when I was around. I was away too much of the time and she had to cope as best she could.'

'What else is new?'

'I know what you mean. It's what every mother who wants

a career has to deal with. But I never got my part sorted out. It's not that I didn't love Fee. I always have. But I played at being a father. I was there and not there, and I never told the truth. When I went away she'd ask when I was coming back, and I was never honest, always made it seem I wanted to be back as soon as I could. But once I was away I always felt I had to stay on for the next break in the story, and the next. By the time I did get home, she'd stopped believing in my promises. I brought her presents but I knew I was only trying to compensate. She used to look at me with those fabulous hazel eyes, and I felt she was looking right through me.'

'You're being very hard on yourself.'

'I don't think so. When our marriage broke up I started playing the divorced father as well, and I was still doing it up until last week. Taking her on lavish holidays, buying her expensive gifts, as if that made up for everything. But it didn't. There I was with this beautiful, intelligent and articulate young woman and it was like looking at another snapshot. She was my daughter, and yet I felt I hardly knew her. Look what happened in the restaurant. Every time I said something it was as if I had pressed the wrong button. We could have been talking in a foreign language. It makes me feel I've spent my whole life playing games. Sometimes I don't know what's a game and what's real. Maybe there's nothing real about me at all.'

It was a long time since Stewart had made such a declaration, or exposed his emotions so rawly. He felt troubled, as if he had been caught in a compromising pose. Suzanne was looking at him intently.

'I think you're real,' she said. 'I think you're more real each day, and more strong too. I wouldn't have got as far through this as I have without you.'

She noticed the scar on his cheek. Compared to the photograph, it seemed to have bedded in, to be part of him, a mark of his vulnerability as well as a badge of courage. She reached out and brushed it with her fingers, sending a charge through his body. He saw an intensity in her eyes and a wisdom in the incipient time-lines beside them.

He wanted to say they gave her an air of fullness and experience which attracted him, but he couldn't work out how to frame the compliment. He reached out for her hand in gesture of fondness to replace the words he could not find. His arm brushed against the swell of her breast and he let it rest there and she did not move away. He held her eyes in his, looked briefly away, met her eyes again, then closed towards her. She waited for one tense breath then moved towards him in turn. Her lips were parting.

From the kitchen, the oven timer rang. The cannelloni was ready. She could not suppress a laugh. Saved, she said, by the bell.

Forty miles north of Austin, near the town of Marble Falls, Red Kain turned off the highway on to a dirt track that took him to the boundary fence of Jesse Beaumont's weekend ranch. There was a 'Keep Out' sign but no gate, only a cattle grid to guard the track. Kain drove his truck across it without troubling to slow down.

'*Mamas, don't let your babies grow up to be cowboys,*' Kain sang, Willie Nelson keeping him company on the truck's stereo.

A mile beyond the grid, the track climbed a steep rise. Kain paused at the summit to let his dust settle. Below him, a white-painted ranch house and a collection of outbuildings nestled along the dry bed of a stream a mile or so away. Back in Austin, Beaumont liked to boast that the steaks he served at his fancy dinner parties came 'fresh off the hoof', implying he was a cattle man. From where Red Kain sat there wasn't a damn cow in sight. More of Jesse's bullshit, Kain supposed.

'*They'll never stay home and they're always alone,*' intoned Willie.

'Ain't that the truth,' said Kain, in his best imitation of a Texas twang.

From a lock-box behind his seat he extracted an automatic machine pistol and placed it within easy reach. He was not expecting trouble but it never hurt to be prepared. He reduced Willie to whispering volume and drove gently down the far side of the rise. A quarter-mile further on he found the perfect spot for an ambush.

After a blind bend the track divided, and in its fork was a spinney of cottonwood trees where he could hide the truck. Jesse wouldn't know a thing until he came around the bend.

Kain drove into the thicket and switched off the engine. He checked his appearance in the mirror and used his arms to lever himself out of his seat and into the back of the truck. Kneeling on the floor, he unbuckled the straps that held the wheels of a motorised-chair, then hauled himself into it. Anyone watching would have thought his legs were dead.

He picked up the machine pistol and checked the ammunition clip. He placed it in his lap and covered it with a blanket that he wrapped around his knees. He kept the safety catch on because he still doubted there would be trouble. Not once Jesse knew the score.

'You were always on my mind, you were always on my mind.'

Willie had moved on to the next song. Gone all sentimental on him. Kain powered the wheelchair to the rear of the truck and positioned it on the electric ramp, then pressed a button to open the back doors. He remained motionless, inspecting the hollows and the stubby mesquite bushes with his sniper's eyes. Except for a gopher that scuttled away he was entirely alone. With the press of another button, he lowered the ramp to the ground.

The terrain was rough, with cracks and gullies scoring the parched earth, and Kain had to steer carefully to reach the track, grimacing with each jolt. He came to a halt in the middle of the track, facing up the rise. Willie, barely audible now, was still keeping him company when he saw Jesse Beaumont's car crest the summit. Kain put one hand under the blanket and took hold of the gun.

When Jesse Beaumont rounded the bend, he found a man in a wheelchair blocking his path; a man wearing a combat jacket with sergeant's stripes on the rolled-up sleeves; a head of thick curly hair reaching down to his shoulders, with a battered Stetson perched on the crown.

The car slithered to a halt just a few feet short, spitting up dust with its wheels.

'What in hell you doing, boy?' Beaumont yelled, leaning out of the window. 'Didn't you see the sign? You're on private property.'

Kain did not reply. He stayed perfectly still, staring at Jesse, willing him to get out of the car.

'Could have got yourself killed,' Beaumont said. Still Kain stayed mute.

It was not until Beaumont was obliged to abandon the sanctuary of his car, and march up bristling with indignation, asserting that he must be dumb as well as stupid, that Kain finally spoke.

'I've come to help you, Jesse,' he said. 'Come to help you get your boy back.'

Claymore Park Road, Southall, turned out to be occupied by a slip-road leading to the M4 motorway.

'How old's your street map?' asked Suzanne accusingly.

Stewart looked inside the cover. '1989,' he said.

'Maybe it's time to get a new one.'

'I keep meaning to,' he said. 'Let's try Croydon.'

The M25 was the usual jousting-ground, with convoys of trucks running line abreast and boy-racers snaking across the lanes. They drove in silence, as if they had revealed enough about themselves the previous evening. It took an hour to reach the exit marked 'Croydon and London via A23'. Stewart followed the signs guiding him through Croydon's southern suburbs.

'What sort of place is this?' Suzanne asked, as they sped between playing fields, with Croydon's institutional high-rises looming ahead.

'It used to be an attractive Victorian town. Then they pulled down most of the Victorian buildings. Now it's more and more like the US.'

Ahead was a forest of signs: McDonald's, PC World, Toys-R-Us. 'You're saying this is all my fault?'

Stewart laughed. A sign for a restaurant flashed past on the left, then a garden centre, then an aeroplane, then a petrol station.

An aeroplane?

'Jesus Christ,' said Stewart. He switched lanes, swung a U-turn around a traffic island, and drove back the way they had come.

'What on earth are you doing?'

'Over there,' he said.

On the far side of the road, mounted at an angle on a dais so that it looked as if it was taking off, was a twin-engined plane in a blue and white livery. 'It's a De Havilland Heron,' said Stewart. 'It was a passenger plane during the fifties and sixties. They didn't build many. This must be one of the last outside Africa.'

'What's it doing there?'

'Look behind it.'

A few yards back rose the mock-heroic facade of a 1920s building, with square-cut pillars framing a pair of wooden doors. It bore the words Airport House.

'I don't understand,' said Suzanne. 'This is an airport?'

'It used to be, between the wars. I'd forgotten about it. This is all that's left. It's the old terminal building. It was derelict for about twenty years, then it was restored as offices. Look over there, the sign next to McDonald's. Does it say what I think it says?'

'Yes, it does. Croydon Airport Industrial Estate.'

'Are you thinking what I'm thinking?'

'Yes, I am.'

He found a place to turn again. They passed the Heron and took a road named Imperial Way. 'That must have been one of the old hangars,' said Stewart, as a creosoted building loomed. Everything else was new: featureless 1970s offices, a DIY store, a Castrol oil depot. At the end was a yard, guarded by a chainlink fence with floodlights at each corner. Stewart stopped. Behind the fence was a row of articulated lorries. Each bore the letter C painted red and enclosed in a black circle.

'Mr C?' asked Suzanne.

'I presume.'

At the far side of the yard was a two-storey redbrick office building. 'I'll see what I can find out,' Stewart said.

'What if he's there?'

'He won't know who I am. I just want to get a feel for the place.'

The office was strictly functional: a scattering of desks with brown mock-pine tops, a young woman at a computer, a map of Europe dotted with marker pins. A middle-aged man wearing a brown suit stood up expectantly.

'Can I help you?'

'Do you have a brochure?' Stewart asked. 'Showing your rates, that kind of thing?'

'What sort of business are you in?'

'Personal computers. We're looking to build up our export business in Europe.'

'This one should help you, sir,' the man said, handing Stewart a leaflet. 'Do you have a business card?'

Tom patted his shirt pocket. 'I must have left them in the car. I'll fax one to you.'

Suzanne read the leaflet as soon as he got back to the car. 'Here we are,' she said. 'Canning International. We get there first. Managing director, Victor Canning.'

Stewart was clicking numbers on his mobile telephone. Directory enquiries said there was no listing for a Victor Canning in Claymore Park Road, Surrey. He asked for the number of Croydon Library, then called it for the address. Trick of the trade, he told Suzanne. Libraries can tell you a hell of a lot.

It turned out that not all Croydon's Victorian buildings had been pulled down. The library was a red-brick edifice with a mock-Venetian campanile. Inside, beyond a glass atrium, sat a bored receptionist wearing a name tag, 'Debbie'. When Stewart asked to see the Croydon Electoral Register, she pointed at a line of file boxes on a nearby shelf. Stewart and Suzanne scanned the pages until they found Claymore Park Road. The entry for number 47 read: *2487 Canning, Victor J.*

'No Mrs Canning,' said Suzanne.

'Apparently.'

'Never got married? Gay? Divorced?'

'Perhaps he just prefers his own company.' They returned to the reception desk.

'Debbie,' he smiled. 'Does the library keep old electoral registers?'

Debbie looked doubtful. 'I'm not sure,' she said.

'Could you find out?'

'If they're anywhere, they're in the basement.'

'Could you take a look?'

'I'm not allowed to leave my desk.'

'Well, can we look instead?'

Debbie looked even more doubtful. 'It's not really allowed.'

He leaned over the desk. 'Debbie, this is *really* important. You would be doing us an enormous favour if we could just take a quick look.' He gave an impossibly broad smile. 'Please?'

Debbie got up silently and led the way down a flight of stairs. At the bottom she unlocked a door and turned on the light. The room was lined with shelves, with a dusty table at the centre and a stack of packing cases at the far end.

'They should be over there,' she said, before retreating up the stairs.

There were piles of registers going back decades. As they thumbed back through the years, they found that 47 Claymore Park Road had the same spare entry. Until they reached 1986.

2486 Canning, Marjorie
2487 Canning, Victor J

'Divorced?' asked Suzanne.

'Could be,' said Stewart. 'Or dead.'

On another shelf, Stewart found the yellowing bound files of the *Croydon Advertiser*. 'Let's start in 1985 and work forward.'

'What are we looking for?'

'Reports on divorce cases. Death notices. Accidents, suicides.'

Suzanne found it in the *Advertiser* of May 16, 1986.

CANNING (Marjorie) – beloved wife of Victor, mother of Kathleen. Tragically passed away on May 12. 'What is life to me without thee?' Funeral Croydon cemetery, May 21. Enquiries 684 1632.

'I recognise that phrase,' Suzanne said.

'So do I. But I can't place it.'

Stewart went upstairs to dial the number on his mobile.

'Hello,' said a woman, briskly.

'I'm sorry to trouble you,' said Stewart. 'I'm calling about the funeral notice for Marjorie Canning that was in the *Advertiser*. Ten years ago.'

The woman hesitated. 'Yes?'

'I'm doing some research about Victor Canning, and I wondered if you're a relative.'

'Yes, I am,' she replied. 'What's this all about?'

'My name's Stewart, Tom Stewart, and I'm a writer. I'm working on a book and you might be able to help me. Would you mind if I came to see you?'

'You're writing a book about Victor?'

'He comes into it, yes.'

'Have you spoken to him?'

'I'm hoping to.'

'Well, don't bother. Victor won't give you the time of day.'

'That's rather what I thought. Look, I really would appreciate the chance to talk to you, Mrs . . .'

'Mrs Johnson. Mabel Johnson.'

There was a long pause.

'I'm in Croydon now, Mrs Johnson,' said Stewart. 'I could come right away. I wouldn't keep you for long.'

Another pause, and then she gave him her address.

21

Stewart had played the scene a hundred times before.

Step out of your car and into someone else's life. When he was starting out in Birmingham, it meant asking how they felt about winning the prize for the best chrysanthemum, or having a book published about the old local tram service, or losing their job at the engineering factory, or having their child's body pulled out of the canal.

Some wanted to talk, some did not. Some had to be flattered, cajoled, manipulated, until they gave up what you wanted. Some gave you nothing at all. Which would Mabel Johnson be?

She lived in Shirley, in classic suburban hinterland. The front path was bordered by neatly-trimmed rose bushes. The front door had a circular leaded window of frosted glass, with a red mock-deco tulip at its centre. It was opened by a woman with an ample figure, red cheeks and neat rows of grey curls. She wore a kitchen apron printed with the message 'A present from Wales'.

'Mrs Johnson,' he said briskly. 'I'm Tom Stewart. I called you about my book.' He held out his hand and she shook it limply.

'This is Mrs Beaumont,' he added, gesturing at Suzanne. 'It's very good of you to see us.'

'You'd better come in,' Mrs Johnson said. She led them into a room wallpapered with sprigs of blue and pink flowers. 'I'm just making tea.'

She disappeared towards the back of the house, returning in a few moments with a tray bearing a teapot decorated with roses, along with a sugar bowl and a milk-jug inscribed: 'Souvenir of Snowdon Railway'.

'You're very fond of Wales,' said Stewart, experimentally.

'Not really,' said Mrs Johnson. 'Our next-door neighbour

goes there on holiday. She always brings me a present for looking after her cats.'

He reverted to a head-on approach.

'Could you tell me how you're related to Victor?'

'Victor's my nephew,' she said firmly. 'But what's your book about?'

Stewart laughed. 'I'm not quite sure yet,' he said. 'But it's partly about Victor, and the kind of business he's in. I'll know more when I've finished my research. That's why I need your help.'

'So what is it you want to know?'

'Can you start by telling me when you last saw him?'

Mrs Johnson seemed satisfied with his evasions. 'He popped in one afternoon when I was doing the garden,' she said. 'My Arthur was out at his bowls. Said he was just passing. That was last summer.'

'Had you seen a lot of him before then?'

'Once or twice a year, that's all.'

'Well that's not bad, is it? For a nephew?'

'That's one way of looking at it. But not when you've brought up your nephew like your own son. And then his daughter as well.'

Stewart knew now that Mrs Johnson was going to be a talker. Don't rush it, he told himself. One step at a time.

'I see what you mean,' he said, reassuringly. 'So how old was he when he came to live with you?'

'Eleven, to the day. He was just about to start his new school. He looked so smart, in his blazer and his cap. His mother would have been proud of him.'

'Tell us about her.'

'Vi was a lovely girl. Very pretty. But she was always rather frail. We never got to know her terribly well. It was as if Jimmy – that's Victor's father – didn't want her to make friends. She stayed indoors a lot. She played the piano. I only heard her once or twice, but she had a beautiful touch. Then she got cancer. She'd been to the doctor with a pain but the doctor said it was nothing to worry about. When it was finally diagnosed it was too late, of course.'

'What did Jimmy do then?'

'My brother was a lorry driver. Went all over Britain and the continent too. When Vi passed away he tried to find something local but he couldn't – not with anything like the same money anyway. That's when he asked me to help out with Victor. We said yes right away. It was just what we wanted, Arthur and me, not being able to have children of our own.'

Steer clear of that one, thought Stewart.

'How did Victor get on at school?'

'He seemed to do all right at first. Then we started getting letters about his homework. We went up there several times to try to sort it out.'

'What was the problem?'

'I don't think he ever really settled, what with his mother dying and all. Apart from that, we never really found out. That was the thing with Victor – you could never tell what was going on up there.' She tapped the side of her forehead. 'A closed book, Arthur likes to say. By the time he moved out we didn't really know him at all.'

'How old was he then?'

'Sixteen. It was when Jimmy set up his own lorry company. Canning International. He wanted Victor to help him in the business. It happened all at once. He packed up at school without taking his exams and went to work in the office. The next week he just took his things and went back to live with his dad.'

'When did Victor take over the business?'

'He was twenty-six. We knew his dad wanted him to take the reins one day. Jimmy was finding it too much of a strain and his doctor said he should ease up. He worked in the office for a bit and then he moved down to Sussex. That's where he is now, in an old people's home. We still go to see him but he's gone a bit doolally. Sometimes I don't think he knows who we are.'

She drained her cup and replaced it in the saucer. 'Would you like some more tea?'

'That would be great,' said Suzanne, handing over her cup. 'We'd like to hear about Marjorie. What happened, exactly?'

'I was just coming to her, dear.' Mrs Johnson poured a fresh cup for Suzanne. 'Victor met her when she went to work at the company. She was in accounts. She'd only been there about a week when Victor called in and told me all about her. Said she was wonderful, that kind of thing. I was flabbergasted. He'd taken so little interest in women that we were beginning to wonder if he was . . . you know, a bit the other way. But he told me that he was going to marry her and move into a new home. And that's exactly what he did.'

'That was Claymore Park Road?' asked Stewart.

'That's right, dear.'

'He must have really fallen for her.'

'He kept on about how pretty she was. She had these deep brown eyes, they were sort of widely spaced, and dark, wavy hair. He said she reminded him of Kathleen Ferrier. You know, the opera singer? She was his poor mum's favourite.'

'Of course,' said Stewart. 'Didn't she sing "What is . . ."?'

Suzanne cut across him. 'And that's why they called their daughter Kathleen.'

'That's right, dear. It all hardly bears thinking about. Little Kathleen was born a year after they were married. They used to bring her to see me. She was a bonny child, always smiling, the apple of her father's eye. Then Marjorie had the accident. Kathleen had started at nursery school and Marjorie used to take her there in the car. She was on her way back, just coming up to Claymore Park Road, when it happened. There's a very nasty bend and the other driver just carried straight on. Smack into her, head-on. It was so sad. To look at, there wasn't a mark on her. They said at the inquest the impact had snapped her neck.'

'Victor must have been devastated,' said Suzanne.

'That was the thing. He came to the funeral with a bunch of lilies. I remember he put them on her coffin and just stood watching as they covered it up with earth. His face was like stone.'

'So did you make all the arrangements?' asked Stewart.

'That's right. He had so much to do looking after little Kathleen. The one thing he did himself was put the notice in the paper, although he used my phone number. He said it had to be worded exactly right. The next day he came to see us. We had already guessed what he was going to ask. He said we'd helped him once in his life, and now he wanted us to help him again. Kathleen lived here for the next five years. Victor gave us all the money we needed and we tried to bring her up as her mother would have wanted. She had good clothes and nice toys and we did our best to love her truly. But we were more careful this time because we knew one day Victor would want her back, and we didn't want to be hurt again. Sure enough, when Kathleen was eleven Victor said he wanted her home. He said he was getting a housekeeper who could help look after her. We tried to argue with him but it was no good. Once Victor's made up his mind on something, there's no changing him. He just said she was his daughter and he knew what was for the best.'

There was an air of finality in Mrs Johnson's words, as if she was closing the conversation. The cups and saucers clattered as she collected them on to the tray.

'We'd better let you get on,' said Suzanne. 'You've been a great help.' Stewart stayed where he was. He knew there was more.

'But you knew he was wrong, didn't you?' he asked.

'What about?'

'Taking her back. Getting his housekeeper to look after her.'

'It's not for me to say.'

'Suppose she had gone on living with you. What do you think would have happened?'

'She wouldn't have got ill for a start.'

'Why do you say that?'

'I'm sure the housekeeper did her best, but she couldn't give her a mother's love, like we tried to. There were little things at first. Kathleen got these rashes which took a long time to clear up. Then she had a lot of throat infections, one after the other. Next thing was, she went down with pleurisy. She was in and out of the Mayday hospital, over by West Croydon. We saw her there a couple of times. Then she got something wrong with her liver – hepatitis, I think they said. I didn't understand everything Victor said, but there was something children got, something wrong with her blood. He had her moved into a clinic, down in Surrey somewhere. He said the National Health wasn't good enough for her. We haven't been there ourselves. He said he didn't want us to see her any more.'

She stood up. 'Well, that's all I can tell you. Arthur's due home from his bowls soon, and he'll be wanting his supper.'

'Mabel.' Suzanne's voice was firm, and Mrs Johnson looked

at her in surprise. 'Have you ever heard of an illness called CHIDS?'

Mrs Johnson thought for a moment. 'No, dear. I can't say I have.'

In the heart of Westminster, on the eighth floor of number 50 Queen Anne's Gate, Oliver Windlesham, Deputy Under Secretary at the Home Office, viewed the two men sitting in his office with a combination of irritation and disdain.

Thus far they had been responsible for three unmitigated disasters: dragging his minister out of a performance of *Cosi Fan Tutte* at Covent Garden the previous evening, halfway through the second act; obliging the Home Office to spend much of the day responding to a barrage of protesting phone calls from the Foreign Office; and requiring him to negotiate his way through delicate issues of rank and etiquette at Scotland Yard.

Now, to top it all, they were jeopardising his prospect of attending a cocktail reception being hosted that evening by a small but prestigious City bank, to mark the appointment of a former Home Secretary as the bank's new chairman.

He looked at the title page of the folder that lay at the centre of his immaculately polished desktop. 'Operation Shrike?' he read out. 'Shrike?'

'Its a perching bird, sir,' said Detective Sergeant Humphries. 'Pale grey, with black and white markings and a nasty hooked bill.'

'I know what a shrike is, thank you sergeant. But why is it the name of your operation?'

'Because shrikes impale their prey live on thorns and barbed-wire fences, and save it for later. Rather like the target, we thought. You see, the shrike's got a nickname that fits our man perfectly. It's called the butcher bird.'

Windlesham adopted a tone of mild exasperation. 'Could we get to the point, gentlemen? Why is your Operation Shrike upsetting our friends on both sides of the Atlantic? Why, in particular, are you refusing to cooperate with the French police?'

'Commissaire Halard is over reacting, sir.' Detective Chief Superintendent Skinner placed a folder on Windlesham's desk. It contained the entire history of Operation Shrike, and was far more substantial than the file which had been sent to the Home Office that morning by the Assistant Commissioner of Special Operations. That was merely a brief summary. And it didn't have the photographs.

'Perhaps you would be so good as to explain that to me, Mr Skinner,' said Windlesham, the sarcasm becoming unmistakable. 'Because Commissaire Halard isn't the only one who's over reacting, as you put it. So is the French interior minister, so is the French ambassador, so is the FBI, and so, now, is the American ambassador. As a result of which, you might like to know, the Home Secretary is asking whether you have been wilfully obstructive.'

'No, sir. The French asked us to keep an eye . . .'

'Keep an eye, Mr Skinner?' Windlesham opened his folder at the first page and read from a passage side-lined in red ink. 'What the French are asking for – and I quote – is immediate and covert round-the-clock surveillance.'

'Which, with all due respect, sir, is not warranted.'

'Not warranted, chief superintendent?' Windlesham consulted the file again. 'Allow me to remind you. We have a man whose daughter may have been kidnapped, who may have come to London to make contact with the kidnappers, who may be wandering around with a gun that could be crucial evidence in a murder case. Who may, for all you know, use that gun when he finds the people who he thinks kidnapped his daughter.'

Windlesham removed his glasses and fixed his prey with a glare. 'And you're saying, chief superintendent, that surveillance isn't warranted?'

Skinner rubbed the lobe of one ear. 'I think you've just made my point, sir, if I may say so. It's all very iffy. A man whose daughter *may* have been kidnapped. Who *may* be carrying a gun. A gun that *may* be evidence in what *may* be a case of murder. That's an awful lot of mays when we're being asked to drop everything and mount a round-the-clock surveillance operation at heaven knows what cost to our manpower and budget.'

'Go on,' said Windlesham.

'And even if the French, and the Americans, had come up

with information that was a bit more solid, we still couldn't oblige them.'

'Are you going to tell me why, chief superintendent?'

'Because it would jeopardise Shrike, sir. I'm sure you picked up the reference in the French request to the files that Stewart is supposed to have taken from the murdered reporter's flat? The files on Antoine Cabrini's British connection?'

Windlesham nodded ambiguously.

'Antoine Cabrini's British connection is the prime target of Operation Shrike.'

'Victor Arthur Canning, born South Croydon, December 11, 1946,' Skinner began, after Windlesham had demanded 'the essential facts'. He was reading from the file he had retrieved from Windlesham's desk.

'Mother, Violet Doris Canning, nee Draper; deceased. Father, James William Canning, now retired. Victor Canning is the largest importer and distributor of heroin in the United Kingdom. He is also a significant contributor to the national murder rate.'

'A ruthless bastard,' added Humphries, 'if you'll forgive my language, sir.'

That set the pattern. For the next thirty minutes, Skinner and Humphries combined to describe the criminal career of Victor Canning; Skinner, the main narrator, while Humphries added emphasis with apparently unprompted interjections. Privately they called it their 'Punch and Judy show'. They had already performed it once that day, for the Assistant Commissioner of Special Operations. It was the AC who had warned them that Windlesham was 'steaming' because of the disruption the combined protests of France and the United States had brought to his life.

'As far as we know, Canning got into heroin some fifteen years ago to rescue his transport company from financial difficulty,' Skinner said. 'After his father retired from the business, Canning borrowed from the bank to expand the fleet, and couldn't meet the repayments. The solution was put to him by Antoine Cabrini. We have information that Cabrini paid Canning fifty thousand pounds for the first run.'

'Very specific information,' Humphries emphasised.

'Using those proceeds, Canning began establishing a network of shell companies to distance himself from the sharp end of the business. These shell companies, that cannot be traced back to him, operate a number of transport firms, depots, freight handlers, and so on. You get the picture, I'm sure.'

Windlesham did not oblige him with an answer. Skinner pressed on.

'There is nothing to link these companies to each other, nor to any common ownership, and certainly not to Canning. Every time one of Canning's loads has been seized – and we've had our small victories, I might say – we've raided the company concerned and found what?'

'Sweet nothing,' Humphries volunteered.

'Little men, stooges, who know nothing – certainly not who really owns the company. We've been trying to pin some of these outfits to Canning for the last five years, without success.'

Humphries took up the story. 'Canning and Cabrini use these shell companies to smuggle morphine base from the Middle East and Southeast Asia to labs in France and Italy where it's turned into heroin. Then, as often as not, they use the same companies to smuggle the finished heroin to the first-level distributors in the marketplace. Every marketplace. Britain, of course, the United States, France, Germany . . .'

Humphries continued reeling off countries, until Windlesham waved his hand, as if to say 'that's enough'.

Skinner took over again. 'But being a major distributor of heroin is not sufficient for Canning. Like the Colombian cocaine cartels did in the United States, he has also taken over much of the first level of heroin distribution in the UK. And, rather like the Colombians, he has often used violence to achieve his ends.'

From his folder, he produced a glossy, ten-by-eight colour photograph and laid it on Windlesham's desk. It looked like a close-up of a piece of red meat.

'Peter Rodney Archer,' volunteered Humphries.

Skinner placed a second picture before Windlesham. For this shot, the police photographer had pulled back to show most of Archer's body spreadeagled on the pavement. A crimson stain surrounded what was left of his head.

'Manchester city centre two months ago, eight twenty-five in the morning, still the rush hour. A Colombian-style assassination. Two men on a motorcycle. The pillion passenger was the shooter. We found the vehicle the next day.'

He placed a picture of the motorbike on the desk, but Windlesham showed no interest in it.

Skinner lifted the folder and crossed his legs. 'To be frank, sir, Archer was no loss to the world. He was a pimp before he got into heroin, running a string of whores in Manchester. Then he moves to London and the next thing we know, Archer's selling smack – and Canning is his supplier. Then he made the mistake of short-changing Canning, together with another dealer. This man.'

He placed on the desk an image from hell. Windlesham blanched.

'Patrick Fowler,' said Skinner. 'We fished Fowler out of the Thames at Richmond. Somebody shoved fishing hooks down his throat, wrapped up in bits of bread; made him swallow them like he was a carp. The hooks were attached to nylon lines. Three hundred pounds breaking weight. They threw him into the river and snagged the lines on the bank. There was a pretty good tide running that day. Off down the river goes friend Fowler, trying to stay afloat. Then he reached the end of the line, so to speak, and the hooks ripped his insides to ribbons. He drowned, of course. In his own blood.'

Windlesham put his hand to his mouth and coughed.

'Archer ran for it, went back to Manchester, but it didn't do him any good. There have been eleven other killings in this country in the last eighteen months which we attribute to Canning.'

Windlesham raised his eyebrows.

'You have a question, sir?'

'Only the obvious one, chief superintendent.'

'Why hasn't Canning been nicked,' said Humphries.

'I was getting to that, sir. Canning is *extremely* cautious. His control of the heroin business is entirely remote. None of the people who do the dirty work know Canning or anything about him. Canning deals only with lawyers, who act as his cut-outs. He rarely meets them and never discusses anything of consequence by phone. They communicate through computers and electronic mail, using remote mailboxes, all of them located overseas. All their messages are encrypted, and so are all the messages which are relayed down through the organisation – from the lawyers to the lieutenants, from them to their underlings, all the way down the chain.'

Skinner paused, and Humphries knew to stay silent.

'As a result, there are no incriminating telephone calls for us to intercept, no paper records to seize, and very few people in the organisation who can turn informant with much effect. Of course, there are people who must talk to each other but they sit a long way below the top of Canning's pyramid. Victor Canning is as close as it comes to being untouchable.'

Skinner placed his elbows on the file and brought his hands together at the point of his chin in the form of a steeple.

'Now,' he said, 'you will understand that we want Victor Canning very badly. I do not know if he's involved in the French case, though I wouldn't put anything past him. And I understand why the French want us to place Stewart and Mrs Beaumont under surveillance. It is a perfectly reasonable request.'

'But?' said Windlesham.

'But we can't. Not now. Not at this precise moment.'

'Why not?'

'Because, you see, sir, we're this close' – Skinner held the thumb and forefinger of his right hand a fraction apart – '*this* close to taking him.'

He was talking very quietly. 'We have a source, an informant, at the very highest level of Canning's organisation. It has taken us years to get the goods on him, and persuade him where his best interests lie. He's a City solicitor, one of Canning's top lawyers. With what he knows, he can put Canning away for the rest of his life.'

He looked at Humphries as if seeking confirmation, and then back at Windlesham. 'But we need time, sir. In the next forty-eight hours our informant is going to secretly tape Canning talking about another murder he has ordered. And nothing – please God, nothing – must make Canning suspicious. If we place Stewart under surveillance, and he goes anywhere near Canning, then Canning will spot it. He always has in the past. He'll clam up, cut himself off completely. Our informant won't be able to get near him.'

He looked intently at the man who would decide. 'We're *this* close, Mr Windlesham. All we need is a couple more days.'

'What if you fail? What if Canning is involved in this kidnapping business?'

Skinner gave a thin smile. Here he goes, thought Humphries, recognising the signal. Ray Skinner, about to close the trap.

'Then, sir, we will make sure that Stewart gets to the British connection he's looking for. We'll send him in wearing a wire, and see if Canning incriminates himself. It doesn't matter what initial charge we get him on. Just so long as we get him.'

'Either way, he's nicked,' said Humphries.

Oliver Windlesham contemplated the minefield that lay before him. If he acceded to Skinner's request, the minister would doubtless say, 'Well, on your head be it' – and Windlesham had no intention of placing his head on any politician's block. On the other hand, if he ordered Skinner to commence surveillance of Stewart immediately, the responsibility for the likely ruin of Operation Shrike would be his – and Windlesham had no taste for such a burden. What was called for, he knew, was a firm and fast decision that would leave him blameless – and allow him to get to the reception after all. In other words, a compromise.

'You said you need forty-eight hours?'

'The informant is due to meet Canning tomorrow night,' Skinner said.

'Forty-eight hours. Absolute maximum,' said Humphries.

'Well, obviously, the attempt to gain evidence on Canning should go ahead, and you shouldn't begin surveillance until that attempt has been made.'

Skinner felt like punching the air. Instead he said, 'Thank you, sir.'

'And then, as soon as that's done, you will of course give the French your fullest possible cooperation – whatever the cost to manpower and your budget.'

'Absolutely, sir.'

'Whatever they want,' said Humphries.

'All right.' Windlesham made a note on the file. 'Well, that's settled, then.'

Skinner and Humphries stood up in unison.

'Just one thing, chief superintendent. Get your informant to bring the meeting forward to tonight, or tomorrow morning at the very latest. Then, come what may, you can start the surveillance within twenty-four hours.'

Antony Palmer looked down and saw the black water slapping against the quay, and felt the tremors in his stomach. The gap was not wide but the unmarked police launch was pitching heavily against the evening tide. His every instinct told him not to make the leap, to turn back, but that was not an option. Closing his eyes, he reached out an arm and felt the strong hand of the young crewman grip his wrist.

'Right you are, sir. Come ahead.'

His eyes still closed, Palmer took his leap in the dark.

Barely had he landed on deck than he felt the surge of the engine. The launch pulled away from the quay and made a fast 180-degree turn until it was heading east, running with the tide. Palmer gripped the rail, while his unsteady legs got used to the motion, and stared at the jumbled waterfront racing by on the South Bank. Ahead, approaching rapidly, was Tower Bridge; beyond it, the grotesque tower of Canary Wharf, gleaming in the evening sun.

'We need a meet,' Humphries had said on the telephone, crude as always, breaking his promise to never call the office. 'Customs Quay. London Bridge.'

'When?'

'Thirty minutes.'

'That's impossible.'

'Be there.'

Humphries had not added 'or else'. He didn't need to. Palmer knew as well as they did that they owned his soul.

'They're waiting for you below,' said the crewman. 'Mind your head.'

Summoning up his dignity as best he could, Palmer scuttled across the bucking deck and took the stairway down to the cramped chart room.

'Evening, Tony,' said Humphries, a smirk on his fat, red face.

Skinner did not bother with pleasantries. 'Sit down, Mr Palmer.'

'I have to say that your dragging me here like this . . .' Palmer began, but the look on Skinner's face caused his voice to falter.

'Out of order are we, Tony?' Humphries put a hand on Palmer's shoulder and pressed him down into a narrow bench opposite Skinner.

'Your meeting with Canning in the Rose and Crown,' Skinner said. 'It has to be tonight.'

'But that's ridiculous. It's set for *tomorrow* night.'

'Then you'll have to unset it, won't you?'

Palmer felt sick, and not just because of the diesel fumes invading his nostrils.

'But why? You know what Canning's like. He's practically psychic. He'll know that something's wrong.'

'Tonight,' said Skinner.

Palmer felt the sting of tears in his eyes. 'For God's sake, why are you doing this?' He turned to Humphries. 'Why, Bert?'

'Operational reasons,' said Humphries. 'And it's Sergeant Humphries to you.'

'I can't do it. I don't have any excuse to bring the meeting forward.'

'Then you better find one,' said Skinner.

'Damn you, he'll *know*.'

Skinner looked at him with a pitiless stare. 'Let's make sure he doesn't. For your sake.'

21 Claymore Park Road seemed especially impregnable. The street was lined with imposing detached houses, Edwardian at a guess, that could be half-glimpsed among high walls and the foliage of lime and chestnut trees, made ghostly in the flare of the sodium street lamps. Canning's had the air of a fortress: an iron gate set in an arch, to be opened only by remote control or from inside, with a gravel driveway leading to a creeper-covered frontage. As Stewart pulled up outside, his car was bathed in light from a pair of halogen lamps set high on the side of the house.

He moved away and parked on the far side of the street. 'We have to talk to him about Kathleen,' Suzanne said. 'I'm wondering just how much he knows about CHIDS and what's likely to happen to her.'

'I really don't think we should get into that,' said Stewart. 'Let's just stick to the subject, which is Kain.'

'Don't you see? It's the perfect opening. It goes, "Mr Canning, you don't know us, but we need your help. And we may be able to help you in return." If we don't follow that line, what are you doing to say when he opens the door?'

Stewart shifted in his seat. The debate had occupied most of their journey from Shirley. '*If* he opens the door. Let's just see what happens. Once we're inside, we can see how it goes. The first problem is how we get to the front door.'

'There's an entryphone,' she said, pointing back at the house. 'In the wall beside the front gate.'

Stewart sat for a moment, steeling himself for the encounter. 'Let's go for it,' he said.

They both got out and he had just locked the car door when he sensed a movement behind him. As he turned, the barred gateway opened. There was a crunch of gravel, and a Ford Mondeo swept through the gateway and headed down Claymore Park Road.

'Back in the car,' Stewart shouted. He fumbled for the door-lock then threw himself into the driver's seat. The car was already moving as Suzanne's door slammed shut. The Mondeo was fifty yards ahead but at the top of the road it had to stop to allow a double-decker bus and a line of cars to pass. Stewart jolted to a halt behind it. In the glow of his headlights he could see broad shoulders and the back of a round, close-cropped head. The Mondeo accelerated out of the junction, slicing ahead of an oncoming car and bringing the squeal of brakes and the blare of a horn. Stewart tried to follow but the gap had closed. He watched impotently as the Mondeo contoured a bend and was lost to sight.

'Bollocks,' said Stewart.

'Do you think he knew we were following him?'

'Hard to tell.'

'Did you see the sticker in the rear window?'

'All I made out was the word "Hope". Was it one of those ads for a church?'

No, not a church, she told him. 'It must have something to do with Kathleen. It said "Hope Clinic".'

Antony Palmer was naked again. His back rose in a gentle mound, with irregular fawn blotches appearing as oases in the expanse of his flesh. His buttocks were like two collapsed folds of blubber. His head was tilted forward in a position of repose, that of a man who has found peace at last.

At least, that was how he seemed from behind. From in front, Ray Skinner observed, whatever peace Palmer had finally achieved was at a terrible price. In the glare of police floodlights, in the yard of the Rose and Crown in West Norwood where his body had been dumped, there was a wildness in his eyes that conveyed the final tormented moments of his life. His mouth gaped, the stumps of his teeth showing in a sea of blood. The message was clear: This is what happened to traitors.

It was less than six hours since Skinner and Humphries had dropped him back at the quay; sent him on his unhappy way still protesting: *He'll know*.

Skinner's face was deathly white in the lights.

'Steady, guvnor,' said Humphries, though he shared Skinner's rage. 'There was nothing you could do. It's fucking Windlesham's fault.'

Skinner wasn't listening. He had turned and was walking back to the car.

'We can still get the bastard,' Humphries called, hurrying to catch up with him. 'We're still in the game. It's not over yet, Ray.'

'Not by a long chalk,' said Skinner.

22

The tang of disinfectant mingled with the sweet scent of the carnations Stewart carried into the Hope Clinic.

'These are for Kathleen,' he said to the receptionist.

'Kathleen?'

'Canning.'

'Of course, sir. Do you know where to go?'

'Just remind me, would you?'

She pointed across the polished hallway. 'Down the corridor to the right. Room nine.'

'Is Mr Canning here?'

'Not yet. He's usually comes around midday.'

Stewart set off across the hallway.

'Sir? Would you mind?'

The receptionist was holding out a pen. 'You haven't signed the visitors' book.'

The page was headed 'Hope Children's Clinic'. The spidery grey typeface had the same discreet air as the clinic itself, surrounded by pines and rhododendron bushes at the end of a lane in Surrey *rentier* territory. Ruing his failure to anticipate the problem, Stewart signed with the first name to enter his head: Sam Arbuthnot. As he started down the carpeted corridor, his flowers seemed hugely theatrical and a nurse looked at him curiously as she passed. The door to room nine was closed.

The corridor was empty. He turned the door handle and went in. The room was shaded, with pale light filtering in through venetian blinds. In a bed at right angles from the wall he could see a head sunken in the pillow. There was a pale, drawn face framed by dark curls and her eyes were closed. He stood and listened to her laboured efforts to breathe. She looked innocent and vulnerable, and he thought of Fee.

Check the waste-bin, Suzanne had said. It was in the corner, beside the door. Inside was a flat, green rectangular packet marked, in white lettering: 'MycoGene'. Stewart slipped it into his pocket.

Get her chart. Look on the end of the bed. She was right again. A clip-board was hanging from the bed-rail. He riffled through the pages, finding graphs and scrawled notes, but they were barely legible in the subdued light.

He took the papers and cautiously opened the door. The corridor was still deserted. The reception desk lay to the right. Stewart went left. Beyond the turn at the end of the corridor, nestling in an alcove, was a photocopier. A light on the control panel was glowing green. Green for Go.

Stewart placed the first sheet of Kathleen Canning's medical records on the glass of the copier, pulled down the lid, and pressed 'Print'. Nothing happened. He pressed the button again. Nothing again. He lifted the copier lid, closed it, and pressed for a third time. Frustratingly, enragingly, still nothing.

'Your code.'

A nurse with close-cut hair and a quizzical smile was standing behind him.

'You have to enter your code,' she said.

Stewart smiled back. She was clutching a single sheet of paper. 'Is that all you need to do?' he asked. 'Why don't you go first?'

He memorised her code as she tapped it into the copier keypad. When she had disappeared, it took him no more than five minutes to copy the file. When he replaced it in Kathleen's room, she was still asleep. He closed the door and headed for the entrance hall.

'Excuse me.'

Stewart hoped the call was aimed at someone else.

'*Excuse me, doctor.*'

The call was louder this time. He turned and saw the nurse with short hair waving a sheet of paper.

'You left this on the copier.'

As he walked towards her, she was eyeing his clothes. 'You are a doctor, aren't you?'

'From the Mayday,' he said. 'Must rush, I'm meeting the registrar in reception.'

He took the paper from her hand, and forced himself to walk at an even pace along the corridor towards reception.

Suzanne was waiting for him in the car, which she had parked under an ancient Scot's pine. As she thumbed through the photocopies, she had no difficulty with the doctor's handwriting, and spent more time examining the graphs. As she reached the last of the papers, she shook her head.

'It looks like she's got hepatitis X. And CHIDS.'

'How serious is that?'

'Serious serious. The big question is, are they giving her MycoGene?'

'It's not a question any more,' said Stewart. He pulled the MycoGene packaging from his pocket and placed it in her hand. Resignation was written on her face.

'What's on your mind?' he asked.

'Listen, Tom, there's something very troubling going on. Three years ago, we heard about some cases of children with CHIDS not responding to MycoGene. That wasn't unheard of, as MycoGene doesn't guarantee a cure. But what was strange was that these kids had a range of symptoms very like Kathleen's. Worst of all was that, like her, some of them went on to get hepatitis X. The FDA came in and investigated but it could find nothing to link MycoGene with those abnormal cases. The thing about hepatitis X is that it's cryptogenic, meaning that in most cases no one really knows what causes it anyway. After that the incidence declined, although there have still been isolated cases of hepatitis X cropping up. It looks like Kathleen's one of those.'

'How bad is that?' Stewart asked.

'It means she's dying.'

Stewart heard her voice break. It was the voice of a mother, contemplating the death of any child. He said nothing, thinking of Kathleen's head sunk deep in the pillow. On the far side of the car park, a dark blue Mondeo pulled up. A tall, heavily-built man, got out and headed for a gap in the trees.

'It's Canning!' Stewart said.

Stewart flung open the car door and hurried after him, Suzanne following. Canning was striding towards the rear of the clinic. They caught up with him just as he reached a small side door.

'Mr Canning,' Stewart panted.

Canning looked at him nervelessly.

'Mr Canning, my name's Tom Stewart. We need your help. Our children are missing and may have been kidnapped.'

Canning was still motionless. His eyes were impossible to fathom.

'There's someone who may know where they are, and we've been told there's just a chance you could help us to reach him. Do you know Red Kain?'

Only Canning's lips moved. 'I simply have no idea what you are talking about.'

Canning turned away; the subject was closed. Suzanne pushed past Stewart just as Canning was opening the side door.

'I'm so sorry about your daughter, Mr Canning. I know she has CHIDS.'

Canning paused in the doorway.

'I know a lot about the illness,' Suzanne went on. 'There are some things which have happened to Kathleen I just don't understand. But if there's anything I can possibly do to help, I will. That way, maybe we can help each other.'

'You can't help Kathleen,' Canning said.

She put her hand on his arm as if to hold him back. 'How do we know, unless we try?'

Stewart saw Canning pull away, then incline his head towards hers. He seemed to say something, but Stewart could not make out the words. The door slammed shut, and he was gone.

Suzanne looked stunned. 'What did he say?' Stewart asked.

'How did he know my name?'

'What do you mean?'

'He called me Mrs Beaumont.'

The ground was opening up like a chasm. Stewart suddenly felt dizzy.

'There's more,' she said. 'He told me we were wasting our time, there was no point asking him all these questions.'

'Was that all?'

'No, he said one more thing.' Her face was like chalk. 'He said, "Mrs Beaumont, you should go home to Texas. If you want answers, you'll find them in Austin".'

Part Four

23

Phil Brady shivered. Beyond the brown-tinted glass of the FBI's field office, the city of Austin simmered in the searing Texas heat. The pink granite dome of the state capitol building reminded him of the yolk of an egg that someone had cracked on to the pavement to see if it would fry. He remembered the field office in Arizona he had been posted to early in his career, where the temperatures would soar past 120 degrees and you were drenched in sweat the moment you moved a muscle. Thank God for air conditioning, he thought, even if his Texas colleagues had turned it up so high it felt distinctly chilly.

Brady swung his chair back so he was facing the bank of monitor screens again. They were blank.

'Any news on the pictures, Harry?' he asked.

Harry Gonzales, the FBI's Supervisory Resident Agent in charge of Austin, was leaning back in his chair, stretching out his legs so that his tan leather boots made him look even more of the archetypal Texan than Brady had remembered.

'Nothing yet,' Gonzales grunted. 'But we'll have it fixed soon, won't we?'

A lanky young man in denims was moving his hands over a console of knobs and dials.

'Won't we?' said Gonzales again, louder this time.

'It's coming, Harry,' said the technician. At that moment one of the screens flickered into life. It showed the ramp leading down into a parking garage, with a street door to one side. The door opened and a man emerged, walking silently past the ramp and out of the frame.

'Harry?' said Brady.

'Relax, Phil,' said Gonzales. 'That's not him. How are we doing for sound?'

The technician was still adjusting dials. 'Still no dice, Harry,' he said. 'The problem's inside the console. If I try to go in there now, you'll lose the picture again.'

'Jesus Christ,' said Gonzales. 'We get in all this hi-tech stuff and it doesn't work. Just be sure you keep the pictures coming.'

'Got it,' said the technician. On screen, the door opened again and Gonzales sat upright. 'Target in view, Phil,' he said. Brady watched as a tall man with a mane of white hair emerged from the side door and strode easily past the ramp.

'Come on, boys,' said Gonzales, as if to encourage his unseen team of watchers, stationed in surveillance vans in the centre of Austin. On cue, the camera swung to follow the walker. 'He's heading down Congress,' Gonzales told Brady. 'That's away from the Capitol. He must be baking in this heat. He'll pick up a cab any moment now.'

As Brady watched, the man waved one arm as if beckoning to someone out of shot. The camera panned left to show a red and white cab pulling into the kerbside. The man stooped to talk to the driver, then climbed into the back of the cab. As it pulled away, the camera angle widened to show it merging with the mid-afternoon traffic.

Gonzales pointed to a second monitor screen. At first Brady saw only a phalanx of cars heading into the camera but then he saw the red and white stripes of the cab.

'You've got another van on Congress?' he asked.

'Three in all. Two main, one back-up, in case we get another target. We should be so lucky.'

'Where's he headed?'

'We'll know soon enough,' Gonzales said. 'Last time he went to the bus station. Time before, it was Town Lake. First time, it was the Johnson Library.'

'Always the same pattern, right?' asked Brady.

'Never varies,' said Gonzales. 'He drives downtown, parks his car, gets a cab, drives somewhere or nowhere, gets out, speaks to nobody, gets another cab, picks up his car and drives back to the office. That's apart from the first time. He just went round in a big circle, didn't get out at all, and ended up where he started.'

'Any particular cab?'

'No. Whatever happens to be passing.'

Gonzales was concentrating on a third screen. The picture was jerky and there were blotches obscuring part of the frame. 'Goddammit,' he said. 'How often do I have to tell these guys to clean the windshield?' The FBI driver was playing a skilful game, keeping two cars distant from the cab to make sure he wasn't spotted. 'Knows his stuff,' said Brady.

The camera glimpsed an overhead sign marked I–95. 'He's heading north,' said Gonzales. 'My guess is the airport. It'll be easier for us once he's on the freeway.'

Brady crossed the room and filled a white plastic cup from the water cooler. On his way back to the console, he picked up a blue file from a table.

'This is good work, Harry.'

'Tell you what you wanted to know?'

'Most of it. I certainly understand how he managed to get the White House so fired up.'

'Some pull, huh?'

'That's politics,' said Brady.

'That's Texas,' said Gonzales.

In the interval since Brady had asked Gonzales to look into the background of Jesse Beaumont, he had certainly spared no effort. The file Brady had studied on the plane from Washington the previous evening painted a compelling portrait of a Texan business leader and political operator apparently blessed with formidable financial prescience, and a raft of contacts to ease his path.

Beaumont had a resounding military record, having flown bombers in World War Two and fighters in Korea. When he quit the USAF in 1954, he used his military renown to raise the capital he needed to set up Beaumont Airfreight. Twenty years later he had judged the precise moment to sell his company to one of his major competitors, using the proceeds to move into property and real estate just as the Texas property boom began. He had shown similar foresight in progressing from property into medical hi-tech in the late 1980s. At the same time, he had skilfully forged his political networks, spotting the revival of the Republican party in what had been traditional Democrat territory and becoming one of its most assiduous fixers and fund-raisers. He had proved tireless at organising dinners, shaking hands, pulling levers, calling in favours, all to help grease the wheels of the state's political machine and advance his own business interests.

His key political alliance was with Saul Bates, formerly an ambitious state legislator who had been elected a US senator in 1968. As Bates moved up the political ladder, eventually becoming chairman of the Senate Appropriations Committee, which settles the budgets of a host of Washington agencies, Beaumont had profited from his contacts and influence. Zoning laws were eased, loans materialised at sensitive junctures in his business ventures, opposition from regulatory agencies was tempered in his favour, demonstrating the eternal truth that politics is about debts and obligations, about paying and receiving dues. Reading Gonzales's report, Brady easily understood how it was that a well-placed phone call or two from Jesse Beaumont could persuade the White House to take up the case of his missing grandson with such alacrity.

Brady also understood how important that grandson was to Jesse Beaumont. There was little doubt that he was determined to build a business dynasty that would enshrine the Beaumont name through the generations, in the true Texas manner. Larry, his son, with whom he had set up BioGenius, was intended to be the first keeper of the flame. Then had come the tragedy of Jesse's life, when Larry had died in a plane crash five years before.

So the mantle of succession had passed to his grandson, Josh – even though he was not much more than a boy, and even though the rumour in the company was that young Josh was not exactly living up to his grandfather's expectations.

'It could be a motive,' Gonzales had reported by phone. 'A way to get at Jesse, for money or revenge.'

'Keep an eye on him,' Brady had responded.

If asked to justify why he was consuming FBI resources in this manner, Brady would have made a case based on his long experience of juggling competing hypotheses: keep them all in the air, never rule anything out. True, there was a strong theory on offer. A British writer had persuasive evidence that a former American marine, a decorated hero of the Vietnam war, was in reality the killer of his own commanding officer; and it was this allegation that the marine was determined to suppress.

This made Josh Beaumont an innocent victim caught up in the crossfire: what a marine might call collateral damage. But something was telling Brady that the story, however plausible, seemed incomplete; could he really ignore the presence of a seriously rich US businessman, who had the clout to call in favours as far as the White House? Sure, nothing quite added up. But when Gonzales reported the curious pattern of Beaumont's movements, Brady knew he had to come to Austin to see for himself.

'It's the airport,' said Gonzales. On one of the monitors, the cab's indicator was flashing as it slowed to take a ramp marked 'Robert Mueller Airport'. There was a brief image of Beaumont in the back, apparently engrossed in something he was reading, as the surveillance vehicle moved ahead.

Another surveillance van had moved in behind the cab. Gonzales was watching closely as it came to a stop by the kerb outside the arrivals terminal. To Brady, it seemed as if the hum of the air conditioning had intensified.

'Audio!' yelled Gonzales. 'We need sound.'

'No can do,' said the lanky technician. 'There's nothing else I can try without closing down the whole system.'

Beaumont climbed silently out of the cab. Brady saw an arm reach out from the driver's window to accept the fare, then give a brief wave of thanks. As the cab pulled away, Beaumont straightened up and turned towards the terminal.

'Taking a flight?' suggested Brady.

'Unlikely,' said Gonzales. 'He's not carrying anything. Not even a briefcase.'

Beaumont looked at his watch then walked into the terminal building, his broad back disappearing into the gloom.

A telephone rang. Keeping his eyes fixed on the screen, Gonzales picked it up, then said: 'Okay, stay on the line. We've lost audio.'

He cupped the receiver and told Brady: 'Beaumont's at the newsstand, just looking at the magazines. No contact so far.'

Gonzales put the receiver back to his ear and provided a running commentary. 'He's checking his watch . . . Now he's walking away. Didn't make a purchase . . . Still hasn't met anyone . . . Okay, he's heading for the exit. He's coming through . . . now!'

Beaumont was back in view on the monitor. He waited on the pavement while his eyes adjusted to the sunlight, then looked left and right before walking towards the waiting line of cabs. He climbed into the yellow Checker at the head and leaned forward to speak to the driver. The cab pulled away, with the surveillance vehicles in stealthy pursuit.

They followed Jesse Beaumont all the way back to Congress, where he paid off the cab and picked up his car. Then they followed his car back to BioGenius. As far as Brady and Gonzales could tell, it had been an entirely pointless journey.

How do you tell someone their father may have been murdered? As Stewart walked through the Washington streets towards Dupont Circle, he knew this was going to be the worst part of all.

It was the moment he had been dreading. The encounter he had been postponing ever since learning about Kain; the reason he had not returned Luke's messages, until Luke's tragedy had been overtaken by his own and he had tried to push Luke from his thoughts. But once he knew he had to go to the US in search of the truth about Fee, he also knew it was time to settle with Luke: time to level with him, time to tell him the score.

At least the first part was over. When he called Luke from London to say he was coming to Washington and had news to impart, Luke had insisted on knowing what it was about.

'There's no way easy way to tell you this,' Stewart had said, and by the time he uttered the words – 'I'm sorry, Luke, he's dead' – they were superfluous.

'I knew it really,' Luke had told him. 'At the same time I didn't want to know. At least it's over.'

They had not said much more. Stewart had promised he would tell Luke everything when he arrived, which would also help to explain why he had not told him anything before.

He had slept badly. The jet-lag would have seen to that, but as he lay counting the hours to his rendezvous, he found himself rehearsing his explanations in an endless loop. As he played through the dialogue, Luke would break in to pose all the questions it was his right to ask. They prompted other questions in turn which Stewart himself was only just beginning to formulate.

'Your father died at Khe Sanh. He died a hero, as the official history says. But he wasn't killed by the North Vietnamese. He may have been killed by one of his own men. That man was Red Kain . . .'

'Why haven't you told me this before?'

'That's what I've come to explain. I've been worried out of my mind. As I told you when you reached me in France, my daughter's disappeared. Since then I've found out that she's been kidnapped. And the man who did it was Red Kain.'

'Was she kidnapped because of your book?'

'Yes. Well, I think so. I think he did it to stop me writing it. At least, that's what I used to think. Until yesterday. Then I found out something extraordinary, something I find it almost impossible to believe.'

'Whatever are you talking about?'

'It's very complicated, Luke. I'll try to lay it out for you . . .'

Washington was showing the usual signs of Sunday morning life: solitary male joggers wearing bandannas and headsets, women jogging amiably in pairs; dog-owners with their charges and their pooper-scoopers; the odour of coffee. Luke lived in Riggs Place, three short blocks north of Dupont Circle. He must have been looking out for Stewart, because he opened the door while Stewart was still a few paces away. From their previous encounters, Stewart had pictured him wearing a loose college T-shirt and baggy tennis shorts that ended just above the calves of his muscular athlete's legs. Instead he was dressed in smart navy slacks and a laundered dark-blue check shirt, open at the neck. Stewart realised he had dressed to hear about his father's death.

'Good to see you, Tom.'

Luke drew Stewart across the porch with his grip: a quarterback's hands, Stewart remembered. He led Stewart into his living room. From his first visit, Stewart remembered it as a room shared with two other young men, lawyers like Luke, with its over-stuffed chairs and scatter cushions, its bank of stereo equipment and the posters on its walls. Someone had made an attempt to tidy it ahead of Stewart's visit, for the magazines which had undoubtedly been scattered across the floor were neatly piled on to a side table. There was a photograph on the mantelpiece which Stewart knew well: it showed Barney Lewis in his uniform the day before he left for Vietnam.

Stewart settled into one of the chairs and Luke handed him a mug of coffee.

'I've got so much to tell you, Luke,' he said. 'I hardly know where to begin.'

He began by telling Luke something he already knew: that Fee had disappeared. He gave Luke an outline of what had happened, so that he could get it out of the way, and so that Luke would understand why he had not spoken to him before. He was moved by Luke's expressions of sympathy, even though he knew he was waiting to hear about his father.

'I'll tell you more later,' Stewart said. 'Now I'll tell you about Barney.'

There was a stillness in the room, as if it had taken on the air of a mausoleum, while Stewart approached the moment when he had to reveal to Luke what he had seen under the green tarpaulin on the hillside in Vietnam. The morning chatter from the streets drifted in through the window, but it belonged to another world, a continent away from the field on Hill 861. Stewart saw himself walking across the clearing again, saw himself being led under the tarpaulin, saw the relics being lifted from the packing case.

'There was some of his equipment,' he said. 'Part of his fatigues, a water bottle.'

'What else?' Luke asked.

'Part of the skull, some fragments of bone. That's about it.'

'Then how do they know it's my father?'

'Because the skull is Caucasian, and the remnants of equipment were American. Battle fatigues, water bottle, both military issue. Barney was the only American not accounted for. It has to be him.'

'Are they quite sure? Beyond any reasonable doubt?'

'When I left they were still looking for more fragments of skeleton so they can carry out DNA testing. That would make it absolutely conclusive. But they're sure within any reasonable definition of the word. I wouldn't be telling you otherwise.'

Luke settled back. For a minute, maybe two, he stared past Stewart to the open window, to the plane trees, their leaves idling in the morning breeze. 'So be it,' he said at last. 'What else can you tell me?'

Stewart told Luke about Red Kain, leading him along another journey, this time from Hill 861, through the official archives of the marines, to the Last Chance saloon in Bangkok. As painstakingly as Barney Lewis's mortal remains had been displayed before him on Hill 861, he laid out the evidence which pointed to the final question he had to ask: was it Kain who had killed his father?

'If that's true, you're saying he was murdered,' said Luke. Stewart was grateful that he had used the word first.

'That's what I believe,' he replied.

'In cold blood?'

'I can't prove it yet.' He was bracing himself for Luke's response. Instead Luke asked, with preternatural calm: 'So where is my father now?'

'His remains are still in Vietnam. But once the search mission is satisfied nothing more is to be found, they'll be sent to the army's identification lab in Hawaii. That's where they'll carry out the DNA testing, and you'll be asked to provide a blood sample for comparison. Then they'll be sent to Washington. Your father will be buried, with full military honours, at Arlington. You see, Luke, in the end it doesn't really matter how he died. What matters is that he was a hero and you can be proud of him. As proud of his father as any son is entitled to be.'

The phone rang but Luke ignored it. The ringing stopped and Stewart supposed that one of Luke's roommates had answered it elsewhere in the apartment.

'Now tell me more about Fee,' Luke said.

The question came as a jolt. Stewart realised that for an hour, at least, he had been immersed in someone else's troubles, not his own. Except that they were his after all, because of Kain . . . As Stewart embarked on his own story, he had a sudden sense of *déjà-vu*, a premonition that he had sat in this room and told this story before. Was it the jet-lag, or was it that in talking about his quest for the truth about Barney Lewis, he was talking about his quest for Fee? And was it that, in talking about the man who had probably murdered Luke's father, he was talking about the man who had murdered his daughter? Because even now there was no proof she was alive. Even now it remained an assumption, a hope, that she had not been dumped over the side of the *Symphonie* the day after it left the bay near Villefranche.

As he began to talk, Stewart's thoughts seemed to fracture, so that there was no connection between his words and what he was seeing in his mind. The key episodes appeared like a series of tableaux, illuminated by a beam of light, passing before him. His angry parting from Fee outside the restaurant, the last time he had seen her alive. Looking through the drawers in her bedroom. Seeing her photographs, learning the name of the yacht on which she had been abducted.

He looked at Luke and realised he was listening intently. He forced himself to focus on his own words, grateful that he himself had not broken down. With his impressive composure, Luke deserved that.

'And Kain was the one?' Luke was saying. 'He's the one who kidnapped Fee? You're certain of that?'

Stewart could hear the lawyer in Luke, gently testing the strength of his belief, just as he had over his father's remains.

'It's not one hundred per cent,' Stewart admitted. 'But it's close enough to make no difference.'

They fell silent. He watched Luke, who first watched him, then turned away. Stewart suddenly felt intense compassion that he had had to listen to the story of his father's death, compounded by another person's grief.

'I'm truly sorry,' Stewart said. 'Sorry I had to tell you, sorry I couldn't tell you before. Sorry for your father too. He was a fine man.'

Luke stood up. For the past half-hour he had been nursing a can of Diet Coke, which suddenly seemed fragile in his muscular hands. Stewart pictured him crushing it and smashing it on to the table. Instead he placed it carefully in a waste-basket and picked up a bunch of keys.

'Let's go for a walk,' Luke said. He was halfway down the front steps before Stewart reached the front door. Stewart closed the door and hastened to catch up with him. The burghers of Washington were now out in force, the Sunday *Washington Post* under their arms, trying to decide whether to take brunch at the Belmont Kitchen or the Dakota, or at El Caribe, where fumes of garlic were wafting into the air.

They walked in silence until they reached a park, where they sat on a bench beside a creek. On the far side, young men and women were playing touch football. The ball rolled down the slope into the water. There was a commotion as a man waded in to fetch it without removing his trainers.

'There's more,' Stewart said, when the noise had subsided.

'I want to say something first,' Luke replied. 'Like you, I'm not sure where to begin. I just want to say how grateful I am to you for finding the truth about my father and for giving it to me straight. My mother and I have heard so many rumours and false promises and lies that we had no idea what to believe. Now I hope we can put this thing to rest. I don't know how my mother will take it when I tell her all of this. What I hope is that it frees her to get on with the rest of her life.'

The shouts of the football players dwindled as their game moved to the far side of the field. 'I feel angry, too,' Luke went on. 'It's true, I was upset that you didn't call me. Now I can see it doesn't make any difference. At least I went on thinking my father might be alive.' Luke had stood up from the bench and was looking away from the creek. The football players had gone.

'It's still hard to put all the pieces together,' Luke was saying. 'But I feel sorry too. Sorry that my search for my father became your search, because you have been dragged into something you could not have imagined. And now you've lost your daughter too.'

Luke turned to face him again.

'Kain is my enemy as well as yours, right? So let's search for him together. At least let me help you find Fee. What can I do?'

'I don't know, Luke,' Stewart replied. 'Because I'm not sure what I believe any more. Forty-eight hours ago I thought I had some certainties to cling to. Now nothing is clear. You'd better hear me out.'

What was strange, as Stewart related what he had learned during two days in London, was how clinical his recitation sounded. Each time before he had told how Fee had disappeared, his emotions were drained. This time he felt more like a scientific researcher assembling the evidence that would test an intriguing new hypothesis.

Another child is missing, he said. His name is Josh and he's the same age as Fee. His mother is an executive at a biotech company in Austin. This boy and Fee were together when they disappeared. Previously I had assumed that Kain grabbed the boy as well because he was in the wrong place at the wrong time. Now I'm not so sure. When I was in London, I learned something very strange. I was trying to contact Kain, and I went to look for a man called Canning who was supposed to know him. I found out that Canning has a daughter who is suffering from an illness that is treated with a drug called MycoGene. The drug isn't working, and the girl is dying. And MycoGene is manufactured by the biotech company which Josh's mother helps to run.

Stewart wondered how far-fetched his exposition was sounding. 'Are you with me?' he asked.

'So far,' Luke replied.

'I couldn't see where all this was leading,' Stewart went on. 'So I went with the boy's mother to see Canning. He wouldn't tell us anything at first. Then right at the end he said the answers were in Austin.'

'Meaning?'

'At first it made no sense. But when we talked it over, we realised what Canning could have meant. Perhaps he was blaming MycoGene for what's happened to his daughter. Perhaps he was telling us this was the reason for the kidnap. I still have no idea whether Canning had anything to do with it. But I'm beginning to think that Fee might not have been kidnapped because of my book after all. The book may have nothing to do with this. It could be that it was Josh the kidnappers were after, and Fee was the innocent bystander, not him.'

Luke's forehead was furrowed in concentration. 'But how does Kain fit in?'

'I simply don't know, and I can see no way of finding out. The only way I can take this further is to find out if there was something wrong with MycoGene. Something that could have hurt Canning's child.'

'What does the boy's mother say?'

'She's even more baffled than me. She says there's nothing wrong with the drug. There have been a few cases showing adverse effects, but none were directly linked to MycoGene.'

'Suppose she's wrong about that. Did she mention any lawsuits?'

'Not to me.'

'You see, if there's anything wrong with it, there should be a product liability suit somewhere along the line. I guess you know what they are.'

'Someone trying to screw money out of the manufacturers?'

Luke smiled. 'I guess that's the bottom line.'

'I didn't know that was your territory.'

'It's not. But it shouldn't be too hard to find out if there's anything going down. You're not the only one with contacts, you know.'

24

The queue for taxis at the New Orleans airport was interminable, and Stewart was too impatient to join it. He was also too exhausted: from the draining encounter with Luke, the dash to National airport for American Airlines' early-evening flight to New Orleans. He went back into the terminal and rented a car. When he asked how to get to the Cotton Exchange, the Hertz agent gabbled a set of directions as she ringed the location on a tourist map of New Orleans.

'You going there now?' she asked.

'Why?'

'Lock the doors.'

After Stewart had cut through the French Quarter and turned west on to Canal Street, traversing the shadow of the Superdome, the traffic thinned. He pressed on. Following the curve of the Mississippi, he skirted rows of warehouses, then towering cranes servicing the bulk tankers moored alongside the docks, their floodlights blazing as dusk darkened the sky. He reached the waterfront and, attempting to remember the agent's instructions, turned right on to Basin Street. The warehouses looked deserted now. He took another right, then a left, and was lost.

He smoothed out the crumpled tourist map and laid it across the steering wheel. He could not find the switch for the interior light, so pushed open the driver's door until it came on. A deep metallic sound echoed from a distant quayside. He peered at the map, attempting to read the minuscule street names, until he finally deciphered the words: 'Cotton Exchange'. He eased the car back into gear, took a left and a right, to find a gaunt eight-storey building rising at the end of a cul-de-sac.

At first it seemed a proud monument from a bygone era, but as he neared he saw that it appeared to have been gutted by fire, with cracked and broken windows signalling its neglect. He noticed a glow of light coming from a window on the second floor, and realised that the first two storeys had been renovated. He parked as close to the entrance as he could and found a line of brass plates next to the door. The end one read: *Morton Mintz, Attorney at Law.* He pushed the bell beside the entryphone. The response was brief and gruff. 'Mintz.'

'It's Tom Stewart. I'm the British journalist Luke Lewis spoke to you about this afternoon.'

'Come on up.'

As Luke had warned, Mintz was immensely tall. He also had a stoop, as though he was burdened with the sufferings of his clients. Luke had warned him about that too: few product lawyers could match Mintz's ability to convey the sense of righteousness with which he confronted the major corporations – the airplane and auto manufacturers, the asbestos millers, the pharmaceutical companies – across the courtroom.

Time and again, jurors had been swayed by his pleas for retribution against the wicked, coupled with his demands for punitive damages. Whether it was all a lawyer's act, or whether he really felt his clients' pain, was a matter of debate among youthful admirers like Luke. What was certain, and where Luke warned Stewart not to be deceived by appearances, was the thorough way he prepared his cases, which was equally decisive in turning them his way.

The warning was timely. What first struck Stewart, as he followed Mintz into a brick-walled room, with its restored and polished wooden beams, was the tide of paperwork swamping the pair of long tables at its centre. Don't be fooled, Luke had said. Mintz's research may look a mess. But if he's ready to file a liability suit, you can be sure that he's found, if not the actual bullet, at least the smoking gun. And as Luke had discovered, in an intensive hour on the phone working his legal networks, Mintz was working up a class-action lawsuit against BioGenius Incorporated of Austin, Texas.

'Will he talk to me?' Stewart had asked.

'Try stopping him,' Luke replied. 'If he thinks you're going to write a big piece about him and his case, he'll give you everything except his fee. Publicity is how he gets his cases. It's his life blood.'

'You're interested in MycoGene?' Mintz asked Stewart, after they had occupied two chairs at a corner of one of the tables. 'What have you heard?'

'That it can harm children,' said Stewart.

'And where have you heard that?'

'In Britain. I'm wondering if it's another thalidomide.'

'In Britain, right? You people did a fine job on thalidomide. Were you on the *Sunday Times*?'

'I was,' said Stewart, 'though not as part of the thalidomide team. But I can see the parallels with MycoGene.'

'There's one big difference' said Mintz. 'Thalidomide was a rotten drug, at least for pregnant women. MycoGene is a good drug. Look at the trials, look at the data. It's helping thousands of kids.'

'Then why are you planning to sue BioGenius?'

'You're not hearing me,' Mintz said. 'I said MycoGene was fine, not BioGenius. It's a good drug, produced by a bad company. And when I say bad, I mean bad as in wicked, evil bastards.'

For a moment, Stewart saw Mintz across a courtroom, making his opening speech to the jury. 'That's a very strong statement,' Stewart said. 'Can you back it up?'

'I don't make statements I can't back up,' Mintz said. 'What do you know about gene-pharming?'

'You'd better assume I know nothing at all.'

'The first thing you probably don't know is how to spell it,' said Mintz. 'It's pharm with a P H – as in pharmaceutical. That's one of the keys. We're talking a mix of science and profit. We're also talking the arrogance which leads humans to believe they can manipulate the animal world to their advantage. The trouble is, as a scientist once said to me, the animal world turns out to be far more complicated than humans think. Have you heard of the Beltsville Pig?'

No, Stewart admitted.

'That's a major-league example. Back in the eighties, scientists at a government lab near Washington injected growth hormones into some pigs. They'd tried it first with mice, and they grew to twice the normal size. So they thought it would work with pigs, and bring enormous profits for the farm industry. The pigs grew, but not in the way the scientists wanted. They were deformed, riddled with disease and so heavy they couldn't support their own weight.'

Stewart remembered the passion with which Suzanne talked of Larry, and the idealism he had brought to the development of his drug that would cure children of CHIDS. 'What's this got to do with MycoGene? I thought you said it was a good drug.'

'It was. And it is. That's to say, it was at the beginning, and it is now. It's what happened in between that concerns me. That's where we get into evil.'

'You keep using that word,' said Stewart.

'You're about to hear why.'

What Stewart heard first was an explanation of the mysteries of genetic engineering, presented by someone with the gift of explaining science's most complex details in terms a jury could understand. Some of it was familiar to Stewart, from what Suzanne had told him at Le Bosquet; some of it was breathtakingly new.

The part of Suzanne's account Stewart remembered most clearly was how Larry had manufactured a protein, spyrone, which played tricks within the body's immune system – its defences against disease. 'It was a key moment of inspiration,' she had said. Spyrone had provided a camouflage for the core of the body's defences, known as the T-cells, sparing them the ravages of the invading CHIDS virus.

'That was brilliant science,' Mintz told Stewart. 'The guy who gets the credit is Larry Beaumont, who founded the company with his father, Jesse. He was barely out of college, yet he came up with a genuine scientific breakthrough – to the extent there were plenty of sceptics who doubted it could be real. But it sailed through its clinical trials and thousands of sick kids whose parents had given up hope began to get better. BioGenius called the drug MycoGene, and spread the word that it was a miracle cure. Usually when I hear pharmaceutical companies talking like that, I want to throw up. For once, they were right.'

'So what went wrong?'

'In a way, BioGenius was a victim of its own success. The

company was stuck with the problem of how to produce enough spyrone to meet the demand. It made the first batches synthetically, in its laboratories. That was the stuff it used for its initial tests. But they needed far larger amounts, which was when they switched to gene-pharming. Larry knew all about the Beltsville Pig, of course, but this was different. Instead of tampering with an animal's growth genes, he aimed for something far simpler. That was to find a way of inducing an animal to produce spyrone in its milk. Animal milk already contains a lot of natural proteins, which humans consume as a matter of course. All this meant was adding one more protein.'

As Mintz told it, Larry set out to do just that. There were good precedents. Researchers in Scotland had already found a way of altering sheep's genes so that their milk contained a protein called AAT, used for treating emphysema. Larry used the same techniques to construct a sheep's gene with two genetic codes: one for making spyrone, the other to target the sheep's mammary glands. He injected the combined gene into a sheep's embryo. Several generations down the line, sheep were born whose milk contained spyrone. What was more, the quantities far exceeded anything which could be produced in a laboratory.

'That's gene-pharming,' Mintz explained. 'And it secured the company's future.'

Mintz reached into the morass of paperwork on his table to show Stewart how the company's fortunes soared. There were analysts' reports, brokers' tip-sheets, clippings from the *Wall Street Journal*, all talking of the BioGenius breakthrough, the FDA approval, the 'buy' recommendations. BioGenius's stock price doubled, then doubled again, and again.

'Then things started going wrong like you wouldn't believe. First off, Larry Beaumont died in a plane crash, which to my mind deprived BioGenius both of its finest scientist and its ethical core. Jesse brought in Larry's widow, Suzanne, to help him run the company, but she knew little more about gene-pharming than you. Then the herd got sick. It was mastitis, inflammation of the udder, and it hit more than half the sheep. No one's quite sure why. But my scientific friend tells me that tampering with the sheep's genetic make-up had left them vulnerable to an epidemic of this kind. The bottom line is, their supplies of spyrone began to dry up. Literally. It put the company in deep shit because MycoGene was in widespread use and the stocks were running out fast. If it couldn't keep pumping out the drug, kids would start dying again, and the company would be ruined.'

Mintz was becoming more restless, shifting his long legs beneath the table. He stood up and paced the room, as if to release the energy his exposition was generating. Stewart wondered if he preferred the full audience of jurors. But it seemed that Mintz's agitated state reflected the fact that he was embarking on a phase of speculation, and was uneasy that he no longer had the full facts on which to base his case.

'We're not entirely sure what happened next,' Mintz said. 'But what we think is this. When the herd was hit, they went back to their original laboratory stocks, thinking there would be enough to see them through for the next three months or so. But when they got the bottles out of the chill-store, they were in for a shock. They tested the spyrone and found that there were some tiny alterations in the molecules making up its chemical chain. The best guess is that it had simply degraded over time.'

Stewart felt a tingle in his limbs. It was the tingle he got as a journalist when he managed to penetrate an official version of events, and was about to discover that the truth was different. 'So what did they do?' he asked, although he had already guessed the answer.

'They went right ahead and used it. By doing so, they took a terrible chance, because they didn't know what effect these molecular changes would have. Sure, they reasoned that the changes were insignificant, the risk was minimal, all the usual justifications corporations sell themselves when they're about to gamble with people's lives.'

'So they lost the gamble.'

'Of course. Some of the children on MycoGene got worse instead of better. Turned out that instead of protecting the immune system from attack, the defective MycoGene seemed to encourage the CHIDS virus to attack it more viciously than ever. We think it only affected a handful of children, ones who were prone to liver damage, which is not a normal consequence of CHIDS. The kids with healthy livers, the vast majority, continued to do fine. But the vulnerable ones were hit by a very nasty form of hepatitis.'

'We're talking hepatitis X,' said Stewart.

'You know about that?'

Stewart nodded.

The rest of the story, said Mintz, was a mix of speculation and fact. It still wasn't clear when BioGenius knew its gamble had failed. All this time it had been working to fix the mastitis problem and finally cracked it. The gene-pharm herd was nursed back to health and it stopped using the defective laboratory supplies. 'The FDA became involved at this stage, because they heard about the apparent increase in adverse effects, and ordered fresh trials. They also went into BioGenius to check out the paperwork but by then, we suspect, someone had tampered with the records, so that no one on the outside knew about the switch to the synthetic supplies.'

Mintz had stopped pacing the floor and was holding himself steady, looking at Stewart. 'What else can I tell you?'

'How much of this can you prove?' Stewart asked.

'Most of it. We should know more after the discovery process, but that's still some way off. We're hitting them with a suit in a few weeks, and we'll file for discovery soon after. You can bet they'll fight every inch of the way, and it could be months before we get a single document. But we'll get there in the end. Once it all comes out, it's just a question of how many zeros the jury puts on the number.'

Stewart gazed at Mintz for a moment, then looked away. So much had been said, there was so much to absorb, and he wanted to give himself the space to reflect.

'I'm not sure you quite believe me,' Mintz said. 'It's a lot to take in.'

'Yes, it is,' said Stewart. 'But I don't doubt what you say. At least, it all seems very plausible. It's just . . .'

Mintz dropped a file in front of Stewart. 'It's all in there – dates, summaries, pleadings. Why don't you take a look while I go to the can?'

As Mintz left the room, Stewart opened the file. There were pages of tightly-spaced text, columns of figures and dates. His mind was in overload mode already: his eyes scanned the text without understanding it. He looked at the index, and saw an item headed 'Plaintiffs'. He turned to the page and saw a dozen or so names in a list.

Robert Michael Aldridge
Jane Michelle Brunner (Estate of)
Alan John Brampton Jr
Kathleen Marjorie Canning
Andrew Paul Harris
Howard Peter Hunt III (Estate of) . . .

He almost missed it. *Kathleen Canning*. A cistern flushed, and Mintz came back in. Stewart felt a rush of adrenalin as he closed the file.

'There's a lot of useful stuff in there,' he said.

'I can let you have a copy,' Mintz replied.

'Tell me about your clients. Are they all from Louisiana?'

'Do you know what a class action is?'

'I think so,' said Stewart.

'We've got clients from all over the US, and we're going to sue BioGenius in a federal court. They come from half a dozen states already, and more could turn up. Now, and this could be of interest to you, one of our clients comes from England. It's mostly thanks to her father that we've gotten this far.'

Stewart's pulse beat faster. 'Tell me about him,' he said, calmly.

As he built his case, Mintz had cast his net ever-wider in the search for clients. The first parents to come to him – they had a boy aged fifteen – were from Baton Rouge. The cases rippled out from there, first through the southern states, then, as he followed his practice of advertising for clients, from anywhere in the US. Finally he placed an advertisement in the London *Times*. The person who called was from a British law firm, and said he would be with Mr Mintz the next day. The man who arrived in New Orleans wearing a Savile Row suit, exquisitely tailored to conceal his expanding waistline, together with a grey silk tie, was Antony Palmer.

Palmer told Mintz about his client. Her name was Kathleen Canning, and she was ill with CHIDS even though she had been taking MycoGene. Her father, Victor Canning, was determined to find out if his daughter's illness was an anomaly or whether there was some more sinister explanation for her worsening condition. He was also very wealthy. Once he had concluded that Mintz shared his determination to get to the truth, Palmer explained, he was prepared to finance any inquiries Mintz deemed it necessary to make.

'I thought he was putting me on at first,' Mintz told Stewart. 'But there was nothing about him to suggest he had a sense of humour. It was one of those offers you simply can't refuse. Normally I work on pure contingency. I finance the case and take one third of the damages if I win, zip if I lose. Call it a gamble, call it payment by results – either way, it's a powerful incentive. But at that point we had nothing more to go on than a couple of hunches. So I decided to take up Mr Palmer's offer. That's how we've moved from a couple of hunches' – Mintz nodded at the table – 'to all this.'

'Does Kathleen's father know everything you've just told me?'

'Of course. He's paid for it, after all.'

'What about your sources. Have you got someone inside BioGenius?'

'I've laid out almost everything I've got for you,' said Mintz. 'But you must know that's one thing I can't tell you.'

'I'll do my own research on the company, of course. But what else can you tell me about BioGenius?'

Mintz rummaged through the documents on the table again and handed Stewart a brochure with a glossy blue cover inscribed BioGenius Inc.

'It's their annual report,' said Mintz. 'Must have cost them plenty.'

Stewart opened it. Greeting him from the first page was a photograph of Jesse arm-in-arm with Suzanne. Behind them was a statue, seemingly in granite, of a mother cradling a child. The picture was captioned: 'Jesse Beaumont, co-founder and President of BioGenius; Suzanne Beaumont, Vice President for Marketing and Corporate Affairs.' Both were smiling as they looked confidently into the camera.

'Pretty schmaltzy, huh?' asked Mintz.

'Jesse and Suzanne,' Stewart cut in. 'They run the show, right?'

'They're the ones.'
'And they had to know about this?'
Mintz laughed, a mix of amusement and sarcasm.
'Absolutely.'
'Both of them?'
'Of course.'

It was past midnight, Stewart saw from the dashboard of his Hertz car, by the time he left Mintz. The light in the window was still aglow, the only sign there was another human within miles. *They had to know*. The words – his words – were a mantra, insisting on being heard through his tiredness. He did his best to concentrate as he reached the T-junction at the far end of the street, where a one-way sign compelled him to turn right. As he looked for an intersection taking him back towards the Hilton Airport Inn, the streets were like canyons, their sides formidably sheer. *Both of them*. He took another right and found himself staring at two yellow rings cast by his headlights on a grimy brick wall. By the time he had reversed out into the street he had lost all sense of direction. He opened the driver's door to make the interior light go on and fumbled for the map. The network of streets made no sense. *Both of them had to know*. He closed the map and headed into the night.

How did they do it? As he gulped a scalding cup of coffee, Stewart watched the New Orleans commuters parading briskly through the departure lounge. In contrast to their spruce turnout, he felt jaded and exhausted after catching little more than four hours' sleep at the Airport Hilton. It was six thirty. Still twenty-five minutes before his flight left for Austin. There was a bank of payphones on the opposite wall. He found a number in his address book, calculated that it would be an hour later where Rachel was, and made the call.
'Rachel?'
'Hold on. I'll just the close the door.'
He heard her heels on the kitchen floor.
'Where are you?' she asked when she came back on the line.
'New Orleans.'
She didn't ask why. But then whenever he'd called her since

Fee disappeared, she seemed to have lost all capacity for surprise. 'What's happening now?' she said.

He related Mintz's revelations as succinctly as he could, pausing now and then for questions that never came.

'Rachel, are you there?'

'What are you going to do?'

'I'm going to confront her.'

'And then?'

'If what Mintz says about Canning is true, I guess I should tell the police.'

'Tell the FBI,' Rachel said. 'You do it, or I will.'

They let the silence hang. He said his flight was showing last call and he had to go.

'Please, Tom. You can't take this any further alone. Tell the FBI.'

'After I've talked to her.'

'Promise?'

'Promise.'

He was about to ring off when she told him she was going back to London.

'What about your mother?'

'Mom's doing okay. Not great, but okay. I want to be back home. I feel so far away from Fee.'

'When are you leaving?'

'Tomorrow, or the day after.' She hesitated. 'Tom, I'm glad if this isn't about your book.'

'It's still my fault.'

She didn't contradict him.

25

'*On the road again, just can't wait to get on the road again . . .*'

King Willie's anthem playing on Radio KASE 100 FM, Red Kain hollering along. July 4 is officially 'Willie Nelson Day' in Austin, courtesy of the Texas Senate, but, hell, the folks at KASE dedicate the whole damn month to him.

'*Seeing things that I may never see again . . .*'

Kain drove lazily down Bee Cave Road, took the turning to Town Lake, and headed for the marina. It was still before nine in the morning, and the parking lot was almost deserted. He hauled himself into the back of the truck and released the wheelchair from its shackles, beginning the routine that had become second nature to him. It was like he'd been crippled for most of his life.

The lake glittered, two sailing dinghies scudding across its surface. He powered the wheelchair across the lot, up a wooden ramp and along a deck that hung out over the water. The few joggers he encountered, the folks sitting at tables sipping coffee in the sun, Kain greeted as though he knew them.

'Hi, there . . . How're you doing? . . . Hell of a morning, ain't it.'

Most responded in kind. Now and again he caught a look of gratitude, as though he was being thanked for his cheerfulness: for not allowing the sight of his disability to spoil this perfect morning.

He pressed on until the deck widened to a toytown replica of a town square. There was a fountain, surrounded by tables and chairs. On three sides, small boutiques sold brightly coloured casual clothes and souvenirs. He found a spot in the shade and waited for one of the impossibly pretty young waitresses to come and give him a thousand-watt smile.

'Hi,' she said. 'What can I get you?'

He smiled back at her while she looked at the campaign ribbons on his combat jacket, and the tattoo of a rampant scorpion on his bare chest. 'Maybe a Dr Pepper,' he said.

'Coming right up.'

'Say, is there a phone around here?'

'Sure,' she said. 'Over there by the drugstore. One of them's especially for . . .' She broke off, embarrassed.

'For us disabled folk, right?' He reached out and touched her tanned arm, as if to tell her it was all right.

There were three phones attached to the wall, one of them set low for people in wheelchairs. He put a quarter in the slot. Nathan Yannuck answered on the second ring.

'Hey, feller, what's happening?' said Kain.

'Not much. What do you need?'

'I need another ride, good buddy,'

Kain told him where he was.

'On my way, Red Bird,' said Yannuck. 'Be there inside twenty minutes.'

Kain checked his watch, inserted another quarter and dialled again. When he heard Jesse Beaumont's voice he said 'Scramble' and hung up. The call lasted less than two seconds.

SPEED IT UP, the message from Raven had said.

Well, Redbird could do that. No problem. Jesse was a plum, ripe for picking.

Sipping on his Dr Pepper, Kain grinned amiably as he watched the pert waitresses in their short shorts. His mind was on other things.

He imagined Jesse in the back seat, telling him he must have shit for brains; Jesse still trying to find an angle he could work, some way out. And Red up front, apologising, giving him the middle-man routine: 'Well, Jesse, I've told them that. I've told them, "Hey, guys, you've got to be reasonable". But they ain't listening, Jesse. They ain't listening one little bit.'

Jesse would whine and bitch, and threaten fucking Armageddon – and Red would just drive and let him blow off steam.

Finally Jesse would concede as to how it just might be possible, given a little more time.

Except there was no more time.

'You saw your grandson? Doesn't look too happy, does he?'

He imagined looking in the mirror, watching Jesse's face turn red.

'Look, I hate to tell you this, but they've moved up the deadline. Saturday, the kid dies.'

'Well, you've sure got a lot to smile about this morning,' said the waitress. 'You want another Pepper?'

Red as a chilli pepper. That would be Jesse's face when he heard about the deadline.

'You're keeping mighty pretty company, I must say,' said Nathan Yannuck, who, by Kain's watch, had arrived five minutes earlier than he'd predicted. 'Seems a shame to take you away from here.'

They exchanged high-fives and some farewell banter with the waitress. Then Yannuck was pushing Kain back along the deck. When they were out of sight of the town square, the two men exchanged places.

'About an hour?' Yannuck asked, settling himself into the chair and handing Kain a bunch of keys.

'An hour should do it,' said Kain.

As he walked towards the parking lot, he jingled the keys in time to another of King Willie's greatest tunes, playing in his head.

This time they had audio. Today, the glitch was somewhere else in the system.

'Can you believe this shit?' said Harry Gonzales when the picture on one of the three monitor screens dissolved into jagged black and white stripes. Brady nodded as if to say, Only too well.

Gonzales leaned towards a microphone on the console and pushed the transmit button. 'Bobby Clark? Are you hearing me?'

'Loud and clear, sir.'

'Bobby, have you been messing with that damn camera of yours?'

'No, sir. It's working fine at this end.'

'Well, it ain't working fine at this end. You'd better . . .' Gonzales was about to tell him to let another surveillance van move into the lead when all the monitors went blank.

'Terrific!' snorted Gonzales in exasperation. 'What did I do that was so bad?'

He slapped the nearest monitor sharply but it didn't help.

'Bobby, we've lost all pictures. You're going to have to talk us through this one. Let me know when he gets off the freeway.'

'Will do.'

'I'm gonna find the tech boys and kick some ass,' Gonzales told Brady, heading for the door. 'For all the good it'll do me.'

The phone on the console rang and he paused. 'Go ahead, Harry,' said Brady. 'I've got it.'

'Okay, he's exiting on South Congress.' Clark's voice came loud and clear over the speaker.

'Brady.'

He heard the disconcerting echo of his voice bouncing off the static of a bad transatlantic connection.

'Mr Brady, this is Detective Chief Superintendent Ray Skinner.' The voice was unmistakably English. 'New Scotland Yard in London. Criminal Intelligence Section.'

'I know who you are,' said Brady. It came out as coolly as he'd intended.

'Yes, well, I was ringing to apologise. For the misunderstanding.'

Misunderstanding? The nerve of the guy. Brady took a swat at the nearest monitor, which flickered into life then steadied. Jesse Beaumont's Lincoln was making slow progress down a congested South Congress towards the Capitol.

'You're talking to the wrong person,' Brady said.

'You mean Halard? Oh no, that's all squared away. She knows she can expect our fullest cooperation from now on. Didn't she tell you?'

'She told me what you said.'

'Looks like he's going to park,' Clark's voice boomed over the speaker. The Lincoln was signalling a right turn.

'Say again?' said Skinner

'Right now I'm running a surveillance op.'

'I won't keep you long. I just wanted to bring you up to speed. There have been some very interesting developments.'

'I'm listening.' The Lincoln was disappearing down the ramp of the parking garage Beaumont always used.

'You know about Canning?'

Brady allowed that he did. Halard had faxed him the summary of Operation Shrike that Skinner had belatedly supplied to her, even though it was marked 'Not For Distribution – For Your Eyes Only'. Ignoring Skinner's request was her token of revenge. 'After the stunt he pulled,' she told Brady. 'He can . . . What is it you say?'

'Go to hell?'

'That too. I was thinking of whistle Dixie.'

Skinner's account of the operation against Canning had explained why he'd refused to place Stewart and Mrs Beaumont under surveillance in London, but it hadn't suggested any definite link between Canning and the disappearance of the children.

'Canning's definitely in the frame,' said Skinner.

Not yet, thought Brady, watching the monitor, waiting for Jesse to emerge into the light. What he said was: 'Go ahead.'

'Canning has a daughter who's ill. In fact, she's more than ill. She's dying. And she's dying of a disease that's supposed to be cured with one of those new biotechnology drugs. Or, if not cured, at least slowed down.'

'Here he comes,' Clark announced. Beaumont emerged from the garage entrance and stood blinking in the sun.

Skinner had paused for effect. 'Guess who makes that drug, Mr Brady?'

Brady blinked, as if somebody in the room had let off a flash bulb. 'I think I'm looking at him, Mr Skinner,' he said slowing his speech for effect. Clark's voice intruded again and Brady concentrated hard on what Skinner was saying.

'Yes? Well, listen to this. The day before Stewart and Mrs Beaumont flew to America, they went to the clinic where Canning's daughter is a patient. At least, Stewart did, but I'm betting she was with him.'

'How do you know?'

'From his description. Tall, lanky, scruffy – you can hardly miss him. He signed the visitors' book with some Mickey Mouse name, then wandered around pretending to be a doctor. A nurse spotted him copying some documents, almost certainly Miss Canning's medical chart, which he'd nicked from the bottom of her bed. One of the pages is missing. The nurse found it on the photocopy machine and gave it back to him just as he was leaving. My guess is he'd already replaced the rest of the chart and didn't want to risk going back to the girl's room. So he stuffed it in his pocket and scarpered.'

Beaumont was standing on the edge of the sidewalk like a man looking for a cab.

'We picked up on all of this today when my people followed Canning to the clinic and began making inquiries,' Skinner continued. 'We're now on him round the clock, by the way.'

Better late than never, thought Brady. 'Good,' he said.

A dark blue Chevy with the livery of 'Vet Taxicabs' emblazoned on its side had pulled up to the kerb, and Beaumont was climbing into the back. Something nagged at Brady, but he was distracted by what Skinner was saying.

'I don't know what Kain has got to do with all this, or Stewart's book, or his daughter. What I do know is that if Canning blames the Beaumonts for what's wrong with his daughter, you don't need to look any further for your motive. And I wouldn't count on him demanding any ransom, either. What Canning always looks for is revenge.'

Gonzales hurried back into the room with an anxious tech agent in tow. They stopped in surprise when they saw the now-functioning monitor, which showed the cab as it turned east on Congress and headed towards the University of Texas.

'How in the world . . .' Gonzales began. Brady held up his hand.

'Listen, Mr Skinner, have you told Commissaire Halard all this?'

'I couldn't get hold of her today. She's been in Paris apparently, and is now on her way back to Nice. As soon as we've finished this call, I'll fax her a full report. With a copy to you, of course.'

Of course? Brady let it go, though he knew there had to be a reason for Skinner's new-found spirit of cooperation.

'There's one other thing,' Skinner said. Here it comes, thought Brady.

'We're tapping Canning's phones. He hasn't said anything to excite us. In fact, he hasn't spoken to anybody except the clinic, checking on his daughter's condition. But he has transmitted the occasional short burst of data, which we've intercepted. The trouble is, it's encrypted.'

Brady groaned. 'Don't tell me,' he said. 'He's using PGP, right?'

'So the experts tell me. I thought you'd know about it.'

Brady knew about it all right. It was the bane of the FBI, and of other law enforcement and intelligence agencies that try to eavesdrop encrypted telecommunications. There isn't an encryption code that can't be broken, Brady told Skinner. But PGP came damn close.

'It stands for Pretty Good Privacy, which is some computer nerd's idea of a joke,' Brady said. 'It uses two mathematically-related codes, one to encrypt and one to decrypt, and you need to know both of them. The government here tried to ban it, but then some deviant in San Francisco uploaded copies on to the Internet, so just about anybody with a computer and a modem can get hold of it.'

Brady was no longer watching the monitor. Gonzales tapped him on the shoulder and pointed, just as the cab drew up in front of the Johnson Library. 'Same as the first time,' Gonzales said. 'Except then he didn't bother getting out.'

Beaumont was standing by the driver's door, handing over the fare. Brady was about to tell Gonzales there was something nagging at him, something he couldn't quite tie down, when Skinner said: 'Hello? Are you still there?'

'Sorry. I got distracted.'

'I was saying, is it true these codes can sometimes be broken?'

'Sometimes, though it's not something we're anxious to advertise.'

'Of course not.'

'It depends on the volume of traffic there is to work with, and how often the users change the codes. Sometimes it's just dumb luck. We crunch it through the computers and see what comes out at the other end.'

'I was wondering . . .' Skinner let the rest of the sentence hang.

'If you want to send the intercepts across, I can ask the guys at the National Security Agency to take a look.'

'That's what I hoped you would say.'

It took them a few minutes to decide that Skinner would send the intercepts to Washington in the diplomatic bag: long enough for Jesse to enter the Johnson Library; long enough for Clark to report from inside that Jesse had neither met nor spoken to anyone; long enough for Jesse to check his watch and re-emerge, looking impatient.

'By the way, we're still calling it Operation Shrike,' Skinner said. 'Since the target hasn't changed. What about your end?'

'I'm thinking about Wild Goose Chase,' Brady replied as he watched Jesse flagging down a cab with blue and white markings.

'What about Mrs Beaumont? What's she been up to?'

'Not much since she got back. She spent all yesterday at her home. Went to her office this morning. Jesse was at business meetings in New York until last night, so she hasn't seen him yet. He hasn't been to the office today. He was still at home when he got a call telling him to scramble.'

'Scramble?' Skinner said, sounding surprised.

'That's what the caller said. In fact, that's all he said. Ever since, Beaumont has been leading us around in circles.'

'Any sign of Stewart?'

'We found his name on the passenger list for a flight from Washington to New Orleans on Sunday night. Where he is right now, we have no idea. We probably won't unless and until he takes another flight.'

'Either way, I think you'll find that Jesse Beaumont, and not Stewart, is the key to this.'

'I think that's right,' said Brady.

By the time Brady put down the phone, the focus of their speculation was paying off the cab on South Congress, ending another pointless journey where it had begun.

It wasn't until the late afternoon that Brady finally hit on what was bugging him. That was after he had received and absorbed Skinner's admirably detailed report; discussed it with Halard, who didn't entirely buy Skinner's theory – 'It's what he wants to believe, Phil, isn't it? Another way to get Canning'; and insisted on viewing the tapes of all of Jesse Beaumont's mysterious journeys.

'Jesus, I'm stupid,' he told Gonzales, taking the blame. 'Vet Cabs. That's what we've been missing. Five of the nine cabs he takes are Vet Cabs, and it's *always* a Vet Cab he takes on the outward leg.'

'But a different Vet Cab every time, Phil.'

'Yeah, but was it a different driver every time? I've got an awful feeling the answer's going to be no.'

It took Gonzales three telephone calls to establish that every vehicle in Vet Cabs' fleet had been adapted, so that each one could be driven by those who had no use of their legs, as well as those who did. Whole or disabled, they were all Vietnam veterans who operated the business as a help-each-other co-operative. They didn't each own or drive an individual cab – they all owned them all. So when you turned up for work, you took the next cab in line. That was part of the founding philosophy.

'You want me to pull the records, find out who was driving those five cabs?' Gonzales asked.

'Not yet,' Brady said. 'Just pray to your god they do it one more time.'

26

There was a thud so loud it seemed to jolt his body. Stewart woke to find he had a grade one headache and was still wearing the clothes he had lain down in to take a nap. How long ago? He looked at his watch in disbelief. Ten hours. It felt like ten minutes. What had caused the thud? Did it come from the corridor? Or outside the motel? He had no idea.

He pulled back the bedroom curtain and saw only a cream stucco courtyard, with three walls of windows identical to his own. A kettle sat on the window shelf. He tore open a pack of instant Supreme Colombian and tipped it into a polystyrene cup as he waited for the water to boil. He felt clammy and his armpits were rank from his unintended sleep. He stripped off his clothes and stepped into the shower, turned the heat as high as he could bear, in a bid to blanch away the languor his body still felt. He sipped the coffee. It was so bitter he grimaced as it hit his throat.

He decided not to telephone Suzanne. 'Everything all right?' he had asked when he called her from Washington on Saturday night.

'Up to a point,' she'd said. 'At least I'm back in my own home. Jesse's in New York. I shan't see him before Tuesday. I'll start checking for adverse reactions when I get to the office on Monday. If Kathleen's doctors reported anything unusual, it should be in our records. Good luck with Luke.'

What could he say now? Morton Mintz says MycoGene was contaminated, children have died, and you must have known? He thought back to the moment they had sat outside the Hope Clinic, when she finally knew that Kathleen Canning was being treated for CHIDS, and she had told him about the glitch in the MycoGene results. Did she really not know anything more? Had everything between them been an act?

Including their moment of intimacy at Wapping? And her kiss – more than a token, Stewart thought – when they said goodbye at Gatwick airport?

Dusk was shading the hotel stucco when the taxi arrived.

'Been to Austin before?' the driver asked.

'Nope,' said Stewart.

'We'll swing by Congress Avenue Bridge.'

Stewart assumed this was some minor rip-off, a tourist route to bump up the fare, and could not be bothered to argue. He settled back and began composing himself for the moment he saw Suzanne open her front door. Ahead the grey cement span of the bridge stretched across a sheet of water. An undulating black curtain rose from its superstructure, its edges changing shape constantly, parts of it breaking away and then reforming to join the main mass. As it climbed, it turned on its end, so that it hung like a shroud above the bridge. It went on swelling in size, then began to fragment into a myriad parts, becoming a cloud that spilled out over the city.

'What on earth?'

The driver chuckled. 'Bats, pal. Mexican free-tails. Supposed to be one and a half million of them. They hang out under the bridge all day, and go scouting for food at night. Listen.'

He stopped and wound down his window. There was a shimmer of sound, a high, eerie echo, suspended in the air.

'Weird, huh? Happens every night, 'bout this time.'

'How long do they stay out?'

''Til they're done hunting, I guess. They're mostly back by dawn.'

Stewart felt like a predator too, as daylight disappeared over Town Lake, with its placid streets, lined with scarlet oaks, and the lawns merging around single-storey homes with their covered boardwalk patios, mimicking a Texan ranch-house. After paying the driver, adding a decent tip for the bats, he walked up a winding stone path towards the white steps of a front porch. He had a sense of foreboding, a sense that he was on the point of confronting something still more terrible than anything before. Suzanne opened the door.

'Tom. Why didn't you call ahead? Are you okay?'

'I'm fine. We need to talk.'

She led him into a kitchen lined with countertops and cupboards painted green and primrose yellow. There was an oak table with a vase of poppies in the centre. She pulled back a chair. 'How have you been? What happened with Luke? You want coffee?'

'I've just had some, thanks,' said Stewart.

'How about tea? I found somewhere in Austin that sells Lapsang.'

'No thanks,' he said.

She studied him for a moment. 'Are you sure you're all right?'

'I need to ask you some questions.'

'What kind of questions? Is there something you've found out?'

Stewart sat at the table. 'This is difficult,' he said. 'Before we get into that, could we go back over some old ground?'

Suzanne was looking puzzled. She switched on the kettle. 'I'm going to have some tea, even if you're not. Why don't you just tell me what all this is about?'

'I will in a moment,' Stewart promised. 'But could we sort out the old stuff first?'

Suzanne nodded, her bewilderment giving way to alarm.

'You remember telling me at the Hope Clinic you thought there might have been a problem with MycoGene? Because you started getting reports of adverse reactions?'

'I did say that,' she agreed. 'But I also told you that nothing definite was ever found.'

'Would you mind telling me again?'

'The FDA got in touch with us about three years ago. It sent us a formal notification of what it calls a significant number of adverse reaction reports. We were on to them already, because we'd picked them up through our physician monitoring programme. But it certainly caused a stir. Trouble was, it made no sense because any problems like that should have shown up in the original trials. The fact is, they didn't.'

'What kind of problems?'

'A variety. Some children had gone down with gastro-enteritis, which can be fatal. That kind of thing. But the most common factor was hepatitis.'

'Which is what Kathleen's got?'

'Well, hers is acute. Most of the reported cases weren't so bad.'

'How many were there altogether?'

'I'm not sure. Twenty or so, maybe one or two more.'

The kettle boiled and turned itself off.

'What happened next?'

'The FDA ordered a Phase Four trial, which is where they keep a close watch on a large group of patients who are receiving the treatment. In our case there were five hundred, and they were monitored for a year. Nothing showed up. So far as I recall, there were around a dozen cases of hepatitis A, but that's infectious hepatitis that you can almost always trace back to contaminated food. What Kathleen's got, and what we were worried about, is hepatitis X, which is a killer, as it can keep coming back until it destroys the liver. But we hadn't had a single case of hepatitis X in the original trials, and we didn't get a single case in the Phase Four trial. When it was over, the FDA gave MycoGene a clean bill of health.'

'So MycoGene is not the reason Kathleen's dying. That's right?'

Suzanne was becoming indignant. 'Of course it's right,' she insisted, her voice rising. 'Just stop and think, will you? If MycoGene had hurt Kathleen in any way, do you think they'd still be giving it to her?'

'That's not what I've been told.'

'Then it's about time you told me who you've been talking to. If that's not too much to ask.'

'Just one more question, then I will. The MycoGene you produce today – it's the same as when you started?'

'Of course.'

'The formula's never changed? Is that right?'

'First off, it's not a formula, unless you're talking about the compound it's presented in. The key ingredient is spyrone. That's the protein Larry identified, which turned out to be so effective against CHIDS. He started by synthesising it in the lab, then when he needed larger quantities he turned to gene-pharming, with sheep. We've been making it that way ever since.'

'So it's always been the same?'

'That's three times you've asked that question. I don't know how many more ways there are of saying this. If we'd changed it, it wouldn't be MycoGene, and we'd have to get it approved all over again. So yes, it's exactly the same. And no, it hasn't changed. Now, in heaven's name, tell me who you've been talking to.'

'Victor Canning's lawyer.'

She stared at Stewart in disbelief. 'Canning's lawyer? What the hell are you saying, Tom?'

'What I'm saying is that Canning's got a lawyer who believes his daughter is dying because she took MycoGene.'

Suzanne steadied herself against the counter. 'That's ridiculous, quite ridiculous. Surely you realise that?' She looked at him closely, scanning his eyes. 'My God,' she said. 'I think you actually believe it, don't you?'

'I'll lay it out for you,' he said, in a neutral voice. 'What he said.'

'I think that's a very good idea. Then we can forget all this crap and get back to finding our children.'

Her voice was bordering on contempt. He realised there was no turning back.

'The lawyer's name is Morton Mintz, and he works out of New Orleans. That's where I was yesterday. The way he tells it, four years ago you – BioGenius – hit problems in the gene-pharming herd. Over half the sheep got mastitis, and the supplies of spyrone were cut. You still had some synthetic spyrone in store, from Larry's original experiments, and you used that to make up the shortfall. Trouble was, the synthetic spyrone had degraded, but you took the chance and used it anyway. It wasn't such a bad gamble, but you lost. The result was that at least fifteen children have died, or are dying. One of them is Kathleen Canning.'

Suzanne shook her head slowly as she absorbed what Stewart was saying. She clenched her arms more tightly, as if she feared she was losing control. 'This is such garbage. Surely you can see that?'

Stewart remembered the table in Mintz's office, covered with documents and files; the pleadings, with their closely-typed text, the schedules, the dates. 'Mintz says he's got all the evidence to make his case. He's a product liability lawyer, and he's going to sue BioGenius for every cent it's got.'

'You keep ducking the question. Do you believe him or not?'

Stewart heard Mintz rehearsing his arguments, felt the passion behind his words. 'It's a very strong case,' he said.

Suzanne swallowed hard. There was passion in her eyes too. 'Now you listen to me.' She was almost shouting. 'I don't give a fuck about his case. What is crystal clear to me now, though I can scarcely believe it, is that you think I'm involved in this. It's fantasy, Tom, fantasy. Do you really think I'd gamble with children's lives?'

'Of course not,' Stewart said, but Suzanne was not to be denied.

'Have you stopped to think for more than two seconds what your accusation means? It means that ever since we found out Kathleen had CHIDS, I've been lying and cheating to you. That everything we've done since was an act. That nothing between us was real, and there wasn't a word of truth in anything I've said. All because some lawyer with a good courtroom act knew how get under your skin.' She looked at him hard and cold. 'I really thought you were better than that.'

Stewart was chilled by her ferocity. He was embarrassed too, knowing he had been caught up in Mintz's logic, forgetting that Mintz did not know Suzanne as he had come to.

'Suzanne,' he said. 'I'm sorry to have doubted you. Of course I trust you.'

'Thank you,' said Suzanne, coldly.

'The fact remains that Mintz says he has evidence of wrong-doing at BioGenius, and he's getting ready to use it. More important still, Victor Canning believes it too. He believes that MycoGene is killing his daughter. And that's what we have to deal with.'

Suzanne was still shaking from delivering her onslaught. She turned the kettle back on and waited for it to boil, then made her tea. 'Look, wouldn't it be best if you went back to the beginning and told me everything that's happened since you got to Washington?'

Suzanne came and sat at the table. There, Stewart took her with him on a journey back to Luke's apartment, where he had related the story of his father's death; out into the park, where he had talked about Fee; back to the apartment, where Luke had worked his contacts and tracked down Mintz; then sent him to New Orleans in dread of what he was about to learn. He told her about the tall, persuasive product liability attorney, with his passion for detail and his certainty that he was right; his hints that his most damning evidence came from a source within BioGenius. Then he came to Canning, and his own malignant suspicion that he was not relying on Mintz to achieve retribution against BioGenius, but was taking the law into his own hands.

'You're really saying that Canning had our children kidnapped to get back at BioGenius? Because of what he thinks we've done to Kathleen?'

As gently as he could, Stewart told her: 'I'm saying he had Josh kidnapped. Fee was taken because she was there too.'

Suzanne had a sudden moment of clarity, so strong it brought almost a sense of relief. 'Then it's obvious what we have to do. We have to show Canning he's wrong.'

'But what if he's not? What happens then?'

'He *is* wrong. I'd know if it were true. And I don't.'

'Could they have done it without you knowing?'

'I can't see it. Every scientist working there was Larry's friend. They're all so loyal to each other. And to Larry's memory.'

'What about Jesse?'

'I can't believe that either. I know he's not perfect. He's a businessman, a politician, he cuts corners, he's always been on the make. But he lives for that company. He and Larry built it from nothing. You know that.'

'But what if the future of the company was at stake? What if withdrawing MycoGene meant the end of BioGenius, and of everything he and Larry had achieved?'

'Even so,' she said. But there was less certainty now.

'Could we talk it through? Hypothetically speaking? Could Jesse have done this without your knowing?'

'It would be really hard. It's such a small company. I hadn't long started there, of course, and I was heading up marketing development and public relations. My training was in business administration, not science. But I knew most of what was going on, particularly as Jesse made it so clear he didn't trust anyone else.'

'What about the spyrone supplies? Who was in charge of those?'

'Now that *was* something Jesse took a close interest in. Said you always had to look after your supply lines. Something he said he learned in the war.'

'How many other people were involved?'

'Just a couple, maybe. Not more.'

'What if something like this did happen, and you'd found out about it?'

'I'd have called in the FDA. The next minute.'

'Even if that meant the end of the company? The end of everything Larry had worked for?'

'No question. And so would Larry. We're talking about children's lives. Larry created BioGenius to save them, not put them at risk.'

'And the same goes for you.'

'Of course.'

'And Jesse would know how you feel.'

'I guess.'

'Then he had to keep it from you.'

'But how? In God's name, how?'

'I'm not the one who can answer that.'

'And you're saying I am.'

Stewart did not reply. Her tea, barely tasted, stood lukewarm in front of her.

At night, the headquarters of BioGenius Incorporated was a brooding place: futuristic, angular, with walls of dark blue glass that reflected the moonlight, and the headlights of Suzanne's Lexus. She pulled into a bay marked *S. Beaumont VP Marketing & Corporate Affairs*, and reached in her purse for her key-card.

Stewart said: 'Doesn't that create a record whenever you use it?'

'So?'

'So he'll know what time we came here.'

'If you're wrong about Jesse, it doesn't matter,' she said, opening the driver's door. 'If you're right, I don't care.'

He followed her across the parking lot, half-expecting to hear the snarl of a guard dog, even though she'd told him that no guards or dogs would come running. Unless they triggered the alarms.

She inserted her card in a slot beside the front door and Stewart heard the soft click of the locks. Inside, she crossed the half-lit atrium to the far wall where the lights of the control panel for the alarms glowed red. Again she inserted her card and punched in a code number. Stewart held his breath until the lights turned to green.

'All set,' she said.

'What's that?'

Above him a granite mother gazed into the eyes of the granite baby she cradled in her arms.

'Woman and Child,' Suzanne said. 'In the style of Henry Moore. Jesse likes to say it embodies what we're all about here at BioGenius – the care of children. Sets the tone.' There was an edge to her voice. She had said enough on the drive from Town Lake to reveal that her reluctance to believe Mintz's claims was on hold. The acid of doubt which had eaten into Stewart was now working on her.

Outside, a patrol car marked 'Cedar Creek Security' cruised into the parking lot and paused behind Suzanne's car. 'Come on,' she said briskly as she began to climb the circular staircase.

He followed her to the first floor and through two sets of doors that also needed her card. At the end of a short corridor she opened a door bearing her name and said, 'Welcome to the vice-presidential suite.'

As Suzanne flicked on the lights, Stewart had a momentary impression of a business space softened by a woman's touch: cream curtains, a sofa with cushions, a photograph on her desk. She dumped her purse and keys and moved swiftly to her work-station, where she clicked a mouse to activate the screen.

'What are we looking for?' asked Stewart.

'Inventories.'

With a flurry of keystrokes she brought up an endless list of files.

'This was all supposed to have happened around four years ago, right?'

'That's what Mintz said.'

She opened one file, then a second and a third, and split the screen so that all three were visible. 'He's got a problem,' she said. 'Take a look.'

Stewart leaned over her shoulder, felt her hair brush the side of his face. On the screen were row upon row of figures. 'What are they?'

'Stock control reports, month by month, 1990 through 1992. The first column shows the amount of spyrone we had on hand at the beginning of each month. The second shows how much came from the herd during the next thirty days. The third tells us what we used during the month, and the fourth what was left at the end of it.'

'And?'

'You said the supplies from the herd went down. This says they didn't.' She pointed at the second column. 'The supply is pretty much constant. The only variations are up.'

Stewart felt flustered, but only for a moment. 'But if those figures include the synthetic spyrone that Mintz says was used to make up the shortfall, wouldn't they stay the same?'

'Let's take a look.' More rapid keystrokes, and a new file appeared. Suzanne gave a brief, derisive laugh.

'What's so funny?' Stewart asked.

She pointed to a column of figures. Below it, alongside a date, were the words: 'Stock destroyed.'

'Mintz is talking horseshit,' she said emphatically. 'They can't have used the synthetic spyrone. It was all destroyed five years ago. Before Larry died.'

Stewart felt a surge of conflicting emotions: relief that his suspicions were wrong; anger that Mintz should make such destructive allegations. Then he saw that Suzanne was also confused.

'But this can't be right,' she was saying. 'They *can't* have destroyed the stockpile.'

'Why not?' Stewart asked. 'Why not, if they didn't need it any more?'

'Larry was far too careful to rely on just one source of supply. He knew that the gene-pharming programme could hit problems somewhere down the line, and he wanted to keep working on a synthetic alternative. He needed the original stockpile for his experiments, and he also wanted to know how long you could keep synthetic spyrone before it degraded. That stuff was priceless to him. He'd never have let it be destroyed.'

She turned back to the screen. 'The truth has to be in here somewhere. It's just a question of finding it.'

What she was looking for now, he couldn't tell. File after file was opened and then discarded, until the images on the screen became a blur. From the photograph on her desk, a man with a mop of thick dark hair was watching with laughing, mischievous eyes. Stewart didn't need to ask if this was Larry. He crossed to the window and looked down into the parking lot. The patrol car had gone.

'Goddammit,' said Suzanne to herself. 'Let's try another route.'

There was a rapid chatter of keys.

'That's weird,' she said. The chattering resumed.

Another pause. 'It's happened again.'

'What's happened again?' he asked, returning to look over her shoulder.

'I'm trying to see if there's anything on e-mail about destroying the stockpile. We regularly purge the system but there's a separate archive going right back to day one which should show what happened. Nothing gets removed from that. Trouble is, I can't get into it.'

She typed an access code and hit the Enter key.

Red letters flashed on the screen: ERROR! ACCESS DENIED!

'You can't deny me, butthead.' It took Stewart a moment to realise she was talking to the computer. 'I've got a system administrator's code.'

She tried again, with the same response.

'Somebody's changed the protection level,' she said.

'How? Who?'

'I don't know, but I aim to find out.'

Stewart followed her into the next-door office where, from the cluster of photographs adorning the wall behind Jesse Beaumont's desk, she removed a picture of Richard Nixon to reveal a recessed safe, guarded by a combination lock.

'You know the code?' asked Stewart.

'Larry's birthday,' she replied tightly. 'Unless he's changed it.'

The door opened. She gave a grunt of satisfaction and began pulling out envelopes and folders. 'Somewhere here should be the master access code, which can't be changed. Not without taking down the entire system.'

She found a compact notebook, bound in grey leather, and flicked through the pages. 'Paydirt,' she said, as she found the code.

Sitting at Jesse's computer, she logged on to the system and began to negotiate the path to the archives. At first, Stewart watched her face in the flickering light of the screen, her brow furrowed with concentration. Then he started looking through Beaumont's files. He had just discarded a folder containing columns of figures – to do with share prices, he guessed – when she uttered what sounded like a cry of pain.

'What is it?'

'Listen to this.'

Leaning forward, she began reading from the screen: 'Kaufman to JB . . .' She broke off. 'Kaufman was brought in as chief scientist. After Larry died.'

She began again: 'Kaufman to JB. Per the interim proposal. On reflection, I think it better not to mix synthetic spyrone with the diminished gene-pharmed supplies in order to make up the deficiency, since there is a slight risk this might cause contamination of the entire batch. I recommend that two discrete batches are manufactured, one from each source of spyrone. This will also allow us to more easily monitor for any adverse reactions, in the unlikely event that any should occur.'

Stewart crossed to the computer and scrutinised the text on the screen. 'When was it written?'

'Four years ago. A year after Larry died. Do you see what it means?'

Stewart did, but he wanted to hear it from her.

'Tell me.'

'They didn't destroy the stockpile. They used it. Then they covered it up by changing the records. Everything in here's a lie.'

Her voice was strangely subdued, mechanical almost, as if she was reciting the account of a tragedy.

'You're sure that's what it means?' he asked.

'Of course I'm sure.' This time the feelings were breaking through.

Stewart had an envelope in his hand, lifted off the pile from Jesse's safe. As if to distract himself from Suzanne's impending anger, he unclipped the metal fastener on the back and peered inside. He saw a glossy surface, then a streak of colour, and realised it was a photograph. He tipped it on to the desk.

They saw them simultaneously, the startled faces of their children, their fear intensified by a camera's flashlight. Dirty and dishevelled, they were kneeling side by side on a stone floor, holding a newspaper in front of them. Stewart could make out Fee's yellow T-shirt, stained and grimy: so that's what she was wearing, he thought, almost irrelevantly, as he remembered Halard's questioning an aeon ago. Although Fee's eyes carried a touch of defiance and Josh remained impassive, Stewart was overwhelmed by their poignancy and vulnerability. The newspaper was the *Daily Express* and he could just make out the headline: Express man dies in Riviera blast.

27

It was that time when the city seems dead. There were a few trucks pounding along Route 71, but once Stewart had turned off and started threading a way through the suburbs, there were no other cars, no people, no visible life. Only the stop lights, flicking irrelevantly between red and green, suggested some human purpose to the deserted landscape.

Stewart looked at Suzanne. She'd said she didn't trust herself to drive. Her face was set and she was biting into her bottom lip. She was the angriest he had ever seen.

'Okay?' he asked.

'No, not okay,' she replied. 'That bastard. That evil bastard. He *knew*. He knew our children were alive, and he didn't tell us. I could kill him. I really could.'

The houses were larger now, set back from the road, and just visible in the orange glow of the street lights. A high yellow brick wall began on the right. 'Take the next turn,' said Suzanne. Stewart found a horizontal barrier pole blocking the way. Next to it, in a pool of light, was a recessed signboard inscribed, in gothic lettering: West Lake Hills. A man wearing a fawn shirt and trousers stepped into the light, pulling on his cap as he did so.

'Can I help you folks?'

'Ben,' said Suzanne. 'Would you let us in?'

'Oh hi, Mrs Beaumont. I didn't see you there. My, you're out early. Come to see Mr Beaumont, I guess. You want me to call ahead?'

Suzanne shook her head. The barrier lifted and Stewart was driving along a cement carriageway punctuated every 100 yards with the largest road-humps he had ever seen. As the car crawled over them, its headlights picked out clusters of trees looming out of the darkness, with the outline of isolated houses beyond.

'We're here,' said Suzanne suddenly. 'Up this driveway.' Stewart stopped in front of a pair of white garage doors. To his surprise, a light in the house was on.

Suzanne had slung her purse over her shoulder. She took out a key and opened the front door. Stewart followed her in. A man with flowing white hair, wearing blue slacks and a blue, open-necked shirt, appeared in the hall.

'Suzanne? What in the world are you doing here? Do you know what time it is?'

'Of course I know what time it is. I want to know what's going on.'

'What are you talking about?'

'I'm talking about this.'

Suzanne took the photograph of Josh and Fee from her purse and held it in front of him, no more than a foot from his face.

'Honey,' he said. 'I can't see without my glasses.' Suzanne and Stewart followed him into a room off the hall. Stewart noticed that he was limping. Beaumont picked up a pair of glasses from a desk crowded with papers and looked at the photograph in the beam of an anglepoise lamp.

'Where did you get this?' he asked Suzanne.

'I found it in your safe.'

'My safe?' Beaumont put the photograph on the desk and glowered at his daughter-in-law. 'What the hell were you doing in my safe?'

'We'll get to that. Why haven't you told us about this before?'

Beaumont looked across at Stewart. 'Who's us? You haven't introduced me to your friend.'

Stewart suppressed the instinct to offer his hand. 'I'm Tom Stewart,' he said. 'The girl in that photograph is my daughter.' Beaumont stared at him and Stewart wondered if he had heard. 'She's called Fiona. She's seventeen. The same age as your grandson.'

Beaumont nodded. 'Honey, could we sit down to talk about this?' he asked Suzanne. He moved behind his desk and settled into a leather chair, resting his elbows on its arms. Stewart saw that Suzanne's face was taut with barely-restrained fury.

'Stop stalling me, Jesse. I want to know how you got this picture. Ever since our children disappeared, you've let Tom and me go on thinking this was all about his book, and all that time we've been living with the fear that they were dead. An hour ago we found out they were alive – or at least they were when this picture was taken. Who gave it to you? Where are the children now?'

'Please, Suzanne. It's okay, they're still alive. But I don't know where they are. I swear.'

'So where did you get this picture?'

'A guy gave it to me. The kids have been kidnapped, and this guy wants money. A ransom.'

'How long have you known about this?'

'Five days. I got bushwacked going up to the ranch.'

'And you haven't told us?'

'I'm sorry, honey. Truly. Half the time I didn't know where to find you. The other half I've been trying to raise the money. They want a lot – a hell of a lot.'

'How much is a lot?'

'One hundred million dollars.'

Beaumont spoke the words deadpan. Stewart sensed for a moment that he had paused for effect. He saw Suzanne's mouth drop open, and felt his legs weaken. He feared he would never see Fee again.

'A hundred million? That's just ridiculous. Are these people crazy?'

'Why don't you both sit down and I'll tell you the whole story,' Beaumont said. 'Then you can tell me whether these people are crazy or not.'

Stewart was glad of the seat. Suzanne stayed on the edge of hers, waiting for Beaumont to begin. Stewart sensed an undercurrent that must have always coursed through their relationship, with Beaumont perpetually bidding for control.

'It was five days ago,' Beaumont began. 'I was driving out to the ranch when I saw a guy in a wheelchair. I had to stop because he was blocking the track.'

'In a wheelchair?' asked Suzanne. 'How did he get out on to the track?'

Beaumont raised his hand as if to forestall further questions. 'Hear me out, honey. I couldn't see how he had gotten out there, or how he was going to get back. He said, "I've come about your boy." He said he was only there as a messenger, but the people who had Josh say there's a ransom. He didn't know how much it was but he'd contact me again when he did. Plus he gave me a warning. He said I wasn't to go near the police. He knew these people and they'd kill Josh in a second if I did.'

Beaumont paused, as if waiting for his words to sink in.

'That was it?' asked Suzanne.

'Right. The first time, that was it.'

'Did he say anything about Fiona?' Stewart asked.

'That came later,' said Beaumont. 'I've met the guy four times since. Not out near the ranch, but in a cab. Turns out he's a Vietnam vet who drives for a vet taxi firm in Austin. He'd pick me up and we'd ride around and do the business. He said that was in case the Feds were watching. The second time he phoned through and picked me up on South Congress. That's when he told me about the hundred million.'

'So when did he talk about Fiona?'

'Not until he gave me the picture. That was yesterday. When I asked about her he said she was an incidental – that was the word he used – but if I paid the hundred million, I'd get her back as well.'

'This man, what did he look like? Tall? Muscular? Short blond hair?'

'He wasn't anything like that,' said Beaumont. 'I've told you. He was a cripple. Hippie-looking feller.'

'A hundred million dollars,' said Stewart. 'That's just absurd.'

'That's what I told him. The third time we met I said I might just be able to raise fifty million dollars, but even that would take time. He said that was too bad, because it wasn't going to be enough. I asked him to tell them to be reasonable, but he said these are not reasonable people. In any case, he said, this isn't about children, it's about you. They're out to destroy you.'

Suzanne had been keeping herself upright in her chair. Now Stewart saw her ease her shoulders and lean back, as if she was trying to relax. Then he remembered what she had in her purse.

'Destroy you?' she asked. There was an exaggerated note of amazement in her voice. 'Why would they want to do that, Jesse?'

'The vet said it was to do with the company. He said something about a shortage of drugs and kids getting sick as a result. I don't think he knew what he was talking about.'

'Perhaps he didn't,' said Suzanne. 'But perhaps the people behind him knew. And perhaps I know too. This is about what happened four years ago, isn't it? When the sheep got mastitis, and we nearly ran out of MycoGene?'

Stewart was watching Beaumont now. There was a flash of surprise in his eyes, then it was gone.

'I guess quite a few people got to know about that,' Beaumont said evenly. 'But it was just a glitch. No big deal.'

'That's bull, Jesse.' Suzanne's words were like ice. 'We know what really happened. When you lost production of spyrone from the flock, you used the old synthetic stock to make up the deficit. There was something wrong with the synthetic spyrone but you went ahead and used it anyway. That's why the kids got sick, and that's why these people are coming after us now.'

'Honey,' said Beaumont. 'What do you take me for? This is all horseshit. Where are you getting this stuff from?'

'We got it from Morton Mintz.'

There was a roar from Beaumont. Stewart thought at first it was a cry of pain, but then he realised that Beaumont was laughing: laughing from his belly, so that his body shook.

'Morton Mintz? Honey, *please*. I thought for a moment you were serious. Mintz is an ambulance-chaser, trying to make a buck out of other people's grief. He's full of crap. Come *on*.'

'Mr Beaumont,' said Stewart. 'Mintz is not full of crap. I was with him in New Orleans on Sunday, looking through his files. He knows what you did. He's been working on this for months, building a product liability case against BioGenius. He says you must have known there was something wrong with the spyrone, and he's going to sue you for everything you've got.'

'Listen, son,' said Beaumont. 'You're from England, right? I don't know how much you know about the law in Texas, or anywhere else in the United States. But lawyers like Mintz launch these liability cases as often as they scratch their balls. Maybe English law is different. But over here you can't just shoot off your mouth. You need a little thing called proof.'

Stewart felt his anger rising. 'Oh, he's got proof all right. He's also got a client in England called Victor Canning who thinks his daughter's dying because of you. We think Canning is behind the kidnapping.'

'Canning? Who the hell is Canning? You're not making any sense, boy.'

'It's no good, Jesse,' said Suzanne. 'Your bluster doesn't work any more. We also have the proof. You asked me what I was doing in your safe. I was looking for the access codes after you'd changed them. So that I could find out how you kept up MycoGene supplies through the mastitis outbreak. When I got back into the system, I found the whole story in the backup file.' She felt in her purse and flourished a computer disk at Beaumont. 'It's all on there.' Beaumont reached out for it. 'It's yours,' she said. 'We've made other copies, of course.'

Stewart knew that he was witnessing a new struggle for control: not between Beaumont and Suzanne, but between Beaumont and his inner feelings. He watched Beaumont absorb what Suzanne had said, wondered how deeply it had penetrated, and – he was forced to concede – was impressed. Beaumont held his countenance like a mask. Yet he was betrayed by the dawn, which was seeping into the room. Previously Beaumont had remained in the half-shadows outside the beam from his desk lamp but now the early-morning light threw his face into sharper relief, amplifying the lines at his eyes and whitening his hair.

'What was I do to, Suzanne?' Beaumont asked at last. 'Everything was going so well. MycoGene was a hit, HaemoGene was in the pipeline, and BioGenius was the hottest stock around. Then we got hit by the mastitis. At first we didn't think there was a problem. We were backed up with three months of synthetic spyrone in the freezer, and the veterinary guys reckoned they could sort out the mastitis in that time. But when we tested a sample of the synthetic stock, we could see its composition had changed. Question was, did it matter? I talked to Kaufman, asked him what the risks were. He said it was odds-on the stuff would be okay.'

'That's not how I read it,' said Suzanne. 'What Kaufman said in his e-mail was that he didn't want to make the call.'

'That's what he said first off. Then I called him into my office and told him he couldn't duck the call. The whole future of the company was riding on it, and I had to have the best scientific advice. That's when he said the spyrone should be safe to use.'

'So you pressured him until he told you what you wanted to hear?'

'No,' said Beaumont. 'He was the chief scientist so it was his call. Remember I didn't have Larry to turn to any more.'

'Keep Larry out of this,' said Suzanne, quietly.

'That's just what I couldn't do,' Beaumont replied. 'Think what would have happened it we'd withdrawn MycoGene. You know that the treatment only works if you keep on taking the drug. So, first off, a lot of kids would have died. Second off, the company would have gone down the tube, taking HaemoGene with it. End of BioGenius, end of Larry's dreams.'

'Larry would never have taken a chance like this.'

'Maybe not. The point is, he wasn't around to ask. I had to make the decision, based on what Kaufman told me. I knew it was a gamble, but I thought it was a good one. If I didn't take it, we were lost anyway.'

'Even that's not true,' said Suzanne. 'Yes, the company would have been in trouble. But we'd have kept our reputation for being straight and telling it like it is, and we'd have pulled it back somehow. Instead, you bet the company, and you've lost. The price may be two more children's lives. *Our* children's lives.'

'Maybe I called it wrong,' Beaumont conceded. He looked Suzanne in the eyes, then Stewart, then back to Suzanne. 'If I did, I'm truly sorry. For everything this has led to. It's my mistake, and I'm ready to pay the bill. If that means the end of BioGenius, so be it. Hell, I've started up a bunch of times in my life, and I'm not too old to start again. But there's one gamble I'm not going to take, and that's on the kids' lives. What these people want, they get. Whatever it takes, the kids come home. I give you my word on that.'

'Jesse, we don't have a hundred million dollars.'

'The trust does,' he said. 'I've pledged the stock.'

'No, you can't,' she said, her voice rising. 'That belongs to Josh.'

'Honey . . .'

Stewart was bewildered. 'I'm sorry. I don't know what's going on.'

She turned on him. 'I told you before,' she snapped. 'All the stock in the company is in trust for Josh. It's what Larry wanted.' She turned to Beaumont, pleading: 'Jesse, you can't.'

He stiffened his back. 'Honey, what damn use is it to the boy if he's dead?'

She flinched, but he didn't let up. 'Anyway, it's not your call. I'm the trustee, and hell will freeze over before I'll let my grandson die. I'm not giving the stock away, Suzanne. I'm just pledging it for a loan. You and me, we'll just have to work our butts off to make sure it gets paid back. This is for Josh. To get the boy back. And Mr Stewart's daughter.'

They were the words Stewart wanted to hear, and he was overwhelmed with relief. They would pay the ransom, without caveat or quibble. Fee and Josh were coming home. Then Beaumont was speaking again.

'There's one more thing I have to tell you. When I met the vet yesterday he told me there's a deadline. We have to deliver the money by Saturday, latest. Otherwise . . .'

'Otherwise?' Stewart asked.

'Otherwise the children die.'

Stewart went numb. He heard a sigh escape Suzanne's body. 'Did they really say that?' she asked.

'That's what they said.'

'Jesse. I want to know exactly what they said.'

'They want it paid in negotiable securities – bearer bonds, as good as cash. The handover is to be in Washington. Don't ask me why. They didn't say. What they did say is that the kids are somewhere in Europe. After we've handed over the bonds we have to go to Amsterdam. Some place called the Hotel Pulitzer. That's where we'll get the call, telling us where the children are.'

Suzanne looked wildly at Tom. 'We have to go to the police. I'm going to call them right now.' She reached for the phone on Beaumont's desk.

He put his hand on the receiver. 'Honey, we can't do it. I've been through this a thousand times. First thing I thought when the vet bushwhacked me was to go to the FBI. Hell, more than that: call in more dues from Senator Bates, get the White House on the case, send in the Marines, whatever it took. Then I thought some more, talked to Bates, and realised all of that was off the menu. We have to pledge the stock to raise the money. But if one word about MycoGene gets out, the FDA will close us down quicker than you can blink. Then the stock dives through the floor, the pledges are worth zip, and we can't pay the ransom.'

'So what happens next?' There was resignation in Suzanne's voice.

'I've just about done raising the money. It's been like chasing possums up a tree. I've rounded up every favour I'm owed, and bagged the last one in New York on Sunday. Once the legal eagles have finished up the paperwork, we get the money. That should be tomorrow, day after at the latest. The bonds are ready and waiting down at the bank. All I have to do then is get them to Washington, and hand them over.'

He hesitated. 'Except I can't.'

Stewart felt as though he was riding a roller-coaster.

'Why?'

'Because the Feds are watching me. The vet reckoned he spotted them at least twice. Didn't matter to him, of course, because they thought I was taking a ride to meet the kidnappers, instead of doing all the business in the cab. But they're still all over me like flies on shit. If I go to Washington myself, they'll come meddling and God knows what will happen to the kids then.'

He hesitated again. 'So Bates is going to do it for me.'

Another lurch on the ride. 'That sounds like a pretty big favour you've called in.'

'Not big enough. He'll take the bonds to Washington, but he won't make the drop. That's down to somebody else.'

'Who?' Stewart asked, although he already knew the answer.

'That's what I was trying to figure out when you two walked in.'

'We have no choice, do we?' Suzanne asked, looking at Stewart.

'No,' he replied.

Beaumont took off his glasses and placed them on the desk. 'You'll need to take care up there. These are dangerous people. You'll also need to look out for the FBI. I'm not sure how much they've figured out, but they're not going to stand by and let you hand over one hundred million dollars to these assholes, not without wanting to get in on the act. So if they get on to your tails, you're going to have to shake them. Think you can do that?'

Stewart felt his head nodding, as though shaking the FBI from his tail would be the easiest thing in the world.

28

The Jefferson used to be Brady's favourite Washington hotel. It was cosy and intimate, with staff who were permanent fixtures and always remembered your name. It was reasonably priced too, and he would recommend it to visiting cops from overseas. Halard had stayed there several times. Now, most of the old staff had gone, and the room-rate had gone through the roof. None of that had deterred Stewart and Suzanne Beaumont. His question, however, was not so much what they were doing at the Jefferson, but what were they doing in Washington?

He had been on their trail for two days: ever since Gonzales had woken him in his Austin hotel room to say that Jesse Beaumont was receiving visitors – his daughter-in-law and an 'unknown white male' – in the dead of night. From the description provided by the night watch at West Lake Hills, Brady knew the UWM had to be Stewart. The watchers had followed him and Mrs Beaumont when they left two hours later; followed them to her house, then to his motel, then to the airport, where they had boarded a Continental flight to Washington. Brady had been convinced that they were on their way to a rendezvous with Kain, and he and Gonzales had followed them to DC on the next flight. Now his certainty had gone.

In Washington, more FBI watchers had followed Stewart and Mrs Beaumont from the airport to the Jefferson, where they took a suite and hung a 'Do Not Disturb' sign from the door. In the evening they had gone to the Vietnam memorial, pausing just once as they passed along the wall, and then dined with another UWM, who turned out to be Luke Lewis, son of Captain Barney Lewis, a name on the wall and the principal subject of Stewart's book.

The next morning they had visited the Hirshhorn Gallery, an oasis of calm in downtown DC, wandering among the sculptures in the garden. Brady and Gonzales were there too, Gonzales extravagantly disguised as a tourist from Texas, in baggy shorts, a Houston Astros baseball cap, and a T-shirt proclaiming 'Remember The Alamo!' (The back – favoured by Gonzales and other Americans of Mexican descent – bore the slogan: 'Remember Who Won?'). Stewart and Mrs Beaumont seemed absorbed in their own world. 'You think they're an item?' Gonzales asked. 'What with them sharing a room and all?'

Brady didn't care. It was what they were up to that gnawed at him like a bad tooth. When he saw Stewart slip away to make a call from a payphone at the Hirshhorn – a phone the FBI was not monitoring – he knew it was time to find out. He slipped past Reception at the Jefferson and rode the elevator to the third floor. As he watched the floors glide past, he found himself rehearsing his moves. It was a habit he had fallen into since guesting at some training courses at the FBI academy, passing on his experience of countless interviews with 'non-cooperating witnesses'. Take control from the start; pledge unstinting help; embarrass them for not co-operating; hit them with something they don't know you know; find out what you need to know; finally, secure their co-operation. In this instance, that meant helping the FBI get to Kain and whoever was behind him; plus bringing the kids safely back home, of course. If they still wouldn't play ball, the next rule was to scare them half to death with some killer revelation. Well, he could certainly do that, courtesy of Chief Inspector Skinner of New Scotland Yard.

Mrs Beaumont answered the door. 'Couldn't you have called ahead?' she protested, as he showed her his badge and steered her into the sitting room.

'Who the hell are you?' said Stewart.

He calmed them down, then told them he was there to help them get their children back.

'I'm glad to hear it,' said Stewart. His tone was sarcastic. He and Suzanne Beaumont sat together on a low sofa. Brady chose a high-backed chair so that he was looking down on them. Take control.

'First off, our number one priority is to see that Josh and Fiona are recovered safe and well.' Pledge unstinting help. 'Catching the perpetrators is secondary. Are we clear on that?'

'No, we are not clear,' said Stewart. 'Our strong impression is that what matters most to you is catching Kain. Nothing that's happened so far makes us believe our children's interests come first.'

Brady leaned back in his chair. Embarrass them for not cooperating. 'But you can't have got that impression from the FBI, Mr Stewart. Because you chose not to come to us, or tell us what was going on in Austin. You left us in the dark, and that's made our job far more difficult. Even so, we've done nothing to jeopardise your children. Or do you think we have?'

'I don't know what you've done.'

'Well, we've found out a few things for a start,' Brady said. 'We know that Kain's demanding a ransom. Which means this is not just about your book any more.'

'Go on,' said Stewart neutrally. Brady couldn't tell whether he had been impressed by what he had just been told. He settled his gaze on Suzanne. He was going to have to wing it now, converting his suspicions into statements of fact.

'We know the kidnappers have been in touch with your father-in-law on at least four occasions, and that he has been conducting negotiations to pay the ransom.'

Stewart intervened. 'And they spotted your surveillance,' he said. 'You don't think that was jeopardising the children?'

It was a good riposte, but Brady was ready. 'I don't know if they spotted us or not, Mr Stewart, but I doubt it. Criminals always think they're being followed. But I want you to take note: We left them alone. We could have pulled them in, no problem. We did not. Even though you had refused to confide in us, which meant that we were flying blind, we were not prepared to put your children's lives at risk.'

They were both nodding: 'Fair point', they were conceding.

'And Victor Canning hasn't been arrested either.'

That shook them up. They were no longer nodding. They

didn't know he knew about Canning. Pick up on what Skinner had told him by phone in Austin, use it to move in hard.

'I need to ask you something, Mrs Beaumont. Is Canning justified in believing that MycoGene is killing his daughter?'

'Certainly not.' Stewart had intervened again – rather too quickly, Brady thought. 'So why does he think that?' he asked.

'It's hard to say,' Stewart replied. 'Except that I could understand why any parent would look for an explanation of why their child isn't getting better, and MycoGene's a useful target.'

'I presume Canning told you that himself. After you got into Kathleen's room and copied her medical chart.'

Stewart took that one in his stride. 'He said something to that effect. We spoke to him outside the clinic. He wasn't specific, but he did say if we wanted to know what had happened to our children, we should go to Austin.'

It was Brady's turn to nod, as if none of this was new to him. But now he had it confirmed: this wasn't about Stewart's book. This was about revenge – Canning's revenge.

'How much are they asking?'

'A hundred million dollars.'

A hundred million was what Stewart had said. This time it was Brady who had to maintain his composure. 'Payable how?'

'Negotiable securities. Bearer bonds.'

'And you're here to hand them over?'

'Yes.'

'To Kain?'

'We assume so. We'll know when the bonds arrive this evening.'

The details were flowing now. 'Who's bringing them?'

'A friend of Mr Beaumont's. A senator.'

Not to hard to guess that one. 'Must be Saul Bates,' said Brady confidently. 'Where are you meeting him?'

'At the Vietnam memorial.'

'What time?'

'We don't know yet. He's going to call.'

'Then he tells you where to meet Kain?'

'That's right.'

'And then?'

'We get a call telling us where to find our children.'

'Where?'

Stewart looked puzzled. 'That's what we don't know.'

'No, where do you get the call?'

'Here. At the Jefferson.'

'And you're going to do this with no proof your children are alive?'

'Of course not,' said Stewart. 'We've seen a photograph of them. It was taken last week. They were holding a newspaper, so we know the date.'

Brady leaned forward in his chair again. Now secure their cooperation. 'I appreciate your telling me all of this. Now I want to explain what we're going to do. When you go to meet Bates, I'd like you to carry a tracking device, a transmitter that will let us follow your movements. It'll be installed in a briefcase, the same briefcase you'll use to take the bonds to Kain, once Bates has told you where to go.'

'And then?'

'We follow Kain.'

'What happens if he junks the case and just takes the bonds?'

'That's a chance we'll have to take. But we've set up this kind of thing before. Once people get their hands on the money, it's surprising how careless they can be.'

Stewart gave an ironic laugh. 'You think Kain is going to get careless?'

'Could be, Tom. But either way, the briefcase puts us in the starting gate. We'll know where he is right then, and we'll follow him as far as we can. It'll give us time to set up other surveillance too.'

Brady thought he was making headway with Stewart. But it was Suzanne who spoke next.

'Suppose they find the transmitter? What happens to our children then?'

Still work to do, Brady thought. Time for the killer revelation. 'How much do you know about Canning?'

'What's that got to do with anything?' Stewart asked.

'I'm coming to that. First tell me what you know.'

'We know he runs a transport company. It's in London, we've been there. And he smuggles heroin.'

'All that is true,' said Brady. 'But only up to a point. This is not some small-time doper we're talking about. Canning's a major, major violator. One of the biggest heroin dealers in Britain. He kills people too – at least a dozen so far the Brits know about. Almost certainly there's more.'

Brady was looking at Suzanne. 'News to you?' he asked.

She gulped and nodded.

'Just so we're clear who we're dealing with,' Brady went on. 'And there's another thing. Kidnapping is a federal crime and we can't ignore it. Least of all can I turn my back while you deliver a hundred million dollars to Kain.'

'So you're saying you'll arrest us?' Stewart asked.

'I'm not saying that. What I am saying is I'll put twenty agents outside the Jefferson, and you won't go anywhere without them.'

'So we can't deliver the ransom – is that the point?'

Brady ignored the question. 'Surely you must see that the best way is we work together. If you carry the transmitter, there'll be no agents in sight. Kain gets to walk away with the bonds, and he can keep walking, wherever he likes. We don't make a move until Fiona and Josh are on their way home.'

'And if they don't let the children go?'

'Then you'll certainly need us. At least this way, we should find out where they're being held.'

Stewart looked at Suzanne, who nodded. 'Then that's what we'll do,' he said.

So it was over. Brady told them to call him as soon as they heard from Bates. A technician would come to the Jefferson to give them a briefcase fitted with the latest miniaturised transmitter. When Stewart looked sceptical, Brady assured him they were almost infallible. He had just one question left.

'You must like the Jefferson,' he said.

'Why do you ask?'

'It's changed, hasn't it?'

'I used to stay here a lot. Came back for old time's sake, I suppose.'

Brady walked back to the FBI building, gave him time to think. As he played over the meeting in his mind, something about it nagged at him like a tooth that still needed fixing. Hadn't it all been too easy?

* * *

'Did he buy it?'

'Looks like it,' said Stewart. 'What did you think of him?'

'Not much,' replied Suzanne. 'He came across like he was doing us a big favour, but he was pretty hard underneath. He certainly knew how to get under my skin when he wanted to. That stuff about Canning was scary.'

'Cops are like that,' said Stewart. 'Hit you with stuff you don't know. Try to shake you up so you'll do what they want.'

'Do you trust him?'

'Same answer. Not much. I still think that what matters to him is nailing Kain and Canning.'

'So we stick to the plan.'

'Nothing's changed.'

'What do we do with the briefcase?'

'I think that's clear now, don't you?'

Suzanne said she was going to shower, perhaps take a nap in her room. Stewart still felt too on edge to settle down. There was a long piece in the *Washington Post* about the future of genetic engineering he knew he should read, in the hope of learning more about what had gone wrong at BioGenius. He had started reading it before, but given up. He tried again.

The unpredictability and complexity of the natural world is at least as problematic as regulatory obstacles or opposition from animal rights campaigners. Still his mind declined to absorb its meaning. Perhaps a shower would help. Suzanne had disappeared into her room – no sound from within – and he let the water wash over him for a good five minutes before emerging in one of the Jefferson's white towelling dressing-gowns. He ensconced himself in an arm-chair and tried the article one more time. But this time his thoughts returned to the plan he and Suzanne had devised, wondering where it could go wrong. He knew they were taking a risk. But still he wasn't ready to trust Brady, or any other of the police officers who persisted in assuring him of their good intentions.

He laid the *Post* on the floor and allowed his head to rest against the back of his arm-chair. He remembered his dream of climbing along the ridge of the mountain in Vietnam, when

Fee had called to him from out of the mist. The telephone rang and it was Bates, terse and to the point.

'Six-thirty. Where we arranged. Don't be late.'

'I won't be,' said Stewart, and the line went dead.

'Was that him?'

Suzanne's call came from beyond her half-closed door.

'Suzanne?'

'It's okay. Come on in.'

The curtains were drawn and the room was in shadows. She was lying in bed, one bare arm resting on the covers.

'The meeting's on,' Stewart said. 'Three hours time.'

'And Brady?'

'I was about to call him.'

'Why don't you do it from here?'

He dialled Brady's direct line from the phone beside her bed. The conversation was as brief and functional as the last.

'We need to pack up to leave,' Stewart said as he replaced the receiver.

'What time's he coming?'

'Five-thirty. Gives us two hours.'

'Are you sure we're doing the right thing?'

'There's no moment since our children disappeared that I've been sure of anything. This is as much of a gamble as everything else. But what choice do we have?'

'That's what I've been wondering.'

'Are you having doubts?'

'Sometimes I feel as if I'm out at sea in an open boat. It's like that now. I feel bewildered and lost. And there's no-one we can trust. Not Kain, not Brady, not Jesse.'

'We do have each other,' Stewart said.

'I know we do,' she said, 'and I'm beginning to realise how much that means to me.'

He reached across the counterpane. She took his hand and held it tight. She was looking at him intently but in the shadowy light Stewart could not fathom her eyes. For a second or two there was nothing, and Stewart wondered if he had made a mistake. Then she met his lips with hers. At first he did not know if this was a kiss of consolation, of compassion for their shared plight. Then he sensed the charge which told him it was more.

'Come here,' Suzanne said, and lifted the bed cover. As he slid beneath it, he felt his dressing gown part. She rested her head on the pillow. He held himself away from her, wondering and waiting, but she was waiting too, holding herself still. He touched her shoulder, then let his hand course down her side and into the hollow of her waist before rising again across her hip. Then he felt the ripples of her ribs and the cushion of her breasts. He brushed her nipples with his fingers and felt her desire stiffen in measure with the quickening of his own.

Always at this moment he felt poised between the impulse of his desires and the inhibition of revealing himself to a stranger for the first time. Then the two merged, and the revelation strengthened the desire. Then he would try to balance his own pleasure with his desire to bring pleasure to the stranger who was indulging her own desires too. Sometimes selfishness won, and he left the stranger to satisfy herself. Sometimes he felt their desires merging as the stranger became a partner and their skin touched and brushed and mingled, so that it felt as if they had become one. That was happening now. Suzanne was breathing harder and he cupped her head as if to shield her from the night and the pain that was threatening their lives.

'Suzanne,' he said. 'Suzanne, Suzanne,' elongating the syllables, savouring her name, 'Suze Ann.'

He was moving into her now, felt her tight at first, then ease herself open, warm and yielding. The stranger was welcoming him, bringing him in, taking him home. He wanted to say he loved her, but that wasn't quite right. He wanted her to know that he shared her anguish and her grief, and that the knowledge that they were not alone brought some respite. He didn't say that either, but he wanted the locking of their bodies to say it instead. He was exploring her now, feeling her out, far inside, his rhythm quickening. He wanted her to have a moment of pleasure that would be theirs, wanted this to be a moment of intimacy and strength that separated them, however briefly, from the world beyond the bedroom door. The pain would return to claim them but not now, not yet. For now they and their moment, in the darkness, with the sheets of Suzanne's bed the ground on which they lay, were all that mattered. They were moving together, muscles clenching, her holding him in, him wanting to go deeper and further, finding her limits and pushing beyond. They were in the present, not the terrors of the past and not the uncertainty of the future, and they were together, coming together ever more strongly, together as one in defiance of what awaited them beyond and outside. She was gasping and he was searching for the strength to sustain their togetherness. The force was outside him now, outside his control, and it grew and mounted and then it broke and ebbed and he heard himself struggle to find his breath as if from afar.

He saw a man nestling in the cusp of some rocks and knew it was himself, and knew he was nestling against a woman and knew it was Suzanne, and he heard her breath subside with his own. He reached over and drew her to him and then relaxed his hold, and then stroked her face and felt her perspiration on her forehead and in her hair. He knew he wanted to shield her and knew he wanted her to hold him for as long as they could before they had to break apart and go out and face the world. He wanted to say all that and he knew he could not find the words but knew he had to speak, and he said: 'Suzanne.'

She murmured something in reply but he did not know if it was words or just a sound. Her eyes stayed closed. Then she spoke again.

'How much time do we have?'

Stewart knew the spell was broken and they were two people again and the pain would return.

29

If talking to yourself was a sign of madness, Stewart mused, the men in white coats would be coming for him soon. 'Heading down 17th,' he said, shortly after leaving the Jefferson. 'Farragut Square,' he next said. 'Crossing Pennsylvania Avenue,' as the White House loomed. 'Outside the Corcoran,' as he passed the pair of stone lions crouching at the art gallery's entrance.

Despite Brady's admonition, Stewart fingered the top of the pen that was lodged in the top pocket of his shirt. The pen made him feel self-conscious too. Brady, when warning him not to touch it, had assured him that no one, but no one, would realise that it was a disguised radio-mike. But it was hard to believe that he was not attracting attention. And could Brady and his team even hear the stilted commentary they had asked him to provide? This was supposed to let them check the accuracy of the tracking device secreted in the handle of his black leather briefcase. But whether the mike was even working, Stewart had no idea.

He crossed Constitution Avenue and turned along the edge of the park. In other circumstances, it would have made a pleasantly indolent sight, with people strolling across the grass or sitting on the marble surround of the Reflecting Pool. But which were FBI agents? The twenty-something couple deep in conversation as they walked parallel with him thirty yards away? The middle-aged man in a floppy hat with his dachshund and pooper-scooper? Brady had promised him that the watchers would keep their distance and allow the gizmos to do their work. But would they really show such self-restraint?

True, Brady seemed to be straight – or, at least straighter than most. But it was the straight cops, not the obvious chancers like Desiry, whose lies were the hardest to detect. There was only one rule worth following, as he and Suzanne had reminded each other after Brady had left the Jefferson: trust no one, apart from ourselves. As he prepared for his rendezvous with Bates she had kissed him softly and assured him: we have each other. He remembered the darkness of the bedroom, and how strong they had seemed together.

'Approaching the memorial,' Stewart said. There were more people now, converging across the park at a cluster of trees where Stewart glimpsed the blackness of the Vietnam memorial. He briefly registered the irony that the very place where his quest for Red Kain had begun was now to be a key staging-post in his search for Fee. In the crowd around the wall Stewart saw the same solemn faces, some fresh and innocent, others weary and lined, that had so moved him more than two years ago. Then he found the bench he had been sitting on when he first spied Luke Lewis attempting to make sense of the engraving of his father's name in the marble. It was occupied by four teenagers in baggy trousers and baseball caps but a bench alongside was free.

Stewart took a copy of the *Washingtonian* magazine from his briefcase. 'In place,' he said, tilting his head to bring his mouth closer to the pen. 'Five minutes ahead of time. No sign of Bates.'

Then Stewart saw a venerable head bobbing towards him through the crowd, the shock of white hair familiar from the photographs Brady had asked him to study. He closed the *Washingtonian*, held it purposefully against his case, and stood up.

'Senator Bates. I'm Tom Stewart.'

'Can you prove that?' Bates barked. 'Got your passport?'

Stewart removed it from the briefcase. Bates opened it, looked at the photograph and handed it back.

'Let's sit here,' he said, taking a place on the bench, facing the marble wall. 'Damn shame,' he said. 'All those lives wasted.'

'It's a very moving place,' said Stewart, as he sat down beside him.

'Should never have happened.'

'The war?'

'Losing it.'

Stewart didn't feel like responding. 'Let's get on with it,' said Bates. From inside his jacket he produced a bulging brown manilla envelope. 'The bonds are in here,' he said.

'When I leave, you're to take them to Howard Johnson's Motor Lodge, 2601 Virginia Avenue. You know where that is?'

'Opposite the Watergate.'

'You'd better put them in your case and take a cab. You don't want to be walking the streets like that.'

'I'll be fine, senator,' Stewart assured him.

Bates took a key-card from his pocket. 'Room 336. It's in your name, just go right up. Put the briefcase under the bed, then get the hell out.'

'Are you saying there'll be no one in the room?'

'You've got it. Just park the bonds, then leave. Get another cab and go wherever you're going. That's it. Remember, room 336. It's not marked on the card.'

'Three three six,' Stewart repeated.

Bates stood up, leaving the envelope beside Stewart on the bench. 'Damn shame,' he said, looking at the wall again. 'Give me a few minutes, will you?' He soon merged with the evening walkers as he headed down the path towards Constitution Avenue, where his limousine waited. Stewart picked up the envelope and nursed it on his lap until Bates had disappeared. Then he, too, set off across the park.

Barely a quarter-mile away, a van sporting the livery of the Washington Gas & Light Company was parked on the corner of 23rd and C streets. Inside, out of sight of any curious pedestrians, sat Brady and Gonzales, together with two technicians – one wearing earphones, the other scrutinising a monitor-screen showing a map of the Vietnam Memorial and the surrounding park.

'He's gone awful quiet,' said the technician with the earphones.

The second technician kept watching his screen for signals from the briefcase. 'He's not moving either.'

'Give him a moment,' said Brady.

Gonzales finished speaking into a mobile phone. 'Everyone in place.'

'Nobody inside the hotel, right?'

'Right,' said Gonzales, jabbing at the screen. 'I've set up a perimeter here, here and here.'

Brady turned to the technician with the earphones. 'You getting anything?'

The technician contorted his face in concentration. 'The signal's very muffled. Maybe he's put the mike in his pocket.'

'What's he playing at?' said Gonzales.

'He's moving,' said the second technician.

On the monitor, a flashing white dot was moving away from the Vietnam Memorial. 'At least it's functioning,' said Brady. But then, instead of turning north towards Constitution Avenue as they expected, it continued east.

'He's heading away from the Howard Johnson,' said Brady.

'In Christ's name what's he doing?' Gonzales asked.

'Maybe he's looking for a cab,' said the first technician.

'In the Reflecting Pool?' said the second.

Brady watched the dot moving steadily further eastward. 'Any agents got him in sight?'

'You said you didn't want him eyeballed, Phil.'

'I know I did, Harry. Damn. Let's check it out.'

He pushed open the back door of the van and jumped down to the street. Half-walking, half-running, he and Gonzales reached Constitution Avenue and turned in the direction taken by the dot.

'Can't see him anywhere,' said Brady. 'What's the van saying?'

'He's still ahead of us,' said Gonzales, who was listening through an earpiece. 'Let's cross.'

They dodged across Constitution Avenue and ran to the 17th Street intersection. 'We should be alongside him right now,' he panted.

Brady leaned against a railing, his tie askew. 'So where the fuck is he?'

Gonzales spoke urgently into a microphone concealed in the sleeve of his jacket. 'He's continuing on the same route,' he told Brady. 'Looks like he's headed for the Washington Monument.'

Walking now, they took a diagonal course across the grass to the towering obelisk. A dozen people were standing around its base or sitting on its mound. Stewart was not among them.

'Over there, Harry,' said Brady. 'The bag lady.'

An elderly woman in bedraggled clothes was rearranging her

bundles of possessions, some in plastic shopping bags, some bound with string, on a battered supermarket trolley. Tucked in beside them was a black briefcase.

They strode across to the woman. 'Federal agents,' said Brady, showing her his badge. 'You're in possession of stolen property. We need that case.'

As he reached into the trolley, she snatched the case and clung it to her chest. 'No you don't, motherfucker. It's mine.' Heads turned around at the monument as she began screaming. Some watchers came to take a closer look.

'Back off, folks,' said Brady, brandishing his badge. Gonzales wrestled the case from the woman's grasp and snapped open the catch. Inside was a copy of the *Washingtonian* magazine and a pen containing a radio microphone. Back at the Washington Gas & Light van, the two technicians heard a torrent of abuse exceeding anything the woman had uttered.

Room 337, the Howard Johnson Watergate Motor Lodge, opposite Watergate, Washington DC: A guest who had registered as Dr Marcus Scott lay on a queen-sized bed watching a mute television screen where the final images of a police drama were being played out. A sniper was trapped in the bell-tower of a church while members of a SWAT squad held him in their sights. The sniper crawled to the edge of the tower and loosed off a burst of semi-automatic fire before being shot, toppling over the balustrade and tumbling to his death.

'The dumb fuck,' he said, with feeling. As the credits slid past, he checked his watch and blanked the screen. Beside the television was a black medical bag. Scott pulled open the Velcro flaps and removed a stethoscope. He moved to the door connecting with room 336 and listened with his stethoscope for several minutes. Then he replaced the stethoscope in his bag and took out a leather key case. Inside was a line of thin steel picks with a variety of slots and teeth. He tried one in the door-lock but it did not move. He selected a second and this time he succeeded. He opened the door and stepped through.

Once inside, he remained still until he was finally sure no one was there. He bolted the main door and turned on the light. Room 336 was identical to his own: the same queen-sized bed, the same television, the same fake mahogany surfaces. He lifted the counterpane on the bed. Nothing underneath. He reached under the bed. Again nothing. He sat with his knees drawn up and surveyed the room. He pulled the counterpane off the bed, followed by the rest of the bedding. Nothing. He pulled the bed away from the wall and upended it. Beneath was only the same brown carpet that covered the rest of the floor. He opened drawers, peered inside the wardrobe, yanked open the curtains. Still nothing. He went into the bathroom and tugged down the shower curtain, lifted the top of the lavatory cistern, pulled out the panel beneath the sink. Nothing, fucking nothing. He returned to the bedroom once more, his anger bursting through.

'You fuck,' he said. 'You're fucking dead.'

He returned to his own room and was closing his medical bag when a telephone rang. At first he thought it was his phone but when he lifted the receiver he heard only the dial tone. He crossed back into room 336 and picked up the receiver. A man's voice asked: 'Kain?'

'No,' he lied. 'Who's this?'

'Listen, Kain. I have a message for you. You don't get the package until you produce the children. You want the package, be in Amsterdam the day after tomorrow. The Hotel Pulitzer, three in the afternoon. Don't screw up.'

'Who the fuck is this?'

The dial tone again.

The cleaners had been and gone long ago, clattering their way through the offices as they emptied the waste-bins and vacuumed the FBI's well-trodden steel-grey carpets. Brady had embarked on a search for coffee which was interrupted when he was summoned along the corridor to see Assistant Director Jim Miller, who was not best pleased at being compelled to stay late to help sort out the politics of Brady's operation. It was all, as Gonzales was telling his Austin office, verging on disaster.

First place, Gonzales recounted, Stewart had disappeared, most likely taking the bonds with him. Second place, the Beaumont woman had checked both of them out of the Jefferson and gone off with some guy in a Mustang, who wasn't Kain. Sure they were sure, Gonzales insisted. 'From the description, he was half Kain's age. Then someone got into the room where the drop was supposed to go down and trashed it to hell.' No, the surveillance crew didn't pick up on them, going either in or out.

And how was Brady taking it?

Brady had just come back into his office. Gonzales looked at him and ground out a smile. 'You tell me,' he said into the phone. The voice in his ear was saying Brady must be spitting blood. 'Got it in one,' said Gonzales.

'What did Miller say?' asked Gonzales, as he put down the phone.

'He wants us to lay off Bates for tonight. I think he's getting worried this thing's going nowhere. Sounds like he wants to play it by the book.'

'Can't say I'm surprised,' said Gonzales.

'You want more coffee?'

'Hell, no. I'm shot full of caffeine already.'

Brady burrowed into the cupboard beneath the coffee maker. 'Where's Betsy put the stuff?'

'There's more,' said Gonzales.

Brady looked up. 'Tell me about it.'

'Beaumont's disappeared, too. He's not at home and his secretary hasn't heard from him since yesterday morning.'

'Are your people certain?'

'No question, Phil. Hide nor hair. Jesse's gone.'

'That's all we need.' Brady gave up his search for coffee. His tie was askew, his face was slack. Gonzales could not remember seeing him so tired before. 'We'll have to go for an APB on Beaumont. All agencies, arrest and detain. Let's do it now.'

'On what charge?'

'I don't know. We'll think of something, and worry about the details later.'

'Accessory to kidnapping? Interstate flight?'

Brady ran his fingers through his hair. 'None of it'll stick, but it'll do for now. I just want him picked up. And put out an airport watch for Stewart and Mrs Beaumont. National, Dulles, and don't forget Baltimore. I want all passenger manifests checked, domestic and international.'

'We're not going to find too many airline folks around this time of night.'

'I know, but I want it started as soon as they open for business.

Get a team lined up now. I want every flight checked going back to 6 p.m. last night, and every flight out for the next three days.'

Gonzales picked up the phone to call the night-watch commander in the Washington field office. Before he could dial, Brady said: 'One more thing. You should get back to Texas and take hold of the investigation. We need to understand how this went down. Pull Beaumont's phone records and check on everyone he's called in the last ten days.'

'I'll get the first flight,' said Gonzales.

'I want you to crawl all over that taxicab company – Vet Cabs, whatever it's called. More I think about it, the more I'm convinced that's how Kain did it. Used one of the drivers to conduct the negotiations with Beaumont. Or maybe he was the goddamned driver. Anyway, lean on them.'

'You've got it.'

As Gonzales made his call, Brady was continuing his search. He gave a grunt of satisfaction when he found Betsy's stash of coffee in a filing cabinet. He was opening a packet when the fax machine came alive.

'Did you ask for a list of rental cars?' he asked Gonzales.

'Yeah, all the major companies,' Gonzales replied. 'In case the Mustang turned out to be a rental.'

Brady pulled the list from the machine. 'Take a look.'

The fax was from Avis, listing all Mustang rentals in the Washington area in the previous seventy-two hours. There were only six. The most recent was for a Mustang rented at National Airport the previous morning, and returned to Dulles twelve hours later. The name on the contract was Luke Lewis.

'You think we should wake him up?' asked Gonzales, reaching for his jacket.

'Damn right I do,' said Brady.

Four thousand miles away, Dominique Halard yawned. Another night spent trying to marshal the endless theories and permutations criss-crossing through her mind. Another morning back at the Prefecture, fortified by coffee that grew viscous as it stewed in the pot. Two days before, she had moved aside the trestle tables and laid out the case files on the floor, end to end, in lines of parallel paper canals. She had done this once before, on an investigation into a sequence of murders in the Paris *banlieu* of Saint-Denis. It had helped her find connections she had not seen before, and three gangland hitmen were now doing hard time in Les Beaumettes, France's toughest prison. This time, as she paced up and down the canals, the links would not come.

Halard had no doubt Cabrini had ordered Sail's murder. But by staying in the restaurant, eating yet more oysters until it was over, he had provided himself an inviolable alibi. And though Desiry had beaten the bushes in Marseille, Lyon, Bordeaux and even Corsica – anywhere Cabrini had cousins or criminal connections – there was no trace of the hitman, or his driver. 'Probably a couple of punks hired off the street through cut-outs,' Desiry had gloomily decided. 'Probably never even heard of Cabrini.'

'Okay,' Brady had said on one of his repeated calls in quest of an update, 'but what about the boat? It can't just have vanished.'

'Phil, we're doing everything we can.'

So they were. For six days, spotter planes from the *Police de l'Air et des Frontières* had scoured the Mediterranean as far as the North African coast, looking for a two-masted yacht matching the *Symphonie*. Along the entire southern coast of France, from Menton to Perpignan, gendarmes had checked every port and harbour, every inlet and creek, while their counterparts in Spain and Italy had continued the search further west and east.

With no result.

So, risking the ire of the minister – whose patience was stretched thin – Halard had pleaded for reinforcements from the French navy and air force, and started the hunt again. This time her 'stop and search' description included yachts with one mast as well as two, on the guess that the kidnappers might have disguised *Symphonie* by removing the mizzen mast.

'Damn it, Phil, there are simply too many boats out there at this time of year,' she'd told Brady.

There was a snap in her voice which surprised him, but he assumed it stemmed from her frustration.

'How many?' he'd asked in his methodical way.

'I don't know, and I don't care,' she fired back. 'All I know is that we can't find it, or the children. At this moment, we are precisely nowhere.'

Perhaps to placate her, Brady had owned up to his own failures: his failure to realise until too late that the ransom negotiations with Jesse Beaumont had been conducted under his nose in the back of a taxicab; the failure of the NSA to crack the encryption codes that Canning used for sending and receiving messages; above all, his failure to anticipate that Stewart's agreement to cooperate was a blind, and that he might bolt with the ransom.

'I did warn you about him,' Halard had said.

'Yeah, you did,' conceded Brady. 'And in writing.'

Halard had since regretted the sour turn the conversation had taken. Her instinct was to call him back and make amends but it was the early hours of the morning in Washington, far too late to disturb him. Tired of pacing the paper canals, she leant against a desk, sipping Badoit and playing through the shifting hypotheses on the kidnap. How the Vietnam Book Theory had given way to the Sick Daughter Revenge Theory, and how the British cop, Skinner, claimed to be fully on board, now that he saw the chance to nail Victor Canning.

She didn't trust Skinner, or his sudden conversion. 'Let's just take him at face value,' Brady had advised. She had agreed but her doubts remained, adding to her fear of losing control. A refrain kept insinuating itself into her mind: 'Running on empty'. The title of a movie? The lyrics of a song? She couldn't be sure. But it just about summed up how she felt.

Another call from Brady snapped her out of her musings.

'For God's sake, Phil. What time is it there? Two thirty?'

'We've got a lead,' he said. 'The guy who collected Mrs Beaumont from the hotel was Luke Lewis. Then he drove to the Arlington Bridge where Stewart was waiting to take over the car. Lewis says he bailed out at that point and has no idea where they were headed. In fact, he claims to know nothing, other than that Stewart asked him to rent a car and do what he did. I think he's lying, but that doesn't matter for now. Since we know the rental car was returned to Dulles airport last evening, my bet is they're in the air.'

'An international flight?'

'Can't tell. We're rousting all the airlines to get a look at the passenger manifests. Assuming they're using their own names, we should know in a couple of hours. At most, four.'

'I'll be here,' Halard said. 'And Phil . . .'
'What?'
'Get some sleep.'

Brady called again at six o'clock his time.
'We've got them,' he told her.
'Tell me.'
'Beaumont's in London. She got into Heathrow on British Airways a couple of hours ago. I've got Skinner looking for her now. And Stewart's with you. In France.'
'They split up?'
'Yeah. He left Dulles forty minutes after her on Air France. Landed at De Gaulle ten thirty your time, so he's got a ninety-minute head start. Think you can find him?'
'It won't be easy, Phil.'
Brady assumed Halard was talking about the new ease of travel in western Europe, where border posts are little more than gestures, customs checks have been abandoned, passports are superfluous. In fact, as she told him, her difficulty lay in persuading the minister to allocate yet more resources to a case that was reeking of failure.
'Jesus,' said Brady.
'A lot depends on where Stewart's gone and how. If he's on his way back down here, there are flights just about every hour to Marseille and Nice. Or he could come by train, in which case we can still pick him up when he arrives. The airline checks are no problem, and I can organise a watch on the railway stations down here. For anything in Paris, I'll have to get on to the minister.'
It took Halard two hours to reach him, and he tersely agreed that twelve Paris officers should be deployed to Charles de Gaulle. Equipped with photographs of Stewart and Kain, they questioned airline officials, car rental clerks, taxi drivers, and booking clerks at the train and bus terminals. But many of the staff had started their shifts that afternoon, by which time Stewart was long gone. It was just before midnight, as Halard prepared to leave the Prefecture, her mind dazed with fatigue, when Brady called once more.
'Any joy?'
No, she told him. None at all.

Part Five

30

Stewart sat on the terrace of the Hotel Pulitzer, drinking lemon tea and wondering how it was, given it was a perfect summer day, that the world inland racing dinghy championship was about to be staged on the neighbouring canal. The dinghies were there all right, tiny craft with brilliantly-coloured sails, blues and reds, yellows and greens, drifting across the narrow stretch of water bounded by a humpbacked bridge at each end. The banners announcing the championship had been suspended among the plane trees that gave Amsterdam its bucolic air. But where was the wind?

Stewart looked at his watch. The race was due to start at three o'clock: five minutes to go. He looked at the sky; still not a cloud in sight, so no prospect of a sudden hurricane either. By chance, three o'clock also happened to be the time of his rendezvous with Kain. If he came, of course. Stewart was suddenly aware of the terrible gamble he had taken. Standing up a killer and kidnapper in Washington, summoning him to a meeting in another continent. And what if Kain refused to play ball?

Out on the canal, four boats had formed a line abreast. Spectators were clustered on the bridges and along the canal bank. A man was poised on the apex of the bridge, a blue flag in one hand, staring at his watch. Stewart glanced at his, as the seconds counted down to three o'clock. There were still fifteen seconds to go when the starter flashed down his flag. From the far bank, a klaxon sounded, its echo resounding from the canal walls.

Still the boats were not moving. But then came a sound Stewart knew from the mountains, of a gust of wind, gathering in strength as it approached. The dinghies' sails filled and they edged forward. Stewart saw a bank of turbofans, six in line, mounted on a boom under the arch of the bridge, the engines rising to a whine as they gathered speed, the fans driving air down the enclosed space of the canal. The dinghies skittered across the water as they headed for the bridge at the far end, encouraged by whoops from the spectators.

'Can you believe that?'

Red Kain was standing beside Stewart's table, following the boats with his eyes, shaking his head in amusement. His dyed blond hair was little more than stubble, accentuating the broad sweep of his forehead. He wore reflecting sunglasses that hid his eyes and his nose was broader than Stewart remembered. It was the smile on his lips which seemed familiar, from that pool-side conversation at Le Bosquet, when he had extracted the information he had needed as precisely as if he had been using a scalpel.

He pulled out a chair, its feet shrieking on the tiled floor of the terrace, and sat opposite Stewart. 'Do you like them?'

'Do I like what?'

'Sailboats.'

'They don't do a lot for me,' said Stewart.

'Thought you were the adventurous type,' said Kain. 'Personally, I can't see the point of pissing around on a canal. Give me the ocean any time. Go where you like. Go where nobody knows where you are.'

Kain was repeating his Le Bosquet act too: behaving as if they had met by chance, sharing their amusement at the spectacle, whether it was this bizarre race, or the woman in the green bathing cap gliding down the hotel pool. Stewart had that distanced feeling again, reminding him of the time he had given evidence in court in support of the victim of a mugging, and he felt apart from the proceedings, as if he were a watcher, not a participant. This time he had a sense of *déjà-vu*, or something like it: an illusion that he was a character in a story, and that he knew the plot, and how it would end.

Kain asked a waitress for a beer. He lit a cigarette and exhaled, the smoke drifting towards the plane trees, only to be whipped away by the wind from the fans.

'That was quite a stunt you pulled.'

'Glad you liked it,' said Stewart.

'Why Amsterdam?'

'Amsterdam was your idea, remember? It was where we were supposed to wait for the phone call after you got the ransom. I just changed the order of events.'

'Cute. Your daughter's history now. You know that, don't you?'

'That's bollocks, Kain. If that's true, why are you here?'

The waitress brought a beer, together with a glass on a tray. Kain swigged the beer from the neck. 'So, where are they?'

'Where are what?'

'The bonds?'

'Where's my daughter?'

'You give me the bonds, you get your daughter.'

'You've got it wrong, Kain. First I get my daughter, and Mrs Beaumont gets her son. *Then* you get the bonds.'

Kain laughed. 'You want me to make you say where the bonds are? Is that what you're telling me? Because believe me, I'd know how to do it. Is that what you really want?'

'Forget the threats, Kain. I don't have the bonds, and if you thought I'd bring them to Amsterdam, I've overestimated you. The bonds are somewhere you can't reach. If anything happens to me, they're handed over to the police. The only way you can get them is if I see Fee and Josh first.'

Kain swallowed more beer and brushed his lips with the back of his hand. 'I take it you've seen the picture? The one we sent to Jesse?'

'What about it?'

'What about it is you know what will happen to your kids if you carry on fucking me around.'

Stewart stood up. He saw Kain tense, as if steeling himself for a fist fight. Stewart reached into his pocket and pulled out a handful of coins. 'I'm going to pay for the drinks, then I'm going down to the lobby to call the police. This is where you start running, Kain.'

Kain grinned. 'They spiked that piss you're drinking? You've got some nerve.'

Stewart leaned forward, both hands on the table, until he could see his reflection in Kain's tinted glasses. This time he really was watching himself.

'Show me Fiona and Josh,' he heard himself say. 'Show me

they're still alive, and I'll give you the bonds. If you don't, I'll burn them. That's the deal. It's as simple as that.'

'Sit down,' Kain said, but he had lost his bluster. Stewart was impressed at the effect of what he had said. Was he playing a part? Or was this the real Tom Stewart?

'Tell me something,' Kain said. 'How do you know my name?'

'The FBI. They worked out you were Carlson.'

'How?'

'Does it matter?'

Kain ground his cigarette into the ashtray.

'So, the cops put you up to this?'

'I'm not working with the cops. They wanted me to work with them, try to trap you, but I decided to go my own way.'

'Sure you did,' said Kain.

'It's true. Otherwise they'd be all over you by now.'

Kain flicked at the neck of the beer bottle with his fingers, but his eyes never left Stewart's face.

'Look, Kain, understand one thing. I don't care what happens to you, and I don't care about the money. So far as I'm concerned, Jesse Beaumont is no better than you are. If it costs him one hundred million dollars, fine. All I care about, all that matters, is getting the children back. You want the money, show me the children.'

'How did you get here?'

'A plane to Paris, then the train.'

'Under your own name?'

'I just bought a ticket. They didn't ask for a name.'

'The plane, for Christ's sake. Did you use an alias?'

Stewart sensed they were nearing the crunch. 'No. I had to show my passport. I've only got one. Unlike you.'

'Then they'll be on to you. No question.'

'Then we'd better get moving,' said Stewart.

Kain leaned back in his chair. Stewart looked towards the canal, where the race was becoming ever more frenetic, as the helmsmen tacked back and forth, jousting for leeway in the restricted space. The whoops from the spectators intensified. The klaxon sounded again, announcing the end of the contest. Stewart had no idea who had won.

* * *

The ball kept low, skidding off the side wall, but Brady was ready. He lunged to his right and smacked a hard half-volley, turning his wrist to give the ball loft. Coming back at him, it soared back over his head and reached the rear wall on the full. He let it bounce then sliced it into the corner, forcing himself to sprint to the front of the court to play the next shot. He didn't make it. The ball died at his feet.

There was a joke at the club that Brady liked to play squash against himself to make sure he won. But that was to misunderstand the man. He was far from the most competitive member, languishing near the bottom of the squash ladders, though that was partly because the demands of the FBI forced him to default on so many games. At times he liked to play these solo matches because they were free of the intensity of the league matches, testing himself by seeing how long he could keep the ball in play, stretching his muscles to keep them in trim, allowing the cares of his work to fall away. In that brief, self-contained interlude within the court's four austere walls, he could forget the agency, forget Kain and Canning, forget his ragged conversations with Halard – and almost forget the pressure to find the kidnapped kids. In the shower afterwards, as the fatigue in his muscles drained away, Brady closed his eyes to maintain the spell a moment longer. He did not even mind the banter.

'Hey, Phil, why don't you play yourself at doubles?'

'Yeah, that way you could win twice over.'

Then came a louder call. 'Hey, Brady! Phone!'

It had to be Halard. Did she have news? He grabbed a towel and jogged to the phone booth in the club lounge. There were no preliminaries

'Stewart's in Amsterdam,' she said. 'Or he was this afternoon.'

'How did you find him?'

'I put out a Europe-wide bulletin.'

'And what?'

'The Dutch police did a hotel check. Found Stewart registered at the Pulitzer since yesterday morning. That's the good news.'

'Go on,' said Brady.

'He checked out this afternoon.'

'Shit. Anything else?'

'There was another man with him, Phil. The way the receptionist described him, it has to be Kain.'

The implications were racing through Brady's mind.

'Phil, are you there?'

'I'm trying to figure this out. You think he's paid the ransom?'

'Not yet. There's more. From Skinner. Suzanne Beaumont is holed up at Stewart's flat in London. She's not going anywhere, and she's not making phone calls. She got a package this morning, Federal Express. Guess where it came from?'

'Washington,' said Brady. He knew where this was going.

'Dulles International, to be precise. It was left in the Fed-Ex drop-off box in the departure terminal on Wednesday night. Pre-paid with a credit card in the name of Tom Stewart. Addressee, Suzanne Beaumont, care of Tom Stewart, 48 Pennington Street, London E1. Weight of package: four pounds. Description of contents: documents.'

'At least we've found the bonds.'

They left Amsterdam at six, Kain driving the car he had hired before coming to the Pulitzer hotel. He handed Stewart the rental company map and asked him to find the way south towards Utrecht. After leaving the canals, Stewart directed him to the Dutch motorway but when they reached an elevated section there was no slip-road to give them access. They drove along a wide street between tall apartment blocks and found a flyover at the end. Stewart told Kain to take a left and pick up the Utrecht route at the next intersection.

'Don't fuck up again,' said Kain.

'It would be a lot easier if you told me where we're going,' Stewart said.

'You'll find out soon enough,' said Kain. The traffic was lane-to-lane, heavy trucks mixing with evening commuters eager to get home. Kain was gripping the steering wheel, looking less relaxed than at the Pulitzer. He jabbed at the radio buttons and was rewarded with a mosaic of European languages and relentless pop music. 'You people never heard of Willie Nelson?' said Kain.

Stewart felt it was like a scene from a marriage: a couple

trapped in a car, arguing over whose fault it was they were lost. He was tempted to abandon himself to this familiar domestic role, as if he was being blown along by fate and it didn't matter where he ended up. Then he realised this was a dangerous illusion. This wasn't an episode from some other story, it was real, and he had to use this enforced proximity with Kain to learn all he could about him. When the endgame was played out, as Stewart knew it would be, he had to be on top of it. Of one thing he was certain: he was going to find his daughter, and he and his daughter were going to come out of this alive.

As he watched Kain tail-gating the car in front, he tried to divine what was in his head. There weren't many clues to be gleaned from his behaviour in Amsterdam. From the Pulitzer, where Kain had never left his side, they had walked to the car parked on a meter. Kain had told him to dump his baggage in the boot while he retrieved a shoulder-bag. They crossed an arched bridge where whores were parading in their micro-skirts and headed down a street lined with porno book-shops and cinemas to a Thai café where the barman greeted Kain with a nod. Kain made calls from a payphone, his eyes on Stewart all the time. Upstairs in a shabby apartment, he removed a laptop computer from his shoulder bag and plugged it into the wall socket. He opened it and tapped at the keys, his stubby fingers jabbing at the close-packed keyboard.

'What are you up to?' Stewart had asked.

'You should eat something. We're hitting the road soon.'

'How far do you expect to get tonight?'

'Doesn't matter. So long as we're out of here. The cops could pick up on you coming to Amsterdam any time.'

Stewart shrugged. In fact, on this, he and Kain had the same agenda. If Kain were picked up, he could be held on any one of a dozen counts, not excluding kidnap and murder. Stewart wanted nothing more than to see Kain brought to justice, yet knew he had to help him stay free. If Kain were arrested, they could not complete the ransom delivery, and Fee would die. Whichever way you cut it, they were in this together: a Faustian pact, which could only be broken at the end.

Kain was fidgeting with the radio again, taking his eye off the road. The speedometer was past 120 kph. The stop-lights on the car ahead glittered in the dusk and Kain had to brake hard.

'Do you have to drive so fast?' Stewart asked.

'We've got a deadline to meet.'

'If you keep driving like this we won't make it at all.'

'Quit whining,' said Kain. 'You're getting on my nerves.'

They spent the night in a German motel just off the autobahn near Essen, sharing a cell-like room that was almost bare of furniture save for two bunk beds that seemed to have been constructed from lengths of scaffolding, painted blue and red. Kain locked the door and kept the key. It turned out he snored. In the morning they stopped at a service station for coffee and rolls and Stewart insisted on buying a Michelin road atlas. They were on the E35 that runs north-south through Germany, following the eastern bank of the Rhine.

Where were they headed: Switzerland? Italy?

'I told you,' said Kain. 'Shut the fuck up.'

Stewart wondered if they were bound for Nice, taking the longer route to stay out of France until the last stretch. Supposing for all Halard's hue and cry, Fee and Josh were being held near where they had disappeared? And the *Symphonie* was a decoy, to make it appear they were much further away? He realised that couldn't be so, as it was only through the chance discovery of Fee's camera that they knew about the *Symphonie* at all. So where were the children? As Halard had admitted, *Symphonie* could have sailed anywhere in the Mediterranean. Stewart looked through the atlas, counting the countries with coastlines within reach. There were no fewer than eight in Europe, from Gibraltar to Turkey, plus the whole of North Africa. There were the islands too: Sicily, Sardinia, Corsica, Cyprus, the Balearics, Malta, plus the Greek isles and islets, scattered like pebbles across the blue of the map. He closed the atlas and put it on the back seat.

'What about Olivier?' Stewart asked. 'What part did he play in this?'

'Who?' asked Kain.

'Olivier Lavar. Josh Beaumont's friend.'

'Some friend,' said Kain.

'Meaning he got Fee and Josh into the yacht for you.'

'That's him.' Kain was grinning as he watched the road. 'What a creep.'

'How much did you pay him?'

'A few thousand francs, that's all, plus a couple of fixes. Asshole was a coke freak.'

'Was?'

'Coke don't fix it for him no more. He's fish food.'

'So you drowned him.'

'Accident, way I heard it. He fell overboard.'

Kain grinned again, and Stewart felt he had just peered through a crack into a darkened room, obtaining his first intimation of what drove this man. 'Was that your idea, or Canning's?'

'Who's Canning?'

'Come on, Kain. Canning's the man. The one who set this up, who's paying you to do all this.'

'I don't know any Canning,' said Kain.

Stewart persisted. 'The one whose daughter's dying, and wants revenge against old man Beaumont. Wants to destroy him by destroying his company.'

'Shut the fuck up,' said Kain.

It occurred to Stewart that Kain might not even know who was calling the shots; if he had been hired as a mercenary, there could be a cut-out to prevent him ever knowing. He decided to test the idea with the most sensitive question of all. His stomach was already lurching. 'There's something else,' he said. 'Why didn't you kill Fee too?'

'Orders,' said Kain. 'Message came through. Keep the girl alive. Suited me. Could be extra bait. Could be a bargaining chip. Give us something to trade. Guess that makes you the lucky one. Now shut up.'

It sounded plausible, Stewart thought, even though his stomach had lurched again. And maybe Kain really didn't know Canning. But if he was acting on orders, it finally disposed of his book as a possible motive. But did Kain even know about it? He would leave that for now, wait for the moment to come.

After Baden-Baden, there was a new landscape: hills to the left, the plain of the Rhine to the right, with fields of wheat and oilseed and vines, farm villages clustered round square steeples, and stretches of woodland to block the view. The traffic had thickened through the morning, with trucks sometimes line-abreast, Dutch holidaymakers towing trailers and caravans, BMWs and Mercedes, hurtling down the outside lane, lights flashing to clear their path. Kain had settled to a steady speed and Stewart's eyes were closing for a doze.

They never saw the deer that burst from the trees on the far side of the autobahn. By some miracle it made it across the north-bound carriageway, cleared the central barrier and landed directly in the path of a truck. The truck jack-knifed as its driver hit his brakes, going into a sideways skid and then toppling over, spewing its load of pig's carcasses. Some drivers managed to avoid the debris but others piled into the truck or other cars, to a cacophony of crunching metal and shattering glass. Kain had braked as soon as the truck started its skid and was down to 30 kph when there was an impact and the windscreen crazed before their eyes. Shards of glass filled their laps to reveal a pig's carcass lying across their bonnet. Kain was still bracing himself against the steering wheel when they were rammed from behind and shunted into a car in front.

'Jesus,' said Kain. 'Sweet fucking Jesus.'

'We've got to get out,' said Stewart. 'In case the petrol tank blows.'

Kain's door was jammed but he shouldered his way out. They dodged through the wreckage and clambered up the embankment beside the roadway. They looked back to see the truck splayed across the road like a barricade. Fifty or more cars littered the tarmac behind it, some intact, others wrecked. Some people had clambered out of their cars while others were trapped inside. There were shouts and screams, but no bodies as far as Stewart could see.

He ran back down to the road where a woman was pinned behind the steering wheel of her car, whose bonnet was compressed to almost half its length. There was blood on her forehead. Stewart tugged at the door but it wouldn't move. The windscreen had shattered and he looked for something to clear away the fragments so that he could pull her out.

'What the fuck are you doing?' It was Kain, who had seized his arm.

'What does it look like I'm doing?'

'Are you crazy? We have to get out of here.'

Klaxons blaring, the first police were arriving in their green and white Opels. Then came an ambulance and a fire engine, and a helicopter thudding overhead.

'We can't just walk away from this,' said Stewart.

'That's exactly what we're going to do. Cops start asking for papers, we're dead.'

Other drivers had come to help the trapped woman. The police were already talking to drivers, looking at documents.

'I have to get the computer,' said Kain. 'It's in the trunk.'

The rear end of the hire car had buckled and the boot was jammed shut. Kain found a tyre lever in a nearby wreck and smashed at the lock of the boot.

'*Was tun sie denn?*' A traffic cop in a sand-coloured uniform and a peaked cap was approaching Kain. '*Ist ihre Auto?*'

Stewart had forgotten most of the German he had once learned. But he knew that the cop was asking if this was Kain's car.

'*Nicht unser Auto,*' said Stewart. It's not our car. '*Ist ein . . .*' He could not remember the word for hire car.

'*Nicht ihre Auto? Haben sie Papieren?*'

He wants our papers, Stewart told Kain. 'They're in the fucking trunk,' Kain said.

Stewart waved his hand. '*Kein Papieren,*' he said. '*Sind im . . .*' He pointed at the boot.

'Let's blow,' said Kain.

'We have to face this out,' said Stewart.

'We can't take the risk,' said Kain. The cop stood his ground, looking from one face to another.

'We're getting out of here,' said Kain, looking at the cop but talking to Stewart.

'*Entschuldigung?*'

'We have to stay,' said Stewart, but Kain was already edging away.

The cop had a whistle in his hand. In a blur of movement, Kain planted his right leg behind him and pushed him to the ground. As the cop lay there, stunned, Kain knelt down and cradled his head in his right hand. He seemed to be looking into the cop's eyes and for a moment Stewart thought Kain was tending to his injury. But then Kain grasped the man's jaw in his left hand and gave it an abrupt twist. There was a sharp crunching noise and the man lay still.

Stewart was still trying to make sense of what he had witnessed when he saw Kain picking his way through the wrecks. 'You fucking idiot,' Stewart said, mostly to himself, and then hurried after him. The two men reached the top of the embankment together. Ahead was a field of vines, which Kain was already scanning, and beyond that a line of trees.

'You killed him, Kain, didn't you? For fuck's sake, why?'

Kain ignored the question. 'There's a path beside the vineyard. Once we reach it, don't look back.'

Through the melee on the autobahn, Stewart saw another patrolman running towards the wreck of their car. He disappeared from view, and Stewart realised he must have knelt down. Kain had reached the path and Stewart followed him, stumbling on the uneven surface. Suppressing his instinct to run, he was relieved that the trees were coming nearer with every step.

'Hal-loo. *Hal-loo.*' The shouts were coming from the top of the embankment. He heard a whistle, shrilling across the vineyard, and more shouts: '*Achtung! Halte!*'

He knew what that meant. Several men in uniform were scrambling down the embankment. Stewart pushed aside the fronts of the first pines and saw Kain ahead, a shape through the trees.

'Fuck it, Kain. Run!' Stewart had to dodge low beneath the branches as he tried to pick up pace, jumping draining ditches, running along a gully, his feet sinking into boggy ground. Kain was still in front, panting hard, crashing through the trees. Then they were on a track, with a cluster of farm buildings 100 metres ahead, a red-roofed farmhouse with a several outhouses and a tall barn alongside.

'We'll hole up there,' yelled Kain.

Stewart had visions of the German police searching the barn, using pitchforks to prod the hay, and of being forced from their cover and into abject surrender.

'No, Kain,' he shouted. 'Wait, for fuck's sake, wait.'

Two all-terrain police vehicles, dark green with oversize bulbous tyres, jolted to a halt outside the farmhouse. A short way beyond, a tractor was hauling a plough across a field that had been left fallow since the previous autumn. It reached the far side, then turned back, excavating a tidy row alongside the first. A patrolman walked towards it, waiting until the tractor reached the end of the field. He called up to the driver, who was wearing a pair of greasy overalls and a battered straw hat. The tractor stopped.

'*Haben sie jemand gesehen? Jemand im kurzen?*'

Have you seen anyone? At least, that's what Stewart thought he said. He didn't understand the second part, but the answer had to be no. Keep it short and sweet.

'*Nein, niemand.*' He shook his head. Kain, who was sitting beside him, wearing wellingtons and dungarees, stayed still.

'*Sind sie sicher? Ganz sicher?*'

Stewart knew he was quite sure. He pursed his lips in a moment of contemplation, then nodded his head.

'*Danke,*' said the officer.

Stewart knew that in German, 'thank you' was always acknowledged by the word please, although he had never understood why.

'*Bitte,*' he said. The cop returned to his vehicle and continued along the track. The tractor started carving a third furrow as it set off for the far side of the field.

'Good thing he didn't know this isn't the ploughing season,' said Stewart. 'How's your fieldcraft holding up since Vietnam?'

'I do okay,' said Kain.

Stewart remembered from the atlas that the Rhine lay some ten kilometres to the west. Beyond it was France. Whatever else, they had to get away from the German search-parties. The sky was overcast. 'How can we get a bearing?' he asked. 'Without the sun?'

'We use the trees. The prevailing winds are blowing south and east, which gives you an inclination on some trees. Second, the leaves will be fullest towards maximum light, meaning south. That should be good enough to give us a fix. Plus we're heading for the Rhine, so there should be a down slope to follow.'

Stewart drove along the track the patrol car had taken and found it stationed at the first crossroads. The driver was speaking into a radio and Stewart gave a brief wave. A helicopter was buzzing in the distance. Not for the first time,

Stewart had the feeling he was acting a part in someone else's story. An hour or so before he had seen Kain kill a policeman. Now he and Kain were on the run together, as if they shared the guilt and were facing a common enemy. Not me, thought Stewart: I don't kill cops. But he also knew he had to put his moral judgments on hold. There was only one way he was going to get out of this, get to Fee and bring her home, and that was with Kain. The phrase 'Faustian pact' might have been invented for precisely his predicament, and there was no escape.

A quarter-mile on, they reached the cover of another wood. The foliage was changing, the firs giving way to willows and reed beds, the ground more sandy and pebbly. The track merged with a tarmac road and, a few paces beyond the junction, a road sign bore a horizontal black line and the words: *Grenze 500 metres*.

'It's the border,' said Stewart. 'Just ahead. With luck we'll be able to drive straight across.'

They breasted a rise to see the road winding towards a bridge. Blocking the entrance to the bridge was a striped red-and-white barrier. Half a dozen cars had stopped in line, and a pair of policemen were talking to the driver at the head of the queue. They lifted the barrier and waved him through.

'What do you think?' asked Kain.

'Not a chance,' said Stewart. 'We've got no documents for the tractor, and with my German we'll never talk our way across.'

A cop was watching curiously as Stewart reversed the tractor and headed back down the track. A short distance on was a fork and they took the right-hand branch. In another 100 metres the track veered right and they were on the bank of the Rhine. Stewart stopped.

The river, 200 metres wide by Stewart's reckoning, was dark green and flowing strongly. At its edge was a sign showing a skull and crossbones and the warning: *Schwimmen verboten. Grosse Gefahr*.

'No swimming,' said Stewart. 'Big danger.'

'I get the picture,' said Kain.

From the direction of the bridge, car engines were coming to life. The thudding of the helicopter was growing louder.

31

'They're in Germany,' Halard told Brady.

'You've found them? Great news.'

'Not so great,' said Halard. 'They've killed a cop. There's a manhunt in progress. If the Germans find them, it's all over.'

Brady sat at his desk. 'You'd better tell me the whole story.'

The German police liaison officer had called Halard at 6 p.m. He began by reciting the details of an autobahn pile-up – three serious casualties, a host of walking wounded and cases of shock – then moved to the nub of his concern. Two men involved in the crash had killed a German patrolman, who had been found beside a rented Volkswagen. Several witnesses had told how one of the men had pushed the patrolman to the ground and expertly broken his neck.

The two men had escaped across the fields, so far evading capture. The German police had broken into the boot of the car and found documents identifying one of the fugitives as Thomas Stewart, one of the subjects of the alert Halard had posted at the European police centre at Schwenningen in Germany the previous day. The other man was presumed to be the second subject of her alert. The Germans wanted to know anything and everything that might help assist in their capture. Now. *Bitte.*

This had led to some delicate negotiations. Halard explained that the two men were the subject of an international surveillance operation with vital humanitarian considerations, and requested that they not be arrested.

'Impossible,' snorted the German official. 'These people have killed one of our policemen. If it had happened in France, what would you do?'

Halard dodged the question. Abandoning her officialese, she explained exactly why it was vital that Stewart and Kain should be followed, not detained. 'Two children's lives are at stake.'

'Impossible,' the official said again. The most he would concede was that, once Kain and Stewart had been caught and questioned, the French might be permitted to speak to them.

'You're confident you'll find them?' she asked.

'Absolutely,' said the official.

'Where do you think they are?'

'They could be heading anywhere. Switzerland perhaps, if they've stolen a car. If they're still on foot, they might have gone to ground, or they could be heading your way. If they're thinking of getting into France, the Rhine's in the way. We've posted patrols on every bridge, border post and boatyard. There's no way they can cross.'

'In other words,' said Brady to Halard, 'it's a disaster.'

'Worse,' said Halard.

'Dominique, I'm coming over. I'll make some calls to State to see if we can pull political weight on the Germans, but I doubt it'll make any difference. I've checked the airlines and there's an Air France flight out of Dulles at seven twenty tonight. Is there anything else you can do?'

'I'm getting people into place on our side of the border in case they do make it across. The Germans may think it's impossible but they don't know this pair. We're relying on local resources at first and some of these places out in the sticks are hard to move. But we'll have full cover by the morning shift tomorrow. Say nine o'clock.'

'Will you let them run?'

'Of course, and hope they lead us to the kids.'

'What are the Germans going to say when they find out?'

'Don't ask, Phil. I feel enough of a shit already. There's something else. They found a laptop in the car and said we could have it in return for my cooperation.'

Brady felt a surge of adrenalin. 'Kain's?'

'Could be.'

'If we can read it, it could give us a serious lead at last.'

'That might be too much to ask.'

'There's a good connection from Paris down to Nice. I should be with you by noon.'

'Let's hope it's not all over by then. For the children's sake.'

The helicopter was directly overhead, the hammering blades swaying the tree-tops like wheat-fields in a storm. Stewart, peering from the cover of a spruce fir, saw it dip across to the far bank, then work its way upstream towards the border post on the bridge.

As the noise subsided, he heard rushing water. Two hundred metres downstream he could see a ripple stretching across the river.

'I think it's a weir,' he told Kain. 'Let's take a look.'

As they approached, they saw how the river surged over a concrete wall perhaps two feet wide. At right angles below the wall, breakwaters divided the water into a series of pools, churning with whirls and eddies. There were four in all, each some fifty metres wide. Put another way, each measured two lengths of an average swimming pool. A second skull-and-crossbones sign planted on the river bank spelled out the dangers. Kain had his back to it as he sized up the weir, his muscular shoulders hunched, his forearms tensed.

'It's like Le Bosquet,' Stewart said. 'There and back, four times.'

'Then we can do it,' Kain replied.

Kain said they should wait until dusk. They returned to the tractor and drove it as deep as they could into a thicket of undergrowth. Close by they found a pile of polythene bags abandoned by some farmer, and Kain showed Stewart how to fold his clothes inside one, then place it in another which he sealed so that it was full of air. Kain found some twine, too. 'Use that to tie the bag to your waist.'

The light dwindled through the trees, and Stewart could see half a dozen crows, silhouetted against the dusk, in the uppermost branches of a pine. Kain watched as he lowered himself into the water, the concrete of the weir chafing his thighs. The bag of clothes tugged at his waist as it was carried away on the stream. Stewart paddled at first, testing the current, then broke into a crawl, breathing carefully as he turned his head to the left, looking at the wall. The water bubbled round him but he held his stroke, his muscles powering him through the turbulence. Fifty metres, give or take, should take one-minute-fifteen, one-minute-thirty, nothing to it. He reached the first breakwater and hauled himself out of the water. Kain was still on the bank and for a moment Stewart wondered if he was going to follow.

'If I can, you can,' he called.

'Too right,' said Kain. He too swam rhythmically, maintaining his control. A sudden wave thrust him away from the wall but he increased his stroke and was soon clambering up beside Stewart. The bank they had just left looked worryingly close, as if they had hardly made any progress.

'One down,' said Stewart. 'Three to go.'

He found the second leg surprisingly easy, and began to hope the remaining two stretches would be the same. Then he realised that the weir had been constructed on a bend. Since they were crossing from the inside of the curve, the river would be flowing at its strongest on the far side. He looked back, then ahead: it was the same distance either way, and he felt marooned. He thought about turning back, then remembered the German police, and knew the only way out was on.

For the third stretch Kain went first. He took half a dozen strong strokes, then briefly paddled, before resuming his crawl. As Stewart pushed off behind him his limbs felt heavy and he knew the chill water was sapping his strength. A surge of current pushed him away from the wall. He was only too aware that if he was carried out into the main channel he would be swept for miles before he could regain the bank, with precious little chance of surviving the fatigue and the cold. Hang in there, he told himself: maintain your rhythm, swim through the pain, think of Fee. *Fee, Fee, Fee, Fee.* His inner chant matched his strokes as the third breakwater neared and he could reach for it at last and climb up beside Kain.

He knew, when he looked across the last section, that it would be the worst. The water was seething and he was already deep into his final reserves. He took deep gulps of air in a bid to recharge his muscles until he became dizzy with oxygen overload. Kain was behind him, waiting for him to set off. He paused and paused again, knowing he had to commit himself, reassuring himself that 100 strokes would take him to the sanctuary of the far side, and then he stopped thinking and counting and launched himself into the current.

The turbulence snatched at him like a creature of the deep. He forced his arms through the water, through the pain, kick, kick kicking his legs, driving on with every ounce of his being. Fee was calling him on: *you can make it, do it for me*. Ten metres to go, then five – a dozen strokes more, that was all it would take. Through the spray he glimpsed a jetty with steps tantalisingly close. The current was carrying him past but he grabbed the bottom step and closed his hand tight around it, taking deep breaths and urging himself to hold on. He hauled in his clothing bag and reached for a higher step, ready to pull himself ashore.

'Stewart!'

It was Kain. Stewart could just hear him above the rushing water. 'It's cramp!'

He was still ten metres short, his face contorted with pain. For the barest moment, Stewart willed him to be swept away downstream, carried to his death, then knew he had to help him if he were ever to see Fee again.

He plunged back into the maelstrom just as Kain's head was submerged by foam. Stewart seized his shoulders and turned him on to his back, kicking furiously to stay on the surface, his muscles burning. He felt Kain trying to work with him as they drove themselves back to the jetty. They were close now, the bottom step almost within reach. Stewart reached out for it but missed. He had nothing more to offer, felt himself relax as he gave in to the current, gave into whatever it wanted. But Kain was still fighting and he swung in the water to grab the step. His arm locked with Stewart's and together they hauled themselves in. Then they were on the steps, crawling up on to the jetty, subsiding like beached fish, hearts pounding, Stewart breathing so hard he feared he would rupture a chest muscle.

'Goddammit,' said Kain.

As Stewart's breathing subsided, the cold of the night struck into Stewart's bones.

'Hell, Kain, we've got to find shelter.'

A hundred yards down the bank, barely visible beneath the

trees, they came to a low, timbered building. The door creaked open to release the earthy odour of farm animals. Through the shadows Stewart made out a cache of hay and a fireplace with kindling wood and chunks of coal. Against a wall was a battered chest of drawers, with a brown metal pot, a half-eaten packet of biscuits and jar containing the congealed remnants of some instant coffee.

'We can stay here for a bit. Try to get warm,' said Stewart.

'I'll buy that,' said Kain. He pulled open his plastic bag and removed his clothes. Inside them was another smaller bag containing his wallet and passport, and a lighter. He flicked it alive.

A fire was crackling and Kain's face was mottled with red shadows. 'Shouldn't we move on?' Stewart asked.

'Too risky,' Kain said. 'We've no idea what's out there. Better make a recce in the morning.' He loaded more wood on to the fire, which spurted a shower of sparks.

'Nice swim,' he said.

Stewart remembered the phrase.

'That's what you said at Le Bosquet. After you'd taken Josh and Fee.'

'No hard feelings, huh?'

'Come off it, Kain. You take my daughter and I'm supposed to like you? Say it's okay?'

'Feel what you like. For me, it's nothing personal.'

'So what is it, Kain? You're saying you don't get a kick out of this? Fucking over people's lives?'

'I thought we understood each other. We're in this together. My people get the bonds, you and the Beaumont woman get your kids back. It's a deal. Provided it works out, no-one needs get hurt.'

The fire crackled again. Kain motioned Stewart to stay quiet. He went to the door and listened. There was only the ceaseless flow of the river, broken momentarily by the cry of a screech owl. He returned to the fire.

'How did you know I was in Nam?'

'There's a lot I know about you.'

'How come?'

'I told you at the hotel, Kain. I'm a writer. I've studied the

Vietnam war. Especially Hill 861. You were there, weren't you?' It was more of a statement than a question.

'That was a fucking long time ago.'

'What have you done with your Bronze Star?'

'Stop shitting me, will you? What is this about?'

'It's not about anything. I've read your citation. I've often wondered what it was like on the hill that night.'

'It was like shit. It was like nothing. I was a marine. I did what I did.'

'What about Barney Lewis?'

An ember shot from the fire. Kain brushed it from his arm. 'What about Barney Lewis?' he asked.

'What was he like?'

'A damn fine marine. One of the best.'

'And having to leave him behind?'

'There was no way to reach him. Could have cost us a platoon just to try.'

'Do you regret that?'

'Of course. But we had no choice.'

That phrase again. Stewart knew almost everything there was to know about Hill 861, of course. He had imagined the rain, and the mud, and the ambush, and the fusillades of fire, and the cries and moans of dying men. He was also getting a sense of how this was going to end.

'How many people have you killed?'

'In Vietnam? Dozens. Who knows?'

'What's it like?'

'You have to do it.'

'In what sense, have to?'

'If you're a soldier, it's what you do.'

'But you enjoyed it?'

'Depends.'

'On what?'

'On whether they deserved to die.'

'Enemy soldiers are doing a job too. The same as you.'

'And they'd kill me. It's them or you. Simple as that.'

'And after Vietnam? You're a mercenary, aren't you? Doing anything, smuggling, drugs, kidnapping? As it comes?'

'It's like Vietnam. It's what I do.'

'For anyone who pays?'

'You got it.'
'Killing too?'
'If I have to.'
'These people you've killed. Did they deserve it too?'
'Not for me to say.'
Stewart could hear the river brushing past the bank outside, flowing into the night, into the heart of darkness.
'Is there anything you believe in? Good and evil? Or just yourself?'
'I believe in my buddies. In whoever's picking up the tab. In what I do. That's the point, Stewart. I'm a pro.'
The glow from the fire was subsiding as Stewart pushed on. 'And when you kill,' he persisted, 'what is it like? When you twist the knife? When you snap the neck?'
'It feels how it feels. I don't think about it. I do what I do.'
'And you're good at it.'
'That's why people pay me. I don't fuck up.'
'And you enjoy it.'
'I'm not paid to enjoy it. I'm paid to be good at it.'
'But that's not all, is it? Tell me what it's like when they're dying, and you look into their eyes.'
Kain did not reply, and Stewart knew he was closing on the truth. 'I saw you when you killed that cop.'
'I had to do that. If we'd been arrested, your daughter would be dead.'
'That's not what I meant. I saw you holding his head. You were watching his eyes when you broke his neck.'
'That's bullshit, Stewart. It didn't matter to me whether he was dead or alive. What mattered was he was down, disposed of, out of our way. That was all.'
'That wasn't all. I saw you, Kain. You wanted to see the moment his lights went out.'
Kain was silent, and Stewart knew he had seen into his soul. If Kain had been merely a pro, perhaps they could have dealt. But Kain was more than a pro. He was of the night, a killer who relished his work. Stewart also knew that Kain would not hesitate to kill anyone who stood in his way. In theory, it should be possible for him to hand over the bonds in return for Fee and Josh, and then they could go their separate ways. But

he was beginning to sense that this was going to come down to a final duel: him or Kain for the life of his daughter, and he was going to have to show the same ruthlessness as Kain. He had one question left. He didn't know if he was going to find an answer yet, but he wanted to prepare the way.

'My book's nearly finished,' he said.

'Your book?'

'I told you, I've been finding out about Vietnam and Hill 861. In fact, I'd been trying to find you. To ask you some questions.'

'Some coincidence, huh?'

'I searched everywhere. I went to Quantico and the Vet Administration, and I spoke to your buddies from Hill 861. I even went to Bangkok and left messages for you at your bar.'

'Must have been after I left.'

Kain stretched his arms above his head. 'I need some shut-eye,' he said. 'You take the first watch.' He lay down on his side, facing the door.

In the dying glow from the fire, Stewart watched his breathing deepen, heard him snore.

Why not ask me, Kain? he said, but only to himself. Don't you want to know why I searched for you? Or what it was I wanted to ask?

It's because you know already. You know I want to know about the execution of Barney Lewis.

32

'Erstein,' read the sign where the houses began. 'Twinned with Minster Lovell.'

Stewart had played cricket at Minster Lovell, an over-neat village near Oxford, with an immaculate village green, restored drystone walls, and a sandy stream flowing beneath a hump-back bridge, where trout flickered among the shadows. For a moment he was back in England, playing out a ritual in white flannels against a green background, as if nothing had changed.

But it had. He was walking through a French village with a hired killer, escaping a manhunt, trying to rescue his daughter. It had taken half an hour to reach Erstein from the barn, walking at the edge of a tarmac road, turning off at a roundabout when they saw the village. It had the same prettified air as Minster Lovell, its main street fringed with cherry trees, the houses decked with pots of geraniums. Ahead was the main square, still somnolent, and beyond it a railway station. It was 6.15 a.m.

'We need a car,' said Kain.

The only candidates Stewart could see were lodged on driveways, some behind gates. The station car park was bare.

'We can't chance it here,' said Kain. 'Let's see where the train goes.'

The station was deserted but a timetable showed a train was due in about fifteen minutes, *direction Colmar*. There was nothing to show where or what Colmar was. Beside the closed booking office was an automatic ticket machine. Stewart fingered his wallet with its credit cards but there was no cash dispenser in sight. In view of yesterday's events, riding a train without a ticket hardly merited worrying about.

The train, two coaches long, clattered in on time. There

were four people at the far end of the carriage Stewart and Kain joined, and no ticket-collector. Stewart watched the countryside slide past, grain fields mixed with maize and sunflowers. The sky was clear and he could see the German mountains on the far side of the Rhine.

'What's happened to the French cops?' he asked Kain. 'I thought they'd be out looking for us.'

'My guess is they don't know we're over the border,' said Kain. 'Looks like the Germans haven't found the tractor yet. Then they've got to work out how we crossed the river.'

'They will.'

'Forget about the cops. You've got bigger problems. We missed a deadline yesterday, and that means your daughter's in trouble. So's the Beaumont kid. I have to let my people know where we're at. They think something bad's happened to me, they're not going to hang around.'

Colmar turned out to be a sprawling industrial town with a bustling railway station. The train arrived at 7.15. They crossed the booking hall and found themselves at the edge of a square, with an ornate hotel on one corner, and beside it a bus. The direction-board read: *Aeroport.*

'Like it,' said Kain.

There was a bank on the far side of the square and Stewart extracted 500 francs from the cash machine with his credit card. They returned to the station and spent forty francs in the men's washroom buying themselves sachets containing soap, toothpaste, a one-shot razor, and a minuscule hand-towel. After ten minutes, Stewart judged that they looked a little less like escaped prisoners-of-war.

'We need to find a hardware store,' said Kain. Five minutes' walk from the square, a *bricolage* was already open, and Kain selected a pair of pliers, some insulating tape, a glass-cutter and an aerosol can of plumbers' sealing foam. The cashier packed them in a stiff brown paper bag. Back beside the station, the bus driver was warming his engine as they climbed aboard.

'Why the airport?' Stewart asked.

'Best place for picking up a car,' Kain said. 'See them park, watch them take off, and you know they're not going report it stolen all day.'

A twin-engine turbo-prop was waiting on the tarmac when the bus reached the airport. A handful of passengers got off and headed for the terminal, a compact white building with frosted windows. There were half a dozen cars in the parking area and several more arrived as Kain and Stewart were leaving the bus. Inside the terminal, the passengers had joined a short queue at the check-in desk for a flight to Lyon. 'Give me some change,' said Kain. 'I need to use the phone.'

Stewart crossed to a snack bar, bought two cups of coffee and watched the check-in line dwindle. Several last-minute passengers walked in briskly as it was being called, and hurried on to the plane. Its engine whined as it taxied towards the runway. Kain sat down beside Stewart.

'Tell you what we're going to do,' he said. 'When we've seen that mother take off, we're going to walk out to the parking lot, very easy, very casual, and find ourselves a ride. Just do what I tell you.'

There was no barrier or attendant at the car park. A grey-green Audi 100 was parked at the end of the line. 'That'll do,' said Kain. 'Just make out like it's ours.'

He approached the driver's door, then handed Stewart the brown bag from the hardware store. 'Talk to me. Act like we're buddies. I'm going to make out I've seen something wrong with the indicator light. Now say something.'

'I'm becoming very interested in you, Kain. As a practitioner of the illegal arts, I mean. Is there anything you wouldn't do?'

'Oh, come on, this is chickenshit. You never hot-wired a car? No, I don't suppose you have.' Kain laughed and clapped Stewart on the shoulder, as though he had just told a joke. 'Thing is, now they have these alarms, and electronic blocking, and whatever, you have to take a couple of precautions. Talk to me, you fuck. Nod your head. Point to something. Don't just stand there like a fucking thief.'

Stewart pointed at the front bumper and said, 'It looks perfectly okay to me.'

Kain peered down at the light assembly. 'I think you're right. But any good folks watching us don't know that, do they? They think there's something here needs fixing.'

'Now what?'

Kain rolled up the sleeves of his shirt, then lay down and eased himself under the car.

'You want to hand me the aerosol?' he said.

Stewart heard a snap as the top was removed, followed by a prolonged hiss. A car pulled up and parked two spaces away. Its driver, a middle-aged man, looked at them without curiosity as Kain emerged from beneath the car and stood up.

'They ain't made the car that can't be stolen,' he said. He was smiling again. 'All it takes is time. Spray should be rock-hard in a minute or two. That's taken out the siren. Now we get into the car.' He stood beside the driver's door. 'Face me, fold your arms, and start talking. No shit this time.'

'How much are they paying you?'

'No shit, I said.' Kain had the glass-cutter in his right hand, working it in a circle across the driver's window.

'Five hundred thousand,' said Stewart. 'Six hundred thousand. Seven hundred thousand. Eight hundred thousand. Nine hundred thousand. Getting warm? One million. One million one hundred thousand. I'm not, am I? I'm not even close. Come on Kain, how much is it?'

The indicator lights had started flashing but the alarm siren was barely audible. Kain was reaching into the car through the circle of glass he had just removed. He opened the driver's door and pulled the bonnet lock. He moved to the front of the car, lifted the bonnet, and snipped a cluster of wires. The flashing stopped.

Stewart looked towards the terminal. 'I told you,' said Kain. 'No worries. Anyone sees us, we're just fixing our car.'

'What if the police come?'

'Not a chance,' said Kain. 'Cops are never around when you need them.'

He was inside the car, working a line of screws along the steering-wheel housing. He pulled the housing free, exposing a cat's cradle of multi-coloured wiring. He selected three – one red, one black, one green – stripped them of their plastic coating, and placed the bare wires together. The starter motor fired and the engine coughed to life. Kain bound the three wires together. 'Always start well, Audis,' he said.

He opened the driver's window, got out of the car and gripped the steering wheel. He tested it briefly, jerking it back and forth against its security lock. Then he rammed it down with all his force. There was a shredding noise as the lock broke.

'Get in the car,' said Kain. 'I told you it was ours.'

He eased the Audi into gear and drove slowly out of the car park, resting his arm on the door sill, heading out of Colmar.

There was still the same rhythm in Brady's stride, but he was looking older, when he arrived at Nice airport. Halard was waiting for him on the tarmac with a patrol car and they kissed on both cheeks, once, twice, in French style. His eyes seemed weary, his skin slack, and while she put it down to the transatlantic flight, followed by the leg from Paris, she sensed he had changed since their time in Washington four years before. She knew enough of the infighting at the bureau, the squabbling among government agencies, to understand how it could wear a good agent down. Yet he seemed as motivated as ever, skipping the pleasantries to ask her what news she had.

'There's no sign of them,' she said.

'I guess no news is good news,' said Brady.

'I'm getting to know these two. Whatever the Germans say, my feeling is they've made it across the border. Which is what we want, of course.'

'All we have to do is find them.'

The road from the airport was clogged with summer traffic. Halard told the driver to use the siren, but hardly anyone pulled over to let them through. She told him to turn it off.

'The citizens still showing the same respect for the forces of law and order, I see,' said Brady. 'I'm glad nothing changes. Any news of the computer?'

'Good and bad. The good is, it decodes automatically, so we can read all the messages.'

'The bad?'

'There's nothing to tell us where the kids are. All we've got are messages written in a kind of code – 'Red bird has landed', 'The bird is in the nest', that sort of thing. It's pretty obvious what the last one means but it doesn't help us and it's not going to incriminate anyone in court. Canning signs himself 'Raven' and Kain is 'Red Bird', we do know that. They're all dated and signed, so we can follow the sequence. But as for getting us to the kids – forget it.'

'Where's the computer now?'

'The Brits have got it. Skinner's intercepting Canning's messages and decoding them through the computer, so we have some idea of what's going on. At least, that's the theory. Skinner's getting pretty itchy, because Canning hasn't sent or received anything for the past two days. He does keep looking in his mailbox – Skinner's traced it to Zurich – but then he disconnects. Looks like he's waiting for a message from Red Bird.'

'Kain,' said Brady, and Halard nodded. 'Why don't we send Canning a message ourselves? Pretend it's from Kain and see which way he jumps?'

'I thought of that, but it's very risky. Suppose Kain's in touch with Canning some way we don't know about. If Canning knows Kain's lost the laptop, and the next thing is he gets a fake message signed Red Bird, he'll know we're on to him. At the moment we've still got the advantage of surprise, and we don't want to blow it.'

'Something for later, maybe. What else is Skinner doing?'

'Taking care of Mrs Beaumont.'

'With all his normal charm, I guess,' said Brady, with unaccustomed irony.

'He wants to nail her to the wall, as he put it, but he's agreed to hold off until he hears from us. Sooner or later someone's going to collect the bonds from her, or tell her where to deliver them, and that's when we go in. He was ready to buy that.'

They had reached the Promenade des Anglais. Since Brady's stint as the FBI's liaison officer in France, ugly new hotels had risen to scar the seafront and the Casino Ruhl had gone. Yet not so much had changed. The Négresco still resembled a vast white wedding cake, and Brady recalled the most expensive lunch of his life, with a bejewelled matron at the next table feeding her poodle *filet mignon* from a silver dish.

'What's your news?' Halard asked.

Halard thought she detected a blush of embarrassment. When this man – or his crew – made mistakes, it hurt. 'We know a lot more about how Kain pulled his stunt. He had an old Vietnam buddy working for the vet cab company, guy called Nathan Yannuck. Whenever Kain wanted to meet Beaumont, he borrowed whichever cab Yannuck happened to be driving. All this is coming from Harry Gonzales, who's been working his ass off in Austin. Makes me feel like a jerk.'

'Don't be so hard on yourself, Phil. Hindsight's always twenty-twenty. What does Yannuck have to say?'

'Not too much. Claims to have had no idea why Kain wanted his cab. At least he's identified Kain for certain, so that gives us one good witness – if we ever find Kain.'

'What about old man Beaumont?'

'He chartered a plane to Miami, then he vanished. It's an easy place to vanish from. He doesn't show up as a passenger on any flights out of Miami, though Harry's people are still looking. Meantime Harry's been working on what Beaumont was up to before he skipped town.'

Gonzales had gone equipped with warrants to search Beaumont's home at West Lake Hills and his office at BioGenius, and another to force the phone company to provide a list of all his calls. With the documents he had found, Gonzales had reconstructed precisely how Beaumont had raised $100 million: the stock he had pledged – held in trust for his grandson – the banks he had tapped, the favours he had called. He had also identified which bearer bonds Beaumont had purchased, and from where. A full list of the serial numbers was being circulated to every bank and brokerage-house that dealt in bearer bonds, not just in the United States but throughout the world.

The car had reached the end of the promenade and was darting through the alleyways of old Nice. A few blocks short of the Prefecture, the driver surprised Brady by making a left turn.

'Thought we'd have a quick lunch,' Halard said. 'There's a neat place not too far away. Nothing fancy, but I know what you like.'

The radio crackled into life.

'Boss?'

It was Desiry.

'Go ahead,' Halard said.

'Two things,' said Desiry. 'The Germans have found a

stolen tractor hidden in a wood by the Rhine. It's close to a weir, and they're beginning to think these guys might have been crazy enough to try and swim across. They're searching the river now, in case they didn't make it.'

'Number two?'

'I think they did make it. We've been monitoring car thefts from that area on our side of the border. Some guy parked an Audi at the airport at Colmar this morning and his wife was supposed to pick it up. When she gets there, no car. Colmar sent down a patrol and they've just reported back that two men were seen with the Audi. Acting like it was theirs, trying to fix something under the bonnet. The descriptions fit Kain and Stewart, close enough. We're putting out an all-points now.'

Sorry about lunch, Halard said.

Kain was driving more carefully now, watching the mirror, keeping to the speed limit, signalling to overtake.

'Can't afford to get stopped,' he explained. 'We've pushed our luck far enough.'

'That's one way of putting it,' said Stewart. His sense of being in a dreamlike state returned: he had survived a crash, seen a policeman killed, nearly drowned in the Rhine, helped to steal a car; now he and Kain were coasting along a motorway on a sticky summer morning, watching the thunder clouds build on the horizon, hoping it wouldn't rain, like a couple of friends setting off on holiday. He remembered holidays with Fee and Rachel: Fee's laughing face as she destroyed a sandcastle with her spade; Fee pleading for ice cream; climbing a modest hill in Cork together, stopping to gorge themselves on blackberries on the way, reaching the top just as the drizzle descended, so there was no view. She was puzzled, wondering why they had bothered, but he said how proud he was of her, and her wet clothes clung to his as he gave her a hug.

Stay focused, he told himself. Concentrate on making sure nothing else goes wrong. Don't provoke him, like you did at Colmar. He readily assented when they stopped for petrol and Kain said they should eat. He picked up cutlery for Kain when they queued at the cafeteria. He handed Kain change at the next *péage*. He wanted Kain to relax and see him as his ally. So much still had to go right. The children had to be alive,

Suzanne had to deliver the bonds, they had to stay clear of the cops until the children were safe. And lurking beneath all of that was the time bomb he had planted by asking about Hill 861. It was going to be the test of his life.

The Colmar road joined the main autoroute at Beaune. Kain pulled on to the hard shoulder and studied the mirror.

'Problems?' Stewart asked.

'Just checking,' said Kain. 'In case the car's been reported stolen.'

'You said the owner wouldn't get back to Colmar until tonight.'

'Never hurts to assume you're wrong.' He waited for a gap in the traffic and pulled back on to the carriageway. 'We're on our way. On our way to see your kid.' He gave a grin so broad that Stewart sensed the manipulative thrill behind it.

'Why won't you tell me where she is?'

'Why won't you stop fucking asking?'

The call came from the Beaune *péage*. Alerted by the *Police Nationale*, responding to Desiry's APB, a cashier reported to her supervisor that a grey-green Audi 100 with the correct registration number had just passed through her booth. The supervisor notified the nearest *Gendarmerie*, which called Halard in Nice. The back wall of the Prefecture office was covered with maps.

'They're on the A-6 heading south,' said Halard, pointing to the map for the *Saône et Loire département*. 'That puts them 150 kilometres short of Lyon.' Halard told Desiry to ask the Gendarmes to put an unmarked car on the next exit ramp, thirty-two kilometres south, in case the Audi turned off.

'They've got ten minutes to be in place, so tell them five,' she said.

As Brady studied the maps, tracing the A-6 with his finger, Halard called the next *Gendarmerie* post herself, requesting spotter cars on every bridge and exit ramp as far as Lyon. She also asked for two unmarked cars to tail the Audi along the A-6. 'Don't let them spot you,' she warned. 'Stay at least two kilometres back.'

'Are they cooperating?' Brady asked, knowing only too well

that cooperation between the Gendarmes and the national police was usually minimal, at best.

'For once,' she said, joining him at the maps.

'What's your feeling?' he asked. 'Where are they going?'

'Maybe Lyon, maybe further south. If it is further south they can pick up the A-7 on the other side of the city.' She showed him where the *Autoroute du Soleil* began carving its way through Provence. 'Then, here,' she said, moving on to the next map, 'they have a choice. They can either keep going to Marseille, or they can turn east and come all the way . . .' Her finger had stopped on Nice.

They looked at each other.

'Right under our noses,' said Halard.

'I wouldn't put it past him,' said Brady.

She was on the phone again, calling the ministry to ask for *Le* RAID to be placed on full alert and flown to Nice.

RAID is one of those comfortable euphemisms with which nation-states like to shield the true purpose of their emergency para-military squads, poised to deal with such unwelcome intrusions as terrorist sieges and kidnappings. The four letters stand for *Recherche, Assistance, Intervention, Dissuasion*. Its research is into the latest developments in high-technology weaponry and surveillance equipment. Assistance is tautological, since it invariably means intervention; and the intervention, like the dissuasion, is almost always violent. Since its formation in 1985, RAID had 'resolved' more than a dozen sieges and incidents of hostage-taking by the simple but terminal expedient of killing the perpetrators.

Within an hour of Halard's call they were in the air to Nice, where they would await further instructions – confident, as their commander promised, that no matter how demanding the circumstances, there would be a successful outcome.

'That's what they always say,' Halard remarked to Brady.

'Don't tell me,' said Brady. 'It's not getting them to go in that's the problem. It's holding them back.'

'Still, it's good to know they'll be here. Let's hope we don't have to use them.'

Desiry was coming towards them.

'They've just been eyeballed again. Passing Macon. That

puts them about fifty kilometres short of Lyon. The tail cars are in place.'

'Assume they're coming here, or hereabouts,' said Halard. 'How long have we got?'

'Depends on the traffic around Lyon, but five hours, maybe six.'

'Let's make sure we're ready for them.'

To conceal the hole he had cut in the glass, Kain drove with the driver's window down, and the hammering of the wind was giving Stewart a headache. Kain had fallen silent again. His jaw was set and he was checking the mirror almost continuously.

'Notice anything?' he asked.

'Like what?'

'No cops.'

'Thank God.'

'Maybe.'

Kain pulled into the inside lane and let his speed drop to under 100 kph.

'Take a good look,' he said. 'Watch for anyone coming up fast then slipping in behind us.'

Stewart turned in his seat, unfastening his seatbelt, and watched the procession of cars pulling out to overtake.

'Not so far,' he said.

Kain dropped to seventy, bringing hoots of complaint from the drivers forced to slow down as they waited for their chance to pass.

Now they were doing fifty. 'Haven't seen a cop since before Beaune,' Kain said. 'It's like they called them off in case they spooked us.'

Five hundred metres back, there was a flash of headlights as a grey car swerved into the inside lane behind them.

'Christ,' said Stewart. 'Did you see that?'

Kain, who had kept one eye on the mirror, nodded in satisfaction.

Down to forty five. The grey car crept up on them, then dropped back. It was a Peugeot. Stewart felt his stomach in knots.

'What do we do?'

'Point is, what do they do?' Kain was accelerating again.

Through the rear window, the grey car was becoming smaller. Then its indicator flashed as it pulled on to the hard shoulder.

'Maybe it wasn't the police,' said Stewart. 'Maybe there was something wrong with the car.'

Kain had pushed his speed back up to 130 kph.

The Lyon *péage* was 1,500 metres away.

'Get ready,' he told Stewart. 'I don't want to wait for change.'

Stewart did not enquire why. There was a line of tollbooths ahead, with drivers jostling for the shortest queue. Kain took his time, working through the traffic to the outermost lane. Stewart looked out for the Peugeot, but couldn't see it. There were no cops to be seen either. When they reached the booth he handed Kain the ticket and the cash for the toll.

'*Au revoir*,' said the cashier.

'Hold on,' said Kain.

The barrier lifted and the light flicked from red to green. Kain eased the car forward, then stamped on the accelerator. Twenty yards ahead, a gap in the central reservation – used by service vehicles – was blocked with a line of cones. The Audi's tyres squealed as Kain wrenched the wheel to the left and sped through the gap, sending the cones flying. He paused at the northbound booth, pulled a ticket from the dispenser, and then they were through, moving through the gears, the rev counter in the red zone, the speedometer hitting 130 kph and climbing.

'*Shit!*'

Halard looked at Desiry in astonishment as he slammed down the phone.

'Inspector?'

'They've lost them.' He hurried to the map. 'They're heading north like a demon. Must have spotted the tail car. Kain hung a U at the *péage*.'

Desiry kicked out at a chair, which almost overbalanced. 'They've got a five-minute start, and three exits they can take within the next twenty kilometres. They could go anywhere.'

'Can't the spotters pick them up?' asked Brady.

'We don't have any to the north. Not any more. They stood down as soon as the Audi passed them. No one expected those assholes to be coming back. The *Gendarmerie*'s trying to scramble them again now, but they won't get back in position in time. Not if Kain intends to leave the autoroute.'

'Any planes about?' Brady asked.

Halard did her best to sound brisk as she told Desiry to call the Air and Frontier Police at Lyon. Did they have a spotter plane on standby?

'Fat chance,' said Desiry, as he made the call.

Brady and Halard stared at the map, counting the roads, major and minor, around the first northbound exit the Audi could take. There were a dozen within a five-mile radius, leading to a dozen more, spreading across the Rhone valley like veins of fat in a cut of meat. It would take an army of police to cover them, and it needed to be on the move now. Brady knew it was hopeless, and he knew Halard knew it too.

Desiry had finished his call. 'They do have a plane ready to go. What they don't have is a pilot. Thirty minutes to airborne was the best they could offer. I told them to go fuck themselves.'

'Inspector . . .' Halard began.

Brady cut across her. 'I'd have told them the same. Let's get them in the air anyway. We've nothing to lose.'

33

Cumulo-nimbus clouds provided a towering backdrop as the Audi climbed a wooden gorge carved by a stream. They cleared the trees and crossed an expanse of scrubland. Then, where the road broke sharply left, Kain headed straight on along a track that climbed to a small plateau. At the top Stewart saw a windsock, tattered and grey, hanging limply in the humid air. Beyond it was a large corrugated shed and beside that a single-engine plane, white with red flashes on the fuselage and wings.

'You sick shit!' he exploded.

Kain grinned.

'All that business on the autoroute. Was anyone following us? Or was it just a game?'

'We'll never know,' Kain said.

He drove across the field and into the shed where a man was sitting on a barrel of aviation fuel. He was small and wiry, wearing greasy overalls and a tartan beret.

'I was getting worried about you, pal,' he said in a heavy Scottish accent. 'Any problems?'

'Nothing for you to worry about,' said Kain. 'You just worry about flying the fucking plane.'

The Scotsman levered himself off the barrel and looked at Stewart. 'You awright, Jimmy?'

'My name's Tom,' said Stewart coldly.

'Nae bother, pal. Just being friendly.'

He led them out of the shed and scanned the sky. The clouds were assuming the shape of a thunderhead, darkening fast. 'Best get going. There's weather ahead. Unless you want to wait.' He looked at the clouds again. 'It's up to you.'

'Let's move it,' said Kain.

Passively now, Stewart followed him to the plane. It had a flimsy door set in the fuselage and seemed alarmingly small. Kain gestured to Stewart to climb in. There were just four seats two beside the controls, two behind. Kain took the co-pilot's seat and told Stewart to sit in the back. The pilot clambered in after them, tugging the door shut.

'You file a flight plan?' Kain asked.

''Course I did. What do you take me for, a fucking cowboy?'

'Where to?'

'Biarritz. I've always fancied going to Biarritz.'

He chuckled as he turned on the ignition. 'Please make sure that your seatbelts are securely fastened, and that your tray tables are in the upright and locked position,' he said.

'Cut it out,' said Kain.

Stewart had flown in small planes before, but this seemed astonishingly casual. The pilot pressed the starter button, holding it down while the propeller turned, hesitantly at first, then becoming a blur through the windscreen. As the roar built to a crescendo, the plane vibrated and strained against the brakes. Then they were bumping across the field towards a dirt runway. The briefest of pauses, the throttle shoved forward, and they were bouncing, lifting, then dipping, before soaring away. The pilot was working overtime, flicking switches and adjusting the trim with one hand as he nursed the joystick with the other. Below, Stewart saw the airstrip dwindling, then glimpsed the autoroute, with cars scuttling along like beetles.

The horizon yawed violently as the plane hit the clouds. It was tossed around in the mist, rain spattering the windscreen, wipers churning, the engine straining as the plane angled into a steeper climb, the interior shuddering as if it was near the end of its strength. There was a flash of light, more cloud, then they were in clear air. The shuddering subsided. Beneath them was a carpet of cloud with the sun gleaming into the cockpit from diagonally to the right.

Diagonally to the right . . . Stewart looked at his watch. It was four thirty. At midday, the sun lay due south. At nightfall, due west. Halfway between midday and nightfall meant the sun was in the south west. That meant they were heading southeast, towards the Mediterranean. Which would put them on course for Nice, where all this had begun. Surely not?

Kain turned and grinned again, then mouthed something Stewart could not hear above the roar of the engine.

* * *

The Audi had vanished. Reports were flowing into the Prefecture from the Gendarmes, who had set up a twenty-five-kilometre perimeter around the autoroute exit, and from the Air and Frontier Police, flying patterns over a much wider area. All that they did was to prove a negative. They could not find the car.

The demands were flowing in too. The commander of the RAID team, who had been ensconced in a hangar at Nice airport, insisted on knowing where his men should be deployed. From Paris came demands from the minister to be told what the hell was going on.

Unsmiling, Halard sat at her desk, urging the searchers not to give up, requesting RAID to be patient, assuring the minister she took full responsibility for what had gone wrong. Brady sat nearby, wondering how much more she could take. She looked up and saw the concern on his face.

'What do you think?'

'I think it's time for plan B,' Brady replied. 'Suzanne Beaumont. She's all we've got.'

'Skinner's been on again,' she said. 'Several times. He wants a crack at her.'

'I think he's right. She just might know where Stewart and Kain are heading, though I doubt it. There are also the bonds, of course. Kain will have to send her instructions soon, telling her what to do with them. Whether he breaks cover or not, that'll give us a chance of getting back on his trail.'

'That's what Skinner is supposed to be waiting for.'

'Yes, but I don't think we can sit and wait any longer. We need to get a grip on this. Let Skinner go in there and start asking some serious questions. Right now, it's our only shot.'

Halard ruffled her fingers through her hair.

'I still don't trust him, Phil.'

'He's what we've got.'

Impact Graphics occupies one of Austin's less distinguished buildings: a low, single-storey office, fronted with bare white concrete, a single-pane green glass door, a gravelled parking lot. Customers who arrive to place or collect their orders for brochures, art-work and other items of graphic design come and go without undue excitement.

Except for that particular morning. Shortly after ten, Texas time, the door burst open and Harry Gonzales sprinted across the gravel to his car. He fumbled for the ignition with one hand and grabbed the radio-mike with the other.

'I'm coming in,' he yelled, as the engine revved up and he wrenched the gear lever into drive. 'Find Brady in Nice.'

'Where in Nice?' asked the operator. 'What time is it over there?'

'Just find him, will you? And patch me through.'

Stewart realised he had been asleep. It was six-thirty. The sun was lower, and further to the right. Not Nice after all. They had to be over the Mediterranean. He struggled with his mental geography. If they continued southeast, they would soon be over Italy – or would they? What about the islands? Sardinia? Corsica? Sicily? No, not Sicily, too far south. Any others? He couldn't remember. The clouds were still spread beneath them, rippled like a snowfield after wind.

Kain sat immobile. The pilot checked the gauges and fiddled with his instruments, the engine droning on in a monotone. Stewart felt his eyes closing again.

It was sudden activity that roused him. The pilot was tuning his radio and showing an aviation map to Kain. Stewart strained to see it, but its Perspex cover was reflecting too much light. The pilot spoke into his headset and Kain, who was wearing one too, nodded. He looked briefly over his shoulder, saying something Stewart could not catch, and gave the thumbs-up sign. He eased back the throttle, so that the nose of the plane dipped. Stewart realised he had said: 'Going down'.

The plane lurched as it was swallowed by the cloud. Again the engine tone rose and fell as the propeller lost its grip in the pockets of turbulence. When the plane broke through the cloud base, they seemed alarmingly close to the ground. A mountain ridge stretched to the right, with trees petering out at mid-height and ochre rocks above. Ahead was a stony orange plain, dotted with shrubs. An airfield came into view, in line with the end of the ridge. The plane banked and started its final approach. Stewart lost sight of the runway in the moments before it touched down, then came the slap of the tyres as they bounced once, twice, before settling. For all his accumulated air miles, he could not suppress an exhalation of relief.

Figari. That was the name, painted in black capital letters, across the white concrete terminal building. Where was Figari? Italy, surely? Sardinia? The plane scuttled across the tarmac, away from the terminal towards a black creosoted hangar. It taxied to a halt and the pilot shut off the engine.

Kain climbed out of his seat and opened the door, beckoning Stewart to follow. A dry and dusty heat was rebounding from the mountain ridge. Beyond the hangar was a line of stunted pines. The whine of the engine lingered in Stewart's ears, then they cleared and he picked up the piercing call of a jay.

'Thank you for choosing to fly with Tartan Air, pal,' said the Scotsman, with a mocking smile. He had removed his beret, to reveal traces of ginger hair across a pate that was gleaming with sweat. 'I hope you enjoy your stay.'

Stewart was suddenly incensed but Kain grabbed his arm and led him to a battered van parked beside the hanger, its number plate obscured by mud. The rear door was open and Kain pushed him inside. The door slammed shut. Stewart lay on a dusty blanket spread across the floor. Through the thin metal partition, he could hear voices from the driver's compartment. One was Kain's, the other had a rhythm Stewart did not recognise. The van jolted forward and the gears were grinding as they picked up speed. Stewart no longer tried to guess where they were going, resolving to conserve his energies for whatever trials were to come.

They travelled for the best part of an hour, the van twisting and climbing, then descending, the road surface becoming bumpier. At last they stopped and the engine died. The rear door opened. Stewart clambered out, catching a scent of the sea, of salt and ozone, and saw a steep yellow cliff to one side. He was plunged into darkness again, as a cloth hood settled over his head.

A hand grasped his wrist. Stones underfoot gave way to wooden boards, then what could have been a gangplank, and then he was stepping on to another wooden surface. A hand pushed down his head. 'Three steps,' said Kain. He was pushed along a passageway and another door closed. There was a muffled shout from Kain.

'Take off the hood.'

Stewart saw he was in the forward cabin of a boat. There were two bunks, a bucket for a toilet, and chinks of light through a porthole. He knew at once he was on board the *Symphonie*.

'Kain,' he roared.

'I'm listening,' said Kain.

'We had a deal. Where's Fee?'

'Tomorrow, fuckhead. Tomorrow's the day,' said Kain. Stewart knew that he was grinning.

Part Six

34

Suzanne lay on the sofa in Stewart's flat, doing her best to follow the intricacies of the Lebanon war. In his book, Stewart had performed heroics in disentangling the endless battles, from the street-by-street warfare to the amoral manoeuvres of the superpowers, but somehow the words kept failing to register. She knew it was best to concentrate on such a task, rather than dwell endlessly on Josh and Fee, but her fears kept intruding. Where were they? How were they? Where was Tom? The worst of all was not knowing.

Stewart's entryphone buzzed across her thoughts. Suzanne felt a frisson of alarm. Stewart had told her not to open the door unless she could be sure who was outside – adding, rather too easily she thought, that there shouldn't be any callers anyway.

She crossed the room and pressed the speaker button. Before she could say anything, a brisk voice responded.

'It's the police, Mrs Beaumont. Would you let me up?'

'The police? Which police, precisely?'

'Detective Chief Superintendent Raymond Skinner. From New Scotland Yard.'

'What is this about?'

'I'd prefer to tell you when I come up.'

'Do you have ID?'

'If you let me up, I'll show you.'

She released the catch and waited until Skinner arrived outside the door of the flat. When he rang, she looked through the peephole and saw a hand with bulbous fingers proffering a card with a photograph and what looked like an official seal.

'Mrs Beaumont?' said the same brisk voice.

'What is that?'

'It's my warrant card.' He passed it through the gap. There

was a photograph of a man with thin lips and neatly-parted hair. The inscription confirmed his name and rank. The badge was inscribed 'Metropolitan Police'.

She released the catch and Skinner walked in. His mouth was closed so tight that his thin lips had almost disappeared into his face, while his neat parting was held in place with hair gel. His eyes were set so deep she could not tell what colour they were. He was wearing a grey lightweight three-piece suit, with a discreet blue tie. She noticed his manicured fingernails but he did not offer his hand.

'Very nice,' Skinner said.

'Excuse me?'

'We were wondering what this place was like from the inside. We've had you under armed surveillance for the past forty-eight hours.'

'Why?'

Skinner crossed to the window and looked out.

'Still safely in place,' he said. 'You've nothing to fear. So far.'

'Why have you been watching me?'

'Don't be so naïve, Mrs Beaumont. Surely you realise the danger you're in?'

'Who from?'

'Red Kain. Victor Canning. Any one of the thugs they might decide to send here. But rest assured, we've had our people outside ever since you took delivery of the bonds.'

'I don't know what you're talking about.'

The moment she said it, Suzanne knew it sounded like a cheap line from a movie. She instantly regretted feeding Skinner such an obvious opening. He moved away from the window and fixed her with his eyes. They were grey, like his suit.

'Dispatched from Dulles International on Tuesday night,' she heard him intone. 'Prepaid with a credit card in the name of Tom Stewart. Marked documents, weight four pounds. Addressed to Suzanne Beaumont, c/o 48 Pennington Street, London E1. Delivered here at 9.14 on Thursday morning. That's what I'm talking about, Mrs Beaumont.'

Suzanne did not answer.

'And where are they now?'

'I'm not prepared to say.'

'At a friend's house? In a tin box under the bed?'

'It's no good, I'm not going to tell you.'

'How about in a safety deposit box at Mr Stewart's bank?'

She knew that Skinner saw her blush.

'No need to be embarrassed, Mrs Beaumont. The point is, wherever you think the bonds are now, you're almost certainly wrong.'

'I don't understand what you're saying.'

'No, I don't suppose you do. The fact is, the parcel that was delivered here on Thursday did not contain the bonds.'

'But it did. I saw them and counted them.'

'That's what I'm trying to tell you, Mrs Beaumont. You only think you saw them.'

Suzanne had a sudden premonition of what Skinner was going to say. It was to do with Jesse. Although she tried to give nothing away, Skinner registered the flicker of doubt in her eyes.

'I think you're with me, aren't you Mrs Beaumont?'

'Get to the point, will you?'

'That's right. The bonds you have aren't bonds at all. They're fake. Copies, Mrs Beaumont, nothing more.'

Suzanne felt as if she was losing the plot. She remembered something Tom had said. Police tell the truth when it suits them. They lie for the same reason. 'I'm not buying it, Mr Skinner. Not without proof.'

Skinner placed the tips of his fingers together: like a praying mantis, she thought.

'You know a company called Impact Graphics, don't you?'

She couldn't place the name.

'They're in Austin, about a mile from your office. They produce your annual reports.' Now she knew.

'As you may know, they have some very fancy copying equipment. High-quality laser stuff that can turn out replicas as good as the originals.'

Suzanne waited for Skinner to go on.

'At ten forty last Tuesday morning your father-in-law collected the bonds from the First Bank of Austin. At eleven fifteen he arrived at Impact Graphics. He spent an hour in the copy room with one of those fancy laser machines. He went in with one package and he came out with two.'

Skinner paused again. Again, Suzanne waited.

'The numbers are very interesting, Mrs Beaumont. As I'm sure you know, there are 250 bonds. When he was at Impact Graphics, your father-in-law made 251 copies. Take a look.'

Skinner handed her a sheet of paper. 'The FBI faxed it over from Austin last night. As you can see, it's Impact's invoice for services rendered – 251 copies at $8 each. Looks like he spoiled just one sheet. It's made out to Mr J. Beaumont, BioGenius Incorporated. I daresay it'll be waiting on your desk when you get back.'

Suzanne handed the invoice back.

'Shall I tell you about the paper?' Skinner asked.

'If you must.'

'It was a special order he asked Impact Graphics to get in. Delarue Woven Stock. Weight, 150 grams. That's exactly the same paper they use for bearer bonds.'

'Is there anything else?'

'I don't think we need anything else, Mrs Beaumont. I think that's all the proof we need. Or are you still saying you think the bonds in Mr Stewart's safe-deposit are genuine?'

Suzanne wanted to protest, wanted to argue that just because Jesse had copied the bonds did not mean he had given the copies to her and kept the originals himself. But she knew, to the point of certainty, that it was the copies that were sitting in Tom's bank on Tower Hill. She knew, because of his duplicity over the MycoGene trials. She also knew it fitted the Jesse Beaumont she had long suspected but never quite seen, ruthless and amoral in his pursuit of wealth and power; and shameless about using other people's money to further his own ends. The impact of what Skinner had told her was like a hammer blow, pushing her off balance, as its full implications struck home. She sat down, doing her best to maintain her composure. She wasn't prepared to break down in front of this caricature of a policeman, with the calculating way he had played her, like a fish on a line.

'What does Jesse say about all this? I presume the FBI have asked him.'

'That's a very interesting point, Mrs Beaumont. There's nothing the FBI would like more than to have chat with your father-in-law.'

Yet again, Suzanne watched this man set up his traps.

'You see, he's not in Austin any more. Shortly after he gave the bonds to Senator Bates – or should I say the *copies* of the bonds – he chartered a plane to Miami.'

'And?'

'So far, the FBI has no concrete proof that he left Miami.' Skinner unfolded a second sheet of paper and held it in front of Suzanne. 'Unless you count this.'

He handed it to her, saying it had been sent to the FBI the previous night. There were figures on the paper. Figures for very large sums. 'What this shows is that yesterday afternoon someone presented 250 bonds for payment at the Intercontinental Bank of Commerce in San Juan, Puerto Rico,' Skinner said. 'That someone then requested an electronic transfer of one hundred million dollars to an account in the Cayman Islands. From there – who knows? It could be in a dozen different banks by now. The document is formal notification of the transaction. It even lists all the serial numbers of the bonds. If you want to check them, that is.'

Now she lost it. *He's betrayed Josh,* she thought. *The grandson he wanted to take his own son's place. Sacrificed him to his own greed.* Skinner was talking, but his words had no meaning. It was if a charge of electricity was surging through her body, so that she felt like exploding with rage.

'Mrs Beaumont? Are you all right?'

'That money belonged to Josh. It was being held in trust for him.'

Skinner shook his head, then drew in his breath. 'Well, there's a thing,' he said. 'Who can you trust these days?'

Suzanne derived a morsel of consolation from the fact that she had at last told him something he didn't know.

Suzanne sat on the sofa, clenching her hands, doing her best to keep them still. Skinner was facing her on a dining-room chair. Although his tone was gentler, he was as remorseless as ever. She felt a rising fury at her predicament: at the unforgivable wrongs Jesse had committed, at this policeman who seemed to take a perverse pleasure in baiting and shaming her.

'You know Mr Brady was not best pleased when he found you had done a runner.'

'I don't know what you mean.'

'Made an undertaking to the FBI which you broke within two hours. The truth is, you never had any intention of keeping it in the first place. You must have set it up long before Mr Brady even met you. What on earth was your game?'

Suzanne saw no choice but to tell him now. As calmly as she could, she explained the plan she and Tom had formulated on the flight from Austin to Washington just five days – was that all? – before. How they knew the FBI would be watching them, and how they expected Brady to call. How they resolved they could not trust the police or FBI to put the interests of their children first. How they had decided to turn the tables on Kain, to dictate how and when the ransom would be paid. How they had separated at Dulles airport and sent the bonds – or what they thought were the bonds – to London by Federal Express. How Tom had gone to Amsterdam to meet Kain, and demand to see for himself that the children were alive. And how they had agreed that Suzanne would wait in London; wait for Tom to call and tell her where to deliver the bonds.

Skinner was shaking his head. 'Dear me,' he said. 'Lord spare us from amateurs.'

'Don't patronise me, Mr Skinner. None of this might have happened if the police had taken us seriously from the start. The French weren't interested and we were getting nowhere until Jesse got on the case, getting questions asked in Washington'

'That's as may be, Mrs Beaumont. But Mr Brady was certainly taking you seriously in Washington. Or trying to, until he realised you'd taken it into your heads to go it alone.'

'We didn't trust him to put the interests of the children first.'

'What he told me is that he gave you an absolute promise there would be no move against Kain until the children were safe.'

'What he didn't say was what would happen if Kain didn't lead you to the children. If he just tried to walk away with the ransom. What would have happened then?'

This time it was Skinner, faced with Suzanne's anger, who remained silent.

'Come to that,' she went on, 'what do you want most? Find my son? Or arrest Victor Canning? He's become an obsession for you, hasn't he?'

Skinner looked at her coldly. She had taken a chance on goading him and suspected she had struck home. She also suspected he would take his revenge.

'I don't have obsessions, Mrs Beaumont. I'm a police officer; I do what I am required to do by law. The simple fact is that because you and Mr Stewart decided to go your own sweet way, it's likely that none of us will get what we want: either find the children or arrest the people who kidnapped them. And that's because it's all gone terribly wrong.'

Now what? Suzanne's rage was becoming fear.

'Yes, Mrs Beaumont. The day after your Mr Stewart and Kain left Amsterdam, they had a crash. In Germany, on the autobahn.'

She gasped. 'Is Tom hurt?'

Skinner delayed perceptibly before answering. 'I don't suppose he's too badly injured. Otherwise he wouldn't have got away from the German police.'

'What on earth do you mean?'

'Kain killed a police officer. Mr Stewart is wanted for being an accessory to murder.'

Was there no end to the horrors? 'I don't believe it,' Suzanne protested. 'Tom wouldn't be mixed up in anything like that.'

'Perhaps you don't know him as well as you think. The next thing our heroes did was to steal a car in France. He's in a lot of trouble, Mrs Beaumont.'

'Do you know where they are now?'

'Somewhere near Lyon in the south of France. For the moment we've decided to let them run. See where they lead us.'

There was a scream in her head, fighting to get out. 'Please,' she said. 'You can't arrest them. You know what would happen. The children will die.'

'What happens next, Mrs Beaumont, depends entirely on you. This time you have to cooperate fully with us. No more games.'

'What do you want me to do?'

'We want you to do exactly what you and Mr Stewart agreed in the first place. When you hear from him, you will take the bonds wherever he tells you. But this time you'll be working with us. We want you to wear a transmitter that will allow us to follow you. It'll be just like the transmitter Mr Stewart was carrying in Washington, except you won't be throwing yours away.'

Her mind was racing. Was there still a chance of escape? Skinner divined her silence.

'Don't even think about it, Mrs Beaumont. Let's take it step by step. First of all you're wondering, do I have to hand over the bonds? Yes, because if you don't, the children will die. Second, if I manage to shake off the police, could we still go it alone? The answer's no, because Kain's not going to give you back your children until he's had the bonds checked. When he finds out they're fake, he's not going to be very pleased. So you'll need us to be *very* close by.'

She knew something about bonds. 'Won't he have to take them to a bank to get them verified?'

'Yes, he will. And that provides us with our opportunity. It'll be at least a day before he finds out they're fake, and that's when we go in. We don't know exactly how Kain intends to play it, but we're drawing up plans to cover all contingencies right now.'

'Who's we, exactly?'

Skinner gave his thin-lipped smile. 'Me, Mrs Beaumont. Plus Commissaire Halard and Mr Brady. All the ones you didn't trust.'

It was over now. 'What happens next?'

'You carry on waiting for Stewart to call. We know he hasn't done so yet.'

No need to ask how Skinner knew.

'We'll be listening day and night. As soon as we know where he wants you to go, we'll finalise our plans. Until that happens I'm going to move a woman police officer into the flat. She'll take care of everything there is to be done, from shopping to answering the door. You don't go anywhere, and you especially don't go near the windows. Meanwhile the officers from the anti-terrorist squad will stay on guard outside.'

'Isn't that overdoing it?'

Skinner leaned forward in his chair. 'Not in the least, Mrs Beaumont. I know the people we are dealing with. Especially Victor Canning. Perhaps he is an obsession for some people. I think that Mr Brady has already told you he's one of the most vicious criminals in Britain. But did Mr Brady explain anything about his methods? They're not pretty, Mrs Beaumont. The last of his victims – correction, the last but one – was pulled out of the Thames. He had fishing hooks shoved down his throat that ripped his insides to ribbons. Canning doesn't mind who he has killed, or how it's done.'

Her rage had become fear. Skinner had her where he wanted.

'In view of what's happened in Germany, Canning may decide he doesn't want to wait for you to deliver the bonds. He may decide to send some people here to get them. God forbid he finds out what your father-in-law has done. Do you understand, Mrs Beaumont?'

Suzanne understood.

Bert Humphries was in his shirtsleeves, deep in the bowels of the Metropolitan Police South London Command Centre in South Norwood, just two miles from Victor Canning's home. Above ground, in the part of the building the public saw, were the usual facilities and offices where the overt business of policing was conducted. Down here, in the subterranean section, were the listening rooms, the communications suites, the bunkers which would serve as a focus of civilian control in the event of an emergency, from insurrection to nuclear attack. It was also where Skinner had decreed that the final phases of Operation Shrike would unfold.

'On side now, is she guvnor?'

'She put on a bit of a show,' said Skinner. 'But I had her sorted by the end. Not that she had any choice.'

Skinner took off his jacket, although he kept on his waistcoat. This far down the air conditioning was not at its most effective, and there was always a clamminess in the air. 'Anything come up from Canning?'

Humphries shook his head. 'Afraid not, guvnor. The intercept's still in place, and we've clocked him calling to check his messages. But that's it. Take a look.'

Skinner walked over to the table where Kain's laptop sat open, its screen a grey glow. Humphries pressed a series of buttons and a dozen lines of type appeared.

'Here we are,' Humphries said. 'Canning's first call at ten fifty-three. Shows his routing to Zurich, his automatic log on, and here he's checking for messages. Does it three times. And here he is logging off. Nothing sent, nothing retrieved. Same as yesterday, and the day before.'

'Bastard,' Skinner said. 'Any phone calls?'

'Two,' Humphries replied. 'One incoming, from the house-keeper, telling him she was going to be late. One outgoing to the clinic, checking on his kid before he goes down there.'

'How is she?'

'Doesn't look too good.'

Skinner cracked his knuckles. 'Doesn't look too good for us either, does it? Not if Victor's gone all shy on us. How are we going to tie him into this?' There was a brittle edge to his tone.

'He'll send a message, sir. He'll have to.'

'What if he doesn't, Bert? What if he never types the words Raven or Red Bird again? What if he doesn't send a message to Kain before this whole bloody thing goes down? What have we got on him then?'

'Sweet F.A.,' admitted Humphries.

'Sweet fuck all it is. Do you think he knows?'

'Knows what, sir?'

Skinner gestured at the laptop. 'Knows we've got Kain's box of tricks. Knows that we can read every word he sends.'

'I don't see how he can. Nobody's called him. Nobody's met him. Nobody who could know what's happened to Kain.'

Skinner returned to his desk where he peered at a fingernail under his desk lamp. One of his tics, Humphries knew, when he was upset.

'I'll tell you something, Bert,' he said through tightened lips. 'If this all comes to an end before Canning incriminates himself . . . If it all goes down somewhere, whether those kids end up alive or dead, and he still hasn't given us what we need, then . . .'

'Then what, guvnor?'

'I am going to be very, very pissed off.'

'Any ideas, sir. Anything we can do?'

Skinner was silent for a moment, his fingers in the familiar praying position.

'Well, there could be, Bert.'

'How's that, guvnor?'

'Let's just suppose,' Skinner mused. 'What if Canning received a message telling him something he didn't know. A message from a person or persons unknown, that provoked him into doing something rash. If you get my drift.'

'You mean something we could pin on him? Something tying him into the kidnapping?'

'Precisely.'

Humphries pursed his lips. 'And what might provoke him, guvnor?'

'Well, Bert. What if he knew the bonds were just copies? What if he knew that friend Jesse had run off with the loot?'

'He'd do his nut.'

'Precisely.'

'Sounds dodgy to me,' said Humphries. 'I mean, if someone did try something like that, there's no telling what Canning would do. He could have the kids killed. Kain would do it without blinking. Then where would our person unknown be?'

'Think about it, Bert. Suppose that by the time Canning gets the message, our Mrs Beaumont's had a call from lover boy? "I've seen the children. They're safe and well. Bring the bonds to such and such a place". Halard and Brady and all the cavalry's in place, and we send Mrs Beaumont in, and Victor still hasn't said a dicky bird, and then, at that very moment, our person or persons unknown drops him the word?'

'So he sends Kain his orders, kill the children . . .'

'And Halard steps in and saves the day. I think she's very competent, don't you, Bert?'

Humphries stared at Kain's laptop. 'I think that any person or persons unknown considering doing such a thing would want to think it through very carefully indeed.'

'I'm sure you're right, Bert,' Skinner said.

Humphries headed for the door. 'I'll get us some tea.'

Moments later the laptop came to life, its tinny speaker

announcing that Victor Canning was once again transmitting data on his line. Skinner walked back to examine the screen.

Message – Id: < [194.216.92.1]) KAA22466
Sender: (Unverified)
Date:02 Aug 1996 14:38:36–0600
To: (Recipient list suppressed)
LOG ON: ***** *** *****
VERIFIED
CHECKING
NO NEW MESSAGES SINCE LAST LOG ON
LOG OFF AT 14.38:47
NO MESSAGES RETRIEVED
NO MESSAGES SENT
OK!

No messages sent and none retrieved. No, not okay, thought Skinner. It was not fucking okay at all.

35

Stewart heard the slap-slapping of waves on the hull. They were on the move. There had been footsteps above his head, the whine of the engine, the clatter of a chain, but the porthole was still covered. If this was where Fee had been consigned, she must have been in terror. But he hoped he knew her well enough to believe she had found some inner strength to draw on to help see her through.

The cabin door opened. Kain was framed by the morning light. 'You can come up on deck.'

Stewart pushed past him, passed through the main cabin and climbed the steps to the cockpit. He knew at once that the boat had been camouflaged. The mizzen mast had gone and the white hull he had seen in Fee's photograph was painted black. He looked over the stern and saw that its name, delicately inscribed in white capitals, was now *Hibou* – *hibou* for owl, he remembered.

They were 400 metres offshore, on a course parallel to a ragged grey cliff, lined with gullies and with a few shrubs clinging to ledges. The sky was overcast and the sea reflected dark green. The waves were flowing fast, their caps flecked with foam. The yacht was running on its engine and the sails were down. The autopilot had the helm. There was no one else on board.

'Still some weather around,' said Kain.

'Where are we?' demanded Stewart. 'Where's Fee?'

'From the top,' said Kain, 'Where we are, you find out when you've seen her. Where she is, she's coming to meet us now.'

'And afterwards? What happens then?'

'Let's do it one more time. First, you see the kids. Second, you deliver the bonds. Third, you get the kids back.'

Stewart reverted to poker mode, determined not to be riled. The boat was pitching more acutely, the waves sliding up the hull towards the deck. Kain went below and from the cabin came the crackle of a radio. Stewart heard him say, '*Hibou* calling *Barracuda*', and guessed he was talking to another boat.

'Not long now,' said Kain with his grin, when he came back on deck. They breasted a wave and Stewart saw the top of a stubby mast, then the prow of a blue fishing boat beating a path towards them. It vanished from sight each time they slid into a trough, bobbing up again as they climbed the next crest. Stewart caught a glimpse of two people standing by the guard rail. Was one of them Fee? A gobbet of spray smacked against his cheek and he ducked. When he lifted his head, the boat had disappeared again.

The next time the two boats were only 100 metres apart. The fishing boat was broadside on, the word *Barracuda* visible on the prow. Then he saw her, a slight figure being led to the guard rail. Her hair was bedraggled and she was clutching a jacket around her that glistened in the spray. She seemed impossibly frail and vulnerable. Stewart wanted to reach out to her with all his being. A visceral roar welled up from deep inside.

'Fee!' His shout was lost on the wind.

'Fee!' he roared again. She was looking at him, a wan face above the waves. He windmilled his arms above his head, 'Fee! Are you all right?'

Her voice was like a reed, thin but strong. 'All right,' he heard. Josh was being led alongside her.

'Both of you?'

'Yesss.' Her answer merged with the hissing of the waves.

'Fee! I love you!' It was another roar, propelled across the water with a passion he had never felt before. Her reply was like a fragmentary echo of his. '. . . love you, daddy . . .'

Then the boats had passed, and he saw her looking back.

'Kain!' he yelled. 'Take us closer!'

Kain ignored him. They curved out to sea while the *Barracuda* turned towards the shore, their two wakes signing a farewell that was quickly erased by the waves. The boat lurched at the apex of its turn and Stewart clung to the hand rail. When he looked again, the *Barracuda* had gone.

* * *

Stewart watched Kain rigging his cellular phone to a speaker in the cabin. The boat was moored to a rickety wooden jetty, with several missing planks and a hand rail dubiously fashioned from a frayed length of rope. An orange dirt track wound uphill from the jetty and disappeared into a line of trees. There were no other boats in sight, nor any other sign of human life.

'It's showtime,' said Kain. 'What's the number?'

Stewart called down the digits from the deck. He heard his phone ringing in London and willed Suzanne to answer.

'Hello?' she said cautiously.

Kain said nothing.

'Hello?' This time she sounded puzzled.

Kain passed the phone to Stewart, his hand over the mouthpiece. 'Don't fuck up.'

Stewart's first words spurted out. 'Suzanne, it's Tom. I've seen the children. They're alive. They're okay.'

There was silence, and he wondered if she had understood. 'Suzanne?'

'Oh Tom. Thank God.' There was a catch in her voice, and she was silent again.

'Suzanne?'

'I'm still here,' she said. 'Where are you? Tell me what's happened.'

'I'm with the man. He wants me to ask you some questions. Are you alone?'

'Yes, I am.'

'Have you talked to the police?'

'Of course not. I haven't talked to anybody. Now tell me about the children.'

He looked down at Kain, who nodded. 'I saw them two hours ago. They were on a boat, and we were about fifty feet apart.'

'How did they look?'

'They seemed fine. Tired, I'd say, and a little grubby. But otherwise fine.'

'Did you talk to them? What did they say?'

'I couldn't hear them too well because of the waves. But Fee said they were all right.'

'And Josh?'

Stewart thought of the pale, impassive figure alongside Fee.

'He didn't say anything. But he was there. He looked okay. Honestly.'

'Where are they now? And where are you?'

'I'm coming to that. First, do you have the bonds?'

'Yes, I do.'

'Then you have to bring them to a place called Figari.'

'Where?'

'Figari.' He spelt it for her.

'Where's that? In Italy?'

'No, that's what I thought. It's in Corsica. In the south, near Bonifacio.'

'*Corsica*? Is that where the children have been all this time?'

'I don't know. All I know is, that's where they are now. The sooner you bring the bonds, the sooner we get them back.'

Kain was gesturing with his hand, a windmill motion telling Stewart to hurry.

'I have to go. Find out about flights. You'll probably have to come via Paris or Nice. I'll call back in an hour so you can tell me which flight you're on.'

'Will you meet me at the airport?'

Stewart did not look at Kain. 'Of course.'

Kain was making another gesture, slicing his hand across his throat.

'I have to go,' Stewart said. 'Do hurry, won't you?'

'I'll be waiting for your call,' she replied.

Kain took the phone and cut the line.

Brady watched as Halard sat forward, scribbling across her pad, a lift in her voice as she fired her questions, an air of satisfaction when she put down the phone. 'That was Skinner,' she said. 'It's Corsica.'

Halard's summary was to the point, as always. The listeners at South Norwood had heard Suzanne answer Stewart's call. Skinner himself had the earphones by the time Stewart told her where to bring the bonds.

'Figari?' asked Brady.

'It's the airport for Bonifacio,' she told him. 'Southern tip of the island. Old fortified harbour town. Deserted in the winter, solid with tourists in the summer.'

'How long have we got?'

'Skinner's booking her a flight now. She'll be on her way to Nice tonight, picking up an Air-Inter flight in the morning which gets into Figari at 10.50. Skinner's going to brief her.'

'Then we can move,' said Brady.

Halard was already calling the RAID commander at the airport, instructing him to take his men to southern Corsica. An oceangoing police launch was standing by in Nice harbour, and they would be there before dawn. 'But stay offshore, beyond the horizon,' she requested. 'Until we know how this is going to go down.'

Brady asked about the land team. Who was going to be waiting for Kain, Stewart and Suzanne at the airport, and follow them – presumably – to where the children were being kept?

'Very difficult,' said Halard. 'The police there can't make a move without the whole island knowing. Anyway, there's not a local cop I would trust. They're either intimidated or corrupted, or both. We'll have to fly in people from here.'

Desiry had found a map and pointed out how Bonifacio occupied a high, rocky peninsula that had commended itself to the town's founders as an ideal place to defend. The old town sat squarely across the most impregnable part, with steep walls and ramparts glowering out at visitors.

'There's something else, boss. That's where Cabrini's cousin Sanpiero lives. It's a very tight place, especially the old town. It's a warren of passages and alleyways; everyone knows everyone else. Start asking questions and it's round the town in no time. If that's where they're headed it's going to be hard for us not to show out.'

'So who goes in?' Brady asked.

'Desiry, for a start.' Halard looked at him, and he nodded. 'Plus five others. Any more's too much of a risk.'

Desiry was assembling his team and making his plans when Skinner called back to confirm Suzanne's flights. Halard said she would book her into the Holiday Inn near Nice airport.

'Fine,' said Skinner. 'But don't let any of your people go near her. I wouldn't put it past chummy to have somebody around, on the flight or at the hotel, to make sure she's alone.'

'Understood. But she needs to be equipped.'

'How are you going to track her?'

'GPS.'

'I'll have our technical boys fix her up with something and I'll send you the frequency. Will you be there for the next few hours?'

No, Halard told him. She was going to run the operation from a sea-going command centre which had been hastily installed on a gin-palace of a yacht called *Concorde*, which awaited them in the harbour. It looked like a toy for the idle rich and – unlike RAID's police launch – could sit off the coast at Bonifacio without attracting undue attention. It was fast – very fast – but they would need to leave by six o'clock.

'That gives us just enough time to buy you something to wear,' she said to Brady when she'd put down the phone.

'What's that supposed to mean?'

Halard looked at Brady's dark grey suit, his white shirt, his dark blue tie, his black lace-up shoes: must be standard FBI issue, she thought. 'You don't exactly look like idle rich at the moment. We need to fit you out in something more nautical.'

'Who's paying?'

'You're here on FBI business, aren't you?'

Brady thought of the bean-counters in Washington and shuddered.

'It's your operation,' he said. 'You're calling the shots.'

'So long as you remember that, the clothes are on me.'

Midnight in South Norwood. The pubs had only just emptied, there was a sweaty queue in the kebab shop, and a group of youths in baseball caps were kicking a beer can across the street. Deep in the police command centre, Skinner was growing more frustrated by the minute. Canning had not checked his messages since early afternoon – and now he wasn't even at home.

'Still away, Bert?'

'Still at the clinic, guvnor. She must be in a very bad way.'

Skinner stared at the laptop. The fluorescent light was prickling Humphries's eyes. He rubbed them, and yawned.

'Okay, Bert?'

'Bit tired, guvnor. That's all.'

'Listen, I'll do the next stint. Find a cot and get some sleep.'

'No, I'm all right.'

Humphries did not move.

'Do what I say.'

Humphries hesitated. 'That's an order, sergeant.'

He stood up and walked towards the door. 'Maybe I'll get some air.'

Skinner removed two sheets of paper from a drawer, the same two sheets he had shown Suzanne Beaumont the previous day. There was a scanner attached to Kain's computer and he fed them in, watching them materialise on the laptop's screen. Then he began to key in a message.

Victor Canning sat motionless in a darkened room. He wore a charcoal-grey suit, immaculately pressed, a cream shirt with a starched collar, a tie patterned in grey and maroon, a pair of highly-polished black leather shoes. His face was cast in the ghostly light of a screen where a tracer was blipping uncertainly from left to right. But he had no eyes for the screen, only for the inert figure, her head sunk in a pillow, in the bed barely a pace from where he sat.

A refrain was coursing through his mind, its cadences as implacable as ever.

What is life to me without thee?
What is life without my Love?

'Kathleen, my love,' he said. There was no sign she had heard him, no movement save for the gentle rise and fall of the bedclothes as she laboured for breath. She had slipped into unconsciousness just twenty minutes before he arrived, leaving him to watch, all feeling flattened, as her life ebbed away. Her pain was over now, and that knowledge diminished some of his own. He remembered the laughing child she had been, innocent and unknowing, unaware of the trials life would hold. He had so wanted to shield and protect her, so that she grew straight and pure, but it was not to be. Perhaps it could never have been; perhaps his own life had been too flawed for that, so that she never stood a chance.

He stood and leaned over her. Her eyelids were fluttering, then for a moment they opened. She seemed to be looking at him but nothing registered in her eyes. All he could see was the reflection of his own, their irises violet in the shadows of the room, the pupils tinged with gold. Her eyes closed, her breathing faded, and she was still.

36

'Madame?'

The cabin attendant was proferring Suzanne a tray. She nodded and he placed it in front of her. Breakfast, on the Air-Inter flight from Nice to Figari, consisted of a roll, a slice of cold meat, a triangle of processed cheese, coffee and mineral water. She had no stomach for eating, nor for coffee: she'd consumed enough caffeine in the seventeen days of waiting and worrying about Josh; her beautiful, slim-limbed Josh. She sipped the water: even that tasted flat and sweet.

She was glad the seat next to her was empty: no need to exchange pleasantries with someone she did not know. She had placed the briefcase containing the bonds on the seat so that it would always be in her sight. Through the window there were only clouds, adding to the sense of dislocation she felt. She had landed at Nice last night in the dark, helping her forget her arrival with Josh, when the Mediterranean had seemed to glisten in anticipation of their coming, and Nice had looked like a magic city, perched between the mountains and the ocean, theirs to share for a precious week. But walking through the arrivals hall had brought it all back, and she felt as though she was in a recurrent nightmare. Even now she had to keep telling herself: this is no dream, this is real; soon you will have to play your part, convince Kain that she'd handed over the ransom and can I have my son back, please.

She shivered: from apprehension, she knew. So much depended on carrying off this monumental deceit. Nothing in her life had prepared her for this moment. How exactly did you train for delivering fake ransoms? She felt alone in a dark and irrational world. Whatever fears she was fighting, she must appear confident and capable, and in command of herself.

Never let the bastards see what you really feel. She nearly choked with the sudden pain of her predicament, remembering Josh laughing and happy, wanting to see that again, and almost overwhelmed by the responsibility she bore.

She remembered Skinner: his manicured hands, his gaunt face, his thin lips, mercilessly wearing her down, until she had no choice but to submit. On his second visit, he had been less triumphal as he told her what she might expect. She and Tom were to behave as if they had never dreamed of cooperating with the police – 'shouldn't be too difficult for you, should it?' he had cracked, with his vestigial smile. She must insist on seeing the children, and she must find some way of warning Tom. While waiting for the rescue squad to come in, they should reconnoitre escape routes or places to take cover, and stay close to their children until the moment came.

'What exactly do you think will happen?' she had asked.

'That's just it, Mrs Beaumont. We can't tell until we know what kind of place Kain takes you to. How many entrances, can we get observation points – that sort of thing. But the French rescue people are very experienced and they'll be prepared for whatever comes. They've never lost a hostage yet, or so I'm told.'

Then came the moment he relished most. He removed a package from his briefcase and unwrapped it, to reveal a black metal sphere, about the size of a fifty pence piece. 'We need you to wear this,' he said. 'So that we can track you when you meet Kain.' Skinner explained that it would transmit a signal via a satellite to a police control room. 'It's called GPS,' he said. 'Global Positioning System. Ships use it for navigation. It's what the FBI were going to use in Washington, until you and Mr Stewart went off on your own.'

Where was she supposed to hide it, Suzanne asked?

'Somewhere on your person, Mrs Beaumont. Somewhere Kain wouldn't find with a body search. Unless he was going to get really intimate with you.'

He waited while Suzanne absorbed his words.

'It's up to you. We usually find it's best to tape it to the inside of your thigh, as far up as you can. Hold it in place with a bit of sticking plaster.'

He watched for a reaction, but she was damned if she would give anything away.

'Best to shave your skin first. Otherwise it's not very pleasant when you take it off.' Remember, he added, not to attach the transmitter until she was on the flight to Corsica, otherwise it would show up on the metal-detector at the security gate. He had left it with her, saying its battery should last a year, unable to stop himself adding: 'Though I'm sure all this will be over long before that.'

Afterwards, she had wanted Tom there to help nurse her bruised feelings, tell her everything was going to be all right. All she had instead was the memory of his phone call, peremptory and disturbing, even though it brought the news she had been longing to hear. She had felt a brief surge of joy before the full portent sank in. Yes, Josh was alive; but not safe. Still captive, still in mortal danger. A danger she was about to walk into herself.

Tom too had sounded edgy and under pressure. She had strained to decipher his words: 'I'm with the man.' She presumed he was warning that Kain was there too. Her heart had thumped as she lied about the police, and she had struggled to keep her voice even as she showered him with questions about the children. Then he had gone, and she felt alone once more. He had been still more curt when he called to find out about her flights, as if Kain were standing beside him with a gun to his head.

She had felt even more alone as the full implications of what Jesse had done drilled home. She recognised now that she'd never fully trusted him, always held something of herself in reserve. She remembered the last time she'd seen him, sitting in his study at West Lake Hills as the light came up, and she thought of a lizard with skin like parchment, its tongue flicking out in quest of prey. She could hear his voice, explaining away the gamble he had taken with children's lives by using defective MycoGene, trying to persuade her it was for the greater good. What could he say now, to explain away his final betrayal of his grandson?

Anger had surged through her, and she made herself think long and hard, to be sure she was not being driven solely by a spasm of hate. Then she had made her decision.

She had made two phone calls from the Holiday Inn. The first was to Morton Mintz. He was surprised to hear from her: hostile at first, then suspicious, then utterly sceptical. But in the end she had convinced him she meant what she said.

'Are you willing to put it in writing?'

'I already have,' she told him. 'It should be with my attorney in the next two or three days.'

Then she'd called Brady at the Nice Prefecture, and waited impatiently while they patched her through to a boat, heading for Corsica she supposed. She told him that the money Jesse had stolen belonged to Josh, and since he was a minor, and she was his mother, she wanted to file a complaint on her son's behalf.

'I want him arrested. I want him charged. I want him prosecuted to the full extent of the law.'

'It would be a pleasure, Mrs Beaumont,' Brady had said. 'But first we have to find him.'

'I know where he is,' she said. 'Or I know who does.'

The plane's speaker system came alive; the captain made an announcement. They were half an hour from Figari, there was clear weather ahead, and the temperature at the airport was thirty-two degrees. There was shuffling from other passengers, and Suzanne realised she had to get into the toilet ahead of the rush. She clutched the briefcase and made it by a nose.

She took out the transmitter and placed it by the sink. Then she undid the roll of Elastoplast she had bought at Heathrow. She was wearing loose, linen trousers she had hastily acquired when she'd first arrived in London. She undid the buckle, letting them fall to the floor, and ran her hand over the band of flesh at the top of her left thigh she had shaved before leaving Stewart's apartment. She bound the transmitter against the inside of her thigh with several layers of the plaster.

She buckled her trousers back into place and craned to look at herself in the mirror. The transmitter felt bulky but it didn't show through. There was a queue when she left, and she heard a male voice say: 'What on earth do they *do* in there?'

Back in her seat, the clouds had cleared, and beige fingers of Corsica's coastline were protruding stiffly into the sea. Now, urgently, she had another decision to face. How was she to tell Tom the bonds were fake? He won't leave you two alone, Skinner had warned; he won't allow you any intimate moments in case you're planning a double cross. She suggested writing a note but Skinner said that was far too risky. 'As soon as you see Mr Stewart at the airport, give him a hug to show how relieved you are to see him, and whisper in his ear. Do it before Kain knows what's happening. That's your best chance.'

Screw you, Suzanne thought. What if Tom didn't understand her? What if his reaction gave her away? A note was far better: she just had to get it into his hands without Kain seeing. It wasn't risk-free, but nothing was, any more; they were too far in now. She took a notebook from the briefcase and inscribed her message in small, careful capital letters. She tore out the page, folded it into two, then two again, and slid it into her pocket.

The captain was speaking again. It was the ritual announcement: starting their descent, five minutes to landing, trays and seatbacks in the upright position, baggage under seats or in overhead containers, seatbelts securely fastened. Always before she had let the words pass harmlessly by; now they were like the prelude to a summary execution. In five minutes she would be leaving the plane, walking into the arrivals hall, greeting Tom, meeting Kain, and being led to whatever fate awaited them.

The plane was descending steeply, then banking for its final approach. It touched down and skimmed past the terminal, slowing and turning at the end of the runway. Then it was taxiing back past the terminal again, towards the arrivals door. There were faces against the glass, turned towards the plane. She looked intently, but could not see if Tom was there. The plane halted and the cabin attendants moved to open the forward door. The captain was making his final announcement: 'Welcome to Figari.'

Canning's shoes lay on the carpet, one on its side. His jacket was draped over the back of a chair, his collar was unbuttoned and his tie was askew. His eyes were open wide, focused on his computer screen, still hardly comprehending what they saw. He had returned from the clinic weary beyond belief from his bedside vigil, yet he knew he could not sleep as his grief took hold.

Mechanically, almost, he had turned on his computer and checked yet again for messages.

'You have mail,' it said. 'Source: Red Bird. Do you want to retrieve it now?' He had typed 'yes' and waited for Kain's message to download; his explanation, Canning assumed, for four days of silence.

Instead had appeared this facsimile document emanating from the FBI, telling how 250 bearer bonds totalling $100 million dollars had been cashed at the Intercontinental Bank of Commerce in San Juan, Puerto Rico. A second facsimile demonstrated that, in Austin three days before, Mr J. Beaumont of BioGenius Incorporated had made precisely 251 copies of a document or documents. Finally came a message spelling out further evidence to prove that Jesse Beaumont had handed his daughter-in-law fake or copy bonds and then fled from the US with the genuine articles. Spelling out, beyond all possible doubt.

Through her heart, His sorrow sharing,
All His bitter anguish bearing

Kathleen Ferrier's lament was flooding the room, helping to mask his pain. He sat motionless until her voice finally soared and died, and the last chords from the strings signalled the end. Then he cleared the screen and began to type.

Suzanne looked on edge as she came into the arrivals hall. Passengers were filing through the entrance doors, hesitating as they scanned the hall for the baggage carousel. Stewart waved from behind the barrier but she was looking for a trolley and making for the carousel. Her maroon grip was almost the first to arrive and then she was heading for the exit, a black briefcase in the basket of the trolley: no need to guess what it contained. Stewart waved again and this time she saw him, waving extravagantly in reply. Stewart moved to meet her, Kain a couple of paces behind. 'No funny stuff,' he warned. 'I'm watching you every inch.'

Suzanne threw herself at Stewart, clasping her arms around

his neck. 'Thank God,' she said, and kissed him hard on the lips. She took both his hands in hers and squeezed them. 'It's wonderful to see you,' she said. Stewart felt her pressing something into the palm of his right hand, a piece of folded paper. Something must have happened, something affecting their children. Had Kain seen? Without looking towards him, he let go of Suzanne's hands and slid the paper into his right-hand pocket, removing his handkerchief to blow his nose. She kissed him again.

'Very touching,' said Kain. 'Let's get out of here.'

They were heading for the terminal doors when Stewart said he needed a leak.

'Where are the bonds?' Kain asked.

'In the briefcase,' said Suzanne.

Kain grinned. 'Go ahead. I'll stick with her.'

Inside the men's room, a cubicle was free, and Stewart locked the door. He unfolded Suzanne's sheet of paper. Her painstaking capitals filled the tiny page.

> THE BONDS ARE FAKE. JESSE BETRAYED US. POLICE KNOW. THEY ARE TRACKING ME. KAIN MUST TAKE US TO THE CHILDREN. HE NEEDS AT LEAST A DAY TO CHECK THE BONDS. POLICE WILL COME IN THEN.

He read it again, absorbing its implications. *The bonds are fake. The police know*. Clear enough. *They are tracking me*. Tracking her how? With a transmitter? If so, where? *Kain must take us to the children. The police will come in* . . . Guns blazing? A shoot-out? Who survives? An apocalyptic vision filled his mind and he pushed it away.

Jesse betrayed us . . . He imagined Suzanne taking this devastating blow alone, and was appalled.

'Stewart? What the hell you doing in there?'

The toilet was flushing, swirling away the torn-up note, as he opened the door. 'Let's move it,' said Kain. Outside, Stewart's eyes met Suzanne's and he was sure she knew he had read the note.

The path to the car park lay through a construction area, with ruts to cross and kerbs to mount. They abandoned the trolley and Kain moved to pick up the briefcase. Stewart took hold of his arm.

'No, Kain,' he said. 'You get the bonds when we get the children. Take us to them now.'

Kain let go of the case. 'I told you before, Stewart. Quit worrying. That's just where we're going.'

Never before had Humphries seen him so incensed. Skinner was standing rigid by the laptop when he returned from breakfast in the canteen, his mouth set so tight his lips had disappeared.

'Problems, guvnor?'

Skinner glared at him, his eyes unnaturally bright. If Humphries hadn't known better, he would have thought him on the point of tears.

Humphries hurried towards the desk. 'Canning sent something at last?' he asked.

Skinner didn't wait for him to get there. He picked up the laptop and hurled it across the desk. It bounced once and skittled over the edge, hanging by the cables that attached it to the scanner and the telephone jack.

'Steady on, guvnor. That's uncalled for.' Humphries put the laptop back on the desk and untangled the cables. 'What's Canning sent?'

'Why don't you fucking read it?' Skinner could scarcely spit out the words.

Humphries did as he was told. When he was finished he didn't speak. There was nothing to say. He stared at the screen, feeling Skinner's eyes on him, thinking of Canning: the clever, devious bastard.

'One, this is Six, over.'

'Hearing you Six,' said Desiry.

'Red Bird is driving a blue Clio 1.6, registration number 0605 VC 02. Rented from Europcar. Visual contact now. Target matches physical description except for his hair. It's much shorter, call it stubble. He's wearing blue jeans, white and blue trainers, blue yachting shirt with fawn *gilet* – looks like a combat jacket without sleeves. Carrying a brown leather shoulder-bag, so possibly armed. Owl and Tomcat on board.

Baggage includes black briefcase. Exiting airport, direction Bonifacio. Three cars between me and targets. All look like airport greeters, so I shouldn't show out.'

'Roger, Six.'

Desiry was in a burned-out house high on the cliff beyond the old town of Bonifacio, its yellowed walls rising almost sheer like a fairytale castle. There wasn't a decent hotel room to be had in town, and after a night in Bonifacio's cheapest *pension*, where the mosquitoes zeroed in on him like kamikazes, he was feeling somewhat jaded. To the front, the cliff fell away to the inlet that framed the peninsula to the north, with slopes rising more gently on the far side. From a side window, Desiry could see a line of stone steps leading down to the old town, with its jumble of roofs crowding together within the walls. The rear of the house, as Desiry had found when he peered through the cracks in a boarded-up door, overlooked what appeared to be a toytown village surrounded by a wall that separated it from some open ground. It had neatly laid-out streets of miniature houses, with their own doors and windows and roofs of green or orange slates, some with fresh flowers on display, all with minute engravings in the stone. At first he had been puzzled, then he understood a sign he had spotted while scouting for his observation point: 'To the City of the Dead'. This was Bonifacio's cemetery.

Halard had been dubious when he told her he intended to station himself in the heart of Bonifacio: how did he know Kain could head into the town? He said they had to take the chance but the odds were good, given that the Cabrini clan, Sanpiero included, were thick on the ground. Desiry had backed his hunch by stationing two of his five watchers in the town. Observer Two was positioned near the top gate, visible from Desiry's observation point. Three was at the lower entrance, half a kilometre further down. Four was by the harbour, which nestled at the inshore end of the inlet. Five was on the approach road to Bonifacio from the airport at Figari and Six – who had just called in – at the airport, with instructions to provide the fullest possible description of Kain, then tail him as best he could. Halard had conceded to Desiry's judgement, reassuring herself that they would also be tracking Kain through Suzanne's concealed transmitter, although there could be problems when she was inside an enclosed space, like a car.

The plan was to follow Kain, Suzanne and Stewart into the hiding place, then wait for Kain to come out. They knew there were only two banks on Corsica where Kain could validate the bonds, both in Ajaccio, the capital, three hours' drive away. He would have to lodge the bonds overnight, so that the serial numbers could be checked. Not that Kain would be around to be told they were fake in the morning. A second team of detectives was on its way from Nice to take up position around the two banks, ready to move against him. Kain's arrest would trigger the rescue, with RAID going in the moment he was in custody.

Desiry allowed himself a wry smile when he heard the strategy: in his experience, such complex plans contained hidden pitfalls which even the most astute controller could not foresee. So far, however, so good. Red Bird was on his way from the airport, Owl and Tomcat were safely on board, and Six was tucked in behind them. Time to report to Halard.

'One to base.'

'Reading you, One,' said Halard.

'We have visual now,' said Desiry. 'Making for Bonifacio. Looks like we got it right. Do you have them on GPS?'

'We had a strong signal ten minutes ago. It's breaking up now. We should pick it up again as soon as she's out of the car.'

The next watcher came in as the Clio reached the outskirts of Bonifacio. 'Five to One,' he said. 'Entering town limits now.'

'Fingers crossed,' said Desiry. Five hundred metres ahead of Five's position was the turning towards the harbour and the old town. He was beginning to feel that the children could be close, very close. Maybe in a cellar in the labyrinth of the old town. Maybe in sight of where he was waiting. Keep coming, you bastard.

The radio snapped alive. 'One, this is Five. Five calling One.' There was urgency in his voice. 'Red Bird has not, repeat *not*, turned into town. He's continuing to the east.'

Shit. Desiry scanned his map. There was a solitary road winding away from the town before dropping to the far side of the peninsula.

'Six, can you follow?'

'Sure. But all the greeters have turned off into town, so I've lost my cover. I'll have to hang back or he'll make me.'

'Screw it,' said Desiry. He called Halard.

'Problems, boss. We're losing them. Do you have them on GPS?'

'It's very intermittent,' said Halard. 'Not enough to plot.'

In the command room of *Concorde*, cruising parallel to the coast two kilometres west of Bonifacio, Halard and Brady looked at each other in disbelief. 'We can't lose them,' said Halard. 'Not now.' The main cabin was stacked with electronic surveillance and detection equipment, computers, monitors, radio transmitters, laid out in a semi-circle beneath landscape windows. Halard and Brady were watching the monitor which was supposed to show the GPS signal broadcasting from Suzanne's transmitter – supposed, in this case, being the operative word.

In theory, the signal, a pulsing cross, should have appeared at the centre of the screen. A line trailing back to the edge of the screen should have shown the track Suzanne had taken. The top right-hand corner of the screen should be showing a pair of coordinates – two six-digit figures which could be matched to the grid lines of a map, showing exactly where Suzanne was. In the last thirty minutes they had received just two readable coordinates, which *Concorde*'s navigator, a man in his thirties with square, rimless glasses, was plotting on a local map. The first coordinate had come as they left the airport; the second, by some quirk, had been transmitted as the Clio breasted a hill on the approach to Bonifacio.

Brady was studying the map. 'We could be okay,' he said. 'That road goes nowhere.' He showed Halard how it dipped down the contours beyond Bonifacio and terminated at a jetty two kilometres beyond.

'One, this is base,' Halard radioed to Desiry. 'Make sure Six holds back. The GPS should pick them up soon.'

Halard and Brady were watching the monitor intently. There was a flicker at the centre of the screen, but it died. A minute passed, then two.

'They must have reached the end of the road by now,' said Halard.

Then the cross appeared, pulsing strongly at the centre of the screen. Ten seconds passed, and the coordinates flashed in the corner. Brady chanted them out and the navigator called them back as he marked his map. For five minutes the coordinates were steady. Then they started to move.

'Must be in a boat,' the navigator said. He had switched to a sea chart and was marking a line out of the inlet, heading south along the coast, back towards Bonifacio.

'Stand by One,' Halard radioed. 'We have strong contact.'

The line was extending by the minute, running parallel to the coast, nearing Bonifacio all the time. Halard felt a tingle of excitement. Brady saw the flush in her face.

'I don't believe it.'

It was Halard. Anxiously, she was trying to adjust the screen. Brady saw there was no longer a pulsing cross, no coordinates either, and the trail behind the cross was beginning to fade.

'Something wrong with the monitor?' she asked the navigator.

'No. The signal's been cut.'

Halard stopped thinking of the signal as a cross on the screen but as a boat, pitching through the sea, with Stewart and Suzanne on board, waiting to see their children, disappearing into God knows where. She felt a sudden welling of compassion that surprised even her.

37

They sat on the bench in the stern of the launch, bracing themselves against the swell. Kain was a pace away, sideways on, watching them, watching the boatman, a broad man with a weathered seaman's face whom he had greeted with a show of familiarity at the jetty. They were close in to shore, working along the line of a monumental cliff, mottled and discoloured, cracked and creased with fissures, blocking half the sky. The briefcase was behind Stewart's legs. Though Kain still wore his grin, Stewart sensed that he was tense, and he took Suzanne's hand. She responded, gripping hard.

A new fissure came into view, larger than the rest, slicing diagonally through the strata layers with their alternating gradations of yellow and grey. Near the bottom it flared open and Stewart saw that it marked the entrance to a channel slanting into the cliff-face. The prow of the boat was swinging round and Stewart realised, to his alarm, that they were heading directly into it. The grey rock was crowding in on them, closing overhead, as the sea heaved along its flanks. Ahead was a blank wall but off to the right was an elliptical opening, like a half-moon on its side, the sea sucking and sighing as it sluiced around it. It seemed too low to enter but the boatman was judging his moment, waiting for a swell to pass so that he could dip into the trough and let it carry them through.

'*A plat!*'

He flapped downwards with his hands. Stewart crouched forward, pulling Suzanne with him so that she ducked just as the launch slipped under the arch. There was another surge and the launch settled and they were through.

At first there was only darkness ahead. Behind, the half-moon of light receded. The clatter of the motor was reverberating around them and although Stewart knew they were in a confined space he had no idea of how high or wide it could be. He was utterly disorientated, as if they were lost in mist on a mountainside, and he felt a familiar surge of anxiety as he strove to locate himself. Then somewhere ahead – he could not yet tell how far away – was a pool of light swimming in the blackness. As the boat pushed on, the light began to separate into three or four distinct sources, that seemed to be weaving patterns between them. Suzanne was stiffening beside him and through her hand he could sense the intensity of her fears and hopes.

The boatman called out and hurled a mooring rope ahead. A hand grasped it and pulled the boat against a ledge of rock. Stewart looked up to see a beam of light shining directly at him, and realised that it came from a man wearing what looked like a miner's helmet, fitted with a lamp. Kain had already gone ashore. Stewart retrieved the briefcase and stepped off the boat, then helped Suzanne across the gap. They climbed a short flight of stone steps and found themselves on a broad rock platform that formed a natural landing stage for boats arriving across the lagoon. At the back of the platform was a line of boulders, with the cave seeming to rise steeply beyond. There were three men with lamps in all, Kain hovering among the shadows between them.

'Fee?' Stewart's call echoed tightly in the confines of the cave. 'Fee? Are you there?'

He heard her first, a voice from the dark. 'I'm here, daddy.'

Then she was walking uncertainly towards him, was in his arms, snuggling against him. He reached around her to cloak her, to protect her, hold her to him, feel her body and her limbs and her beating heart, an odour of sweat and terror clinging to her, his daughter restored to him, clutching so tight she was part of him again. Fee, his Fee.

'I've dreamt of this moment for so long,' he said.

Beside him he could hear murmuring and tears as Suzanne and Josh embraced. He spoke the words Fee needed to hear, even though he didn't know if they were true.

'It's all right, my darling. It's over now. Everything's going to be all right.'

She pulled away and looked at him, her pallor plain even in the half-light, her hair wild and tangled, the glimmer of tears in her eyes.

'Promise?' she asked.

'Promise.'

Kain had the briefcase in his hand. He opened it and looked inside. 'I'll take this now,' he said.

I don't know they're fake, said Stewart. To himself.

'So we go back in the boat together?'

'No,' said Kain. 'You stay here.'

'What are you talking about?'

'You get to leave when I know for sure this paper is real.'

'What else could it be?' It was Suzanne, playing her part. 'Do you think we'd risk our children's lives?'

'I have to check. Strictly business. Like I told him before, it's nothing personal.'

'Then why bring us here in the first place?' Stewart demanded. 'Why didn't you check them out as soon as Suzanne got to Corsica?'

'Because this is going to take a while, and I want the four of you nice and cosy, where my buddies can keep an eye on you.'

The three guards stood in a semi-circle behind Kain, their lights casting his shape in relief, his face invisible in the dark. Stewart could see one of them was carrying a semi-automatic rifle, another a revolver. Fee was crying, and he pulled her tightly into his side.

'How long do we have to wait?'

'Twenty-four hours, give or take,' said Kain.

'Then what?'

'If the bonds are for real, I let my buddies know you're in the clear. Once they're out of here, we let the cops know where you are.'

'No deal, Kain. How do we know you'll call the cops?'

'You've got to learn to have a little trust,' said Kain, grinning once more.

They had worked through all the possibilities. The transmitter had failed: entirely likely. Kain had found the transmitter and thrown it overboard: also likely. The boat had a steel hull and Suzanne had been locked up below, blocking the signal. Could not be ruled out. The boat had sunk. Didn't bear thinking about.

The *Concorde* had moved closer to Bonifacio and Halard stared from the cabin windows at the cliffs 500 metres away. They looked monumental, scoured by wind and sea, raked by grey fissures, daunting in scale, humbling in the way they seemed to mock her hopes.

Grey fissures.

'Phil!' Brady, who was contemplating the sea chart, was startled by the sharpness of her call. 'Those cliffs are limestone, right?'

'Right,' said Brady, without being sure.

'Limestone is porous. Rainwater seeps through from the top, gradually carving a way through. Over thousands of years, I mean. The great potholes of central France are in limestone country.'

'So why the geology lesson?'

'Don't you see? Limestone means caves. That's where they are. They've got to be.'

Brady tried to moderate her excitement. 'Sounds plausible.'

'It's more than plausible,' she insisted. 'It's the only explanation. There's got to be a cave entrance at sea level somewhere near here. I'm going to take a look.'

'Hold on,' cautioned Brady. 'If you're right, Kain's going to be coming out of that rock anytime now. What's he going to think if he sees you snooping around?'

Halard was not to be deflected. 'We don't even know he's in there. He could have left already. Anyway, there's diving equipment on board. I'll put on a wetsuit and a face-mask, carry a harpoon, make me look like a tourist trying some underwater fishing. Even if Kain sees me, he's not going to make anything of it.'

Brady was not convinced. 'Dominique, let one of the RAID guys do it.'

'To hell with RAID,' said Halard. 'The minute their launch comes over the horizon, the whole of Bonifacio is going to know.'

Brady saw streaks of foam along the foot of the cliffs.

'You see that surf? This is dangerous, Dominique.'

'I appreciate your concern,' she said, mimicking an American accent. 'I'll be okay,' she smiled.

Brady nodded, hoping she was right.

'Besides, I'm running the show. Remember?'

As he sat clutching Fee's hand across the table, Stewart tried to imagine what it had been like for her. One of the things about his ex-wife had been her extraordinary sensitivity whenever Fee had been hurt or wronged.

'You feel what Fee feels, don't you?' he had once asked Rachel.

'Why, don't you?'

She was genuinely surprised that he did not possess the same total empathy for his daughter. When he said he would find life intolerable if he carried his family's entire physical and spiritual burdens with him, she accused of him being selfish and uncaring, and they were into another of their spiralling, destructive rows; she trying to entangle him in emotional snares, he doing his utmost to stay detached.

Stewart looked around the room. It was several zig-zag flights of steps above the shelf where they had landed, a chamber that seemed to have been carved out of the rock. The walls had been concreted and rigged with lights, the power line stapled horizontally and running – from the evidence of a distant hum – to a generator somewhere above. Fee had told him that there had to be more chambers higher up, as she had seen the guards climbing a further flight of steps beyond the zigzags. Sometimes, too, people seemed to materialise in the cave without warning. Directly off the room – there was no door – was the space where she and Josh had slept, on a pair of mattresses no more than two feet apart. A couple of blankets lay on each and Stewart could see that Fee had tucked hers under the mattress, in a bid to preserve some semblance of tidiness and self-respect.

'How are you feeling?' he ventured, squeezing her hand.

'Daddy, I'm just so glad we're back together, and we'll be going home soon.'

How was she, really? How had she endured this trial? What strength had she drawn on? The questions flooded his mind. How much had she suffered? What treatment might she need? A medical check-up, certainly. And counselling? He found it hard to imagine the answers, and had a flashback to Halard's persistent questioning at the Prefecture, when she had charged him with knowing so little about his daughter.

The guard in the room shifted in his seat. His buddies were outside, somewhere deeper in the cave. There were raised voices and he could hear Kain's gruff tones in response. Although he could not distinguish the words, there was an edge of tension, of anger, permeating the cave. At one point the guard stood up and looked back through the door. 'Hey, Jesus,' he shouted, but there was no direct response.

'Jesus did the cooking,' said Fee. 'What there was of it.' They had eaten pasta, pre-cooked chicken, bread, cheese, fruit, with supplies arriving by boat every two or three days. She told him it was 'okay, considering'. Stewart suspected she was confining herself to safe territory, saying nothing that would provoke the guards, saving the truth for when they were out of there and she could tell him everything about their ordeal.

She read his thoughts. 'Daddy, how much longer do we have to stay here?'

In a brief, whispered interlude, when the voices outside had become even more heated and the guard's attention had wavered, Suzanne had told him that the rescue attempt would be made as soon as Kain was arrested in Ajaccio. Three hours, maybe four, and they were to get ready by locating whatever shelter they could. But they had not been able to warn the children; and Stewart was not even sure he wanted to tell Fee there was another ordeal to come.

'I'm not sure, sweetheart,' Stewart said. 'But Kain said it would be tomorrow morning. Which means we'll all have to doss down here, I suppose.' He was filled with foreboding, imagining the chaos that would fill the cave when the rescuers stormed in: the shouts, the shooting, the desperate search for cover. He looked at Fee with a great sense of pity for the trial that still awaited her. But he was determined, after all she had been through, that they would survive.

Suzanne was beside Josh, sitting on two chairs against the wall. She was caressing his arm as if to bring him comfort but also as if to reassure herself that he was solid flesh, her son restored to her touch. Stewart became aware that the voices outside had fallen, and he could no longer hear Kain. He must be on his way to Ajaccio and the surprise of his life. Stewart thought of the night they had spent in the barn: the reckless way he had tried to plumb the depths of Kain's soul, and the collusive silence between them when he had implied he knew the truth about the death of Barney Lewis, and Kain had not responded, and Stewart hadn't pressed him. Now he would never know the answer, and there would be no showdown between them. Kain's secret would be safe for ever; as safe as if it had been entombed.

38

Halard was in an inflatable dinghy below the cliffs, nosing its way among the rocks, pushing into coves and inlets. Brady had persuaded her to take a crew member, and although he was alarmingly young, with the mien of a teenager, he seemed expert enough with the tiller, skirting the foam with aplomb. Halard was in the prow, feeling distinctly constricted in the wetsuit jacket she had tugged over her shoulders, a face-mask on her forehead and clutching a harpoon-gun to assist her disguise. A pair of swim-fins lay on the floor of the boat. They rounded a sea-stack, a yellowing pillar on a rock plinth isolated in the sea, and came upon a chamber hollowed into the rock.

'Take us in,' said Halard. The crewman steered into a roofed amphitheatre that arched above their heads, the sea swirling around its walls. At the far end was a tiny stony beach, with a passage beyond it that seemed to burrow deep into the rock. As they neared Halard saw that it led only to a curtain of stalactites, gleaming damply like a monster's teeth.

'Forget it,' she said.

The inflatable swung on the swell and headed out to sea. 'Let's push on,' she said.

They had crossed the estuary beyond Bonifacio's harbour and were working eastwards along the steepest part of the cliff. The sea was running strongest here, jolting them towards the rocks, the dinghy's outboard squealing as it was lifted clear of the water. Halard succumbed to a moment of claustrophobia as she craned her neck upwards, trying to see the top of the cliff towering over her. From a long way above, a deep crack, almost a gully, angled down, splitting the cliff open at its base as if it had been struck by lightning. The gulch at the bottom seemed to cut back against the grain of the rock.

'Anything down there?'

'Don't think it goes anywhere,' the seaman said. They had almost passed it when Halard's professional nerve gave a sharp tweak.

'We'll take a look anyway.'

He was still sceptical as the inflatable nosed along the chasm. Then they saw the opening in the rock, shaped like an upended half-moon, with the sea slurping through.

'We should go through,' Halard said. 'Can you cut the engine?'

'I could. But once we're inside, I'd have to start it up again to get us out. Anyone inside will hear us for sure.'

Halard knew what she had to do. She braced herself against the side of the boat as she tugged the fins over her feet, then eased the mask down over her face. She balanced on the side, facing into the dinghy, then toppled backwards into the water. She paddled with her hands and then flipped with her legs, once, twice, propelling herself under the arch. Three or four more kicks and she was into blackness. Ahead was nothing, absolutely nothing.

She looked back at the light from the arch, reassuring herself that no matter how far she pushed on, she could always find the route out. She allowed herself to float, air bubbling gently from her mouth, before pressing on. Still, at first, she saw nothing. Then the dark was broken by a hint of lights somewhere ahead.

She drifted again, flexing her legs beneath the surface to avoid any further sound, nothing beside the lapping of the water against the unseen walls of the cave. The lights were sharper now. Then came a voice, brief and deep. Every instinct told her she had found the children.

She had to be sure. She rippled her legs again and glided a few metres further on. A light was shining in her direction.

'Hey Jesus. Come here!'

Now she knew, absolutely. Jesus. Jacob Jesus Fairley: Vietnam vet, ex-grunt, fellow-mercenary, partner, ally of Red Kain. The light was being lifted, its beam moving across the water towards her. Her mask! The reflection would give her away. She dipped and curled, diving into the blackness, then drove her legs to propel her towards the sanctuary of the half-moon light.

Fifteen seconds, twenty, twenty-five. She forced herself on, determined to surface beyond the range of the beam. She altered the angle of her kick, steering upwards through the black film above and out into the air, stifling the noise of her sudden frenzy of breathing. Behind, the light was a distant glow. She willed her muscles to relax, treading water with the fins, then swam through the archway and out into the light.

'Base to One.'

'Roger, base,' replied Desiry. He was sitting against the back wall of the ruined house, on the remnants of a stool he had found among a heap of charred timbers.

'We've found them,' said Brady. 'They're in a cave. It's at the bottom of the cliff you're sitting on.'

Brady told him that the entrance was on the far side of the promontory from his position, at the foot of the steepest part of the cliff. 'We're waiting for Kain to come out. We assume he'll return to the jetty and head to Ajaccio from there. Is Six still on station?'

Desiry stood up, looking out across the inlet. 'Affirmative, base. He's at the junction two kilometres back from the jetty. Wherever Kain's going, he'll have to pass his position.'

'Roger, One. The operational plan remains in place. Kain is not, repeat not, to be detained until he gets to Ajaccio.'

'Understood, base. Is the boss with you?'

'She's on her way back. She's the one who found them.'

'Jesus Christ!'

'Say again, One.'

'It's Kain.'

Desiry had glanced down on to the old town through the side window. Near the foot of the steps was a tall, well-built man with close-cropped hair, wearing a sailor's shirt and what looked like a waistcoat, hurrying down the steps leading to the top entrance of the old town. There was a black briefcase in his hand.

'Sure it's him?' said Brady, meticulous as ever.

'Quite sure. He's at the foot of the steps . . . he's approaching the archway . . . he's through the archway *now*.'

'Did you see where he came from?'

'Negative, negative.' Then he was calling up Two.

'Red Bird has just entered the old town at your end. Can you follow him? But do not, repeat not, detain.'

'Roger, One.'

The radio fell silent, although Desiry could hear the static as Brady kept the link open from the *Concorde*. Down below, a fishing boat was chugging its way out to sea; on the far side of the inlet, a tractor was winding its way up a track. Desiry always found these cameos of normality disconcerting when dramas were being played out beyond the public gaze. Then Two was talking again.

'One, I have him. He's thirty metres ahead, crossing Place du Guéridon.'

'Stay with him, Two,' said Desiry, who was circling the name on a map.

'He's heading down Rue de la Mascotte. Passing a fountain. He's taken the first right, into an alley.'

'Can you see the name?'

'Negative, One. But isn't this where the cousin lives?'

'Affirmative, Two. Repeat, affirmative.'

39

Ruelle Grise was a narrow alleyway cast in shade, but it was still stifling after the chill of the cave. Kain counted the crumbling façades until he reached number twelve. The front door was open and he climbed a steep wooden stairway, the briefcase in one hand, holding the banister with the other.

Antoine Cabrini was sitting at a table, the computer open in front of him. His cousin, Sanpiero, was on a chair in the shadows of the room, nursing a glass of pastis.

'It's payday,' said Kain, grinning as placed the briefcase beside the computer. He opened it to reveal two parallel piles of bonds, deckle-edged, their fine blue print strong against a matt grey background. 'So, are you ready? Let's go to Ajaccio.'

'We're not going to Ajaccio,' said Cabrini.

'What's the problem?'

'The bonds are fake.'

'Fake? What the fuck do you mean, fake?' His grin was already fading.

'Take a look.'

Cabrini twisted the computer so that Kain could read the screen. He pressed a button and a document scrolled into Kain's view: an invoice from Impact Graphics to J. Beaumont of BioGenius Inc for 251 laser copies. Next came an FBI report listing the serial numbers of 250 bonds totalling $100 million that had been redeemed in San Juan, Puerto Rico.

'What is this?' asked Kain, straightening up.

'Canning sent them this morning,' said Cabrini. 'I just picked them up. Keep reading.'

Kain studied the screen again.

Dear Antoine:

The two documents I have sent you were delivered to

> my electronic mailbox anonymously. I have absolutely no idea what they mean, or why they were sent to me. I have no knowledge of the transactions these documents describe, and no interest in the matter. I am sending them to you in the very unlikely event that you know anything about this matter, or why they should be sent to me. If you do have any idea, please let me know.

Kain's face was a mix of bewilderment and anger. 'Stop screwing with me, Cabrini. What is this shit?'

'What it is, my friend, is that someone has made photocopies of the bonds in Austin.' Cabrini was speaking dispassionately, any emotion locked away. 'Jesse Beaumont. The photocopies are in your briefcase. The real ones have been cashed in San Juan. Almost certainly by Beaumont.'

And what about Canning's letter, Kain asked? It looked as though someone had tried to set him up, Cabrini told him. But Canning had seen through it.

Kain was seething, kicking out at a chair which scuttled across the floor. 'It's Stewart, isn't it? He's in this somewhere. That fuck! He's dead.'

Still Cabrini gave nothing away. 'You should read to the end.'

Kain turned back to the screen.

> I am sorry to tell you that Kathleen died in the night. It's over. Please thank your family for their help and concern. There is nothing more they can do. May she rest in peace.
> Yours truly, Victor

'So his daughter's dead. So what next?'

'There's nothing next. He's saying it's over. No more killing. Close it down.'

'Like fuck it's over,' said Kain.

Cabrini stood up. 'Canning calls the shots. That was always the deal.'

'You forgot the rest. Canning owes me two million dollars. That was the deal in Bangkok, remember?'

'I told you, it's over. Leave it.'

'Like fuck, leave it. If Canning's not going to pay me, Jesse Beaumont can. And that lying bitch can tell me where he is.'

'Cool it, Kain. Get your brain out of your arse and think. What this means is, the cops are on to Canning and he knows it. That's why he's sent his message in clear, to cover himself. And if they know about him, it won't be long before they're looking for us. Show a little patience. Let's sit down and work this out.'

Kain was moving towards the door. 'I'm not a patient man, Cabrini. I told you that in Bangkok. I said, if Beaumont fucks me around, the kid gets it. It's more than just the kid now. I've fucking had it with all of them. Especially Stewart.'

Kain left the room, his footsteps clattering down the stairs as he headed for Ruelle Grise. Moments later, Cabrini was running after him.

'One, he's coming back up Rue de la Mascotte.'

'Roger, Two,' said Desiry.

'There's another guy with him – wearing a linen suit . . .'

There was a pause, though Two kept his speaker open.

'He's older, thick set, not so tall – thinning hair . . .'

Another pause.

'Christ! It's Cabrini!'

'You mean Sanpiero?'

'No – Antoine.'

'Antoine? Are you sure?'

'Absolutely. It's him, no question.'

'Stay with them, Two. We have to know where they're going.'

'Not easy, One. They're bound to make me. But they're heading your way.'

'Roger, Two. Get back to the house and see what you can find. It's number twelve, Ruelle Grise. Kick the door down if you have to. I'll pick them up when they reach the steps.'

'What can you see, One?' This was Brady, cutting in from *Concorde*.

'Nothing yet, base,' said Desiry.

'Keep it coming, One,' said Brady. 'Something's going down.'

Desiry kept talking as Kain and Cabrini approached his

position through the arch and started up the steps. 'They're moving it . . . At least, Kain is. Cabrini's just stopped for a breather . . . Now he's started again. Kain's about twenty steps ahead.'

'Do you have anyone else in position?'

'Not at this end,' replied Desiry.

'Then get ready to follow them yourself.'

'What are they up to?'

'I wish I knew.'

'They're still coming,' said Desiry. 'More than halfway. Problem is, I can't see all the way to the top. I'll lose them soon.'

'One, this is Two.'

'Go ahead, Two.'

'I'm calling from the Cabrini house. I don't know what the fuck's going on, but I just found Sanpiero in his living room. Lighting a fire.'

'In this heat?'

'He was burning the bonds.'

Halard came into the command room, still towelling her hair.

'It's all going wrong,' Brady told her. 'They know the bonds are fake.'

'How can they?'

'Doesn't matter. The fact is they do.'

Brady had been radioing to Halard in the inflatable as she returned from the cave, bringing her up to date. Now he told her what Desiry had reported. She took the microphone. 'One, this is team leader. Can you still see them?'

'Negative, boss. I just lost them.'

'Then you'd better get after them.'

'Then what?' asked Desiry.

Halard looked at Brady.

'This thing's getting out of control, Dominique. We've got to take them down.'

'Desiry's on his own. I can't send him up against those two animals without back-up.'

'Boss . . . ?'

'One, try and re-establish visual contact, but don't make a move until I get you help.'

'Then what?'
'You take them down.'

Desiry peeped between the boards blocking the door at the back of the house. Then he saw them, Kain still ahead of Cabrini as they hurried across open ground towards the City of the Dead. They pushed open a tall metal gate and set off along one of the lines of mausoleums, their heads bobbing above the roofs.

'They're in the cemetery,' Desiry radioed. 'I'm going in after them.' He half-ran, half-slid down the slope behind the house that led to the cemetery wall, then reached up to hook his hands over the top and haul himself up. As he balanced on the top, he froze.

Just twenty-five metres away, Kain and Cabrini were crossing the street he was looking down. In a moment, they had disappeared from view. He jumped from the wall and dashed to the intersection where they had crossed. Another thirty metres further on, they were just turning right. He pulled a snub-nosed revolver from the holster strapped to his ankle and ran after them. Weapon at the ready, he peered round the corner they had just turned. There was another parallel line of mausoleums, ending in a steep outcrop of rock that formed part of the wall. Deserted.

Movement behind him, a sound. He turned and crouched, revolver levelled.

'Friend,' said Three, his hands in the air. Four was a pace behind him.

They stooped beneath the ornate doorway of a mausoleum modelled on Notre Dame. Three told him that Five was at the entrance while Six was watching the perimeter steps. Two was watching the steps down to the Old Town from his car. Sanpiero was locked in the boot.

'There's nowhere they can go without being seen,' said Desiry. He pointed his revolver down the street that led to the outcrop of rock. 'They have to be hiding down there.'

Desiry went first, moving from tomb to tomb, Three and Four covering him with guns drawn, all peering through the gates or windows, checking doors to see if they had been forced. Nothing. Near the end another street led to the right. Another cul-de-sac. Still nothing.

Desiry took his transmitter from his pocket. 'Base, we've lost them. They've disappeared.'

'Disappeared where?' Halard sounded brittle.

'They haven't left the cemetery, and they're not in it either. We've checked at least fifty tombs. It's as if they've vanished into thin air.'

The thought hit Brady and Halard at the same time. Not thin air. Into the ground. Halard said it first.

'There's another way down to the cave. From the cemetery.' She was already radioing RAID.

'We'll need a briefing,' said the commander.

'There's no time,' Halard told him. 'We have to go in now.'

40

It had to be a dream. Or the same familiar nightmare. Stewart heard Kain's voice, insistent, rasping, full of threat. The guards were talking too, questioning and querulous. Then Kain was back, standing in the room, bulky and menacing, the anger unmistakable through the shadows of his face.

'So, you fucks, you thought it was goodbye Kain? Never see me again? Well, think again.'

Stewart stood up. Fee was shuddering with fear, while Suzanne seemed to wilt under Kain's onslaught. Josh, standing half-behind her, half a head higher, put his arm around her shoulder.

'Get a grip, man,' said Stewart to Kain. 'What are you talking about?'

'Stop that shit. You lied to me, screwed me around, took me for some kind of fool. No one does that. But no one.'

'I still have no idea what you mean.'

'The bonds are what I mean. The fake bonds. The bonds you tried to con me with. So you'd get back your precious kids, remember? I get the bonds, you get the kids?'

'Oh God, Tom.' The cry, half-muffled, came from Suzanne.

'So where's the money, Mrs Beaumont?

'I don't know,' Suzanne pleaded.

'You people,' said Kain, and he spat in contempt. '*Do you think we'd risk our children's lives*?' he said, mimicking her question of just two hours before. 'Ain't that just what you've done?' He gestured at the four of them, standing in the chamber above the landing stage. 'Bring them down.'

One of the guards started down the steps, his helmet lighting the way, Kain close behind. The other two signalled with their weapons that Stewart, Suzanne and the children should follow. They handed Stewart a hurricane lamp and he used it to light the way down the zig-zags. Ahead of them, he realised, was another figure, his face half-familiar in Stewart's lamp. At the foot of the steps he saw that it was Cabrini: Antoine Cabrini, oyster-eater; Antoine Cabrini, killer of Johnny Sail.

'Raven doesn't want this,' Cabrini warned.

'It's not his show any more,' replied Kain. 'Let's have the boy.'

Suzanne stepped forward. Josh tried to pull her back, but she broke free of his grip. 'Leave him out of this,' she said firmly. 'Do what you have to do to me.'

Kain ignored her. 'Now then, Josh. Do you remember your playmate? Olivier?'

Josh said nothing, and Kain pressed on.

'Do you know what happened to him?'

Josh shook his head.

'Come on, boy. You know *something* happened to him, because one day he was there, the next he was gone. Can't you guess where he went?'

'Kain!' shouted Suzanne. 'Stop this *now*.'

Kain ignored her. 'He went for a swim, didn't he? In the middle of the Med, much too far from shore. Ain't that a shame? Shall I show you how it happened? Have ourselves a little demonstration here? Jesus, watch them.'

Fairley kept his weapon trained on the group while the other guards grabbed Josh. Stewart felt rooted to the spot, though his mind was racing: this is all wrong; this shouldn't be happening; it shouldn't be ending this way. He took a step towards Kain. 'Don't do this.'

Fairley lunged at Stewart, striking his chest with the butt of his gun. The pain, more than the blow, knocked Stewart to the ground.

'Okay, Stewart?' said Kain. 'You through playing the hero? Now, Josh, let's see if you can swim any better than Olivier.'

In a flurry of movement, Josh was swept off his feet, one guard grasping his legs, the other his arms. Kain tied his ankles with a length of rope and stepped back.

'One,' Kain called.

The guards swung Josh back, then forward, out beyond the edge of the landing stage.

'Two.'

'Stop!'

Suzanne's shout echoed through the cave.

'For pity's sake, Kain, stop. I'll tell you everything I know.'

'Now we're getting somewhere,' said Kain. 'I guess we can put the swimming lesson on hold.' The guards dumped Josh by their feet, his ankles still tied. Stewart had stood up and Fee was clutching his hand.

'So, Mrs Beaumont, where's the money?'

'All I know is that Jesse took the bonds. He's disappeared.'

'Tell me something I don't know.'

'He went to Puerto Rico.'

'Know that too. That's where he fucking cashed my bonds. What I want to know is where he is right now.'

'Believe me, I just don't know. But there's someone who might.'

Kain pushed at Josh with his foot. 'Tell me more, Mrs Beaumont.'

'There's a US Senator Jesse knows. He's got a hideaway on one of the islands off Puerto Rico. Jesse used to go there sometimes.'

'So where is this island?'

'That's all I can tell you. Senator Bates would know.'

'So I'm supposed to go and look for some fucking politician, just on the off-chance Beaumont's staying with him on some godforsaken fucking island somewhere near Puerto Rico?'

'Please,' she said. 'I've told you everything. Please let Josh go.'

'I don't have time for this,' said Kain. 'Don't have time to fuck around any more.' He pushed Josh again. 'Tell me where the fucking money is. Otherwise . . .'

'Kain,' insisted Stewart. 'Can't you understand she's telling you the truth?'

'Drown him,' said Kain.

The guards picked up Josh by his arms and legs again, carrying him to the edge of the landing stage, the water unseen beyond. Fairley was holding Suzanne back with his gun. Stewart saw her mouth gaping open, silent for a moment, then uttering a shriek that drowned out all other sound as it pierced the darkness of the cave.

* * *

Twenty minutes before, Halard had seen two RAID launches skimming towards her, bouncing violently on the swell. She was already in the *Concorde*'s inflatable, making for the cave, ready to be taken on board when they reached her. Brady had protested again when she said she was going in with RAID but this time she had the perfect riposte. She was the only one who knew the way in.

The lead launch was almost on her. A man was in the prow, wearing a wetsuit and a black balaclava hood with slits for the eyes, together with a pair of night-vision goggles hanging round his neck. He grabbed her hand and heaved her on board. She fell to the deck, legs and arms awry, aware of the eye-slits looking down at her undignified pose. A hand reached down and pulled her into a sitting position. She glimpsed automatic weapons, handguns, stun grenades, a ladder with grappling hooks and a large halogen lamp.

'Commandant Terrenoire,' a man shouted above the noise of the engine. He pulled off his balaclava to reveal a shaven head and a pencil-thin moustache. 'What can you tell us?'

'Not much,' she yelled. 'There are four hostages in the cave – that's the two kids and two adults. As for the opposition, reckon on between four and six, though there could be more.'

She paused for breath. They were almost at the mouth of the inlet, the cave nearing all the time.

'Do they have light in there?'

Halard thought back to her swim. 'Some kind of fixed light and at least one torch. What do you have?'

'Our goggles,' said the commander. 'Mean we can see in the dark. And this.' He pointed to the halogen lamp. 'Are they armed?'

'I'd count on it.'

'What type of weapons?'

'We've no idea.'

'How many caves are there? Just one, or a series?

'Don't know.'

'Is there another exit?

'Looks like there's some kind of passageway up to the clifftop. But we don't know where it starts or ends.'

'Do they have boats?'

'At least one, but we don't know where it is.'

'What kind?'

'We don't know.'

'Is there anything else you can tell us?'

'No.'

'*Merde*,' said the commander, pulling on his hood. He handed one to her together with a pair of thin black gloves: 'So your skin doesn't show.'

A crew member jumped across to the second launch to relay what Halard had said. Then they were at the entrance to the channel slicing into the cliff, with the half-moon entrance at the far end. The commander throttled back as they slid between the walls. Halard held a finger to her lip and he eased the engine to a murmur. The opening looked impossibly small.

'Through there,' Halard said.

'You're joking.'

'I'm not,' she said.

The commander steered into the entrance. There was a jolt as the launch grazed against the arch. He cut the engine and beckoned to the crew to grip the rock in a bid to pull the launch through. The engine housing jammed against the apex of the arch.

'Push down, boys.' The commander showed how, leaning back and flattening his hands against the roof of the archway. The launch lowered perceptibly in the water, then moved forward again. They were beyond the narrowest point now, and Halard looked ahead into the obscurity of the cave. The commander let the boat drift as the second launch manoeuvred through the arch. He put an arm round Halard's shoulder and brought his mouth close to her ear.

'Which direction?'

Halard remembered her swim again, looking back at the entrance to orientate herself, then pointing directly ahead.

'That's where the swell's taking us,' whispered the commander. 'Let's see how far we get.'

Halard saw the glimmer of lights and shadows moving between them. Then it came, a rasping, echoing scream, a woman pleading for her son's life.

41

They must be in hell. Suzanne's scream seemed to have triggered a deafening cacophony, shouts and the roaring of engines, the hammering thunder of gunfire and the whining of ricochets. Then came louder explosions that pained Stewart's eardrums, more shouts and a beam of brilliant, blinding light sweeping the landing stage. He threw himself to the ground, pulling Fee down behind him to be her shield. Kain had moved like an animal, diving into the lee of a rock at the end of the landing stage, yelling 'douse the lights'. A semi-automatic skidded across the rock towards him and he took up a firing position, looking out over the water. The other guards had found cover of sorts among the boulders. Cabrini seemed marooned, as if he was not prepared for this moment, and was uncertain how to respond.

The source of the light appeared to be swooping from side to side across the lagoon, cutting on and off. Stewart glimpsed Suzanne slithering down a ramp towards the water, then reaching up to guide Josh down. The guards had started firing and there was a yell of pain from somewhere out in the lagoon. He heard a woman's shout – he caught the words 'be sure' – and knew it was Halard. Fee was gripping his arm fiercely, digging in her fingers as if he were the only solid thing left on earth. The gunfire was intensifying, and he knew they had to move. The guards were to the right, Kain to the left, flickering in and out of view as the beam raked the ledge. Behind them were the steps that zig-zagged up from the landing stage. A marksman had found Kain's position, and shots thudded into the rock.

'Fee! We have to move.' She heard him and sank her fingers tighter. 'Get up when I get up. Try to stay in front of me, and run to the steps.'

A decision flashed before him. Should they wait for the next sweep of the light, so that they could see the steps? Or bolt in the darkness, so that Kain would not see them go? Kain looked towards them, registering their position. The beam roamed the shelf again, briefly illuminating the zig-zags. Stewart held their image in his mind as he pushed Fee on to her feet and ran towards them. He felt for them like a blind man, gripping the edges and swinging a foot on to them, seeing Fee on them already. The light picked them out and swept on. Darkness again, groping up the zig-zags, fighting for dear life, Fee's life and his.

They had reached the point where the steps led to the living area when Fee hissed at him. 'Dad, wait a moment. There's something we need.'

Stewart was reluctant to release her hand, but she pulled herself free. In a moment she was back and thrust a helmet in his hand; a helmet with a light. 'This is where they charge the batteries,' she explained. She had a helmet for herself which she eased over her head. He copied her, strapping his under his chin. He directed the light upwards, to reveal a line of steps cut into the cliff, rising straight and disappearing beyond the limit of the beam. He tilted his head and the beam moved left and down, revealing a steep rock face below the steps, with an expanse of water fringed with rubble at its foot, rounded rocks that gleamed black in his light.

'Do you think there's a way out up there?' he asked Fee.

She was prospecting upward with her lamp too. 'There must be,' she replied.

The gunfire had reached a new pitch. He hoped, desperately hoped, that Suzanne's escape plan had worked. They carried on up the steps until they reached a rock platform with a wooden door on the far side. He turned the door handle and pushed, then pushed again. It was locked.

It must have been Kain, making sure that no one could leave the cave. For a moment Stewart had an absurd image of returning to ask him for the key. They only had two real choices. Go back down, and face a hail of bullets; or wait to see who prevailed in the battle. If Kain's side won, Stewart was sure he would show them no mercy.

'Daddy, look.'

Fee was at the other end of the platform, directing her lamp deeper into the cave. A natural ledge continued beyond the steps, disappearing into the darkness.

'Let's give it a try,' he said. Even if it led nowhere it seemed to offer a refuge: a place to hide until the battle was over, a place to hide from Kain.

The ledge was broad at first. Stewart took half a dozen steps at a time, keeping the light focused at his feet, sliding his hands along the wall in search of holds. Fee was close behind, confident in her movements.

Then he saw that the cave was narrowing around them and that the ledge led into a crevice just broad enough to pass through. Emanating from somewhere beyond was a subdued roar, like the breaking of waves. He squeezed through the crack and Fee followed. The roar was louder and more insistent now. He took another few steps and, at the limit of his beam, saw the shimmering white mass of a waterfall.

They went closer, stepping through pools of moisture glistening in their lights. The waterfall was cascading from an aperture twenty feet above them, surging down the rock before it arched out over the ledge and tumbled into the depths. Stewart took another few steps nearer, blinking as the spray doused his face. Its roar had intensified, drowning out the noise of the battle below.

'Can we get past it?' Fee called.

Stewart turned back. 'I think we should stay here for now, until we see how things turn out. There was a spot further back where we can wait.'

As they returned to the crevice, the gunfire had become more sporadic, as if the battle was almost resolved.

He didn't pick it up at first. Down below, lights were still flickering, and there was a brief volley of shots. Then he saw a solitary beam climbing the steps towards them. He hoped it was Halard, coming to look for them, coming to tell them the nightmare was over. He felt his weariness falling away as if he were nearing the end of an immense journey.

The light stopped. Stewart supposed that Halard had reached the locked door. Then the light twisted upwards and Stewart guessed that Halard had removed the helmet, perhaps to check the beam. The beam swung again, briefly reflecting a face. Kain's face.

Stewart scarcely dared breathe. He knew Fee had seen Kain too. Whatever the outcome of the battle, he supposed that Kain was making his escape, the key to the door in his pocket and freedom beyond.

The light moved again. Stewart waited for it to veer leftwards and disappear. It did not turn left. It kept straight on. Kain was coming. Coming after them.

42

He wanted to hold her tight again. He wanted this to end.

'What are we going to do?'

'It's all right,' he told her. 'We'll go through the waterfall.'

'We'll be swept away.'

'Don't worry. I know about waterfalls.'

As they edged back towards the column of water, Stewart recalled a trip he had made to Niagara Falls, paying a dollar to follow a tunnel into a viewing chamber behind the most fearsome part of the falls. There was even a balcony where you could step out and marvel at the monumental volume of water tumbling past.

He told Fee to take off her sweater and he stuffed it into his jacket to keep it dry. The spray was drenching them now, but he could glimpse the ledge leading behind the deluge. Sometimes you had to do things without thinking. He took Fee's hand and led her on, willing her to keep her nerve. Water pounded on to their heads and shoulders, pushing them towards the edge, but he gripped Fee's hand more tightly and they kept on walking and then they were through.

'Wasn't too bad, was it?'

She even managed a smile.

Beyond the waterfall, the walls narrowed again. The ledge led almost to the roof of the chamber, feeding into a horizontal slot in the rock that seemed just large enough to crawl through. Stewart fancied for a moment that it led to some kind of sanctuary, a hiding place where they could rest and gather strength. He moved his head, working his lamp back along the ledge. Halfway down, he held the beam still. There was a change in the colour of the rock, no longer the familiar blue-grey of limestone but a gleaming white. Fee's beam was on his face.

'What is it?'

'I'm not sure yet. Let's take a look.'

When they reached the white section of the ledge, Stewart knew his fears were justified. For the next half-dozen paces, the ledge was caked with calcium deposits, the residue of water dripping from the roof above that would one day form a cluster of stalagmites. Although its texture looked uneven, Stewart knew it would be as slippery as ice.

He looked back down the cave, wondering if Kain was still coming, but could not see beyond the waterfall. He peered over the ledge, wondering if there was a way down to the bottom of the cave, but could see only the unrelenting rock steepling away below. He knew that to step out onto the calcium meant taking a hideous risk.

Unless there was some way of reducing that risk. Until now the rock beside the ledge had been smooth and sheer. As he scrutinised the stretch above the calcified section, he saw that a flake of rock around four feet high had become detached from the face, leaning outwards with its top edge running parallel to the ledge.

'Look,' he said to Fee. 'There's a good handhold along the top of the flake. I think we can make it across.'

Stewart turned sidewards on the ledge so that he was facing the rock wall, with his back to the chasm. He reached out and grasped the top of the flake with his left hand, then took the first step out on to the calcium. He felt his foot slide as he moved his right hand next to the left, gripping with every fibre of his being. He felt it shift under his weight and he had a vision of himself clinging to it as it hurtled into the chasm. Then the flake settled. He moved his right foot alongside the left and balanced there as he called to Fee.

'Your turn.' He lit the edge of the flake with his beam. 'Concentrate on where you put your hands and don't worry about your feet. But you must try to pull downwards on the flake. It's not very stable and if you lean outwards, it's likely to come away.'

She came to the edge of the calcium and stretched across, her fingers groping for the end of the flake, tantalisingly just beyond her reach. Stewart leaned out to grasp her left hand, pulling her towards him. She found a handhold and put one foot on the calcium. It slid from under her but her right hand was already moving across to grab the flake. Her arms were trembling but she was holding firm.

'Now copy me,' Stewart said. He slid his left hand along the flake, brought his right hand to join it, watched Fee follow suit. Left hand, right hand. Now it's your turn, Fee. Hold on for all you're worth. Left hand, right hand. And again. This time his left foot touched down beyond the calcium and held its grip. She was by herself, clinging to the end of the flake.

'One more time, Fee. Step out with your left foot and try to grab my hand at the same time.' She was reaching out, her fingertips groping for his, the skin brushing, sinews extended, fingers closing and locking. Then he was drawing Fee across and into his arms, feeling her subside as her muscles relaxed and the tension drained away.

The ledge ahead of them was broader, and the slot in the rock was only ten metres further on. 'See,' he said, 'it's easier now.' But she was looking back.

'Daddy!'

He turned to see where she was pointing. Something had changed within the waterfall. The column of white foam had a spectral gleam at its heart. The gleam was transformed into the beam of a headlamp with a rainbow halo around it and a ghostly figure emerged, shimmering in the spray. Water was dripping off Kain, his face was glistening, revealing his grin. The beam focused on Stewart.

'I'm coming for you,' Kain called.

'Leave it, Kain,' Stewart shouted above the pounding of the waterfall. 'Why don't you just leave it? Why didn't you escape when you had the chance?'

'Waste of time. Your cops will be crawling all over the place up there. Besides, we've got business to finish.'

Stewart thought of saying they weren't his cops. He thought of telling Kain to leave it again. He thought of pushing on through the slot to see where it led, whether to escape or into a trap. But it didn't matter any more. He had to face this, face Kain.

'I'm coming for you, Stewart,' Kain yelled again. 'We're going to finish this.'

Did he have a gun, a knife? It didn't matter. Stewart had

seen him kill with his bare hands. But first he had to cross the calcium.

'Kain, there's something I want to ask.'

'Ask away. This is your last chance.'

Perhaps he didn't know about calcium . . .

'It's about Barney Lewis.'

'What about him?'

'You killed him, didn't you? Shot him in the head with his own gun, up there on Hill 861.'

'So you figured it out. You're a smart guy, Stewart.' Kain was committing himself too, going beyond the point of no return.

'That's why I was looking for you in Bangkok.'

'Not so smart. What's your question?'

'Why? Why did you kill him?'

'Because he was like you, Stewart. He didn't know when to butt out of other people's business.'

'In your case that would be the heroin business, right? You were selling junk to GIs.'

Kain was grinning, edging towards them, getting closer to the calcium.

'You've got a mouth on you, I'll give you that.'

'I want to know why, Kain. What was Lewis going to do?'

'Have me arrested. Court-martialed. Told me that when we were going up the hill. Before the firefight started. Big mistake.'

'You told the others you were going to try and rescue him. Then you took his gun, you made him lie down, and you shot him in the back of the head.'

'Told him first. Told the fuck I was going to kill him.'

'And now us. Why kill us?'

'The same. Strictly business. You know too much about me. Especially now.'

Did he know about the calcium? Stewart was going to finesse it. Gamble that Kain didn't know.

'That's fucking bullshit. It's not business, Kain. It's personal. It's personal because you enjoy killing. You're a sadist, Kain. You're a fucking freak, a psycho. You're a hired killer because that's how you get your kicks. And the biggest kick is looking into someone's eyes so you can watch the moment they die.'

There was a roar from Kain. 'You got the last bit right, Stewart. I'm going to love it, watching you both die.'

Kain charged. Feet dancing along the ledge. Then a step on to the calcium. His foot slid at once, flew from under him, flipping him on to his back, his arm flailing wildly. His hand gripped the flake.

For a moment Stewart thought Kain had saved himself. Then there was a searing noise as his full weight came on to the flake, jerking it outwards, peeling it away from the face. Kain was still clinging to it as it crashed on to the calcium. Then he was sliding over the edge and into the depths, the beam on his helmet spiralling upwards, downwards, out of sight. Kain was roaring again, a roar mingled with the clatter of fragmenting rock. The roar was receding, dying, there was a thud, the roaring was silenced; then an abrupt half-splash, final, conclusive, almost banal.

Stewart stood transfixed, hugging Fee to his side. He focused his headlamp on the calcium, hardly daring to believe that Kain had gone. He peered down the rock face, trying to guess the line of Kain's fall, but had only a glimpse of boulders and a glint of water.

'Fee,' he said. 'He's gone. We're safe. It's over. We're going to be all right.' She was sobbing but she looked at him, a smile overcoming her tears.

There was a curious odour in the air, pushing into Stewart's nostrils. It was like cordite and he knew it occurred when rocks fell. He examined the face above the calcium. Where the flake had been was now a scallop-shaped scar, concave, no handholds at all. Their hand rail to safety had gone. There was no way back.

43

'Fee,' he asked. 'Do they know about this part of the cave?'
'No one ever talked about it,' she said.

If only they knew what was happening back at the lagoon. They could hear nothing above the roar of the waterfall, and no one could hear them. Stewart said they could wait in the hope that the police would come to find them, or they could explore beyond the slot. 'We must be at least halfway up the cliff. It's worth seeing if there's a way out.'

He was sure that Fee detected his unease, but she showed no doubts.

'You always said that doing something was better than doing nothing,' she reminded him. It was a good enough reason to push on.

This time Fee went first. 'I'm thinner than you,' she said. She lay on her side and levered herself through the slot, reaching back to help guide him through. His skin rasped against the rough rock and there was a sudden ache in his chest, where the rifle-butt had struck. On the far side, he found they were at the foot of an oval-shaped passage twisting upwards and out of sight. It was not high enough to stand up in and they had to move forward at a stoop, bracing their calves against the incline. Finally the tube opened into the side of a canyon with water coursing deep in its bed. Stewart could not rid himself of the image of two minute creatures lost in a vast catacomb, taking themselves ever deeper into peril.

The canyon narrowed, with the water splashing around them. They were forced to move sideways, squeezing through the rock. Stewart felt his chest compress and he stifled a groan as the pain intensified, hoping that Fee would not hear. To his relief, the tunnel widened again and then steepened so that it was almost like climbing a ladder. Stewart went first, using cracks and ledges for rungs, the water tumbling past. At the top the tunnel opened into another chamber and Stewart lay on the ground to reach down for Fee's hand. She subsided on to a flat rock, panting hard, her breath vaporising around her.

'I don't know how much further I can go,' she said.

Stewart's foreboding was growing.

'Why don't you take a rest here?' he said. 'I'll push on and see if I can find the way. We must be close to the top.'

'Don't go too far, will you?'

'I won't,' he promised. 'But I think you should turn off your light to save the battery. We can still call to each other.'

Fee watched as her father left, the beam of his light strobing from side to side. She now realised that even during the worst moments she had never doubted that he would come for her, just as she did not doubt he would find the way out now. The intensity of her belief puzzled her, and she wondered why she placed such faith in someone who had been so inconstant in her life. His beam was a point in the darkness, still prospecting for the way out. It stopped moving, then it was growing larger again and she heard the scrunch of rocks as he headed back.

It stopped again, as if Stewart did not know the way. His light was arcing through the darkness, but she was still beyond reach of the beam.

'Fee,' he called. 'Feeee.'

'I'm over here. Over here. Here, here, here.'

She remembered the times when she had been so glad to see him, even after he and her mother separated and he kept re-entering her life, kindling memories of the time everything had seemed so secure. The beam loomed and was lighting her face, so that she knew her father could see the expectancy in her eyes.

'I'm sorry, Fee. It just ends in a rock wall up there. There's no way out.'

Water drenched her face, trickling down the nape of her neck, falling over her body, its heat easing away the sweat and the grime and the fear. Josh had showered first and she had left him sitting on his bunk, drying his hair, as he struggled to make sense of what she had told him. She knew it would be incomprehensible, unfathomable: not just how he had been kidnapped in revenge for his grandfather's unforgivable dishonesty; but how

Jesse had pretended to pay the ransom and then fled from the US with the money, stolen from Josh's own trust fund. She knew, really, that Josh never had liked his grandfather, above all because he made no secret of his disappointment that Josh did not match Larry in his hopes. But she always felt that Josh at least respected Jesse for what he had achieved with Larry, and for continuing Larry's work after his death.

'Don't worry,' Suzanne assured him, homing in on his most profound fear. 'Your father would never have done what Jesse did. Your father was straight and honest and true. That's why I loved him. Just as I love you.'

When she came out of the shower, the towel pulled around her, Josh was still on the bunk, his hair spikey and uncombed. Despite what she had told him, there was a brightness in his eyes – the same brightness she had seen when watching news reports of other hostages released and just glad to be alive, no matter what traumas had yet to be resolved. She sat beside him and he took her hand, then looked at her and said: 'I can't tell you how happy I feel.'

She felt it too. But she still had the ache of wanting to know that Tom and Fee were safe. She pulled on a pair of naval dungarees that Halard had given her and went up into the main cabin. Halard and Brady were both there. Behind them, through the plate-glass windows, the cliffs were losing their texture as the shadows of sunset crept up the rock.

'Any news?' she asked.

'Nothing yet,' said Brady.

'How's Josh?' asked Halard.

'He'll be fine, once we get home.'

The ache deepened, as her sense of powerlessness intensified. She had already told Brady that she had no idea what happened to Tom and Fee. As Skinner instructed, she had spotted a hiding place for herself and Josh, an alcove in the corner of the cave, a short swim from the landing stage. As they slipped into the water, she had looked back to see Tom prone on the landing stage trying to shelter Fee with his body. When she looked again from the alcove, they were no longer there.

The ship-to-shore telephone rang. Halard answered it, nodding as she listened.

'They've taken him to the military hospital at Toulon,' she

told Brady after she replaced the receiver. 'He may not pull through.'

Suzanne looked at her inquiringly.

'One of the RAID guys,' Brady answered. 'Shot in the stomach. It's a miracle he was the only serious casualty.'

'And the guards?' What happened to them?'

'You're sure you want to hear this now?'

She was quite sure. She wanted to hear that they were where they could do no more harm.

'Three dead, one injured – and Kain's still missing.'

'Missing where?' she asked.

'We're searching the shoreline in case he managed to swim out, but the best guess is he's still holed up somewhere inside the cave. We know a lot more about it now. Turns out it was first used by smugglers, and then the Germans built a base in there when they occupied Corsica during the war. The whole system goes a long way back and parts of it are like a labyrinth. We're waiting for some cavers to come in as guides.'

'How did he manage to get away?' Suzanne asked.

'It wasn't hard in all that confusion,' said Halard.

Confusion was right, thought Suzanne. One moment Kain was about to kill Josh . . . 'I still have no idea what really happened.'

Halard said that Suzanne's scream had been the perfect signal. The launches had just entered the lagoon when it came, prompting them to mount their attack earlier than they had intended. The lead boat, with Halard on board, veered left, sweeping the landing stage with its halogen lamp, zig-zagging across the lagoon and turning the lamp on and off to avoid incoming fire. The second launch had headed right into the darkness in search of a landing point. The first guard was taken out moments after they landed.

'It was an easy hit,' said Halard. 'He had no idea where we were coming from.'

'Do you know who the guards were?'

'Three mercenaries Kain hired in Bangkok to crew the *Symphonie*,' said Brady. 'The first one killed was a Brit. He was trying to get a bead on the halogen light.'

'The second guy killed was Cabrini,' said Halard. 'He looked like he had no idea what was going on.'

'Didn't you want to take him alive? Hoping he might rat on Canning?'

'That would have been nice. But he was holding a gun, and that was enough for RAID. They don't mess about.'

As Halard told it, the battle moved into an attritional stage. Kain and the two remaining guards had good cover among the boulders and they were stepping up their fire. RAID were much more cautious, because they were afraid of mistaking Stewart for one of the bad guys. 'Be sure,' Halard had called.

Then in one of the sweeps of the halogen lamp, Halard had spotted Stewart and Fee dashing up the zig-zags. She had lost them after that.

Eventually they killed a second guard – 'guy named Pelican,' said Brady. That left the last one, Jesus Fairley. And Kain.

Fairley was well-hidden, and he'd also worked out where RAID's fire was coming from, so he was giving the second launch a hard time. It must have been then that Kain slipped away, though no one had seen him go.

'We'd like to know what line he sold Fairley,' said Brady. '"Cover me, and I'll cover you from the top?" "I'll come back for you?" They were supposed to be buddies but it looks like Kain's own skin came first.'

It took RAID another thirty minutes to get a good line of fire on Fairley. Eventually two of the team had scrambled up the cliff and worked their way round behind him. They only winged him but he stopped firing, which was what mattered. Halard had got to him first, probably saving him from the *coup de grâce*.

'He's in Toulon too,' said Halard. 'At least we've got one person to question.'

'Does he know anything about Canning?' Suzanne asked.

'I seriously doubt it,' Brady said. 'He was just hired help.'

'So, what's your guess on Tom and Fee?'

They wished they knew, Brady said.

Suzanne's ache would not go.

44

Fee tried to suppress a shiver. She had chilled down while her father prospected ahead, and the cold was seeping into her bones. She snuggled into her pullover: thank heavens it was still reasonably dry.

Her father told her how he had followed the stream towards its source, only to find his progress blocked where it was flowing out from under the wall of the chamber, forming a deep pool. Now he was sweeping the walls and roof with his torch. She watched the beam, but could see no apertures or crevices in the rock surrounding them; nothing to suggest a way of escape.

'Why don't we go back down?' she asked.

Stewart thought of the distance they had come, the treacherous stretches they had climbed, the perils of losing their way, not to mention having to cross the calcium. And what if the bad guys had won?

He did not voice his fears. 'The police must have dozens of people looking for us by now. I think it's safer if we stay here until they find us.'

He sat down next to Fee. He wanted to think, explore the possibilities, work through their remaining options. His mind dwelt on the blank walls his torch had revealed. He remembered Fee's confident look when he'd returned from his futile search for a way out. It was the same look she had given him as a child, before she learned disappointment; the same look she had given him during dinner at Le Bosquet, before she knew he was about to let her down again. He shone his lamp on her and saw again that sweet face, that had grown and changed, so that the child who had been his flesh had become her own person, his but no longer his, independent and free.

'I'm sorry, Fee.'

'There's nothing to be sorry for,' she said. 'I know we'll get out of this.'

'That's not what I mean. I'm sorry I haven't been what you wanted.'

'I think you're terrific. You're a great journalist, for a start.'

'But not so good as a father, right?'

She said nothing.

From the pain of the past two weeks, when every part of him had ached to see Fee again, he had finally learned what it meant to be a father. Fee had known all along and had tried to tell him, but he had not listened.

'I think you know what I mean. Taking your love, giving you prezzies. Buying your love, on my terms. Not there when you wanted me. Only there when I wanted to be.'

She looked at him, her torch illuminating his profile against the dark. He turned to her, saw only the blaze of her light, waited for her to speak.

'I've been thinking a lot about this,' she said. 'What I've been through has made me realise how much I love you, as well as mum. Everything you say is right. But we're here in this place because you love me, and because you came to save my life. Things will be different when we get out. Which I know we will.'

Stewart could hear the stream trickling close by, running its course from the surface to the sea. He thought of the rock wall barring their way out, the pool welling up from beneath it. A terrible idea was rising in him, taking strength, mingling dread with a quickening hope.

'Come with me, Fee. I want to take another look up there.'

She followed him up to the pool.

'It's called a sump,' he said. 'The stream has to dip under the rock to get through. It almost certainly means there's a passage leading to a chamber like this on the other side.'

Alarm was filling her eyes. 'What are you going to do?'

'I'm going to have a look.'

'You'll drown.'

He knew he could not drown, because Fee would die too. 'I won't,' he said. 'That's a promise.'

He asked her to count out loud while he held his breath. He filled his lungs as she began to chant: 'One little second, two little seconds, three little seconds'. She had reached thirty-two when his lungs were about to burst, and he let go. That gave him just sixteen seconds to find the other chamber, if it existed. Because if it didn't, he would need sixteen seconds to get back. To give himself a safety margin, he needed to turn back after twelve, thirteen seconds – no more.

His light was still bright. He knelt in the pool and felt under the wall of rock. All he could tell was that it was smooth, and stretched beyond his reach. He breathed hard, filling his lungs two or three times, then took a final breath and pushed under the surface.

Mercifully the water was deep enough. He was half-swimming, half-crawling, groping along a passage with his hands into the iridescent shaft of light from his helmet, thrusting with his feet, counting in his head: three little seconds, four little seconds, five. Another thrust – seven little seconds, eight. How much further? He was almost out of time. Just one more push. He felt his head clear the water. He was through!

Disappointment surged through him. His lamp was lighting not a chamber but a narrow bell-jar cavity with just two or three feet of space above his head. The air was brackish and stale, and would not sustain him long. He counted ten more seconds, filled his lungs, and ducked into the water again. The passage ran on past his beam, still nothing ahead. Or was there? The roof of the passage was rising and instead of disappearing into the water ahead his beam seemed to be refracting through the metallic underside of its surface. He knew, absolutely knew, that there was air above.

His light went out. Blackness, utter blackness, the dark of the grave. Seven seconds had passed, then eight. Go on without being able to see where he was? Or go back, back to the bell-jar, then back to Fee? Go back, go back. He pushed at the rock above his head, easing himself backwards, and surfaced in the bell-jar with an explosion of air and relief. Still utter darkness. He twisted round and dived again, probing through the nothingness, the seconds fleeing, the rock crude to his touch. He saw the glow of Fee's torch lighting the exit from the passage and knew he was safe. He broke through the surface, stayed kneeling in the pool, lungs heaving for breath.

'What did you find?' she was asking. 'Is there a way out?'

He thought again of the refracted light and the metallic gleam, fighting off doubts, confident in what he had seen. He knew it was the way out, knew he and Fee were going to make it.

'Yes, there is,' he told her. 'We're going home.'

He explained what they were going to do. His own lamp was waterlogged and so he would take hers. When he ducked into the pool, she was to follow at once, staying as close to his feet as she could and watching for the glare of his lamp. It would take ten seconds, no more, to reach the bell-jar. They would stay there for fifteen seconds and then press on for the chamber that surely had to be there. Fear was threatening to take over, fear for Fee; fear for what would happen if he were wrong. He calmed his voice, heard himself saying: 'In less than a minute we'll be through.'

They knelt in the pool, filling their lungs once, twice, and again. He ducked under the surface, reached out into the passage, groping for the rock on either side, pushing with his feet. He felt Fee's hands touch his legs, knew she was there, reached the bell-jar and turned to pull her into the air. She was gasping for breath but he knew that she was strong. He counted down the seconds, held her hand, pointed down with his thumb, let go of her hand as he ducked, saw her duck too. He was pulling and pushing again, searching for the metallic underside of the water and the air beyond. The seconds were expiring but the gleam appeared and he was swimming for the surface, bursting into the air, grabbing Fee's arms and pulling her up with him. They were through.

He lay on his back, his whole being convulsed as he gasped for breath. Fee was beside him, her body heaving, and he placed his hand on her hip. His eyes opened and followed the beam of his lamp. The rock above them had changed. It was no longer shattered but rounded and smooth. There was something different about the air too, no longer dank and stale. He felt it on his cheek, brushing his skin. A draught. A draught of fresh air.

Fee sat up and watched the beam of his lamp. It followed the stream for another dozen paces, until it came to where it flowed from beneath another rock wall. Beside it were steps, real steps, fashioned by humans, carving through the rock. He stood up and helped Fee to her feet. Then they were climbing the steps together, Stewart dipping his head so that his lamp lit the way. Off to one side was a narrow shaft and he knew it was the source of the draught.

Stewart stopped. His beam was reflecting from a blank wall, smooth and polished in the light. He heard Fee gasp, saw hope wavering in her eyes. He reached out to touch the wall, caressing its surface. He pushed gently, then harder, and a section of it swung away.

They crawled through the opening. They were in a cramped ante-chamber, not high enough to stand. A soft light was angling into the chamber, revealing sturdy elongated boxes on either side that looked like coffins. Beyond was a grid. The grid was a gate. They opened it and stepped out to see the moon, a glinting platinum disc suspended just above a jagged skyline. Its rays were slanting along a miniature street, with houses and roofs gleaming in the half-light. A shadowy figure was walking towards them, his head visible above the line of roofs, so that they felt they must be in some imagined world, a childhood fantasy, or the nightmare from which even now they could not awake.

'Mr Stewart,' said Inspector Desiry. 'We're so pleased to see you and your daughter. Welcome to the City of the Dead.'

Epilogue

Kain's battered body was found in two feet of water by a team of cavers the next morning. Three days later, following urgent requests from the FBI and US State Department, Jesse Beaumont was arrested at his Puerto Rico hideaway.

It was Senator Bates who supplied the address, after FBI agents warned him that he might otherwise be viewed as Jesse's accomplice. Beaumont was extradited to the US, to be held without bail in Austin on charges of embezzlement and theft. Most of the $100 million he had stolen from Josh's trust funds was recovered.

The story of the defective MycoGene was reported in the US but the FDA declared that the problem had been limited to one batch of the drug and repeated its earlier assurance that MycoGene was safe. The company was fined, though not punitively, and the stock price survived a temporary dip, with investors eagerly awaiting news of FDA approval for HaemoGene. In line with the instructions Suzanne Beaumont sent to her lawyer from Nice, claims for damages brought by Morton Mintz were settled on generous terms.

Victor Canning retired. After disposing of his entire range of business interests, he moved to southern Spain, having also endowed a research laboratory – the Kathleen Institute – to investigate the causes of CHIDS. The Crown Prosecution Service abandoned any attempt to prosecute him for kidnapping, concluding that it would not be able to build a case based on the enigmatic E-mail messages it retrieved from Kain's computer, or on the final message Canning sent to Antoine Cabrini. Certainly no worthwhile evidence was forthcoming from Jesus Fairley, who said he'd never heard of Canning. Fairley himself would not be leaving France for thirty years.

Detective Chief Superintendent Skinner was suspended pending a disciplinary inquiry into the accusation that he had wilfully sent confidential information to Canning, jeopardising the rescue operation and putting at risk the lives of all concerned. Sergeant Bert Humphries agreed to testify against his former guvnor but the inquiry was abandoned when Skinner opted for early retirement. Phil Brady resigned from the FBI so that he could return to France, where he established himself as a security consultant to US companies in Europe, and renewed his relationship with Dominique Halard, who remained a Commissaire with the Police National.

Suzanne Beaumont and Tom Stewart returned to their respective continents, agreeing to put their relationship 'on hold' until they could find the opportunity to spend time together in a calmer ambiance than before. Suzanne took full charge of BioGenius and Josh announced that he wished to train as a chef.

Stewart resolved to spend the next year writing in his Wapping flat, enabling him to spend more time with Fee, whose decision to pursue a career in the movies he gracefully accepted. He was offered a contract from his publishers to write the story of his daughter's kidnap – provisionally entitled *Red Bird* – subject only to the proviso that he first complete his book about Barney Lewis and the Vietnam MIAs. Six weeks after the start of his interrupted holiday in Nice, he sat down at his word processor to begin the final chapter: 'The Truth about Hill 861'.

Closer

Kit Craig

'When you're a mother, you're a mother all your life. You don't stop being a mother just because they do disgusting things and you don't stop when you find out what they are doing. It isn't what they do. It's who they are to you.'

What do you do when you discover your son is a ritual killer? Respectable, overweight, middle-aged Stella Zax feels that she has no choice but to kill her aberrant child. Then she summons an eager young reporter to her prison cell to explain why. She chose Theo Slate, she says, because he reminds her of her dead son. Whatever her reasons for confiding in him, Theo knows that this is a chance of a lifetime.

But then disturbing things start to happen. Someone wants to get close to Theo. Far too close for comfort . . .

Praise for Kit Craig's previous Headline thrillers:

'Absolutely spell-binding' *Washington Post*

'A tightly wound psycho-thriller written with terrifying understatement . . . riveting and menacing' *Newsweek*

'Genuinely frightening, throbbing with menace and horror . . . outstanding' *Publishers Weekly*

0 7472 4938 5

Guilt

John Lescroart

Mark Dooher has it all. A prosperous law practice. The respect of his peers. A healthy wife and family. But he wants more. He wants young lawyer Christina Carrera to be his lover – and his new wife.

Killing Sheila, after twenty years of marriage, is tough. But Dooher's used to tough decisions. It's what comes next that's hard. The unremitting scrutiny of a head of homicide who, with a terminally ill wife, is fixated on catching Sheila's killer. The hints of suspicion from his best friend and defence lawyer. And worst of all, in the mind of the woman for whom he's jeopardised everything, the woman who's soon to have his baby, there's a growing suspicion of his guilt . . .

'Lescroart has brought so much more to the novel than simply courtroom dazzle . . . first-rate . . . raises the drama to an unusually sophisticated level . . . cracking legal drama' *Publishers Weekly*

0 7472 5457 5